GW00645042

About the Author

Ken Melber is an artist and writer. He worked in education all his life, eventually becoming headmaster of a prep school in the UK. Teaching took him to Uganda, Malawi, Nigeria and the USA and gave him some serious and memorable adventures. He and his wife now live in Yorkshire.

Dedication

For Kate and Steve, and in memory of Joe and Tina

Ken Melber

A BRUSH WITH CHAOS

AUSTIN MACAULEY
PUBLISHERS LTD.

Copyright © Ken Melber (2016)

The right of Ken Melber to be identified as author of this work has been asserted by him in accordance with section 77 and 78 of the Copyright, Designs and Patents Act 1988.

All rights reserved. No part of this publication may be reproduced, stored in a retrieval system, or transmitted in any form or by any means, electronic, mechanical, photocopying, recording, or otherwise, without the prior permission of the publishers.

Any person who commits any unauthorized act in relation to this publication may be liable to criminal prosecution and civil claims for damages.

A CIP catalogue record for this title is available from the British Library.

ISBN 9781786298997 (Paperback)
ISBN 9781786299000 (Hardback)
ISBN 9781786299017 (eBook)

www.austinmacauley.com

First Published (2016)
Austin Macauley Publishers Ltd.
25 Canada Square
Canary Wharf
London
E14 5LQ

Acknowledgments

A big thank you to my wife Annie for being part of this adventure, for coping with the chaos, and for her advice, comments, and encouragement.

1

Again it was hot, it was always hot, the heat replete with humidity that spawned inertia and fatigue. Oh for a fresh breeze. No wonder the 19th century missionaries died like flies, they must have been mad walking around in three layers of woolly clothes whilst trying to gain some Christian converts. Only 40 miles away at the next sizeable town, Lokoja, was a small cemetery adjacent to the now redundant mission station. Wandering around the silent, overgrown garden was a sad experience. The melancholy vines cascaded over tombstones and crosses, reflecting the tragedy of the place. There, carved upon each tombstone, was the name of a European victim of yet another unidentifiable tropical disease. It was heart-breaking to read that some of the young men barely lasted three months before they succumbed, miles from home, hoping that their religious fervour and pious beliefs would see them through. Malaria was substantially more powerful than God in this part of the world, he thought. Even though he was devoid of any religious persuasion he couldn't help but admire the selflessness of those missionaries whose life expectancy was similar to that of the men in the trenches at the Somme.

A kite swooped down on some unsuspecting prey and broke his reverie.

He scanned the area outside his house which stood virtually alone in a sea of tall hyparrhenia grass.

The sky was cloudless and the hills some ten miles away shimmered in the heat. He wiped the sweat from his forehead and felt a rivulet run down his spine. He shrugged and sighed with anxiety, glanced over his shoulder, and served up an anxious smile to his wife. "Stop worrying," he said, "you'll be old before your time. It will come; they promised didn't they?"

"Yes," was her unconvincing response, "but you know what it's like here, they tell you what you want to hear rather than upset you."

Now and again in the distance he could hear the faint sound of a car engine on the Okene to Benin City road, and each time he listened anxiously in the hope that the sound would increase, meaning the vehicle had turned off the main road and was heading for his house. He flopped down into a chair. Next to him was the silent music centre, unable to play the Saturday Night Fever LP that sat idle on the deck, and just above his head was the redundant light switch and a dusty ceiling fan that was skiving again. He stood up and peered through the mosquito netting and the louvered windows. The roofs of the college buildings could be just seen above the swaying grass and three or four acacia trees that obstructed the gravel path to his house.

"Did you hear it?" he quizzed his wife. "I'm sure I heard an engine and it wasn't a car." He watched in earnest. He saw it before he heard it. There, just above the trees, was a growing cloud of fine laterite dust, and then the groan of an engine, the grinding of gears, the banging of loose pieces of metal and the crunch of heavy wheels on gravel. It appeared, rocking from side to side, surely un-roadworthy he thought, but who bloody cares, the water wagon was about to arrive at their house and give them, some four days late, their weekly allocation of 400 gallons of brown lake water. His wife stood up relieved and he ran through the screen door onto the road, waving madly to make sure the water tanker stopped. His flailing, gesticulating arms created an image of desperation, as though he needed rescuing from an invisible assassin.

The decision-making process that had brought them to this place was the result of a memorable invigorating, frightening, anxiety-ridden, original, frustrating and character forming experience in Africa some five years earlier. Four glorious years in Uganda as a teacher at a classy, highly organised and academic school had given him and his wife 'the African bug.' Even though they were settled back in England, both working and into their seventh year of marriage, the lure of Africa was still retained and they found it hard not to get upset and nostalgic when watching some safari programme or a documentary on Africa.

They had gone there during the halcyon days of British overseas educational aid, but now the Times Educational Supplement 'Jobs Abroad' section no longer bristled with Ministry of Overseas Development jobs. Nevertheless, they hoped one day to be able to live there again. A month-long visit to Kenya to see old friends had had them longing for the desirable expatriate life of a fine government house, hot and cold running servants, a decent cost of living, and a teaching post that placed him among the top 2%

of earners in the country. But a settled life, decent jobs, many friends and a hedonistic lifestyle unencumbered by kids, had made another expatriate experience somewhat remote. That is until, whilst getting ready for his night class, his wife phoned. "I'm pregnant," she said. It was December 1976.

2

Only 24 hours ago they were surrounded by the reassurance of familiarity. Their world was ordered, secure and organised and they were comfortable with their circumstances. In many respects they were typical of a middle-class family, albeit one without children, in the sense there was job security and a certain predictability about life; this routine was the result of their circumstances. There was enough spare money to take decent holidays to France or Italy in the summer, but there was no great sense of adventure, no tingling of the nerves or the thrill of excitement generated by the unknown. As much as they loved England something was missing, and they knew exactly what it was.

It is often said that when spending time in Africa, for all its poverty, politics and economic woes, the continent can cast a spell on you. Africa is like a tune in your head that you can't get rid of. It creeps up on you unexpectedly, invading your body and soul, and the smallest image or faintest smell can evoke memories and longing that make you want to return. Why is it that an image of Africa can propagate an indefinable yearning for the place? It is so far removed from the security of Europe, it can be risky, though exotic, it can be both enervating and invigorating. Going to Africa for the first time can be a shock to the system and unlike anything ever experienced before.

It may be to do with the quality of life, especially for a pampered expatriate with his wrap-around verandah, the Club, the garden boy, cook and ayah, or his fine salary that places him near the top of the economic tree. It can be the weather. Yes, there's extreme heat, deluges of rain or long, dry season droughts, but the one universal is the sun and how its warmth and brightness makes everything feel and look better.

There are the miles of open country, the romantic game parks, friendly locals, and the ubiquitous gin and tonic at sunset. But there is also the unpredictability of the continent, the excitement, the apprehension over what's around the corner, the unknown, the erratic and unreliable, and these are the things that make it an exciting place to live. Nothing is certain and many times it's definitely risky. Will there be a delivery of petrol, will the electricity fail, can we get through on this bush road, what tropical illness could strike me down, will the car break down in the middle of nowhere, what if I need a doctor, dentist, surgeon... always what if, and it is in part this uncertainty and sense of adventure and danger that makes expatriates want to return.

'It's so bloody boring driving in the UK,' Karl often used to say. No holes in the road that could swallow a goat, no corrugations that could shake your car to bits, no mud up to your wheel arches or worrying road blocks. Not everyone would miss that, but Karl and Anna did.

Only 24 hours ago Karl had sat with his father in the small front room of his house. He was completely consumed with guilt as he thought about the decision that he and Anna had made to leave England to work in Nigeria. Now that their departure was only hours away he was having reservations about the decision, but all those reservations shrank in comparison to what he was about to impose on his father.

Just why were they going? Yes, a genuine love of Africa and a desire to return to a more adventurous life. Yes, to replicate the wonderful, privileged time they had experienced in Uganda. Yes, to experience West Africa because he thought that its mixture of Christian/Muslim culture would be interesting, but he had done little to really find out about it. He'd obtained masses of information about how challenging Nigeria could be, but he knew, as he reflected on it, that he had mentally looked for the good points and allowed the bad points to disappear like dust in the hoover. Anna had relied on him to weigh up the pros and cons, and he had accepted a position there even though he had some worrying misgivings. And the answer? That was easy. It was all down to money. Money and their standard of living were the deciding factors for his flawed decision-making.

But even though going to West Africa was irrevocable, with the plane almost on the runway and revving up its engines, he knew that he hadn't really thought through his choice. Pound notes floated in front of his eyes and distorted his vision, but what about his father?

There his dad had sat in his well-worn armchair in front of the low glow of the gas fire, putting on a brave face. 'Well, you know best,' he had said

15

on numerous occasions. Karl had wanted his father to say, 'You're doing the right thing, go and have a big adventure, I'll be alright.' But the omnipresent fact that hung around like a nimbus cloud was that only 20 days ago Karl's mother had died suddenly. His dad, the man who had always said, 'The only way I know how to make money is to work hard,' and 'What would I do without Tina?' had aged in the last three weeks. He had sat, leaning forward in his chair, his sleeves rolled up and his labourer's arms resting on his thighs.

Karl recalled that when he was a boy, his dad would come home from working his shift at the steel works and take off his shirt to wash himself at the kitchen sink. His white torso and red arms had clearly defined muscles and a just visible faded tattoo that said 'Mother'. He was now 63 years old and had just retired, giving up work earlier than expected to look after his wife who, for many years, had been prone to ill health. He had a deep sonorous voice with a fine Teesside accent. He was a parsimonious Yorkshire man when it came to money and the way in which he spent it on himself. A few pints on a Friday and Sunday lunchtime were his indulgence. He followed the edict of never spending more than you earn. He refused any notion of credit or hire purchase after being drastically overcharged at the age of 21 when he had bought a bike on what was called 'the never never.' He was always willing to point out that 'never never' meant never gets paid for. But any spare money he had would go on his kids and wife. There was no penny pinching with them, nor was there extravagant abandon, just the sensible approach that if there was any surplus it would go to his family. He was a generous man.

He had sat with his head down, ruminating, not looking at his son but pretending to study the headline in the Daily Mirror that lay at his feet in the hearth. Karl tried to picture what was going through his mind. What did he really think of his son, his daughter-in-law and a future grandchild leaving the country at such a delicate time? He had never said to them, 'Don't go.' He had never ventured a comment about possibly delaying their departure. He just kept on saying, 'You know best, do what is right for your family.'

Karl wanted his father to be like him with his straight talking, to the point attitude. His father and his sister were blessed with common sense. They could simplify a supposedly sophisticated problem, see through the intricacies and come up with sensible solutions. Often when he had mentioned a problem to his dad or sister, he would think to himself, 'Why didn't I think of that?'

His father was educated, but not educated. He left school at the age of 14, and though his formal education went no further, he was a self-educated man who took a real interest in politics and world events and held strong, justifiable opinions about social issues. He was a staunch Labour Party supporter. He was once told he should consider running for Mayor because of his ability to tell stories in a loud, ringing voice full of real presence.

As Karl had tried to work out what his father was thinking, he had been consumed with even more guilt. Just how little consideration had he given his mother when she was unwell before her death? How much had he thought about his father? Had he ever taken into consideration what his dad might have thought or his current circumstances? Had he ever asked for his advice? Had he really thought through the implications of leaving at a time when his dad needed him and his sister to be there.

Karl's mother had died on his and Anna's seventh wedding anniversary. His father had announced his mam's passing with a grim phone call.

And now, 20 days later, he was leaving and it was all for money!

Only 24 hours ago his sister had telephoned and asked him if he could delay his departure. He had answered 'No' on the grounds that if he didn't go when stipulated he would break his contract and end up unemployed and broke. He hadn't even called the Nigerian Embassy to ask for a compassionate delay.

Only 24 hours ago Anna had been with her mother. She had gone to say goodbye and was dreading it, not just because she was leaving her mum but because of the agony of saying the final words as she left. They had faced each other in a warm and cluttered front room, soft with deep chairs, cushions, thick curtains and warm rugs. The fire in the room invited torpor, warmth, snuggling up in a chair reading and day dreaming. It was full of decorative eclectic items from sales rooms; old landscape water colour images in curvilinear frames, a huge dark wooden cabinet full of old letters, a Chinese writing bureau lacquered black and full of delicate inlay, and quirky jars and vases on flat surfaces. A small un-groomed, long-haired dog traipsed across the room leaving a little shower of dog hair and the aroma of dirt. It was early evening in April and the sun was going down, giving an orange glow to the room. The grinding gears of a bus could be heard at the end of the road.

Her mother had recognised the anxiety in Anna's eyes, her apprehension sandblasted in her face.

'Are you sure you're going to be alright?' she said. 'With it being your first I do worry. Where is it you're going to have the baby? I remember when you both went to Uganda, oh you were so excited.'

'I was newly married, Mum.'

'Yes, but you couldn't wait to go, it was all you ever talked about. In fact, we all got fed up of Africa this, Uganda that...'

'Do you remember the tourist brochure?'

'The tourist brochure, yes I do, and I have to admit where you were going looked so exotic, and the school, well, you hit the jackpot there. What a school, what a view and the house you were going into, it looked like a millionaire's place. What a view!'

'It was just a bungalow, Mum, a gift to the school from the Americans.'

'No wonder you were excited. Oh how you loved buying masses of cotton underwear and cool clothes, reading about the Baganda, and Karl trying to learn some rudimentary Swahili. He isn't one for languages is he?'

'No.'

'So tell me about Kaduna, what's your house going to be like?'

'Well I don't really know.'

Her mother had looked at her, raising her eyebrows in a silent question.

'They haven't given us a lot of details.'

'Who are they?'

'The people at the college and in the Ministry of Education.'

She had paused and looked at her mother. It was obvious she wanted to know more.

'They haven't been very good at answering our letters. Karl's future boss has been very good telling him about the education department and giving him details of his role, but as he said he has nothing to do with accommodation. But he was helpful at putting us in contact with the local mission hospital.'

'What is it called? Have you checked it out?'

'Well, yes the best we could, but we were told that lots of expatriates have had their children there.'

'And?'

'It's called Our Lady of the Holy Cross, it's only a mile or two from the college. Karl didn't like the name; you know how he is about religion.'

The sun dropped below the level of the window and the rays caused her mother's face to glow whilst Anna became a silhouette. Her mother had bitten her bottom lip at one side, her facial expression saying *I'm unconvinced*. Anna had remained silent as her mother changed position in her chair and leaned forward to touch her hands. At first it was touch, changing to a caress and then an embrace of her fingers with those of her daughter, the gesture revealing her mother's anxiety.

Unsolicited, Anna said, 'They don't seem very organised in Kaduna. I wish it was the Ministry of Overseas Development we were working for. They were so organised and reassuring... the Nigerians... well, they're not very good and I do have a few little worries, but we're going now.'

'You could always stay here and join Karl when the baby is born.'

'No mum, the reason we're going is simple. Karl gets well paid, we get a free house, we can have a couple of servants helping me, and it means life will be a lot easier there for a new mum than in England. Me not working doesn't matter, Karl gets more than enough. It will be just like Kampala.'

'I remember all those years ago, when was it, how long ago was it? As I said you were so exited you were...'

'I know I was mum, and this is another adventure. Just wait, in a week or so we'll be settled in, I'll be bossing cooks and servants about, and I promise as soon as we've unpacked our bags I'll call you.'

Only 24 hours ago Karl had received a letter from one of their old friends from their time in Kampala. They had kept in touch over the years and had visited each other even though they were at other ends of the country, and now he was working on a contract in Lagos. Tony was a lift engineer working for Otis, an ebullient Londoner, gregarious, with a self-deprecating sense of humour and a propensity for saying it as it is. Karl had read the letter twice, or was it three times, and had decided, rightly or wrongly that he should temporarily keep it from Anna.

Dear Karl and Anna,

You have a nerve following me around the world, I didn't know I was so popular. I ask myself what are you after? Did you loan me money on your last trip to Stretford and you're chasing a debt? How much was it, a fiver? Typical of a tight-arsed Yorkshireman.

Nigeria is expensive. Bloody expensive! I hope they're paying you well or even remember to pay you because the cost of living here, well it makes London look cheap. The government, every strand of it is disorganised, and you'll find out about the dreaded 'dash' soon enough.

I hope you've got decent accommodation because it's normal practice that the Nigerians ask for a year's rent in advance. At least you're not in

Lagos, not that I know what Kaduna is like, you know me, I actually had to look it up on a map.

Lagos is manic, corrupt, expensive, dirty. I could go on, but I've heard from lots of people that the further you get from Lagos the better it is. Kaduna must be half a million miles away, so you'll be alright. Work is fine though I do miss the wife and kids. I decided after two weeks here that they would be better off staying in London rather than sweating buckets here and paying a fortune for a flat or having to sit in traffic all day. I get home once a month, though that's about to change to make sure the wife gets what she needs, sorry Anna, but you know a man's needs. I can't understand why you haven't decided to come out first, get organised, and then get Anna to come.

*After all my good advice I think your baby should be named after me, Antonia or Tony Whixley sounds good. So if you ever get down to Lagos then yes, there'll always be room for you but you pay for the beer we drink. Best of luck and remember Nigeria is **not** Uganda (even though it got a bit hairy there at times). In fact, the whole atmosphere of West Africa is different to that of the East.*

When you wet the baby's head make sure I'm invited, with all your money you can pay the fare from Lagos to Kaduna.

Tony

Karl had stuffed the letter in his case. He would decide later on when they were settled whether he would show it to his wife. A bit deceitful, yes, but he didn't want to see any more anxiety radiating from her.

The hire car had been packed, the house let for twelve months. The mortgage would be paid and the attic had been locked, securing the 50 bottles of homemade red wine he had left to mature in the roof space. He had been seconded from his job and in exactly two years it had been guaranteed that he could take up his position again, coming back wiser, more experienced and therefore a greater asset to the college. Well, he didn't really believe that, but that was the tone of the writing on his secondment letter. *Just think,* he had said to himself, *at least we're going to the warmth, going to the Education Department at Kaduna Polytechnic and we won't have to scrimp and save to make ends meet.* With that thought he had convinced himself that another working trip to Africa was the right decision.

When they had arrived at Heathrow Anna had gone for a wander around duty free. As Karl sat guarding their hand luggage his thoughts had turned again to his father. The date was the 26 April and only three weeks ago his mother had died aged 61.

Could he ever forget that early Sunday morning call? *How strange,* he had thought, *why is the phone ringing at 7am?* His first thought was that his football team captain had cancelled the game or the opposition had cried off. His father answered, his words and his sonorous tone would be indelibly etched into his memory. Three weeks ago she had died and now here he was at Heathrow airport about to disappear for at least a year whilst his dad had to come to terms with the loss of his wife with only the support of his daughter. Was he avoiding responsibility? At this moment in time, he was dragging his wife, four months pregnant, to West Africa. *Did she really want to go,* he asked himself for the hundredth time, and if she didn't, why hadn't she said so? He felt slightly sick at the thought of analysing his decision.

All the options he had never thought of, and why? Because he was afraid of being unemployed for two years and basically it was money. He had convinced himself and his wife that they would never manage financially if they lost Anna's income. But all his friends with young kids had managed. Anna's two sisters had managed. It was just a matter of being careful with the cash, but he didn't think they could manage.

He got out of his seat and taking the hand baggage with him walked to a telephone. It offered him a view of the duty-free shops should his wife wander back and not see him. He made a line of 50p and 10p pieces on top of the phone and dialled his father.

His first words were 'I am really worried about going, Joe' He was actually slightly frightened and the letter from Tony had only enhanced his consternation.

'That's not like you,' was his reply.' His father was sure that his son was clever enough to always make the right decisions and he often used to say, 'Well you know best,' when in actual fact he didn't.

'Dad, are you alright, will you be alright?' knowing full well that he wasn't going to be fine after his wife had died only three weeks ago. He felt guilty for not grieving as much as his dad.

'I'm fine Karl, I'll be alright, your sister is around.'

And I'm not, Karl thought.

'And I'll get to the library like you said, and Sandra will help, now you look after that wife of yours and my grandchild, they're more important than me.'

There was an anxious pause before he added, 'I will be fine, and how long is it before you are both home, a year isn't it, my goodness my grandchild could be walking by then,' and to add some levity he said, 'just think, I'll get to miss all the boring bits when the baby just eats and sleeps. When you get back she'll be able to recognise her own granddad. Now your mam would have been so proud, she was waiting so long for this to happen.'

'Dad, no wonder I feel so guilty, how could I, I just don't want to get on this plane, do you think I am doing the right thing?'

Karl just wasn't sure, but had set his dad up to hear the answer he cherished.

'You know best son; your duty is to your wife not me. Honestly, I'll be fine. Write to me.'

'Of course I will, in fact I'll phone when I get there.'

'Go, have an adventure, perhaps you get leave in the summer, perhaps.'

Guilt constricted him like a python. 'Yes I'll try... Dad...The money is running out... Dad, I am sorry, look after yourself, I will be thinking of you all the time. I'll ring, I promise I'll ring.'

But he never did. It is not that he didn't want to, but Nigeria was not East Africa, or Kampala or Kings College, Budo and he had yet to experience just how different it would be. He was flying to Lagos and not Nairobi and well, the phones just didn't work in Nigeria unless you knew someone who knew someone who had cash and influence. But he was not to know that yet.

3

Earlier they had left their heavy bags at the Heathrow Victoria terminal and decided that before their flight a quick excursion to Oxford Street for some pick-me-up retail therapy was in order. Anna left Karl to his own devices for an hour and went in search of a hair dresser, while unbeknown to her he did the same thing, deciding that he should look as professional as possible when meeting the head of department in Kaduna. He was also very aware that for the next two years he would have a well-meaning amateur cutting his hair or, at worst, Anna sighing with despair as she hacked bits of his hair indiscriminately, giving it a manic asymmetrical look, a bit like Einstein only without the curls.

He had tried doing it himself on one occasion and had ended up with a large, unmissable bald spot which was then commented on by all of his so-called friends; 'It's bare enough for a moon landing,' or 'are you going to build a hut in that clearing in the forest.' He was also referred to as the man with the apprentice tonsure. At least it wasn't as bad as the haircut given to a colleague of his in Uganda, who had decided to have his mane of hair cut at the local market at a price equal to the purchase of one boiled sweet. Ben, ever wanting to support the local villagers, had taken his seat on a chair old enough to have been left by Burton and Speke, which was placed in the middle of the small local market. He peered into the stained mirror hanging from a tree, and proceeded to be the subject of a great deal of hilarious entertainment for all the stall holders and customers as they watched the first muzungu ever to have his hair cut there. The barber obviously wanted to impress and took great care in the placement of his scissors. Unfortunately, he couldn't quite get it right and proceeded to adjust each side so that it was equally balanced in length. Still failing to get it right, with admirable determination that really impressed the onlookers but was rather worrying for Ben, he continued to cut his hair shorter and shorter to the extent that there was more pink scalp than black hair.

The barber had stood back as he finished. He admired his work with a proud, presentational gesture of an open palm and uttered the Luganda equivalent of 'voila!' Ben got up, looked in the mirror and assumed a criminal was looking at him. He swallowed deeply, hiding his concern while thinking of the avalanche of comments that would be waiting for him, thanked the barber, and gave him the equivalent of five pence. The barber was full of pride at his magnificent achievement and gave a little bow because he was overwhelmed that the muzungu was so pleased. The onlookers whooped and clapped with admiration. Ben's colleagues, true to form, had likened him to an escaped inmate from Broadmoor and had told him not to smile at their children for fear of inducing nightmares.

Karl decided he would stick with his wife, despite her tonsorial inadequacies. He saw her coming toward him at the end of Moulton Street to their agreed meeting point. She was smiling and looked radiant. With a light-weight pregnancy dress, a pair of new sandals and a huge tube of Colgate tooth paste sticking out of the bag, they wandered into the Heathrow check-in area in Victoria. The idea was to check your baggage in, get your boarding cards, and take a leisurely double-decker bus ride through west London to Terminal Three. A clever commercial plot, Karl thought, thinking of all the time they'd have before their flight to spend money on useless duty free items at the airport. Judging by the average temperatures in Northern Nigeria all they should be stocking up on was anti-perspirant and sun block.

At the empty check-in desk two young women, elegant and slim in their grey Heathrow uniforms, chatted and laughed. One was wearing a badge that said, 'Hello, I'm Holly' and the other had a partially obscured badge with the name Jeanie just visible. Karl heaved the straining trolley towards the desk and was greeted with a jocular, 'Now that really looks heavy, and that must be the biggest tube of toothpaste I've ever seen. Are you going away for a couple of months?' Jeanie asked.

'Two years actually,' responded Karl.

'How exciting, let me guess, America.'

A shake of the head.

'How about the Caribbean?'

'No, Africa actually,' said Anna, and before she could add Nigeria, 'Hello I'm Holly,' remarked, 'Oh, you're so lucky, aren't they Jeanie?' Her eyes were semi-closed and her head rocked from side to side as she went into a minor rapture. 'How lucky you are, it's something I've always wanted to do. I've got a friend in Nairobi who writes to me about his great life, his safaris, his encounters, his trips to Mombasa. It's paradise there, and so cheap.'

Jeanie said, 'No, it would be Salisbury and Rhodesia for me, even cheaper, and it's got Victoria Falls and all those bronzed rugged white farmers. I can see myself now, my future husband running a huge farm with me by his side in the sunshine.'

'We're not going on holiday, we're actually going to work there for two years,' Karl said.

'Jo'burg?'

'Cape Town?'

'Neither,' said Anna. 'We're going to Nigeria and we're on the flight to Lagos.'

'Lagos,' they said with wide-eyed astonishment, 'Lagos!'

'Hello I'm Holly' and Jeanie looked at each other. There was a minor shake of the head that radiated disbelief. Jeanie looked at their bags on the scales and raised her eyebrows as she carried out the unfortunate duty of telling them that their luggage was massively overweight and that British Caledonian would charge them a fortune.

'British Caledonian did you say?' asked Anna.

'Yes, they're very strict about weight and the size of hand baggage and I reckon that...' she paused as she did a quick mental calculation, 'these bags are going to cost you well over £100!'

'What, a hundred pounds!' exclaimed Karl.

'But we are not travelling with British Caledonian,' commented Anna.

'You are going to Lagos?'

'Yes.'

'Are you sure you're not going with British Caledonian?'

Karl and Anna maintained a united silence.

'You're on the Nigerian Airways flight?' they said, their voices full of disbelief. 'Well the good news is that Nigerian Airlines don't really bother about weight, so you could take another huge suitcase if you had one and it wouldn't cost you a penny.'

'Hold on a moment, I'm not quite sure I know what you mean. Let me get this clear, are you telling me that Nigerian Airlines have no strict policy on how much weight they carry?' said an alarmed Karl.

'Well, I don't suppose it is a policy, but from my experience they certainly fly by their own set of rules.'

'Hello I'm Holly' interrupted, 'And when you're there don't drink the water, even on the flight, unless it's from a sealed bottle, and if you get a bottle make sure it's not bottled in Lagos because...'

'It could come from the harbour,' laughed Jeanie.

'Watch out for fruit as well, there are so many bugs that lay their eggs on the skin. You have to wash it first.'

'That's just common sense,' said Karl indignantly, 'We've lived in Africa before you know, we're not completely naive.'

Then, very slowly, 'Hello I'm Holly' leaned over the counter like some praying mantis and said, with a mischievous grin, 'But you've never lived in Lagos.'

'Nor have you I suspect, where do you get these alarmist ideas from?'

'My former boyfriend was a British Caledonian rep at Ikeja airport and he was always sick with something. Nasty sores, he even had a huge boil on his back. At one point he was wasting away...'

Jeanie joined in the conversation. They were in charge of it and enjoying a little bit of status by spouting their knowledge as though they were seasoned travellers and explorers.

'What about that fungal infection he got?'

'Was that the one between his toes or that delicate area we shouldn't mention?'

'No, I forgot about that, it was in his left ear.'

'Hygiene, that's the problem, there isn't any.'

'Then we'll just have to be careful, won't we,' Karl said loudly and affirmatively, whilst looking for visual nodding confirmation from his wife.

'Pork is a big problem, so my boyfriend said. So whatever you do, don't eat the pork.'

'What's wrong with eating pork, we're not Jewish!'

'Because it could be human,' said Jeanie.

'Human!' they exclaimed in unison.

Karl and Anna were aghast. They looked at each other. They had come to drop off bags, had been told that their airline was happy to fly with too much weight, everything was too dangerous to eat or drink, and most preposterous of all the pork could be human. Even though Karl was full of disbelief he wasn't quite sure and there was that lingering doubt that their tales of woe might have a hint of truth.

'My ex said if you're going to eat meat make sure you watch it being killed, oh and don't eat Brazilian meat it has been on a ship for months and months, and don't...'

'Stop, we've had enough, you're just scaremongering and by the look of it you're enjoying it.'

'Sir,' replied Jeanie, 'I'm sorry, we're just shocked that anyone other than a Nigerian would actually choose to fly with them.'

Anna felt she had to explain. 'We're working for the Nigerian government and they're the ones that have paid for our flight, otherwise, as you said, we would have flown with British Caledonian.'

'Do we get our boarding passes and seat numbers now?' Karl said firmly, getting rather fed up with this conversation.

Holly handed them over, feeling it was her duty to tell the two passengers that they had a right to know one more thing.

'The seat numbers I have given you are a bit meaningless, because quite often it can be a bit of a free-for-all when you board.'

'Another wind up I suppose, just point us in the direction of the bus.' He turned on his heel, not allowing them an opportunity to respond.

Pork, water, seat numbers, all those comments, he muttered to himself, and they haven't even been there. He tutted, took hold of his wife's hand, then put his arm around her as if they were a courting couple, symbolically trying to protect her from the content of the conversation.

As had been predicted at check-in, when they boarded the plane at Heathrow they had to be firm with the stewardess when telling her they had no intention of sitting apart, nor would they sit at the back of the fuselage in the smoking section of the plane, and they eventually got their two dedicated seats together towards the back. In the window seat was a gentleman of huge proportions, some of which hung over the armrest and took up rather a lot of Anna's space. In spite of the fact that thankfully he didn't smoke, the designated smoking area signs were ignored by everyone else. The flight was virtually full, and just when it seemed that they were ready to close the doors shouting was heard from the front of the plane. Karl leaned his head over so he could see up the aisle and there was a large African lady in traditional dress, labouring with a massive piece of hand baggage. Even from a distance it looked far too large to fit in any overhead locker, and from Karl's semi-obscured viewpoint it looked like a spare wheel for a car.

A conversation commenced in which she demanded her rights and the two Nigerian airline employees demanded theirs. There was an impasse, and then a shrug of the shoulders by the male flight attendant who walked purposefully up the aisle and then stopped and opened an overhead locker. His face was full of fury, and as he removed the baggage from the locker his body language said, 'Don't bloody mess with me, I have a problem to sort out!' The portly, well-dressed lady shuffled awkwardly up the aisle and to Karl's shock she was, after all, carrying a spare car wheel and tyre, and not just any wheel – it had the distinct symbol of Mercedes Benz on the hubcap.

The flight attendant, just to prove a point, continued to empty the locker, much to the consternation of the owners of the contents, and plonked them in the aisle. This brought about easily predictable vociferous complaints. Immediately the attendant refused to hide behind a mattress of diplomacy and said, 'Let me do my bloody job,' radiating another don't-mess-with-me look. After monstrous grunting, the steward got a segment of the wheel into the overhead locker but a third of it hung precariously outside, ready to decapitate the man below should it fall.

The flight attendant stared at the huge woman and said firmly and sarcastically, 'Now do you believe it won't fit!' This is when Karl and Anna knew they were definitely not on the British Caledonian flight; politeness, avoidance of conflict, the mind-one's-own business attitude, were nowhere to be seen. Everyone had an opinion and no one had a discreet voice. Everyone within sight of the Mercedes wheel hanging out of the overhead locker became involved, shouting out their advice and opinions. Chaos ensued.

The portly, well-dressed woman was obviously someone not to be physically messed with. After all, she had carried a huge, heavy spare wheel under one fat arm and numerous disintegrating bulging plastic bags with the other. She now stood, arms akimbo, and even she knew that the wheel had to be removed. She tutted in exasperation as she expressed her opinion that the steward had not tried hard enough, and around her half of the opinionated passengers thought she had been hard done by and the other half thought she was an idiot, though one not to be messed with physically.

The wheel was taken down. The steward had proved his point and it was wheeled down the aisle, away from the shocked Karl and Anna, and placed against the door of the pilots' cabin next to a pile of battered cardboard boxes and a huge standard lamp that had also refused to go into a locker.

As things finally settled down, Karl was offered a drink and took it, but what he didn't expect to be given was a huge glass bottle of Nigerian Crystal beer. Anna took her usual tomato juice and Tabasco sauce. The huge man next to her proved he was a man of substance by managing to devour three one-litre bottles of beer and then rather quickly descended into an immovable sleep.

Huge glass bottles on an airplane, the size of a mortar shell and 5.5% proof. Was this a plan to pacify unruly passengers or to get them to go to sleep before the food was delivered? It turned out to be a bit of both. Anna took the tray with its bread roll and vacuum packed cheese, declining the carton of hot food. The stewardess, when asked what was concealed under the tin foil, pulled a 'do you expect me to know everything face' and said that she had no idea. Karl was brave, tried it and discovered that after one mouthful it was unlike anything he had ever seen or tasted before. The huge piece of raw okra, reclining like a corpse, had a threatening look. The foil cover was replaced and Anna and Karl had bread and cheese for supper.

A litre of beer caused him to drift quickly into sleep. The huge man next to Anna was comatose, his belly moving in and out as though he was attached to bellows. The Captain announced that unfortunately there would no film because the projector was temporarily out of order. Anna curled up in her seat, eyes darkened by the eye mask she was wearing, and she too appeared to sleep. The airplane was quiet at last, the shouting of greetings all over had stopped, as had the constant demands for attention from the cabin crew. This was the nosiest flight Karl had ever been on, and he was referring to the humans, not the engines.

He woke up when the plane landed in Kano in the early hours of the morning for a few disembarking passengers. He couldn't help thinking, with Kaduna only a two-hour drive away from the airport, how convenient it would have been if he and Anna could have terminated their journey here. But the reason for their journey to Lagos was so they could be briefed and inducted at the Federal Ministry. They could spend a few days in a nice hotel, Anna could relax, they would get over their fatigue and become acclimatised, and he would have a couple of days no doubt filling in forms. That much was for certain wherever you were in Africa.

They stood up, leaving the portly man to grunt and snore in private, and made their way to the back of the plane. The rear door was open, and even at 4 in the morning the warmth poured into the plane. The first smells to greet them in Nigeria were of aviation fuel, damp decaying vegetation, and dominating all was the unmistakable smell of shit. But there was warmth that wrapped itself around you, that greeted you like an old friend, cuddled you and made you feel welcome, so that thoughts of frost and mist and grey clouds were instantly discarded. It was dark outside with a few unidentifiable lights in the distance, but the warmth and smells were what they had wanted and had been looking forward to.

For most of the time it would be a little hotter than they wanted, he just didn't know that yet!

4

The airport was as grim as a slag heap on a damp winter's day. That was his first impression when he stood at the top of the stairs. In the few seconds before he was unceremoniously pushed in the back, he was aware of the heavy cloudy sky, the run-down flaky green-grey of the terminal buildings and the piles of junk scattered everywhere. *Is this really the international airport?* he thought. He breathed in and his lungs were swamped with humidity and the smell of shit. Running across the tarmac little boys of all shapes and sizes and dressed in all manner of rags surrounded him and the other passengers trying to grab their hand baggage. As the urchins tried to help he thought, *how on earth will they carry the cases of whisky and the car wheel and just what were they doing in the supposedly secure part of the airport?*

The Nigerians had no sympathy with the little boys, they were punched and hit, and one only reluctantly let go of a passenger's luggage when he was assaulted with a walking stick. Karl was tempted to take an aggressive stance and tell them loudly to fuck off, but he thought better of it, remembering the golden phrase that helped one navigate through the experience that was Africa – patience, politeness and persistence.

The immigration man was uncouth and came from the 'I don't give a toss about your school or college.' He gave a stare of resentment and intolerance. *Welcome to Nigeria*, Karl thought.

The wait was interminable. The heat and the damp atmosphere attacked them. He discarded his jacket and turned to see his wife covered in a fine film of sweat. She leaned on the squeaking trolley for support after refusing to pay an airport worker for its use. Bags were being thrown about. Aggressive confrontations were taking place. All around them there was no order and piles of suitcases were strewn about like a collapsed cliff. He made sure that Anna was fine as he left her for a moment and dived into the

31

melee to rescue one of their bags. In a moment of objective reflection he wondered what a first-time-arrival would make of the scene. During four years in Uganda he'd seen nothing like the anarchy all around him. He gave an unconvincing smile of reassurance to his wife and watched as a small boy with a razor blade tried to cut open a case. The boy was grabbed by the hair, shouts of thief filled the air, and as he was dragged away the people around, some of whom were 20 feet away, joined in to give him a kick.

At Customs they were greeted with a wide white smile when he showed the officer his Federal Government status. It took an exhausting hour, and all around was visual chaos. Crooked, dust-covered fans creaked lamentably over a sea of cracked floor tiles and uncollected trash. There were more people than air, everyone was shouting, and as they came into the arrivals hall there was a wall of locals looking for a way to make a naira or two from the arrivals. And always there was the overpowering smell of shit.

He and Anna must have looked vulnerable and lost in spite of the confidence and unconcerned image they tried to project. A tall, dignified-looking European came up behind them and said in a very proper English voice, 'Welcome to the 17th Century. Is this your first time here?' he added. 'Just remember to keep your sense of humour. Where are you going to work, who is collecting you?'

Karl replied, 'We're working for the Federal Ministry of Education and I'm looking for their sign board right now.'

'Don't waste your time,' was the reply. 'You stand no chance of a government organisation picking you up, they're not that organised.'

'But I was told.'

'Never mind what you were told, you could wait here until Armageddon and still nothing would arrive. Where is your posting?'

'Kaduna.'

'Well, best of luck.' He paused thoughtfully, 'Kaduna, that's 600 miles north of here. Typical of the government, couldn't organise the proverbial you-know-what, but there is one thing going for the country, they brew a decent beer. But watch out, this can be a hard place to live.'

'Any ideas?' Karl said forlornly. 'Airport bus?'

'I wouldn't if I was you, and that's even if they're running. Death traps, old death traps.' He suddenly waved and moved towards a man dressed in the archetypical driver's uniform who was waving a placard that said 'Carmichael'. He turned, looked over his shoulder and shouted, 'Sorry old man, can't take you, I'm miles in the other direction. Get yourself a cab before your bags are stolen and be bloody firm and bargain. And don't take any nonsense from the driver!'

Outside the sky was as grey as the terminal ceiling and heavy and heaving with moisture. The humidity could be sliced, and he concluded that the lamentable ceiling fans inside the airport had after all had some effect. He briefly thought about putting his jacket back on; he had wanted to at least look professional and important when he arrived so that the Ministry representative would know at a glance he was a senior education officer and therefore warranted some respect, but he felt totally crushed by the heat. *Some respect,* he thought, *where is the bloody transport that was meant to pick us up?* He pushed the heavily laden squeaking trolley through the landslide of humanity and tried to look calm, cool and unconcerned that he and his pregnant wife were staring culture shock in the face.

'Can you see a taxi rank?' whispered his wife.

'No, just people, lots of people moving about. My god, it's like an ant colony.'

A youth forcibly tried to help him with his trolley. He eased him away, trying not to be unkind or disrespectful. Then came another and another, one of whom tried to grab his jacket. He had moved 30 feet and was surrounded by humanity determined to 'help' him or possibly even remove a heavy bag or two if his attention could be sufficiently distracted. They were being mobbed and they weren't the Beatles. He could feel the sweat trickling under his armpits, his wife looked forlorn, and only five minutes after putting his bags on the trolley he was again questioning his decision making. *What the bloody hell am I doing here with a pregnant wife who's putting on a brave face, weighed down by heat, being shouted at, being accosted by insincere toothy white grins, and breathing in the smell of shit and diesel?*

'Sir, sir, I have a taxi, let me help.' There was an element of calm in the man's face and he seemed to appreciate and recognise Karl's consternation. 'It is just there,' he said, pointing to a sea of higgledy-piggledy parked yellow and purple cars which Karl assumed were taxis. 'Look sir, there sir,' he said, pointing to his left.

Karl look quizzical.

'There sir, the one with the roof rack, very good car sir, I am very good driver, I am Mr Safe, sir. Where are you going? Which hotel? I know them all, very safe I am.'

Karl looked at him, thinking, *well we need a lift, his car looks less of a wreck than the others and he didn't shout* **oyibo** *in my face like everyone else is doing.*

'Sir, are you an oilman? Big business? A professor? I can help, tell me where you want to go.'

Anna had that desperate look on her face and Karl was as keen as she was to get into the safety of a vehicle and away from the relentless human chaos overwhelming them.

'Ministry of Education please.'

'Federal or State? I knew you were a professor, we Nigerians need people like you to help us.'

'Federal, in Ikoyi.'

'Yes sir, I know it very well.'

'Let's just go,' Karl said. The driver assumed some highly welcome responsibility and helped to push the trolley to the waiting car. Anna got in immediately, hoping the doors and windows would provide some protection from the heat, the noise and the chaos. The two heavy bags were thrust in and persuaded to go into the boot, although somewhat disconcertingly the lid was then held down by an unravelled coat hanger that attached it to the rear bumper.

A cardinal error, Karl thought. *We're packed to go and I haven't even negotiated a price yet.*

The taxi driver seemed to read his mind and said, 'I *will* give you a good price, you are here to help Nigeria.'

As far as Karl was concerned the cost didn't actually matter. His priority was to make the 10-mile journey to the ministry, complain gently and diplomatically about the lack of ministry transport to collect them, sign a few papers, get taken to their hotel, and wait for transport or a flight to Kaduna.

The taxi juddered as it started up and moved into the horror that the inhabitants of Lagos know as the 'Go Slow.'

After working for four years in Uganda, during the disturbing time when Idi Amin Dada was in charge, Karl had a lot of stories to tell. He thought himself to be an amateur expert on Africa and as a consequence had become a prolific reader of anything to do with its history. In his suitcase was a huge, half-read book by Thomas Pakenham called 'The Scramble for Africa.'

He had read about Nigeria and its booming economy, its oil exports, the high standard of its fine universities, especially the one in Ibadan, and of course the chaos of the place. Everything he read about Nigeria was devoid of the word tourist. The quickly expanding population meant that unlike in East Africa there were no Amboseli, Maasai Mara or Murchison Falls game parks. All that remained was a single wild life sanctuary boasting a few bedraggled elephants in Yankari game reserve on the plateau near Jos. Tourist just didn't go there and Nigeria was never advertised as a must-visit country for intrepid backpackers. He was thrilled to read about the chaos and excitement of Lagos, and was amazed that a concept such as the 'Go Slow' existed.

Lagos, on the coast of the Bight of Benin, is situated in low-lying swamp land and is renowned for being very hot and sticky. The settlement had grown into a town and inexorably into a huge city that had the predictability of a pile of woollen strands. It had grown without planning, and of course no one could have foreseen the impact of the motor vehicle. The city got to the point where there were more vehicles than areas of road, the result of which was traffic chaos. A daily, damp, dreadful Lagos experience was to be stuck in traffic at mid-day, slowly roasting in one's car in the days before air-conditioning as the heat additionally radiated upward from the melting tarmac.

Something had to be done. The local authorities had a brain wave and came up with a novel solution. An edict was promulgated in which cars with even number plates would only be allowed to drive on the roads of Lagos on Monday, Wednesday and Friday and those with odd numbers had the use of the roads on Tuesday, Thursday and Saturday. Sunday could be used by everyone. The restrictions started at 6am and finished at 7pm, meaning that if your car had an even number you could leave the city on a Tuesday, as long as you were out of the city boundaries by 6am. Of course there was an alternative solution, and that was to pay a bribe to any policemen who happened to stop you.

This system seemed to work well for a few weeks, until counterfeit number plates started being sold. Following the crackdown on that scam, the motor vehicle companies then benefitted because there was a burgeoning of new car sales owing to the fact that owners of odd number plate cars merely purchased one with an even number plate. The traffic situation was only marginally better. The roads were narrow, and it was impossible to make a three-point turn because virtually all of the roads were bounded by huge, deep drainage ditches, which also happened to be convenient places for rubbish as well as being used as public toilets. Traffic lights didn't always work because the supply of electricity was about as predictable as the flight of a butterfly.

At jogging pace, the taxi moved into the glacial tangled mass of traffic. Karl looked at his wife, who was sporting a brave face. He patted her hand and smiled unconvincingly in an attempt to look reassuring. His eyes tried to say we're alright now, but he was very worried about her.

It was hard to tell which side of the road you were supposed to drive on, there seemed to be no order. Vehicles wormed and weaved in and out in the direction they wanted to go and after about five minutes the pandemonium started to subside as they left the anarchic airport entrance and entered the main road from Ikeja, through Ikorodu to the city centre. At last they started to move in a more purposeful way, even as horns blared, engines groaned, brakes squealed, and drivers leaned out of their windows either to greet a friend or yell abuse at someone they considered to be driving badly.

In relative terms, now that they were not being hassled and tormented by undisciplined humanity there was almost a sense of calm in the car. As it moved forward, sometimes at 20mph for 20 or 30 yards, it created, just for a little while, a breeze on the back seat. Karl looked at his wife, colour beginning to return to her cheeks. He leaned forward to ask, 'How long does this journey take?'

'Sir, it is quite good today, I think maybe an hour.'

'And how far is it?'

'About 10 miles.'

Karl tried to inject a bit of levity into the occasion and said, 'I could run and get there quicker.'

The driver laughed. 'I get you there very safe and very quickly, then you can make me happy.'

'And how do I do that?'

'I need a big reward, you oyibos are very rich and I am a humble driver with many children who are always hungry. Just think, I helped with those very heavy cases, you can give me a bonus now if you wish.'

'I'll pay you when you have us safe and sound outside the Federal Ministry of Education.' Karl looked at his watch. 'If you get us there by 9.30, then who knows, you might get your bonus.'

'But I need one, I have many to feed and my arms are weak after carrying your cases.'

Patience, politeness and persistence, Karl thought. 'You need to stop talking and concentrate on the road. This conversation is over!' He leaned over and whispered to his wife, 'I should have kept my mouth shut.'

He found himself wondering where the taxi driver lived, did he really have lots of kids, was it his car or was he merely a poorly-paid driver. The inside of the taxi was customised, with a piece of pseudo-oriental carpet with tassels overhanging the dashboard and a sticker on the windscreen saying 'Fella Forever' which obscured the driver's vision somewhat. The final touch was an inflatable seagull swinging from the ceiling at his right side. He was small and could barely see the road. *I should have been more discerning,* Karl thought.

Whenever the taxi was stationary for more than a minute you could almost hear the heat pour in through the windows, and invariably there appeared, as if from nowhere, a horde of small boys thrusting mangos, bananas, some fried mandazi, newspapers, magazines through the window and shouting for 5 naira.

'How much is that?' Anna asked.

'About £4.'

'What!'

'Businessmen of the future I suspect.'

They were held up at a large road junction for what seemed an eternity. Heat and humidity cocooned them and droplets of sweat fell onto the seat, which they realised was covered in fine dust. The driver was frustrated, seeing his bonus quickly evaporating, and seeing a small gap he accelerated.

Karl looked to his left just in time to see the Volkswagen Combi slam into the side of their taxi. He saw the door suddenly become convex and then he slid towards Anna as the vehicle was lifted to a 45-degree angle. It seemed to hover precariously for a lifetime, and then as the VW bounced back the taxi became horizontal with an almighty thud. The violence of the crash filled the air with dust and he could hear someone screaming. He reached out to comfort and help his wife. Her mouth uttered a howl, her hands and arms shook violently in front of her and she pointed in such a demonstrative way that he just had to look. The shock of the impact had disturbed a colony of rather large cockroaches that proceeded to colonise their feet.

Four legs and feet chaotically stamped on the insects and Karl reached across and opened the passenger door. There was just enough room to get out and he watched as Anna did a manic dance at the side of the vehicle, hoping her gyrations would dislodge any cockroaches. The driver had also got out of the car and was yelling as he headed towards the VW. The stationary disabled taxi was the object of howls of horns and waving fists from windows of vehicles that had been stopped by the accident. The coat hanger had snapped and a suitcase was about to fall out of the boot.

The lowering sky had an ominous look that threatened to burst open and drown them in a tropical deluge, and he and his wife were stranded in a sea of motionless vehicles. The taxi was a wreck. Ignoring the screaming of the two drivers he put his arm around his wife, feeling sick with concern. He pointed to her stomach and asked, 'Is the baby...?'

'Yes, yes,' she replied. Full of tears she said, 'What are we going to do, how are we going to get out of this mess?'

Confused, agitated, worried and upset, he had no answer, but an opportunist glance behind him made him realise that the taxi behind had no passengers. He gesticulated to the driver who suddenly realised he could get a fare. He jumped out to help Karl unload the suitcases and shuffled manfully to get them on the back seat of his car. Karl's driver noticed, ignored the regaling of the VW driver, and tried to grab the cases.

'My passengers,' he screamed, followed by a torrent of abuse to everyone in earshot. He was then grabbed by the burly VW driver who was demanding compensation. Anna got into the new taxi, sharing the back seat with a case, and Karl and his new driver attempted to wrestle the second huge suitcase into the boot, while his former driver made ugly grimaces and threats to Karl and the VW driver. Suddenly he stood still, a pillar of salt and anger. His fists were clenched, he shook with fury and focused all of his febrile hatred on Karl.

'Where is my money?' he screamed. 'I want my money, 100 naira, very bad damage, it was your fault, where is my bonus, give me 200 naira now... my car, it done quench!' He was apoplectic and seething with rage. 'I get the police... I want my money... Give me money.' He leaned past Karl to hurl abuse at the new driver, yelling, 'You thief, you have stolen my passengers... give me money.' The burly VW driver grabbed his shoulder and pulled him back. He too was after compensation.

Karl was sure he had said something like, 'Look at the bloody state of my car you idiot, you crossed the road when you had no right!' in Yoruba of course.

The suitcase was secure in the boot, his wife was secure in the taxi, the traffic started to move and Karl put his hand in his pocket, hoping the two five pound notes he had might calm the situation. The snarling taxi driver stood facing him, their foreheads only three inches apart, and with bared teeth and flying spittle he screamed, 'Give me money!'

It was at this point that Karl remembered that the mantra for getting by in Africa was patience, politeness, and persistence. 'Fuck off!' he said, turning on his heel. As he got into the front seat of the taxi he saw the burly man grab his former driver by the throat. *Welcome to Nigeria,* he thought.

5

As their taxi travelled, albeit slowly, away from the accident, both of them, already exhausted by an overnight flight and the chaos of the airport and then the accident, sighed with relief. But that relief couldn't remove the stifling heat, even though in fits and starts they were moving. Karl, from the front seat, leaned over and took his wife's hand. All he wanted to do was to say sorry. Sorry they were in a sweaty battered taxi in West Africa, sorry for taking her away from their nice house, sorry that he had embarked on a job abroad when she was pregnant and sorry for the uncertainty that this new environment propagated. She smiled back and he was sure she had read his mind. Lines of tension were etched into her face which she tried to eliminate by feigning to take an interest in the views from inside the cab.

As the traffic slowed on the Ikorodu road the driver, who introduced himself as Maximus and was dressed in his traditional and decorative Nigerian garb, interrupted the silence by pointing out the huge Festac arena on the right. He then almost leaned over Karl to point out, somewhat anachronistically, a camel and its owner at the side of an unstable dwelling. Small hastily erected wooden stalls lined the road. The edge of the highway had no exact definition; at times it was a ditch filled with all manner of human and animal waste and detritus or was defined by where the asphalt deteriorated into a ragged edge that crumbled into shacks, shanties and stalls. When the taxi stopped the smell was overpowering and the humidity, almost tactile, hung like a heavy damp curtain. Tables or mats on the earth supported little pyramids of irregular shaped tomatoes, onions and mangoes as well as great piles of yams and bottles full of cloudy homemade palm wine. Adverts from Crystal, Star and Gulder beers were stuck on every available wall along with a huge advert for Nigerian Airways being promoted by a toothy stewardess who was, in Karl's eyes, bloody ugly. *As bad as their food,* he thought. Posters for ointments and tablets to improve your sex life or how to be irresistible to the ladies, how to make your skin lighter and how your life would be complete if you had a boom box the size of a small coffin to carry around with you, a machine that emitted mega decibels revealing you to be cool and rich. Karl actually laughed when the taxi stopped temporarily next to a stall that had an astonishing array of garishly coloured men's shoes, all of which had massive high heels and went up to mid-calf, in a mixture of primary and secondary colours, yellow stars on a purple surface, red on green, orange and blue chequered squares, and they all had somewhere upon them flashes of silver and gold. The owner of the stall even had them hanging from rails like some mad abstract mobile and he tottered around in his own technicolour footwear, only just able to keep his balance. The boots looked as though they had been rejected by Roxy Music. He pointed out the scene to Anna. She too laughed and the driver, wanting to be friendly, commented that they were looking at the latest fashions and also that they wouldn't fall apart in the rain.

'Your madam, master... she is pregnant?' asked Maximus.

'Yes,' was Karl's reply.

'That driver was very bad, he didn't treat you with respect.'

'I know...'

'We Nigerians love children, the more we have the better.'

'Have you got any?'

'Oh yes master, I have three and another on the way. I have much libido and my children show that I am a man.'

Karl looked at him as he readjusted his garment. He gave a huge toothy grin and said, 'Maximus, how old are you?

'Twenty-one master, I am very proud of my family.'

What, three kids, nearly four and you are only 21, well you have been a busy boy.'

Maximus, unsure that he was being complimented, laughed and banged his chest as a symbol of strength and virility. Both hands abandoned the steering wheel.

'How many children do you have at home master?'

'None, this is my first.'

'Really,' exclaimed Maximus in a state of mild shock, a response somewhat disturbing and funny at the same time. 'But master you must try harder.'

Karl, laughed as did Anna, and the brief levity evaporated some of their anxiety and tension.

'Maximus, that is an unusual name for a Nigerian.'

41

'It was my father's wish that I would be a scholar and I would know Latin and Greek, but he wasn't sure that he could afford the school fees so he gave me a Latin name.' He paused,' So that everyone would be impressed and would assume I was clever. My two older brothers are called Pericles and Brutus.'

'Did you go to school?'

'Yes of course, right until I was 13, then we had no more money... but now I have a good job and I hope to get my licence.'

'Licence, licence for what?'

'To drive a car of course...'

Karl and Anna turned and looked at each other and gave a disconcerted smile.

'How long have you been driving?'

'Six years now, so you see I am very safe and experienced and when I get enough money to 'dash' the examiner I will get a licence. Do you think I am a good driver?''

'Well you are a lot better than the one who crashed.'

'He was just a bushman, those Igbiras are stupid and ignorant. How did he get to drive in Lagos? He should be back in the bush hunting bush rats and scratching the soil.'

Igbira?' Karl remarked.

'Igbira, very strange people sir, not nice, not friendly, primitive and not to be trusted... Watch out for them they are no good.'

'How did you know he was an Igbira?

'His voice, he couldn't speak Yoruba properly and he squealed like a parrot. A very stupid people!'

'And whereabouts in Nigeria do to they come from?'

'Right in the middle, master, they are only a small tribe and nobody likes them. We have many Igbira jokes. I'm not sure of the name of their main town but I think it could be Akure or Okene. Where are you going to work, master?'

'Kaduna, the teacher training department of the University of Kaduna.'

As the sun chased the clouds away the high-rise buildings of Lagos became visible whenever there was a gap in the traffic. A huge battered yellow bus, with black heads and arms hanging out of the windows passed them slowly only inches away. They were aware of the stares, the pointing fingers and smiles of greeting and also aware that on the roof on top of a ziggurat of boxes, sacks and cases, another whole society of men and women were hanging on. Dilapidated trucks spewing fumes, coughing like old men, carrying loads way beyond the specifications of the vehicle, lumbered along changing lanes or direction haphazardly to add to the chaos. Noise and fumes were an unwelcome addition to the humidity.

The taxi went over a small rise and there, as far as the eye could see, was acres of shacks, shanties and dwellings constructed mainly of corrugated iron, tarpaulins, cardboard and reclaimed pieces of hardboard and plywood. Their brown roofs were an asymmetric mass resembling a sea of crumpled brown tissue paper. Smoke rose from the cooking fires. The intensity of everything going on around them assaulted their senses and they were left speechless. It's not as though this was their first trip to Africa, they had witnessed poverty and chaos before, but the visual anarchy and bedlam set out before them had a gut wrenching emotional effect. This was all compounded when the taxi stopped for a few moments at the side of a ditch. The smell was appalling and what made their mouths drop open with uncontrolled bottom lips were kids, some as young as three or four, who were scrambling around in the detritus looking for something edible or worth saving. Karl looked at Anna. They shared the same expression. Were they in the first stage of culture shock? They were within arrow shot of the city centre and the corrugated chaos stretched to the horizon. Was this the country that was rich, that was in the midst of an oil boom with all of its associated massive monetary benefits?

They crossed the bridge over the lagoon from the mainland to Ikoyi Island. The word lagoon brings to mind crystal clear blue water, but the water below, rather than possessing clarity and luminescence to excite the soul, was still and languid and looked as though the heavy humidity had caused it to surrender any movement, and thus it resembled a moraine of brown sludge.

6

The taxi crossed the Ikoyi Bridge and made a left turn towards a sign saying Falomo. At last, a touch of architectural order; no slums, fewer vehicles, just utilitarian flats, scruffy offices and government buildings. The Federal Ministry of Education, all eleven stories of it, rose above them. It was as grey as the receding clouds and gave the impression of having been designed by a Soviet architect whose only mission was to save money. Karl could see a porte-cochère through the gates and there was a six-foot wall at the front of the building which surrounded a garden that could be reached through rusty wrought iron gates opposite the front of the building or through the porte-cochère.

The taxi driver drove through the opening, trying to get as close as possible, but his progress was halted by a uniformed security man who frantically waved his arms and pointed to the insignia on his chest as confirmation of his authority. His khaki and green uniform had been starched to such excess that with one wrong move he could have sliced off his arm on the sharp crease in his shorts. He virtually threw himself on the bonnet to get the taxi to stop and pointed behind him at a huge lorry, jammed under the porte-cochère and surrounded by women.

The women, some of whom were carrying babies on their backs, had formed a human chain and were unloading the truck whose cargo consisted of hundreds of boxes of condensed milk. Karl assumed that the idea was to remove the cases at the top of the vehicle so that it could be un-jammed and wondered why didn't they let a bit of air out of the tyres. On closer inspection he could see that the lorry was well and truly stuck. It had slammed into the portico roof and large lumps of concrete were strewn over the floor. They paid off Maximus, their unlicensed driver and, like two homeless people clutching their suitcases for security, Karl and Anna

44

walked gingerly past the army of women, astonished to see that all the condensed milk was being taken up the stairs into the Ministry building.

Karl stopped a man who looked as though he might know what was going on. 'Why are they unloading all these boxes here?' he asked. 'It is the wish of the permanent secretary,' he replied, nodding his head and genuflecting to show his courtesy. 'He runs a very big tin can supply business and his warehouse is full so he gets the lorries to bring the cans here so they can be stored in the corridors and offices. Sometimes he sells the contents at a discount to his staff. He is a very fine man.'

Karl and Anna entered the foyer of the ministry where they found no signs to give them a clue about where they should go. They saw a young European woman coming down the stairs, carrying a small half-caste baby. She was short and blonde, about 28 to 30 years old; there were circular sweat stains under her arms and a film of sweat on her forehead. With her one free arm she swiped her forehead and cheerfully said, 'You look lost.'

Karl mustered a smile and tried to make light of the situation, saying with a bit of feeble humour, 'Someone will eventually tell us where to go.'

'Don't bank on it,' was her reply. She went on to say, 'What are you doing here? And with those cases?' She too tried to inject a little levity. 'You look like refugees with those bags.'

Karl and Anna explained their circumstances and went on to describe the nightmare of their first two hours in West Africa. She shook her head in horror, but she was very impressed that they were off to Kaduna Polytechnic as teacher trainers. She commented that it would have been more sensible of the ministry to fly them to Kano, and then added, 'But this is Nigeria!'

She introduced herself as Helen, formerly from somewhere in London, and said she was about to be sent to Port Harcourt in the Delta area of Nigeria to work as a teacher of English at a secondary school. She was due to leave Lagos tomorrow, and evidently had some friends with whom she and her six-month-old baby would stay that night. In the morning, a ministry vehicle was to collect her and her luggage and take them on the six-hour journey to the Delta state. She had a two-year contract.

'Is your husband...I mean the father of the baby with you?' questioned Anna.

'He bloody well should be,' she said as she threw her head back in a gesture of annoyance. 'But that's a long story.' She was about to continue, but then interrupted herself by pointing at a well-dressed woman wrapped in red and yellow cloth topped by a spectacular head dress. As she walked magisterially past them, Helen immediately crossed the foyer to talk to her. A short conversation took place between the two women, with Helen constantly turning her head in Karl and Anna's direction, resulting in two minions being dispatched to carry their bags to the lift.

The well-dressed woman turned out to be Mrs Obaganda who was in charge of postings and had an office on the 3rd floor. Karl and Anna were about to follow the two porters into the lift but Helen quickly intervened, gesturing firmly with her free hand. She ordered the two porters out of the lift and said, 'Whatever you do, *never* enter a lift in Nigeria. Even if there are 20 floors, walk them, because quite frankly you could be trapped in one for hours, days even.' And on that note she turned away, though not before telling them that they were lucky to get to see Mrs Obaganda so soon since she often did not arrive for work until late morning.

Up on the third floor they sat and waited on two tubular and canvas chairs in an austere office with the atmosphere of a prison waiting room and a rather stale smell. The walls were painted with ubiquitous magnolia paint and the only form of decoration or personalised touch was a framed certificate from the University of Ibadan adorning the wall. One would have expected images of cheery children with big smiles or coloured posters showing students, teachers and kids enjoying 'education.' There was no evidence to say Mrs Obaganda was in a position of importance except for the size of the desk and a big white telephone that stood out like an iceberg on the surface. The desk was huge and covered with towers of files. Behind her chair there were more leaning towers of unstable files as well as two boxes of Carnation Milk. Despite the chaotic nature of the room, they gained the impression that they were in the office of someone who was extremely busy. They sat and waited a bit longer, and a bit longer.

On her eventual arrival, Mrs Obaganda wanted to show she was important and adopted an annoyingly perfunctory and careless attitude towards them. She had a magisterial walk and her authority was such that she expected some lackey to open the doors for her or move her chair when she wanted to sit down. She looked irritated that there were two foreigners in her office as this meant getting down to business rather than being able to adopt a posture of importance while drinking her coffee.

'What do you want?' was her first question, followed by, 'why are you here?' What are your names? Who sent you here? Why do you have those cases?'

Karl and Anna were flabbergasted and truly disturbed. She obviously had no idea who they were, or maybe she was pretending in order to keep them feeling very uneasy. She rummaged through some files on her desk and after scrabbling through the slag heap of paper and cardboard she said she could find no information about them or where they were going or for what purpose they were claiming to have been employed.

Karl gave her the documents from Kaduna Polytechnic. With a wave of an arrogant hand she pushed the file to one side and stood up and sighed with an air of boredom and disinterest. 'I have looked at the Kaduna files and not one of your names is down to work there,' she said forcibly. 'And you say that you are here to teach our teachers.'

Karl was getting annoyed and exasperated and Anna was entering into a state of mild shock. He pointed to the Kaduna documents, as well as one from the embassy in London and another from the Federal Ministry of Education. He located the pertinent paragraph with his finger and said, 'Can't you read it, can't you see it? It clearly says that I have been offered, and have accepted, the post of a senior education officer to teach on the postgraduate teacher training course!'

'Of course I can read, but they haven't told me. They haven't come through me. They are supposed to show me everything, I am the one in charge here, how dare they just appoint anyone without me knowing.'

'Well!' said Karl angrily, 'you know now. My question is, why didn't you know and now that you do know – because it is in black and white in front of you, what are you going to do about transport to take us to Kaduna where there is a federal education post waiting for me?' Looking at the phone on her desk, he said, 'Just pick it up and call Kaduna.'

'The phone does not work! You can't just turn up here and go where you want. That is not how it works.'

'Does anything work around here?' Karl snarled. 'Your representatives in London, at your embassy, appointed me to come to your country to work. Look at their documents!' She tried to interrupt, but he was in full bellicose flow. 'They told me where I would be working. They paid for our flights. They paid for our baggage. And now you tell me you have no idea who we are. What a bloody shambles.'

Things were going very badly. Anna wanted to crawl into a suitcase to be shipped back to the UK.

Mrs Obaganda had obviously never been spoken to like this and appeared shocked that Karl was so critical.

'And the mission hospital in Kaduna has been fully informed about my wife's pregnancy,' he said, handing her a copy of a letter from the Mission.

'Pregnancy,' she uttered, and stood up behind her desk. Confused, thinking this was a sign that the meeting was over, Karl and Anna did exactly the same thing. Her eyes lit up, her face displaying interest rather than annoyance and irritation. It was as though two old school friends had met after years apart or supported the same football team. It was as though a magic word had been spoken, a word of such significance that it rendered all three of them silent. The woman in bright red and yellow topped by her astounding head wear, was transformed from an impatient and arrogant lady into a benevolently smiling one. Karl looked at the two women; there seemed to be a silent electrical contact between them, and the pregnant silence ended with the words, 'Pregnant! Why didn't you say so? Sit down, sit down.'

She shouted, 'Ado, Ado, bring this lady a comfortable chair... now!' Ado, one of her minions, looked bewildered as he nervously said, 'Where from, madam?'

'Just use your initiative, that means no excuses, just find one, and quick, and make sure it has soft supportive cushions.' She paused as Ado looked vacant. 'Can't you see she is pregnant, go!'

That one magic word had created an instant empathy that was propagated by Mrs Obaganda. It was as though a personality switch had been thrown. She ignored Karl who was temporarily of no interest to her and proceeded to talk maternity matters with Anna. Ado evidently (it was later found) removed a fine armchair from the Permanent Secretary's office while he was absent and graciously gave it to Anna. Mrs Obaganda continued to talk, barely pausing for breath, as if she was paid by the amount of talking she could do.

The transformation of the meeting was complete. Karl and Anna now knew she had six kids, she had visited the UK six times and was born in the sixth month of the year. 'Six must be my lucky number,' she said.

Karl dared to interrupt, 'So you'll be sticking at six children then?'

'I'm not sure about that,' was the reply. 'My husband, a big man, has a very big libido and we love children.' Her husband was a businessman, 'imports and exports' they were told, and they were wealthy enough to live near the University of Lagos, an area which Karl and Anna later discovered was rather desirable as well as being strategically gated to keep away thieves and riff raff.

It was as they had thought. She had no idea about the job in Kaduna and alarmingly she actually wasn't sure where it was in Nigeria. Karl explained it was a little south of Kano, the third city in terms of size in Nigeria, but she was still unsure of its whereabouts. She called in Ado who was on his knees looking at files and trying to find some reference to Kaduna. Things didn't look good, and they were compounded when a youth in a green uniform came in and asked Mrs Obaganda for some dead ones. She gave him a yes and instructed Ado to take two files from the top of each skyscraper of paper and manila files and give them to the youth in green. It turned out that the youth in green was given the job of shredding, or in his case tearing up manually, all of the dead files, and once a week he would call into each office to collect them. It was frighteningly obvious that Mrs Obaganda had no idea which files were pertinent, urgent, latent or dead, and she simply ordered an arbitrary number to be destroyed. No wonder she knew nothing about the Kaduna file.

Seeing how tired Karl and Anna were, she shouted at another one of her lackeys and ordered him to organise a driver and car to take them to a nice hotel where they could rest and experience real Nigerian hospitality while she solved the problem of where they were going to work. Following what felt like a long hour of searching and rummaging through papers she told them, rather disturbingly, that they would not be going to Kaduna, and said confidently that she would find another fine posting for them. As much as they would appreciate a night in a fine hotel, Karl hoped that their destination would be sorted out by next morning, although everything he had seen in the Ministry so far did not fill him with confidence.

After two hours with Mrs Obaganda, Karl and Anna walked back down the stairs, followed by the two minions carrying their bags. They were greeted by a frustrated Helen who was still in the foyer waiting for a lift. They found it hard to believe what she told them. Her husband was a Nigerian trying to run a business in the UK and because of money issues he had arranged that his wife, with her baby, some 13 months old, should go and work near his home town in Nigeria and send home surplus cash to maintain him. Karl thought she was mad and Anna thought she was desperately in love.

'Did you have a successful meeting?' she asked.

'Well, yes and no,' was their response, 'everything is so badly organised.' They told her about the dead file man. Helen responded by having a mini-tirade. 'You do realise that the ministry is notorious for inefficiency. It's over staffed. No one seems to be in charge, there is little administrative structure, no department shares information and basically at this moment the place looks like a Carnation milk factory rather the ministry of education. Last week the place was full of Argentinian tins of corned beef.' She gave a big sigh and said, almost to herself, 'The place doesn't fill you with confidence.'

They were interrupted by a skinny driver carrying a piece of paper, who asked for Mrs Mwaka. Helen held her hand up to stop him in mid-conversation and said, 'How about this example of the right hand not knowing what the left hand is doing? It's unlikely that you know, but over the last three months every typewriter in the ministry has gone missing, even the replacements have gone missing, and it was all done by a gang of four who actually lived in a big cupboard in the ministry. They had 'acquired' uniforms and spent all day in the ministry, apparently as bona fide workers who ate, slept, and washed in the building. While they were supposedly working they stole their food, went to meetings, ate in the canteen, helped as porters, and each night when they were locked in they stole a few typewriters every day as well as stationery and furniture. And they got away with it. They were only caught when they tried to sell one to a senior official of the ministry in a bar across the road. When they were arrested they were ushered into the foyer, left for a moment by the two policemen who were occupied with looking at a pretty girl, so off they ran and they haven't been seen since. I suspect the two policemen have a nice typewriter at home.'

'Is this your lift?' asked Karl.

'Yes, about two hours late, but that's typical of the inefficiency here. I assume you know the phrase, 'Only in America?' Well, it was stolen from here. When things are crazy and disorganised here, remember the phrase, 'Only in Nigeria.'

7

Following the long and exhausting meeting with Mrs Obaganda they had eventually been given a couple of bottles of warm Fanta and a packet of Cabin biscuits with the texture and toughness of a floor tile. Tasteless biscuits softened with a fizzy orange drink were a new taste sensation for both of them, and what they really needed was a good dose of Valium after their quite surreal conversation with Mrs Obaganda, but at least she had tried to help after the very fraught first 20 minutes. Their bags were safely with them, having declined the offer to store them with the boxes of Carnation milk, and they had also declined any notion of using the lift to the ground floor, suspecting that they could end up being mummified before the doors were open again. Mrs Obaganda, wielding her authority, had ordered the two rather old men to carry their bags all the way down the stairs.

They were now about to get into an Isuzu people carrier with 'The Federal Ministry of Education' emblazoned on its side. Wellington, their driver, introduced himself. He was skinny and looked underfed. 'Could have done with a bloody good Sunday dinner,' Karl's father would have said. He was all white teeth, big smile, ligaments and sinew. He looked about 17 or 18. He wore the dark green Ministry regulation trousers and white shirt with the initials FME stitched on his breast pocket. Wellington radiated enthusiasm. He asked questions, wanted to know what they were going to do? Where were their children? Every Nigerian they had met seemed to have assumed that if you had a wife you had many offspring. Where were they being posted? Did they like Lagos? Karl cynically assumed his sense of friendliness and inquiry was to induce him to give a big tip.

In his hands Karl held some papers that had been given to him by Mrs Obaganda. Despite the frustrating meeting she had turned out to be most helpful, and though it took her an hour she had been able to ascertain for certain that Kaduna would not be their destination due to the fact that the Embassy in London had failed to confirm their appointment, and as a result someone inexperienced and local had been employed in the meantime. What Wellington clutched in his hands were FME payment vouchers for a hotel in Lagos, and he said he had been told to check on availability on Ikoyi and Victoria Islands.

'I assume that's where all the best hotels are?' questioned Karl.

'Yes sir,' was the reply. 'We will go to the very best... swimming pool, maybe two, air conditioning, its own power supply and very fine chop, I mean food... So I am told.'

'What's it called?' asked Anna.

'The Eko.'

'I read about it in the Rough Guide and that's what it said, but it was ridiculously expensive... In fact, all hotels in Lagos are very pricey.'

'They are not for the common man like me,' commented Wellington.

Just visible through the partially closed wrought iron gates of the FME garden courtyard were the large letters B and A. Karl leaned to one side, squinted in the sunlight, and saw an R and a C. 'Barclays!' he shouted. 'We can get some money and stop at a shop and buy something decent to eat.' He fumbled with his hand baggage to get at his wallet and pulled out two £10 pound notes, waved them at Wellington and told him he would be a few minutes because he was going to change his pounds into naira.

'But masta, they will give you a very bad deal, the banks are not good.'

'Yes, but it seems to be very foolish to be without cash and I know all the hotels give you a very bad rate.'

'How much do you hope to get? I mean how many naira do you want for your pounds?'

'Well, I was advised in the UK that each naira was worth about 50 pence.' Wellington looked quizzical. Karl recognised his lack of familiarity with pence and said, 'I'll get around two naira for each of my pounds.' Wellington looked truly shocked. Anna leaned towards them to see what was going on. All she wanted was a comfy bed and air-conditioning. It was mid-morning, they were in the shade, but it was getting rather hot.

'Masta, wait,' said Wellington. He unlocked the glove compartment, moved a few items, bent over to see more clearly the packed space, and came away with a roll of bank notes. 'Masta, don't go to the bank, they will give you two for every pound and I will give you...' he paused, thought, rubbed his chin and said, 'six, I will give you six for each pound.'

'Six!' Karl exclaimed.

'Six!' Anna said in astonishment.

'Six,' nodded Wellington, and then after a look of uncertainty he said, 'Is that not enough? Masta, that is a very good price.'

'Six, are you sure?'

Yes, Masta, I buy a bit, I sell a bit... I am a very honest man... I do it only for my children, they need many things.'

'Your children?' questioned Anna. 'You don't look old enough to have children.'

'Oh yes, madam, I have three and one is soon starting school, the fees are high and there are pencils and books and shoes and...

Karl held out a hand to interrupt him, wondering if he was telling lies, was this a huge con trick or was it really a decent deal. 'If you give me six naira for every pound I give you, how are you going to make any money?'

'Masta, it is obvious, but I will honestly tell you, I will sell your pounds to someone else for eight naira each, then I become Mr Wellington 33 percent.'

The sun moved effortlessly over the FME and its shadow disappeared. The sun's rays caught the three of them, casting theatrical shadows on the ground. It was almost 11am and the humidity raised its ugly head. A film of sweat was developing under Karl's shirt and his long trousers became conduits of heat. He turned to Anna. She squinted in the sunlight and he noticed that she too had a light film of sweat on her forehead. It must be bloody hot. It was he who was the prince of perspiration and she the dry skinned lizard. A colourful bird alighted in the tree next to the porte-cochère, and remaining perched on a branch it vigorously flapped its wings. *Perhaps it's trying to cool itself down,* thought Karl. They were used to heat, four years in Uganda near the equator, but with a more benign sun whose power was diluted by altitude. Here the air was heavy, it was thick, and even the slightest movement encountered the invisible resistance of humidity.

Wellington took the driver's seat as they got into the Isuzu through the sliding side door and sat behind him near their cases. Wellington slammed the door shut and immediately wound down his window and then leaned over awkwardly and did the same to the window at the other side of the cab. 'What about the air-conditioning?' asked Anna.

'No A/C in this car madam, and I beg your pardon, but myself, and you as well, are not important enough to have A/C. Only the big Ogas get A/C, masta. Don't worry, when we drive the air will keep you cool.'

Karl had reservations; he was quite sure he was about to experience the interior of a fan oven for the first time. Travelling at a snail's pace in heavy traffic was unlikely to keep them cool, and Cabin biscuits and Fanta had not satisfied their hunger and thirst. But they were on their way. He wondered if he should have been more vehement with Mrs Obaganda about their posting, but in retrospect, after the initial alarming statements she had been concerned about their welfare, especially that of Anna, and had genuinely tried to help. So at last they were moving. A quiet room, room service, a pool, decent food and a place to relax for a few days while their posting was sorted out, and conveniently the hotels of Victoria and Ikoyi Islands were only a mile or so from the FME. An easy and quick taxi journey.

Ikoyi and Victoria Islands were a world apart from the traffic mayhem and unruly atmosphere of the chaos at the other side of the Carter and Victoria bridges only half a mile away. The two islands were designated as a GRA, a Government Residential Agency and of course the small level of planning and organisation that spawned meant that big business built accommodation there, as did entrepreneurs, the former trying to make sure their employees had somewhere stable to live and the developers hoping to cash in on the growing numbers of foreign companies coming to Lagos. Big business didn't really want their employees to see the real Africa. They needed to be kept away from the surfeit of carbon monoxide, the noisy horns, the chaos, the danger and the sheer grubbiness of poverty. You couldn't privately rent an apartment on the two islands unless you had two years' rent up front. If that was not bad enough, the rental cost per month was bordering on the astronomical. It was quite simply legalised highway robbery on behalf of the builders who had probably acquired the land through nefarious means.

But Karl and Anna didn't know that yet. The roads were quieter, there was still an ignorance of the highway code and of course fewer cars meant things were better, their driver hadn't leaned out of the window and screamed at anyone, nor had anyone screamed at him for 500 yards.

There were ordered blocks of flats, each of which sported a token guard. There were even gardens here and there, but one couldn't help noticing that just above eye level the roads were caressed with masses of wires. Between each unstable wooden electricity or telephone pole was a tangled disorderly river of wires, some of which hung down alarmingly, almost touching the roofs of vans and lorries. At the top of each pole was a mass of wires as tangled as a mad man's wig, wires of all different lengths and colours, each of which seemed to have no purpose. Wellington caught Karl's eye and decided to answer his unspoken question.

'The Brazilians are trying to sort it out.'

'Who?'

'The Brazilians, masta, they are in Lagos to install the new telephone system.'

'They'll be here for bloody years,' was Karl's response. 'They should rip all those wires up and start again. It's like a jigsaw puzzle without a plan.'

'They have been here many years, masta, and nothing has happened.' And then, to perhaps ingratiate himself, he added, 'It would be better if you British did it, at least it would be fixed.'

Karl decided not to comment. He thought the aerial chaos was so great they should rip everything out and start again.

The Isuzu slowed down at a rather tall building. There was a ramp going up to the front of the building and through the car window Anna could see a sign saying Bar Beach and huge waves crashing onto the sand. As her eye turned toward the horizon she saw a remarkable sight. Ship after stationary ship at anchor just off the coast, fifty, perhaps sixty. She tried to count but then her mind was taken elsewhere as Wellington stopped under a far more splendid porte-cochère than the one at the FME. At last, something clean and ordered. The door was opened by a smartly uniformed hotel employee who genuflected and said, 'Welcome to the Eko Hotel, madam.' He held her hand and helped her from the vehicle.

Karl stood with his back to the Isuzu, looking up at the rather beautiful hotel. He cast his eyes towards the splendid reception area and smiled to himself. Anna also breathed a sigh of relief at the sight of a building which seemed to conform to standards that implied it would stay standing and looking elegant for rather a long time. The entrance alone was a million miles away from everything they had experienced in the last couple of hours. They looked at each other and smiled. He removed the FME accommodation warrant from his pocket and took the first step onto the polished terrazzo floor.

A porter struggled to get their bags out of the car, but was hindered not by their weight but by Wellington who seemed to be either insisting they should stay in the car or he was in charge and he would carry them. Karl gave Wellington a stern look as if to say let the porter do his job. Wellington's response was a barely audible utterance of, 'But, but...'

At the reception desk a well-dressed employee eased a minion out of the way and attended to them.

'How may I help you sir?'

'We'd like a room please, a double room, for my wife and I,' said Karl.

'Yes sir,' was the courteous response. 'And how long will you be staying with us?'

Anna looked at Wellington for advice, thinking that he had obviously experienced this kind of situation before. 'I don't know, madam,' he said, looking slightly embarrassed.

Anna looked at the receptionist and said, 'A minimum of four days.' He looked down, examining the tariffs and pausing first to make sure he was correct, then said, 'That will be 1300 naira with an insurance deposit of 1000 naira. Would you like a sea view or a view of the lagoon, or for another 1000 you could even have a room with a large balcony overlooking the pool?'

Karl gulped. £650 for four nights in the hotel. Thank goodness he wasn't paying. £650 was more than he earned in a month in the UK, and then there was the deposit as well.

The receptionist, noticing Karl's slight alarm, added, 'Of course sir, we can make it a little cheaper if you can pay in dollars or pounds.'

'No, that won't be necessary,' Karl replied. He looked at his wife who also looked shocked at the amount of money it was going to cost the Ministry, but they both dispelled these thoughts as they dreamt of air-conditioning, cleanliness, order, peace and quiet and a bit of luxury until they were sent to their new posting.

Karl took the accommodation voucher from his pocket and handed it to the receptionist, who stared at it as though he was about to handle a piece of used toilet paper. He held it at arm's length with two fingers and gave a long significant sigh. Then, with a look of disdain he strode off to the office behind him. Karl and Anna were both confused. They turned to look at Wellington who responded with a shrug of his shoulders and a look of 'don't ask me, I don't know what's going on.'

A tall, elegantly dressed European came towards them holding the piece of paper. He had dark curly hair, a magnificent suntan, and was wearing a brilliant white shirt that was as starched and as crisp as the Cabin biscuits in their bag. He was tall and very slender. The small nuances of his long theatrical fingers made him look a little effeminate. It didn't help that the inflection in his voice was definitely French or perhaps even Spanish. His English was, nevertheless, perfect, but with a slight southern European accent. He was joined by the receptionist. He delicately adjusted his hair, then carefully cleared his throat before dramatically placing the FME voucher on the desk. He held it with one hand and with the other smoothed it out, paying careful attention to what was written on it, before looking up and looking them in the eye.

'I am very sorry,' he said. 'I am afraid that the hotel is completely full and we don't have a vacancy for...' He momentarily stopped speaking and quickly glanced behind him at the wall on which the rates were printed, and said, '... for at least another 14 days.'

Karl was shocked. He looked at Anna who was also confused, then looked at Wellington who gave another embarrassed shrug. Pointing at the receptionist, Karl said, 'But he has just offered us a choice of rooms.' The receptionist received a barely detectable message from his manager and disappeared into the room behind.

'I am sorry, but he was mistaken.'

'But he told us the price and suggested a room and...'

'Again I have to say I am sorry but he is very new. I apologise for the fact that he inadvertently misled you and I will see to it that he is disciplined.'

'But I don't want him disciplined, we just want a room.'

The manager visibly swallowed and touched his neck, as though his collar was annoying him. He quickly assumed an authoritative stance and then responded. 'A mistake was made. I repeat, I am sorry there are no rooms.'

Karl was not amused. His optimistic mood had evaporated and he could feel his anger building. His wife's eyes were a mass of disappointment and he didn't like to see this, nor experience the fact that one minute ago they had been dreaming of a welcome quiet room and were now being told, somewhat suspiciously, that the hotel was full.

'Hang on a minute, just what is going on, your receptionist, who seemed to know what he was doing, he even looked professional, offered us a price, told us about a variety of rooms we could choose and now you come along and say the place is full. What's bloody going on?'

'Let me explain, sir. It is quite simple. He made a mistake and forgot about the big convention we are hosting.'

'What convention? I see no signs for one. How can you or your staff forget there is a convention on here? What is it, an anti-British convention?' And then, after looking at his wife, he added, 'Do you have something against pregnant women?'

'Of course not, sir.'

'You are lying, one minute we have a room, then we don't because of some invented convention. What is it, a convention of ghosts?'

The manager was getting irritated. His authority was being challenged as was his honesty.

'I get it, I bet you are wanting a back hander,' said Karl.

'A what?' was the response.

'A bloody bribe, or is this hotel one that looks good but is basically full of lies and has a corrupt front desk. Let's not mince words, either the receptionist is an idiot or you are just a liar, and I suspect it's you that is lying because of some dubious monetary requirement or for some reason you're prejudiced against the English.' Karl turned to look at his wife for visual support. He got it. He looked at Wellington who seemed to be cringing with horror. 'So Mr. Manager... you are the manager I assume!'

'I am.'

'Then is there a room or not, or do I have to put up with more of your sleazy lies?'

The manger looked him in the eye, then looked over his shoulder at numerous people who were watching the altercation.

'It is this,' he said in an angry tone, waving the voucher. 'It is useless, it is worthless. Do I make myself clear?' He handed the voucher back to Karl and said disdainfully, 'Just throw this paper in the bin, it means nothing.'

'You what... It's what... But it's from the Federal Ministry of Education!' Karl bellowed.

The manager bellowed back, 'And that is the problem. It is not worth the paper it is printed on. You see sir, they *never* pay their bills,' and pointing at Wellington, he went on, 'and he should never have brought you here. He and everyone else knows that the government, especially the FME, don't ever pay their bills. So you will not be getting one of our vacant rooms unless you can pay cash. And should you have cash sir, then we would refuse your custom because... Well, you seem to be a rather unpleasant man. Good day sir.' He turned on his heels and left.

Their bags were forlornly put back inside the Isuzu. There was a seething silence. Wellington was avoiding eye contact and Karl sat looking resentfully at the infamous piece of paper. He looked at Wellington and recalled the comments of the manager. Did it mean that Wellington was aware that the voucher was useless at the Eko Hotel?

Wellington interrupted his thoughts. 'Masta,' he said. 'I am very ashamed that they treated you so badly. It is terrible, it is not the Nigeria way. That oyibo, he was so unkind, but I am sure the Federal Palace will treat you with respect.'

'Federal Palace?' questioned Anna. 'Is that close to the Eko Hotel?'

'No, madam,' said Wellington, anticipating the question. 'It is a very fine hotel near here. All we have to do is turn left, go down Adeola Odecku Street and it is about half a mile away.'

Karl and Anna looked at each other. *More traffic, no air-conditioning,* they both thought. Again Wellington identified their hard-to-hide consternation and cheerfully said, 'Very little traffic on Victoria Island. I can drive fast and create wind, we will be there in no time.'

And so they were.

The Federal Palace hotel was about four stories high compared to the twenty of the Eko. It was surrounded by mature foliage and it was an unlucky driver who had to park in full sun. The building wasn't ostentatious and had a sturdy, well-built look about it. Anna and Karl, looking around, liked what they saw. Gardens to walk in, birds singing and pavements glorious dappled by strong sunlight and the movement of leaves. They left Wellington and the bags in the car. They smiled reassuringly at each other as they walked up the four steps to the entrance. They were greeted by a doorman clad in braid and sporting real or faux military decorations, and the cool blast of a functioning air conditioning system. This alone made standing in line waiting to be attended to worthwhile.

'We would like a double room please for four or five days.' Karl paused as he fumbled to remove the voucher from his pocket. In the most official voice he could muster, he said, 'We've been sent here by the Federal Ministry of Education... here is their voucher.'

The receptionist smiled politely but a little quiver of anxiety trickled over her lips. She took the document and said, 'Could you wait a moment please?'

'Is there an issue?' blurted Karl. All the officialdom of his prior words had evaporated.

'I'll just be a moment sir.' She turned and had a quiet conversation with a be-suited man behind her.

He approached Karl and Anna. He took a deep breath, cupped his hands together priest like in front of his chest, and then sympathetically said, 'I'm really sorry, sir. I am sorry to tell you that the Federal Palace Hotel no longer accepts their vouchers. In fact we haven't accepted them for over a year now.'

'But! was Karl's futile response.

'You can of course pay yourself and get them to refund you, but my advice is that, well, they just might not pay you. In fact I would go as far as saying they are very, very unlikely to reimburse you.'

'Are you sure?' was Anna's despairing question.

'Madam, we have some beautiful rooms available, but you will have to pay for one yourself and of course, as is the policy here in Nigeria, you will have to pay cash in advance.' He then added, 'You could always try the Intercontinental, it's further along the road a little nearer the Victoria Bridge. But I believe that they too have the same policy.'

Karl was appalled at the state of their circumstances. They had been in Nigeria about five hours and their situation was bordering on surreal. Bags nearly stolen, no food on the flight, involved in a road accident, not recognised at the Ministry, a breakfast of floor tiles and Fanta, and now finding themselves, dare he say it, homeless in Lagos.

'Are you sure about the Intercontinental?' he said, looking at the telephone on the counter. 'Could you ring them up and ask them?'

'I am afraid sir that the phones don't work.'

'But what about that man over there? He's on the phone and that seems to be functioning properly.'

'Sir, that is an internal phone.' He pointed at the phone on the front desk. 'This is the outside line but it has never worked, and I doubt it ever will. We have no ability to phone anyone. Remember, this is Nigeria!'

They slid out of the hotel like two condemned prisoners. Wellington looked apologetic and deeply embarrassed. 'Wellington, did you know this would happen?' said Karl. 'Did you know the voucher was useless?' Wellington's head dropped and his chin touched his chest. His pose said everything. 'Why did you take us to these hotels knowing that we couldn't stay in them?'

'Masta, I wanted you to be in a nice place so you could enjoy Lagos, not the...' He suddenly stopped talking.

'Not the what?' questioned Anna. 'What do you mean?'

'Madam, I want you to stay in a nice place,' he said obsequiously, 'and I will take you there right now.'

'Where is it?' asked Karl.

'It is Ikorodu.'

'Ikorodu, we passed the signs for that in a taxi this morning. Isn't it miles away?'

It did turn out to be miles away, but before they got there they had the traffic and the notorious Nigeria 'go slow' to negotiate.

They crossed the Victoria Bridge, leaving the relative peace of Victoria and Ikoyi Islands behind. On arrival in Ikorodu, Wellington miraculously double-parked outside the Bristol Hotel as he assured them that only recently the hotel had accepted a Ministry voucher. The Bristol Hotel was right in the centre of Lagos Island on Broad Street, which seemed to be a main shopping street. It was directly opposite the Kingsway supermarket and a huge Bata shoe shop. The manager was apologetic as he confirmed that yes, in the past he had accepted the dreaded Ministry of Education voucher but had still to be paid for all of the people who had stayed there.

They headed out once more, making various turns until they were on Catholic Mission Road and were temporarily held up outside the Holy Cross Cathedral. This small bottle neck was a capitalist opportunity for the locals, and the pavements (a rare sight) were covered with food sellers all of whom were shouting out about their wares. It was like medieval England with Simple Simon trying to sell his pies, accompanied by vociferous and noisy competition. Hungry and gingerly accepting Wellington's advice, they accepted something on a skewer. He paid. Was it guilt? A skewer of questionable meat was their first real taste of Nigerian street food. They didn't ask what it was, they just hoped it was edible and that they would survive. They looked apprehensively at the skewers as Wellington disturbingly confirmed that it wasn't grilled rat because the Catholic Church had banned the sale near their church and were told not to worry because there was no long tail or big ears and chopping teeth visible. They were very spicy but tasted fine.

They bypassed the Eko bridge going off to Apapa Docks and slowly crossed the Carter Bridge onto the Ikorodu road. The reality, chaos and madness of Nigeria hit them squarely in the face. The assault of noise, cloying humidity, serious heat, diesel fumes and previously unknown smells grabbed them by the collar and shook them. They had left the semi-normal atmosphere of Victoria and Ikoyi Islands. Below the bridge was the lagoon. It was not the sort of Pacific lagoon that one normally thinks of; no tropical fish here, no transparent, clear blue water, no white sand and swaying bent palms, just an oily black surface punctured with junk, rubbish and even an abandoned car or two.

There was no life in the waters below, just the knowledge that should you fall in, one swallow and you could die. As they reached the top of the hump of the bridge, ahead was line upon line of vehicles, crushed together and looking like the carapaces of hundreds of slow moving beetles; yellow buses, yellow taxis, overloaded trucks, all spewing exhaust fumes into the already polluted air.

The sight was hideous. The Isuzu moved at a glacial pace. The roads either side were crowded with makeshift dwellings of cardboard, tin sheets and polythene. The open sewers at each side of the road were long receptacles for rubbish and human waste. The smell was awful.

A cacophony of skinny kids, all sinew and bone, banged on the windows and tried to sell their wares. Lighters, palm oil, health tablets (long life guaranteed), Tee-shirts, spanners, empty oil cans, love potions, plastic knives, forks, spoons, empty dirty bottles and even at one point a puppy, were pressed against the window of the vehicle in the hope that something would be purchased as a pet or a meal. Faces of kids sent out to sell or beg pressed against the window and distorted lips and bent noses left their sweaty marks. A shirtless teenager, full of brio and dirty dreadlocks, lifted up the windscreen wiper and with his fist beat a rhythm as he yelled, 'Give me money, give me money.' Karl muttered, 'Fuck off.' beneath his breath.

He was actually frightened. Protected only by a thin skin of steel or a couple of millimetres of glass, outside was humanity at its most appalling. To think that on an airplane just a thin skin of aluminium saved you from a free fall of thousands of feet, but what was beyond the skin of the car was, to him, far more dangerous. Yesterday his wife was having her hair cut in the West End of London, yesterday he had said goodbye to his father, and now! Anna looked horrified. How brave she was. He looked at her as she looked down so as not to make eye contact with any of the 'salesmen' outside and he felt ashamed. He had always been worried about coming here, but hadn't had the guts to defer departure until after their baby was born. Just how could he have let this happen? How could he have left his dad so soon after his mam's death? What had happened to his ability to make a sensible decision? He would make it up to her. He wasn't sure how, but he would go out of his way to make their time in West Africa a pleasant one, even though at this moment it didn't seem possible. If he and Anna could be spirited away and placed on a flight to the UK, even Nigerian Airways, he would do it.

Less than six hours in Lagos and they had become emotional wreckage. All the madness they had experienced over the last few hours flashed past him. He couldn't have envisaged or contemplated such a visceral experience. Yes, he was frightened, all he had read about Lagos was true, and it wasn't as though he didn't have any experience of Africa. In Uganda he was happy to walk through the dodgy market area in Kampala and ride home with seven or eight Ugandans in a four-seater taxi; he went through the slums of Kampala to watch football matches at Nakivubo Stadium. He reflected on what this experience would be like for someone who had never experienced the third world.

The snarling teenager was swept off the bonnet as the Isuzu jerked forward and after Wellington had delivered a loud Yoruba expletive. Everything was loud! There was no order outside their metallic haven. Rising above the slums, huge billboards promoted the health-giving values of Nigerian brewed Guinness. A tattered poster the size of a double-decker bus promoted Ambi Extra, a fashionable skin lightening cream, and an image of an air hostess, seemingly picked because she looked fearsome, advocated the charms of Nigeria Airways. How incongruous the posters looked when below them were people who could hardly afford to eat and banked on selling a few paper clips or dud watches or a U2 battery to make a few naira. The Ikorodu road was not only bedlam, it was also a building site for a new motorway to ease the Lagos traffic. 'Built by Dumez' signs were all over; perhaps, Karl reflected, they should be changed to 'Pandemonium by Dumez.' Under every bridge was a settlement, a free prime residential location. There was shade and the down pipes from the road above provided water that was almost clean, but irrevocably there was the manic, tangled, aerial mayhem of telephone and power lines. Alongside them was a truck whose suspension was being punished by a huge number of bales of some unrecognisable vegetation. And clinging to the bales were people, lots of people, women with little kids, old men festooned with wrinkles, their bags and boxes tied with string. Some of them appeared to be five or six feet above the roof of the Isuzu and some appeared to be hanging on for grim death. One slip and they would just be another stain on the road surface.

After nearly an hour and about five or six miles, some traffic was diverted onto a partially completed section of the new motorway and the traffic was now just heavy. Gone was the chaotic cardboard city; the houses were still crowded, but more substantial and made from corrugated iron. Still further on houses appeared that were not in danger of being blown down by a big bad wolf. Wellington turned right onto a bumpy gravel road that was relatively free of cars and flanked by houses of some substance.

Another 100 yards further on there were houses that actually had small gardens. There was still some rubbish in the street but there was less noise and it looked as though the residents actually cared for the road. Wellington braked and made a right turn into a drive that just about accommodated the FME vehicle. He stopped at a detached house with two foot high capital block lettering displaying the words PHIN-O HOTEL, all red against the white walls. Wellington turned around and his grin lit up the cab. 'We are here,' he said. 'You will like it here, Madam Dejonwo is so very kind.' And it proved to be true.

One hundred and fifty yards behind them was the snarling mass of overcrowded yellow buses, precarious people carriers and tentative trucks, but the road outside the PHIN-O-Hotel was, it seemed, a haven of peace. The hotel was a large house with five or six bedrooms; there was no formal reception desk and it was like an English B&B but without the tasteful decoration and sweet smells. The main room was spartan, and a lazy fan stirred the air over the cool floor tiles as slowly as a child stirring dough for its mother.

A lady appeared, dressed in traditional Nigerian garb which was colourful and voluminous and reflected the size of the woman under the swathes of cloth. She paused for a moment and looked at the tired couple who, in perfect symmetry, tried to create a friendly smile. She looked them up and down, came to her own conclusions, and realising that Anna was pregnant immediately became a mother hen. With a loud shout, a servant popped his head round the door and tea and 'food for the lady' were ordered. 'Be quick,' she shouted. Anna was ushered to a chair with a cushion. Karl was temporarily ignored; Anna was given a magazine to fan herself as Madam Dejonwo reached across the room to turn the fan up. Nothing happened, but it was a gesture of kindness and care that Anna appreciated.

Madam Dejonwo fussed. She ordered the bags to be taken to the 'best' room. She introduced herself and wanted to know how two 'oyibos' had been sent to her hotel, because, as she declared, she hadn't had the honour, as she called it, of hosting white people from the Ministry for over a month. 'I will make you welcome in Nigeria,' she said, and she really did her best.

Madam Dejonwo told them she was the sole proprietor of the hotel. She was not encumbered by a husband as he had run off with a young girl years ago. She had five kids. 'All very successful,' she said. It seemed to be the case. As the tea appeared, together with a plate of something very red and steaming, she showed them photos of her children, taking each frame in turn from the sideboard as she explained their whereabouts and what they were doing now. Each photo had a smiling image of a person either clutching their scrolled certificate or donning a graduation gown and in one case sporting a mortar board. Only one picture was in colour, and Madam Dejonwo slowed down as she showed it, a sentimental smile of pride on her face. Did Karl detect the hint of a tear? It was of her daughter, her youngest, her only daughter, exuding happiness, as they were told she was now studying in America and Madam Dejonwo hadn't seen her for two years.

'Don't you speak on the phone?' Karl asked. Her response was one of sadness. She made a melancholy slow gesture towards the phone on the table and hoped he would understand. 'It, it, doesn't...'

'...Work,' Karl said as he interrupted her. He realised he had made a mistake and tried to make up for it by saying, 'I'm sure the system will be fixed soon, we've only been here a few hours and we saw lots of workers mending the wires at the top of the poles.'

Their room was quite large with an attached shower room containing a huge shower head whose holes had been created with the stabbing of a screwdriver. There were two unmatched chairs to sit on, or in Karl's case to throw his clothes on, and a large table against the wall that was an ideal height for Anna's suitcase so she didn't have to bend over. The window looked out on a garden or plot of land that was half filled with stuff that could either go straight to a scrap yard or be sold in some rustic auction house in UK. There were some apologetic stalks of maize and a couple of healthy banana trees, as well as four or five scrawny chickens that were as skinny as marathon runners. The window was half blocked up with an air conditioner the size of a small coffin which alarmingly had an improvised plastic draining tube coming out of the back that was inserted into a plastic bottle on the floor. The device, it turned out, didn't have the power to extract all the water from the humid air and therefore needed the assistance of the Heath Robinson device. It worked. The air conditioner may have made noises like an old man clearing his throat or sounds like a shunting engine but it was emitting cold air. If you closed your eyes you could imagine, apart from the sounds, that you were in the foyer of the Eko or Federal Palace Hotel. Just as they would have made a bee line for the open fire when coming in out of the cold on a winter's day in Yorkshire, they did the same here, wallowing in the chilled air.

After the most mentally exhausting 24 hours they were in a state of collapse. They looked around their room. No sleek designer furniture and tasteful art adorning the walls here, just a mish mash of different styles. 'It's not exactly what I envisaged,' remarked Karl. It was the wrong thing to say. It was blatantly obvious from Anna's expression that the hotel, as clean as it seemed to be and as welcoming as Madam Dejonwo had been, was definitely not what she had been expecting. But it was nevertheless a sanctuary. They sat on the edge of the bed holding hands and saying nothing, knowing full well that any utterance or comment was not going to change their circumstances. Their silence was comforting.

They were to be picked up tomorrow and after a good night's sleep they could arrive fresh at the Ministry to sort out where they were being posted. They were lathered with sadness and anxiety. They smiled wearily at one another and Karl said weakly, 'With luck we'll be out of Lagos tomorrow and on our way, hopefully to Kaduna.'

'Couldn't we just go home?' was Anna's response.

He was at a loss for what to say. 'Come on love, we've only been here 24 hours. I know it's been a trial but once I get working and we're in our own place, things will be better.'

'The place is horrible, the traffic, the chaos, the heat, the driving, the noise... Even this hotel isn't very nice.'

'You mean it doesn't compare with what we would consider to be a decent standard of accommodation,' he responded.

'I mean everything is horrible,' she said with some force, and with that she turned away from Karl and a tear ran down her face.

There was a knock on the door and Madam Dejonwo appeared, her face full of smiles and her big cheeks like beacons of welcome, telling them that food was ready and that the cook had prepared a chicken especially for them. Anna turned around, wiped the tear from her face, and smiled at Madam Dejonwo.

'You like your room?' she said enthusiastically. 'It is the best in the hotel. I know it is at the back of the hotel but it is quieter here and the A/C in this room is much more reliable. But we are in the hands of God and NEPA.'

'NEPA?' questioned Karl.

'Yes, NEPA, it stands for the Nigerian Electric Power Authority.'

'God and NEPA,' Karl replied quizzically.

'If only God was running NEPA, then we would have electricity all the time. If only God was running the country. Cheer up, just wait until you taste my cooking.'

A chicken from the back yard had been sacrificed. Madam Dejonwo had performed miracles with its athletic, wiry flesh and served it with a tasty green heap that was evidently okra under a piri piri sauce that she had tenderly diluted so as not cause a fiery mouth or explosive stomach.

After their meal, and feeling slightly relaxed for the first time in 24 hours, they wandered outside and were hit by the hot, humid air which, even though sweat inducing, was considerably cooler than the FME at mid-day. In the absence of street lights a huge array of stars was visible. They went on forever, static, calming, and revealing beauty that had not been present on their travels through the suburbs of Lagos. They remained silent, holding hands. They needed each other and love, like the humidity, caressed them. They wandered back into the hotel, enjoying the draught from the functioning fan, and then went up to their room where they could luxuriate in the chilly air produced by the arthritic air conditioner.

Anna sighed as she sat on the bed and said she felt better and was sure that after a decent sleep she would be less fraught and emotional about their circumstances. Karl continued to gently reassure her, while hiding his lack of conviction that tomorrow they would know their posting and be able to plan for the future. A refreshing shower would help her sleep she declared as she turned on the water. Sitting alone, Karl tried to be rational and objective. Anna was in the shower and there was no need for him to keep up his brave face. He knew what was wrong, he knew that he and especially Anna had had a bucket of culture shock poured over them. At least she will be more positive in the morning he hoped.

There was a loud scream from the shower room, the door flew open and Anna appeared, swathed in suds and her head shaking badly as she pointed to the floor of the shower room, trying to say something. Words would not come out of her mouth. Karl went to the shower entrance not knowing what to find. A snake perhaps or a scorpion ran through his mind, and then he saw, near the plug hole, two of the largest cockroaches he had ever seen. They imperiously scuttled around wondering who had invaded their kingdom. Anna looked over Karl's shoulder, making guttural sounds. 'Get rid of them, kill them, spray them, do something! before they disappear down the plug hole!'

Karl turned and grabbed his shoe. He flailed at them, and it was then that the insects got into top gear. He swiped and missed, swiped and missed, and just as one was about to disappear it was hit and its body exploded, its creamy slimy bits from underneath the carapace splattered the walls. The second suffered an almost identical fate as it moved like a formula one insect up the slippery tiles. As it was half hit by the sticky shoe, its body distorted and it dropped into the shower tray and continued its drunken escape act. Karl hit it and hit again, bits of legs and feelers were mixed up in slime and the hard shell was hanging from the end of the shoe. It took 10 seconds and he was out of breath. He turned to his wife who was shivering with revulsion and gave her a wet, reassuring hug. All prior thoughts of being less fraught had evaporated.

They were both physically and emotionally exhausted and took to their bed. It was only 9pm and seemed to be a lifetime since they had been at the Victoria check-in desk. Only 24 hours ago they were window shopping in London in smart, clean, functioning shops, and it now seemed to be 24 hours since they had been asleep. They hugged each other for reassurance. The A/C whirred, clanked and stuttered and they drifted towards sleep in the cool room. It was almost cool enough to pull the blankets up to their chins. Karl's reveries were broken as he became aware that the A/C was functioning ever so quietly. But as he listened he thought, *is it functioning at all?* The bedroom was getting warmer. His hand reached out for the bedside light, he clicked the switch and nothing happened. Every few seconds the air got a little warmer and sticky.

In no time the room became uncomfortable and he could feel beads of sweat on his forehead. No torch, no candles, the room temperature around 90F, and they were disorientated. There was a knock at the door. Karl fumbled his way towards the door to see Madam Dejonwo with a huge lantern in her hands, looking like a Halloween image with the light shining upwards. 'This is for you,' she said, handing the fluorescent light to him. 'Sorry about the A/C,' she continued. 'You'll soon get used to NEPA,' she said apologetically.

'That's the electricity company you talked about earlier?'

'Yes. You'll soon get used to it, and they charge so much and they never apologise when the supply is cut off.' She continued without pausing for breath, 'I bet it's not like this in England, oh to be able to touch a switch and know it was going to work.' With her hands indignantly placed on her hips she leaned forward for maximum effect and said, 'You know what NEPA really stands for don't you?' Karl barely had time to shake his head when she declared, with a loud resigned laugh, 'NEPA is known here as No Electrical Power Again!'

Karl had to laugh and so did Anna as she joined them at the door. The air from the corridor felt a little cooler and she asked Madam Dejonwo if it was a good idea to open the small vent in the window above the A/C, thinking to herself that no one apart from a very small child could slip through and get into their room.

'Oh, I wouldn't if I were you,' advised Mrs Dejonwo. 'You'll get eaten alive.'

Anna, still slightly sleepy, didn't quite get what she was saying and repeated, 'Eaten alive!'

'Oh yes, in no time the room will be full of mosquitoes, and I actually think they prefer the blood of oyibos... Sorry, I mean Europeans.'

They slept on top of the bed. The room was hot and uncomfortable. Karl fashioned a fan from a magazine and tried to waft the air about, which proved to be futile as all he was doing was moving hot air from one place to another. They slept fitfully and had it not been for their exhaustion it may well have been another sleepless night.

Before they left for the Ministry the next morning they wrote a note to their friend Tony, who had been working in Lagos for the last year. They asked Madam Dejonwo where they could post their letter and she instantly shuffled off across the room, reached in the drawer for something and then kindly provided them with a stamp. She looked at the letter, hummed and muttered. She tipped her head to one side as she thought and then announced that it was not good to trust the post office.

'Well what's the point of having a postal system?' questioned Karl.

'It used to work when we had post boxes, but they were all stolen, and do you know...?' Lowering her voice to a whisper so that some invisible person couldn't hear, she checked behind her. No one was there so she carried on. 'Do you know that lots of post office employees were sent to prison?'

'What for?' asked Anna.

'I bet they were opening letters and looking for money,' remarked Karl.

'Oh they probably do that all the time, but what they did was worse!'

'Worse!' exclaimed Anna, her face aghast.

'Oh yes. Do you know what they did?' Karl and Anna shook their heads.

'They actually dumped hundreds of bags of mail in the swamp near the airport so they wouldn't have to deliver all those letters. Just think of all those poor people waiting for a letter or those waiting for some important business mail. They should have been shot like the armed robbers on Bar Beach.'

She looked at the address on the envelope.' It is going to Victoria Island I see. Why don't you get your driver to take you to the post office there and put it in the numbered mail box yourself, then you will know your friend Tony will get it.'

8

Over the next two days they were collected by a driver and suffered the slow, sweaty and frustrating drive to the FME in Lagos. Although they posted their letter they were frustrated that they had been unable to give Tony an address he could reply to. Frustration was the outcome of everything they tried to do. They waited to see someone who didn't appear or didn't exist. The people they dealt with were charmingly incompetent, some desperately lazy, and they lost count of the number of workers reading a paper, just talking in social groups, or fast asleep. Mrs Obaganda was apologetic or she wasn't around. In fact on their second day in the Ministry they were sure she was avoiding them. Basically they always felt that they were being told what they wanted to hear. All that came of a frustrating first day at the Ministry was that they were definitely not going to Kaduna but she was sure their posting would be to a Federal Teacher Training College. She tried to play up the idea by saying that the colleges were new and modern and were specially built in four areas of the country that had a shortage of teachers – Yola, Pankshin, Okene and Maiduguri. This seemed to be a step forward but it was also worrying. On the wall of an adjacent room was a huge map of Nigeria. Karl and Anna were alarmed that Maiduguri was in the very far north east of the country and virtually in Chad. Yola was in the extreme sweaty east and virtually in Cameroon. He mentioned Okene to one friendly clerk who shook his head disturbingly as if he knew some deadly secrets, and then uttered the words 'civil unrest and cholera' when Pankshin was mentioned. Karl recalled that Maximus, the taxi driver, had said some disparaging words about Okene, though in truth he couldn't be sure.

Their trips into town with Wellington were an ordeal. In an attempt to extract some sympathy, Wellington made it clear that he had to be up at 5am to get to the Ministry to collect his allocated vehicle so he could pick

71

them up. Anna asked why he was not allowed to take the vehicle home and the reply was that where he lived it was too dangerous to park a government car and too many of his fellow drivers used the government cars as taxis to supplement their income.

On their third day they were' helped' by one of Mrs Obaganda's minions to open a method of payment for their monthly salary. With the help of Sunny J, as he called himself (he was evidently self-named after a Congolese singer), they had to fill in an avalanche of forms. Sunny J told them that only he knew how it all worked and therefore declared often that he was indispensable and would soon be a 'big shot'. In reality he was a spotty, callow youth who was required to do a simple quotidian task. He had a supercilious attitude and Anna found the way he kept leering at her as he leaned over the desk uncomfortable. His breath smelled like an old football sock. For all his so-called expertise, he constantly had to shuffle the papers and re-read them so the correct procedures were followed. They were reminded many times that procedure must be followed.

To prove his love of the Congolese crooner he constantly tapped a rhythm on the desk and hummed some tune as he vacantly stared at the ceiling.

Anna leaned over and whispered in Karl's ear. 'He's such an...'

'...Arsehole,' interrupted Karl.

'Actually,' she replied, 'I was going to be more polite. I thought he was worthy of the word wanker.'

Karl nodded his head in agreement and smiled.

The youth lost one of the forms. It had to be filled in again. He took them away a second time and after about 30 minutes he came back clutching the bouquet of paper and declared that Karl had filled in one incorrectly. It was obvious that he had had to show them to a superior who had found his talents wanting and sent him scuttling back.

From their annual salary of 8,000 naira they were given 800 naira in cash as an advance payment, which they were informed would be paid back incrementally from their monthly salary. The best thing about this two hours of incompetence was that someone, somewhere, lost the forms and they never did get to pay the money back, although this was only discovered sometime later and therefore they couldn't wallow in a little success. They sat around a great deal in the sweaty austere building. They wandered outside into the road and with the notes in their hands bought some Nigerian bread rolls and cheese from a man with a small hand cart. The bread was a shock. It was as sweet as a croissant and the cheese, which was a sunrise yellow, looked awful but tasted, well, cheesy. It was all washed down with the ubiquitous Fanta that was sold in the Ministry.

They had been assured that they would be placed in a proper hotel on Victoria Island later that day. They were told they were going to a prestigious college situated next to a fine hospital, and they would be given a brand-new Peugeot 504. Again they sat about. They grumbled. They were frustrated and felt, rightly, that they were being treated badly by people who were either kind, sympathetic and incompetent, or they were in the hands of charlatans who had no manners and were equally as incompetent. Mrs Obaganda was a member of the first group but even she had lost some credibility. Even so, she had said, 'Don't worry, by the end of the day we will have you placed and it will be my pleasure to make your travel arrangements for the next day.' All of this was accompanied with a big reassuring smile which Karl and Anna knew was meant to give them hope. It was the hope that they would get away from Lagos, as they waited yet again to find out what was going on. They both thought that if the posting was not quite ready, at least tonight they would be in a decent hotel, one with its own power supply, without cockroaches and no infernal four hour journey in a hot Isuzu van to get there. They agreed that they didn't mind waiting another day or two whilst sitting by a pool.

Later in the day, Mrs Obaganda entered her forlorn office. She tried to resurrect a smile, tried to impart a glimmer of hope, but her facial features, in spite of her efforts, told the story. No posting, no decent hotel, no car to drive away in. Karl was approaching volcano status. Anna sank into the chair, looking small and helpless. Karl had so many critical words and expletives he wanted to pour out.

'But!'

'Why?'

'When?'

'What next?'

'What is happening?'

'Yet another bloody cock-up!'

'Why don't you send us back to the UK?'

Fuming and disconsolate they found Wellington and got into the Isuzu. They steeled themselves for another two-hour crawl through traffic mayhem, through mini markets that formed when they stopped, and the gruesome attentions of locals who, in their keenness to perhaps extract a naira or two from the oyibos, pressed their faces against the windows of the car like some live gargoyles, leaving a sweaty stain of damp flesh. They made their resolution. *Bugger Nigeria, we're going home.* Their destination tomorrow would be the British High Commission.

Wellington was taken aback the following day when he was told that the Ministry could wait because they had an important appointment at the British High Commission. Their premises were only a mile away from the grey federal building but light years away aesthetically and in terms of organisation. They were informed that yes, they could be repatriated. Yes, the cost of the airfares was expected to be repaid within a week of their return to England. No, the Commission couldn't return their household baggage to them when it arrived in Nigeria from the UK. No, they couldn't organise their journey to the airport, and yes, they felt Karl and Anna should tell the Nigerians at the Ministry in writing of their intentions. Yes, should the Federal Ministry try to sue them they would defend their case, but they must also remember that any future jobs abroad run by the British Government may not be available to them because of their repatriation decision.

All of this took place in a cool, efficient looking office. The junior diplomat in his smart white shirt and tie was polite, personable and not at all fazed by their request. Tea was served. Real tea. Strong satisfying tea, Tetley's or PG Tips, along with McVitie's chocolate digestives. No sign of the indigestible Cabin biscuits they had been given at the Ministry.

After hearing the story of their first day and about the gulag (his words) that they had been sent to, he was very sympathetic, but he advised that once you left the big towns like Lagos, Ibadan, Kano and Abeokuta things were dramatically more pleasant. Their conversation with him finished with advice to think it over and make a decision the next day. He told them to call in on their way back from the Ministry tomorrow afternoon and if their decision was yes, he would arrange for flights the day after. He did mention, however, that their passports would be taken from them at Heathrow and only returned when the debt was paid.

Their journey to Ikoyi Island the next day seemed to be easier. Perhaps they were becoming inured to the chaos of the trip and perhaps it was the thought that they had a get out of jail card and could, if they so wished, fly back to UK the next day. The former revulsion for the sights they saw from the Isuzu was replaced with resignation and acceptance, and once there was acceptance there was observation. Trying to eliminate the bad smells, the aggressive salesmen, the endless shouts of 'oyibo' or 'give me money,' Karl and Anna were witnessing ground roots capitalism. Everyone had something to sell. It could be a starved chicken thrust at them, a deflated

74

football, a basket of dried smelly fish, a packet of cannabis or even as happened on one occasion a seriously pornographic magazine that was thrust through the open window and waved in front of Anna's eyes. They batted away the small boy who was trying to sell it but they knew that they were becoming resigned to what they saw because they laughed at the incident. Wellington said he was ashamed that it had happened to them and nobly offered to get out and admonish the boy. Of course it was totally impractical and nor did he really mean it because the cars were so tightly packed in the jam that you couldn't open the car door, nor could you unfold, if you had any, the wing mirrors. The salesmen survived under sticks and plastic sheets, houses of cardboard the size of kennels and ubiquitous corrugated iron sheets made into unsteady dwellings. They could be aggressive, taking offence if they were ignored or you said no. Wellington gave them a bit of advice, telling them that in the future, when they had their own fantastic car, they should never refuse to buy a foot pump. Refusal meant that within minutes you would have four flat tyres and then have no choice but to buy one at an inflated price. Better to have one and then pay the seller to pump your tyres even if they didn't need to be done. He then added, 'You can't win though, because it is likely that if you hand over your pump you'll never see it again.'

They had talked for ages and had thought long and hard at the PHIN-O Hotel last night. They realised that as each day went by everything looked less appalling, less threatening. Yes, inured was the word.

They were greeted at the entrance to the Ministry by Mrs Obaganda. She had a smile the width of the Niger and her bosoms, autonomous and slightly out of control, jiggled with excitement. 'Come with me, come with me,' she beckoned, and they followed her to the stairs and up to her office. She read from a piece of A4 paper. 'You will be a Senior Education Officer and after three months you will be made into a Principal Education Officer.' She stopped reading and said, 'Principal Education Officer, not 8,000 but 10,000.'

She picked up the paper again and carried on reading. 'Where was I?' she said, searching the paper with her finger. 'Oh yes.' She paused. 'At the Federal Advanced Teacher Training College in Okene and you will be assessing trainee teachers in the field. You'll need a nice new Peugeot to do that.'

'Okene?'

'Yes, I showed it to you on the map yesterday. It is very new, has lots of new buildings under construction and...'

'It is new? How new? Is it actually functioning as a college or is it just a building site?' Karl said with some cynicism.

She ignored or didn't catch his sarcasm and replied, 'It has been open for four years and they are extending the college to take on more graduates.' She added, 'It is being extended because it has been very successful.'

'How about a hospital?'

'The town has over 100,000, perhaps 150,000 people, and a town that size will have a fine hospital, and Benin City is close by, only 120 miles away.' She added more glorious details and answered more questions. But they made sure not to get carried away by her embellished enthusiasm.

They wandered outside and went under the porte-cochère to the garden to think about what they were going to do.

9

They had been in Lagos for four full days and even though their skins had thickened and their tolerance for chaos and unintentional mismanagement had grown, they were, they had to admit, still in a state of minor culture shock. What would their mental state have been like had they not experienced Africa before? They had eased seamlessly into Kampala, everything was organised: the greeting, the induction, the expectations, the accommodation, the timetable, help on how to purchase a car, pay your bills, get the spouse a work permit, with the added bonus of the welcoming attitude and friendliness of the Ugandans they had met. Yes, there was visual chaos in Kampala, the noise, the traders and hustlers, but it was not aggressive or in your face and overpowering. Their arrival at Entebbe Airport and their two-night stay at a hotel on the Port Bell Road had been organised by the UK government, and they knew which school they were going to. That was the difference. Here in Lagos they had been seconded to the Nigerian government, a word implying organisation but which in Lagos appeared to mean maladministration, with everything being done at glacial pace. They were in the hands of a disinterested workforce. The Federal Ministry of Education was overstaffed, filled with ill-motivated and untrained workers who, even when they felt threatened, tried to do their best. Karl and Anna's situation was a minor irritation to most of them. At best they were ignored and at worst people were just rude.

As they sat in the car with Lagos receding behind them, Karl tried to analyse why their experience had been so disturbing to them. Because they had no control over what happened to them, they were powerless. Of course they hadn't just accepted the incompetence. They had vociferously complained, they had gone to the British High Commission to enquire about repatriation, and they had at all times been aware that Africa required patience, politeness and persistence. He felt that they had crossed that boundary many times. The PHIN-O hotel, with all its faults, had been a haven yet also a prison and they were thankful to have been helped and encouraged by the ever-cheerful Madam Dejonwo. But Lagos had denied them any freedom and they felt as though they had to abide by the rules of an occupying force. There seemed to be no personal space. They had to make physiological adjustments to their own sense of space. They had to redefine what was privacy, and all they got was the room in the hotel. There was no privacy at the Ministry, in the street, a shop. Nowhere to whisper, to think things through, they were always surrounded by teeming humanity. They were objects for exploitation, items of no concern. There was great discomfort in feeling out of place and purposeless. They were outsiders in a very alien environment, with no sense of purpose. It was so unlike Uganda where they had been greeted as a white couple who had come to help the country. Here it was different. The cacophony of urban noise, of hawkers, internal combustion engines, horns, construction work and the constant yelling was everywhere, as well as the ever-present stink from open sewers. They were stared at, watched, followed, grabbed, touched and hassled. There was never a time, until they got back to the hotel, in Anna's words 'when she didn't feel threatened.' Karl wouldn't go that far, but the inertia, the not knowing where they were going, where they would live, what he would teach, had undermined them both. He knew things were bad for him mentally, he had lost his sense of humour, it had been relegated to the back of his mind. When was the last time he had roared with laughter (usually at his own jokes) or told a joke or even just smiled? His mind was saturated with guilt about his father at home, the death of his mam and the constant worry about Anna, and what seemed to him to have been a bad decision to leave their comfortable life in England to work in Nigeria. And to think, he had turned down postings in Brunei and Zambia.

He noticed that their driver had stopped at the side of the road and was insisting that they join him for tea. Images of a quaint, rural tea shop came to mind, the clink of porcelain cups and saucers, crisp table cloths, cleanliness and baking smells. Karl imagined the aromatic taste of PG tips and Anna the golden colour of Ceylon and a slice of lemon. But this was Africa, this was Nigeria, and they were parked at the side of a rough, ill-maintained tarmac road in the middle of Benin State, thousands of miles away from their imagination. At the side of the road sat two large women. Why was it that all middle-aged women in Nigeria seemed to be ample, though voluminous clothes certainly had something to do with that as well as the local ideal that big was beautiful. In front of them was a small wood-burning stove and on top of the small flames and embers was a huge grey galvanised kettle, just like the ones that were dragged around factories in the UK by the essential tea lady.

Wellington's exclamation was aimed at Anna. 'You need to be strong, tea makes you strong, good for the baby, keeps you awake.' He politely insisted that they try a cup. Three plastic mugs were handed to them and with great effort one of the ladies lifted the large kettle and filled their mugs with a hot milky brown liquid. Well, it looked like tea, it steamed like tea, it was in a mug, but there the resemblance ended. Wellington took a swig, smiled with his piano key teeth and uttered a loud, 'Aah!' He made an encouraging gesture to them to try it. Karl and Anna looked at each other while Wellington purchased a small bread roll which he proceeded to dip into his tea. They smiled to each other silently and their eyes said, 'Okay let's give it a try.'

The taste was quite unique. It bore no resemblance to tea as they knew it. It was sweet beyond tolerance as far as Anna was concerned and Karl, who was not averse to doughnuts and other sticky pastries, jerked his head with shock. Neither of them liked it, but it was hot, it was a kind gesture, and they politely tried to finish the mug of liquid. Karl asked Wellington what sort of tea it was, a somewhat naive question, expecting to hear a brand name. Wellington translated, and from the fold of her skirt the woman produced a brown paper packet that held a mass of desiccated leaves and stalks that did in fact look like tea. Wellington smacked his lips, spoke in vernacular to one of the women, and she produced a large tin of Carnation Condensed milk which she added to his drink.

It turned out that the tea, of dubious quality, was boiled in the kettle. A huge amount of sugar was added, and then to give it that milky look, condensed milk was generously stirred in. The concoction was brought to the boil and left to simmer all day and was occasionally topped up with all three ingredients as purchases were made. The empty cups were taken from them, given a quick swish with water and made ready for the next customers.

A few miles further along the road they stopped at a picturesque river bank for a lunch consisting of some bananas and mangoes that Wellington had bought from the tea lady. There were lots of completely naked children frolicking in the water, their faces beaming with health and happiness as they used an overhanging branch as a diving board. They were having a competition to see who could jump or dive in the most mad, daredevil or funny way. The air was filled with shafts of sunlight flashing through the foliage and the sounds of chatter and laughter. Initially they were only interested in showing off, but after a while they became brave and approached the trio, perhaps assuming that two oyibos with a driver and a big Peugeot could be a source of income. Wellington was having nothing of it and his firm voice quickly told them that begging for money here was a waste of their time. The negotiations went on until, with Wellington's nod of approval, one of the kids, still dripping with water, spoke somewhat nervously, directing his words to Karl and Anna. 'I am William, welcome to...' He paused for a second or two, searching for the right words. 'I go to school.' Another boy chirped up, 'Ten and ten is twenty,' and another, 'Where do you live?' But the best was a smaller boy who thrust his way to the front and uttered the phrase, 'There are big red buses in London.' Anna and Karl laughed. It was probably the first time they had laughed out loud since leaving the UK. 'What sort of sentence is that? What a mad way of teaching English,' Karl said. The little boy, eager to impress, pushed himself further forward and said somewhat shakily, 'A happy new year and Christmas.' There they were, in the midst of tropical Africa, in a place of dramatic, bucolic beauty, heat, humidity, trees with leaves the size of garden sheds and butterflies the size of starlings, and a small naked boy was trying to impress them with what he had learned at school. They laughed and laughed and as if they had triggered a switch the little boys, about six of them, laughed hysterically. Even Wellington rolled about laughing.

The laughter evaporated along with their inhibitions. They came up to the visitors and one spoke quietly to Wellington, who listened while looking at Karl as if trying to ascertain from his attitude whether the boy's proposition would be approved. Wellington nodded his head, then turned to both of them and said, 'They want to touch your skin.'

'Haven't they ever seen a...?'

Wellington interrupted before Karl could finish his sentence. 'Yes, they have seen white men before, but they have never touched one.'

'They want to touch me?' said Anna quizzically, asking for confirmation.

'Yes, they are fascinated, perhaps they think if they rub their skin next to yours they will turn lighter and you will turn darker.' At that point he dissolved into laughter and once again everyone fell about laughing, Anna and Karl because they thought it was hilarious and the six little boys because they laughed at people laughing.

Karl thought of the kids he saw going to school in Uganda. They ran past his house every morning and ran back every afternoon, the boys in their ill-fitting khaki shorts and pink shirts and the girls in their hand-me-down pink dresses. The Nakasozi Junior School was about two miles down the hill, and on a couple of occasions Karl had accepted the invitation to visit the place. It radiated happiness and the children glowed with the desire to learn. Upwards of 40 children in the class listened intently, did as they were told, and were either wise enough to know or had been informed by their parents that doing well in school was the key to prosperity. It was always amazing to see the fine concentration level of kids so young.

They were taught English by rote, and their teacher, only just conversant in the language, taught them stock phrases and sentences, just as they had heard only a few minutes ago from the boys around them. 'I want a cuppa tea'; 'The Bobby directs the traffic'; 'Are you well madam?' were chanted in the classroom, and it was easy to assume that if they learnt enough of them they could end up having a conversation. Desks were shared by three pupils, pencils were handed out and taken back at the end of each lesson by the teachers, and exercise books had to be supplied by parents; cheap as they were in the UK, the cost in Uganda was a major sum of money for many of them. He hoped that these Nigerian boys and girls took their education seriously, because having witnessed such fine secondary education in Uganda he knew it really was the gateway to prosperity that was sadly ignored by so many kids in Europe.

The boys came up close, and treating these white people as though they were delicate Ming vases or just very fragile, they caressed their bare arms. They were enthralled by Karl's hairy arms and at one point when he stood up he felt his calf muscle being delicately stroked. It was like some form of ritual. But in the end Wellington had to answer a question, and he did so by taking the arm of the most confident spokesman and placing it against the forearm of Karl and rubbing gently. The little boy, lithe, athletic and with huge fascinated eyes, gave a canyon-like smile and then burst into laughter, as did everyone else as Wellington vigorously rubbed a black arm and a white arm against one another and proudly held them up to show neither had inherited each other's colour.

Eventually Wellington gave them a stern look so they knew the fun was over. They waded through the water, collected their few clothes and disappeared into the trees.

Stopping here had been a welcome break, just as leaving Lagos, its filth, traffic madness, its chaos, corruption and organisational ineptitude was a real relief. Once they had left the Ikorodu Road the city petered out and the landscape became delightfully rural. Whenever the car stopped, sounds that were previously smothered by the loud urban noises of Lagos could be heard: bird song, the wind in the leaves, the buzz of insects, you could hear your own thoughts rather than having to listen to the horns, hooters, inefficient silencers, the slow rumble of traffic, and of course everyone seemingly yelling at one another. What was impressive visually was just how aesthetically beautiful and wonderful the tropical surroundings were. An endless variety of palms, some with feather-like leaves, others pronged like tridents, palms that exploded from the ground like fountains, ones with long sinuous trunks and others with leaves as big as the wings of a small aircraft. The forest smelled aromatic and damp and at times looked almost floral and delicate rather than mysterious and foreboding, and went on and on. Here and there small rural settlements broke the monotony, each of which without fail displayed haphazardly placed advertisements along the side of the road. Some were hand-made and badly spelt. There were notices for the services of the local 'doctor', purveyors of the best palm oil, a food stop with a grass roof – 'Cool Shade Cafe' read one, a drunken lorry with a slogan, 'Christ is watching you' and, without fail, adverts for beer – Gulder, Star and Guinness, all of which were guaranteed to give you good health and also help you to attract fine ladies. People were smiling. It was all a far cry from the city that seemed to be built on aggression.

Once the boys had left and all that could be heard was the noise of a small waterfall a few yards away, Karl drifted into an idealistic yet hopeful reverie about what would happen when they arrived in Okene. They would have a government house, acquire transport, employ a servant to help around the house, and enjoy the pleasant life of an expatriate whilst educating a few trainee teachers. He could watch their baby grow up and Anna would be unencumbered by working so she could give all her time to being a mother and enjoy some security. The thinking bubble of his daydream was punctured by the manic drone of a huge sausage fly zooming around them and then Wellington getting up and telling them it was time to go. They both felt better for being in a peaceful bucolic environment that was an antidote for the almost unbearable tension they had felt for the last five days. Oh how nice it was to laugh again! To think they had actually gone to the British High Commission to see about repatriation. Their Peugeot 504 estate waited for them. Only another 240 miles to go.

The road changed from a two-lane asphalt highway into what Wellington said was a strip road. His definition was perfect. What lay ahead was a strip of tarmac just a little wider than the average car. It meant that with careful driving you could always have your wheels on the smooth part of the road, but irrevocably most of the edges had deteriorated to the extent that where the edges had collapsed it was like forcing one set of wheels over a surface like a jagged knife or where some giant carnivore had bitten lumps out of the edge of the road. Wellington declared that the idea was to build roads at half the price and therefore help more people travel. A bull dozer would demolish a swathe of forest to the width of a two-lane road, followed by a grader followed by a team of labourers, often numbering hundreds (so Wellington said) who poured the hot asphalt onto a surface just greater than the width of a car. There were no foundations and no aggregate underneath. No wonder they eroded so quickly or deteriorated due to heavy lorries, tropical rain and piercing sunshine. But what was really alarming was another car in the distance coming towards you. Ideally, as two cars approached each other they would each pass with one set of wheels on the tarmac, but Wellington explained that there were unwritten rules about etiquette. As far as cars were concerned, lorries didn't move, nor did army vehicles, nor did buses, nor did taxis. There also seemed be another rule, in that whoever had his flasher on first declared his right of way. At times it came down to which driver valued his life the least and therefore refused to move, forcing the other driver almost into the ditch. Now this of course was open to conjecture, but the results could be seen in the many cars lacking wing mirrors, cars with scrapes down their sides, and a wreck at the side of the road every mile or so. Wellington was a better than average driver as far as Karl and Anna were concerned, although they suspected that he modified his driving so as not to give them a heart attack. The car bounced about, veered from side to side, and there was a horrifying swoosh as their car passed within inches of another.

Eventually the palms and tropical vegetation seemed to stop as though there was a line across the land forbidding their further growth. The topography changed and a whole wide vista appeared suddenly as the claustrophobic canopies of tropical vegetation became savannah. Undulating hills and small mountains, rocky outcrops called inselbergs, a few palms, but more acacia trees and lots and lots of blue sky and endless space. The enormity of Africa was on view. It was visually like being given a new lease of life. No towns, no people, just sky, warmth, and a landscape that was crying out to be walked in. They were even more excited when Wellington told them they would be in Okene in twenty minutes. Images of an organised little town went through Karl's mind; he pinched himself and was satisfied by the glorious vista ahead of him. Anna was impressed. After hours of a green kaleidoscope flashing by them on a dodgy strip road there was an element of safety in their positive reaction to the wide-open spaces. They looked at each other, tired as they were after a long journey, and a great wave of relief flowed through them.

Still on the strip road the Peugeot reached the summit of a small hill, to be confronted by carnage. Two taxis, each demanding more than their share of the road, had collided. The result seemed to be an explosion of steel, glass and flesh and two concertinaed vehicles that were barely recognisable. There was just enough room for Wellington to get past. On their left, steam was screaming from a smashed radiator, the windscreen missing where two passengers had been flung through it. One car was on its side, its bodywork distorted into modern art and its surfaces coagulated with blood. There were bodies everywhere and glittering small cubes of glass. Bodies past hope, bodies unrecognisable, and others dazed and shocked and some as mangled as the bodywork of the two taxis that had hit each other at full speed. Unnervingly there was also the smell of petrol.

Karl and Anna were shocked during the seven or eight seconds that it took them to pass by the mayhem and blood bath. Onlookers stood around waving their arms and screaming, some as a reaction to witnessing such horror and others in anger at the stupidity of the drivers.

'Stop Wellington!' shouted Anna. 'These people need some help.'

There was no response from him. She leaned forward and pulled at his shoulder, trying to get him to listen and obey. He turned, giving her an uncharacteristic firm look, and with one hand at the wheel he said, 'Their stupidity is not our problem. If we stop someone may try and blame us and we could end up in a very bad way.'

Some half a mile after they passed the accident, Wellington slowed the car down and parked at the brow of a gentle hill where he gestured for them to get out. The landscape wasn't dissimilar to that of the garrigue in the Mediterranean, with areas of scrub, small plots of vegetation, rocky hills in the distance, palms and acacia trees. A few cattle crossed the road ahead of them, controlled by a small boy in ragged shorts and carrying a large stick. There was a change in the heat. Yes, it was hotter, but gone was the clammy, sticky atmosphere in the air. They could breathe more easily even though they could feel the sun's rays penetrating their skin. A whisper of fresh air and the sound of bird song accompanied them.

'What's the stop for?' asked Karl indignantly. He was still shaken by the carnage they had passed two minutes ago. It was obvious that Wellington had chosen to forget the accident. He was getting ready to address them as he pointed to the top of the hill.

'Those poor people,' said Anna. 'Isn't there anything we could do?'

'No,' was his response. His tone brushed off Anna's suggestion and he seemed eager to tell them about what would be revealed when they crested the hill.

'Are you sure we couldn't help? Perhaps we could...'

Karl's words were interrupted by Wellington. 'We'll tell the police when we reach Okene,' he said.

'But isn't that miles away and...'

'...That's why we have stopped. In 50 yards at the top of the hill you'll see Okene and the teachers' college. We are here,' he shouted jubilantly.

As pleased as Anna was, she was still concerned about the accident. 'Surely we could have offered some first aid,' she implored.

'It is far too dangerous to stop. Those people were hysterical, all they did is look and scream, they didn't really help and some of them will even take the clothes from the dead. Accidents happen all the time here. Stupid people, drivers who don't care. Drivers who can't drive, have no licence or are on drugs. Too many people in the car, bald tyres, no brakes, broken suspensions, and daydreaming instead of watching the road. Driving without sleep. And if we had stopped to help we could have been blamed even though we just happened to be passing. There are too many accidents here. Don't worry, I'll tell the police, they are only a mile or two away. Now come and see this.'

He beckoned them to walk with him up a short slope to the top of the hill. He got there first and theatrically gestured at the view below them.

Oh how different it was to the sweaty tropical jungle of the south. There were open vistas of craggy hills. To their right was a glimpse of a lake and down below, perhaps a couple of miles away, was a town. A red-roofed town. Not the red of Mediterranean roof tiles but acres of roofs of rusted corrugated iron. Just visible in the clear air were a couple of minarets, a couple of towers, presumably churches, and three or four buildings that were more than two stories high. There was no traffic. The road was quiet and they could hear the wind and the whine of insects and birdsong. As tired as they were after being in the car all day, it was a pleasure to witness the space and tranquillity.

The sun lowered itself towards the horizon and started to relax after its day long work out. Wellington, with a huge smile, pointed to the left. 'Can you see those white buildings?'

'Where?' asked Anna.

'Look at the ridge.' He paused. 'Do you see the little bits of white?'

'Yes,' she replied, and then, 'What are you trying to show us, Wellington?'

'The college,' he replied excitedly. 'It is where you will be working.'

'I wonder where we will be living,' muttered Karl.

'I have seen the houses, there are some there where we are looking now and many fine houses in the town.'

'How do you know so much about the place? I thought you had only been here once?'

'People I met told me about good accommodations and the new buildings and new campus.' He looked at them, wanting to reassure them. 'No more horrible Lagos, this is the nice Nigeria. Just think, the next time I come here I can visit you and be your friend and we can wash my car together.'

'Wash your car?' Karl said, with a puzzled look on his face. 'What do you mean, wash your car?'

'It is what we say here. It means we can share a beer with each other and talk about the world.'

'And eat crappy goat sandwiches and piri piri everything and wait for the dreaded NEPA to start,' commented Karl drily, trying to inject some wit into the conversation.' Wellington didn't understand his sarcasm and laughed in a feeble way. Karl felt a little guilty about his comments and thought about how helpful Wellington had been over the last few days. He really appreciated his optimism and small cheerful and encouraging comments. He had disparaged the government, the ministry, the roads, the drivers, hoping that his criticisms – real or invented out of courtesy, would create some empathy with them. It was a bit of ingratiation that they recognised and appreciated.

'Wellington,' he said, in a serious and friendly tone. 'You will be welcome in my house any time, and yes, we can wash your car together.'

Wellington's smile glowed like the setting sun.

10

They passed the sign for the Federal Advanced Teachers College as the sun was setting. The buildings were mostly obscured but a bare patch of land was pointed out by Wellington who immediately stated that the four visible buildings were staff accommodation.

They both strained to see and were not impressed, for what they saw were four small boxes with odd-shaped roofs. Their anxiety levels grew as they entered the town. Where would they be staying? Who would greet them? Would their house be ready? Would there be food in the pantry? The rust coloured town they saw from the top of the hill was exactly that. Hundreds upon hundreds of one story corrugated iron houses. They passed people scurrying home in the twilight. The sun was close to the horizon and blessed the town and especially the corrugated iron roofs. They were aglow with pink, gold and orange hues, that, with the gentle smoke from cooking fires, gave Okene a mysterious look.

They stopped at a substantial two story house with a set of stairs descending from the front door to the yard below.

'Is this where we are going to live?' asked Anna as the last rays of the sun caught the top of the house.

She thought to herself that at least it looked imposing and was a decent, though just acceptable, size compared to the shacks, as she thought of them, that she had seen near the college.

The answer came as a shock to her.

'No you won't be staying here, this is Dr Omega's house.'

'Dr Omega?' she said with a puzzled look on her face. 'Isn't he the...'

She was interrupted by Karl who confirmed what she thought, by saying, 'He is the principal.'

'And he lives here?' was her alarmed response. 'If he lives here, just what sort of houses do the lecturers get?'

Karl got out of the car and joined Wellington at the top of the stairs. He was talking to a young scruffy barefoot Nigerian. It turned out that he was a servant and with Dr Omega being away until tomorrow he was to pass on the message that Karl and Anna had been booked into the best rooms at the Paradise Hotel in the centre of Okene until tomorrow, or the day after if the Doctor didn't return in time.

It was a short journey in the twilight. Very few houses had electricity and the gloom was pierced by newly developed fluorescent lanterns, old hurricane lamps, candles, or fires outside the houses. There was the smell of smoke and cooking. A stray dog barked at a huge cow that had decided to cross the road and small motor bikes carrying two, three or even four people spluttered their way through the town.

The Paradise Hotel was imposing. It was lit up. They had obviously paid the electricity bill. It had three floors and proudly advertised a roof top bar where there was a flimsy rail to stop customers falling off when they had had too much to drink. The hotel stood out because it was painted white. It even had a lamp that shone on the gimcrack name plate, illuminating the word PARADIC and revealing the lost letter and incorrect spelling underneath the title. On the wall was crudely painted the words, 'God and Jesus has blessed the Paradise.'

The owner, Mustapha, was full of enthusiasm as he excitedly welcomed them. He shouted at two teenagers, one of whom was wearing huge purple platform shoes and a pair of shorts, to carry their bags inside. They were ushered through a door covered by a beaded curtain. Another door beckoned and behind it, as described by the owner, was the best room in the hotel. Wellington had skulked off. Mustapha genuflected and proudly presented the 'suite' and Anna, after a quick and scrupulous visual check, whispered to Karl, 'It's a dump!'

He tried to shush her so that Mustapha would not be offended, but her response was to say, 'Don't shush me. That so-called hotel in Lagos and now you have dragged me, and I'm pregnant, half way across the world to stay in this dump!'

Karl tried to pacify her with an apologetic gesture but it was an action in vain.

'Look,' she said pointing. 'There isn't even a door on the toilet, I bet there is no water and next they'll be handing us lamps because the power will fail.' She rubbed her fingers on the grubby white-washed wall, noticing that there was only one small window which looked out onto the street.

'Look, the place is filthy and to think I took your advice and followed you here because we … or you more like it, thought we'd have a better life. Money rules again I see. I don't care what you say, or how much money we would lose, or the fact we have no job in UK to go back to, nor a house for that matter, but we … or I, am going home tomorrow. Do you really expect me to live here, or stay here for that matter? And don't mention the contract you signed, what bloody contract, they have broken it time after time. Just look around, if this is the best hotel in town what is the hospital like. No, no child of mine will be born in this dump!'

'But we are in the middle of Africa,' he whispered.

'Middle of Africa, too right we are, and I'm stood on the bullseye and all the darts are hitting me! The whole place is a dump and I've told you, I don't care what it takes, we are going home!'

She slumped onto the bed. It was irrevocable that they would have to stay the night here. She tried to calm down, taking deep breaths as if the slow movement of her chest would erase the anxiety she felt.

She opened her eye and gazed at the white washed walls; two sconces, each with a tiny light bulb, was the room's attempt at sophistication. Her eyes moved to the ceiling. Each corner of the high room was festooned with cobwebs from a Hammer horror movie, a fan moving them gently as it laboriously fought against the hot air, and she saw out of the corner of her eye an image from the past, one she considered revolting. There, hanging from the ceiling, was a long sticky fly trap. It had done its work and was encrusted like some pebble dashed wall with nasty black and green dead flies. The last time she had seen one of these was when as a small child she had to go on errands to the local corner shop where in pre-aerosol days hung a similar device equally as disgusting. The floor was gritty underfoot. She didn't get undressed, because the bed covers felt damp and as though they had been the recipient of sexual assignments or minor surgical operations. Fat flies resting upside down on the ceiling stared down at her, ignoring the congested fly paper. A mosquito whined past her ear. Her swat was futile. She ignored Karl, pulled down the grubby grey mosquito net and curled up on the bed fully clothed and tried to sleep. She felt dirty just being in the room and for some unaccountable reason, ashamed. If this was the suite, what were the other rooms like?

Karl declined the offer of food. Was it because Mustapha kept wiping his hands on a dirty apron, or that he wasn't hungry. He was actually concerned that some prandial horror would be presented and further upset his wife. In silence he sat on an iron folding chair looking at bare concrete floors with cracked white plaster hanging on to the walls like a desperate climber and a crucifix next to a creased poster advertising Yankari game reserve. The bath room had a brownish toilet, but at least there was running water. There was no door on it, no privacy and their two heavy cases lay unopened next to a wooden rail that would, he assumed, take the place of a wardrobe. He heard someone yelling from an adjoining room and he banged on the wall, hoping his actions would quieten his neighbours.

Anna drifted in and out of sleep, hoping that some of her tension and unhappiness would evaporate. In the normally sublime state of being half awake and half asleep she boiled with resentment. She pictured her husband behind closed eye lids and resented him. Five days ago, they were in London, five days ago life was divinely predictable. There was security, they were surrounded by all their possessions and the people whom they cared for and who cared for them and now after his decision they were in a shit-hole and on a two-year contract. Thoughts rebounded around her brain, arrows of anxiety, rays of hopelessness, daggers of revulsion and frustration and helplessness. She could see no future other than a long trip back to Lagos, the horror of the airport and a flight home to unemployment and humiliation. Another wave of resentment overwhelmed her thoughts and then, in a moment of unemotional clarity, she realised that she had agreed to this decision. Yes, she had understood how life could be easier financially and for her as a new mum having lots of help. But she, like Karl, had not thought it through. Did they ask about conditions in Nigeria? Did they do some real research; did they seek out people who had been there? The answer was no and they really had disregarded the warnings in the couple of letters sent to them by their old friend Tony. What a bad decision. Sleep at last won and overpowered her.

Karl sat with his head in his hands, feeling sad and angry that he was not in control. What had kept them sane had been their support for each other, but the curled-up figure on the bed looked helpless, with waves of resentment like an aura around her. The fan continued to work, the two bare light bulbs created overlapping shadows on the floor and outside only an occasional motor vehicle disturbed the silence. Who would have believed that after Lagos there could be a town that was not overrun with cars? He took his shoes off, silently walked to the bed and gently eased the sandals from his wife's feet, and then he too lay down on the bed to get some sleep.

He woke early and in the light of dawn he saw a polka dot sprinkle of mosquitoes hanging on the net waiting for their bloody breakfast. His big toe was rather swollen and red and it really itched. Puzzled at first, he realised what had happened. Whilst asleep his bare toe must have been resting against the netting and one or more blood thirsty insect had placed its sharp proboscis through the net and taken a Dracula sized sample of his blood. He got up, trying not to touch his swollen toe, and peered out of the window. The pink glow on the clouds in front of him revealed the effect of the rising sun behind the hotel. At 6:30am the road was already full of people walking. To work, he assumed. He opened the bedroom door, walked through the door with the beaded curtain and passed through what he supposed was a dining room. He eased the front door open and felt the pleasure of the breeze and the warm dry air. The door opened on to the main street and he stood on the step. Opposite him women were setting up their stalls, little motor bikes chugged past, two or three people on one push bike, and the occasional car that had suffered many minor skirmishes.

A voice behind greeted him, 'Good morning Masta, did you sleep well? Can I get you something to eat?'

He was offered eggs, that could be done two ways he was told, and bread, and if he didn't mind powdered milk and special food for oyibos called cornflakes, Although the waiter added that he had tried them and found them to be 'insubstantial' and not the sort of food that could give you energy.

Karl was about to order when a slowly moving Peugeot 404 pickup truck pulled up alongside the Paradise.

On its white body work were the letters BICC, and hanging out of the window was a European, with another European next to him.

As the pick-up stopped the driver looked at Karl, then grinned and asked, 'Where are you from? English, German, French?'

'English.'

'Bugger me, what are you doing in the Paradise, you didn't actually sleep there did you?'

'Well actually...'

'Did you hear that Trev, this bloke actually slept there.'

Trev's head leaned over that of the driver and with a gargoyle expression, he said, 'I'm Trev, and my mate here is Jim, nobody sleeps there, well certainly not white guys, but it is a good place to drink beer and Mustapha, actually, when he has power, keeps it cool.'

Jim added, 'We both work for BICC erecting power lines.'

'He always wanted to be involved in powerful erections,' interrupted Trev.

Jim merely shook his head with a gesture that said he had heard that comment far too many times.

Jim went on, 'We have a camp outside Okene and there are six of us, five Brits and an Irishman. Are you here by yourself?

'No, my wife is with me.'

'What, in there!' they said in unison looking up at the facade of the hotel. 'Is she okay?'

'Did he actually say he had his wife with him,' Jim said, looking amazed.

Trev was slack jawed with astonishment.

'She's asleep at this moment.'

Trev momentarily counted and said, 'Two of you, now that means you two, plus us six and the three Germans and the six or seven at the teachers' college … we are doing well. There are, for today anyway, around 18 white guys and 80,000 Nigerians in Okene, the St Tropez of Kwara State. Actually, Okene was originally an Irish settlement.'

'Take no notice,' said Jim, 'I've told that joke too many times.'

'Irish!'

'Yes, you know,' Jim explained, whilst hanging out the front window and ignoring the locals wandering past. 'O'Kene, as in O'Conner, O'Malley etc., geddit?'

'Ah yes, oh I see,' said Karl, slightly taken aback by the carefree tone of Jim and Trev.

'What are you doing here?' inquired Jim.

'We… I'm going to work at the teachers' college.'

'And they put you in here?' was the bewildered response.

Trev and Jim looked at each for confirmation of a mutual decision.

'Listen, we can't have you and your wife in a dump like this, we white guys,'

'Us British!' Trev interrupted.

'We have to stick together. So listen, I am serious here, if you want to, we have spare cabins at our camp, and water, and A/C and electricity. We can't have you staying here when we have a decent clean place with all the amenities you need. What do you think? And it's free and you can stay until the FATCO sorts you out.'

'FATCO?'

'You know,' interrupted Trev again. 'Federal Advanced Teachers College Okene,' emphasising the capital letters.

'Well,' muttered Karl. He stuttered and then answered the invitation, 'I … we … suppose, yes we could.'

'Suppose, well it is up to you, you are welcome, and your wife. You're both more than welcome to stay with us until the college gets you organised.'

'Are you sure?'

They looked at him somewhat exasperated.

'You can always stay with Mustapha and his dubious hygiene, his ratty food and real ratty friends, you know, the ones that run around or...' said Trev.

'Yes,' was followed by a nervous pause, 'Yes, I, we would be happy to join you for a while.'

Karl immediately made a mental note to not mention the word rat in front of Anna.

'Right, it's a done deal. So we'll be back here about 6pm to pick you up. Most evenings, we all get together to have a drink on the roof top bar, right here, so get ready to get your money out.'

As they drove away Trev yelled out of the window, 'And tell Mustapha we want the beers extra cold! Bye.'

Karl went and woke up Anna as she stirred. Excitedly he tried to explain what had just happened., Still sleepy, she was either unimpressed or wasn't awake enough to take in what he had said.

In a mumble she tried to repeat very slowly what she thought she had heard. The result was a face full of scepticism and a hint of resentment.

She sat on the edge of the bed looking forlorn, her knees together and her arms stretched out before her resting against her knees like a girl in a Munch painting. Karl actually knelt down in front of her, held her hands in his and carefully repeated the conversation with Jim and Trev.

Anna looked around, her head moving slowly like a radar dish as she examined the 'suite' in the Paradise. Grubby flaky white walls, Spartan furniture, the damp smell and their door-less toilet was what she saw.

She felt dirty, alone, despondent and saturated with unhappiness. Colonial dreams of privilege, hot and cold running servants, cheap baby care and a nice house had disappeared like effervescence.

'Fine,' she said 'We'll go, anything other than this dump.' She paused, 'It will be only a night or so until we can get sorted and fly back home.'

An hour later, Dr Omega's car and driver came to pick them up.

11

A white Peugeot 504 estate car was waiting for them outside the Paradise. Anna had quickly packed the small amount of clothes from the previous night and they both dragged their baggage to the hotel entrance. Mustapha hung around them with a face full of concern. *What is he worried about?* Karl thought. Was he waiting for payment? Did he want positive feedback from his first international guests in months? Was he concerned that they hadn't finished their breakfast? He didn't really care, but he had to admit that Mustapha, though working on a different level of hygiene and efficiency, had tried his best. Breakfast was a bowl of cornflakes imported from the UK, but unfortunately the long sea journey had taken its toll. The flakes were soft and smelled like a ship's hold and sea water. The milk was reconstituted from dehydrated powder from a huge tin with NIDO written on its side, and on a small plate next to their bowl was a lone fried egg, its yoke like sunshine peering through the fog of fat under which it hid.

'You don't need your bags, madam,' said the driver in a somewhat surly manner. 'There are too many of them and nowhere to put them at the college.'

Anna responded immediately. 'What do you mean?' she said, her face full of concern. 'I am certainly not leaving them here, they could get stolen or sold and anyway we need them since I assume we're leaving the Paradise Hotel.' Glancing at the flaking white paint behind her, she gave him a disdainful look and carried on, 'We'll take them, I would feel better if they went straight into our college accommodation.' The driver didn't like what he heard and clearly showed it with a facial contortion.

Karl gingerly interrupted, 'Perhaps it's best we leave them here. You know, just in case something goes wrong. We are in Africa after all.' She was about to interrupt but Karl went on. 'Let's leave them here with Mustapha, he seems okay, and then should we go off with Trev and Jim tonight when they finish work we'll have all of our belongings.' She gave him a 'look', a piercing look, a look that could make milk go sour. Was it anger or exasperation or was it anxiety? He surmised it was all three as she ignored the bags, got in the back of the car and slammed the door. The driver had to be told once more that the bags were not staying in the hotel and he needed to load them in the car. He banged about, huffing and puffing and looking resentful and muttering under his breath. Karl had no time for tantrums. *He was only the bloody driver and he needed to do as he was told,* he thought.

The Federal Advanced Teachers' College was three miles out of town going south on the road to Auchi, the next town some 40 miles away and then on to Benin City for a further 80 miles. On their left, they passed a turning for a new steelworks that was being built at Ajakuti on the banks of the river Niger some 30 miles away. The houses, all grass, tin or mud, petered out and the topography became rock and scrub with the occasional acacia and palm tree. What a relief it was to drive through open spaces with attractive vistas again rather than being hugged and squeezed by the canopy of the tropical forest that had seemed to go on forever. The road wound up a gentle hill, and the landscape of rusty tin roofs bathed in the mist of hundreds of breakfast fires slowly receded behind them.

The driver spoke and told them that he drove everywhere for Doctor Omega and therefore he was a man of some status and recognition, not a porter. Karl and Anna ignored his moaning tone. He was driving a little too fast in a small act of belligerence and made sure to make a sharp right hand turn up a gravel road, past the partially obscured sign board and into the college itself. They passed some single-storey, long buildings resembling barracks on the left. Through the tall hyparrhenia grass they saw a tennis court ahead and next to it a white structure with a Mediterranean-type tiled roof and a huge antenna that ended 15 feet above the roof, before eventually arriving at a double door that announced the Administration department.

'Well it's not Kaduna Polytechnic,' whispered Karl.

'It looks like an army camp to me, but not that it matters because if I get my way we'll be on our way home in 48 hours, or even 24,' was her firm response.

Dr Omega's office was like a doctor's waiting room. The man himself sat behind a substantial desk, while around the walls of the office were chairs full of people waiting to talk to him who had arrived at his office on the off chance he would have time for them or who had been summoned at short notice, or had a specific appointment time which proved to be worthless, as was shown by Dr Omega's first action in front of Karl and Anna.

He stood up, speaking in both Yoruba and English and told everyone else to clear the room. He then courteously dragged two chairs from against the wall, placed them in front of his desk and beckoned them to sit down. 'I am delighted to meet you both and I will immediately apologise to you, in case the ministry didn't do so, about the mix up with your posting and the delay you have had in getting here.' His English had African intonations and Karl was sure he detected a hint of a North East accent in the way he pronounced his words. 'I am sorry about the Paradise, I only found out about your imminent arrival late yesterday and it was the best I could do at such short notice.'

Dr Omega was a short, round man, portly or very portly being an apt description. He looked like a man who sat a great deal and ate a great deal. He was balding, and the folds of his neck fought their way for freedom over the collar of his ironed white shirt and tie. His jacket hung over the back of his swivel chair and his stubby hands revealed knuckles like walnuts. He had a kindly face and big brown reassuring eyes, and a smile that formed his cheeks into tight round brown balls. He introduced himself as Dr W.H. Omega, then immediately silenced their thoughts when he said, 'No, I don't mind being called Dr Who behind my back, but to you and everyone else I am Doctor Omega, and before you ask, the initials W and H are my secret.' Maintaining his big, relaxation-inducing smile, he continued speaking.

'And of course I know the BBC and Dr Who. I did my five years in the United Kingdom.'

'Where did you live?' asked Anna.

'Can you guess?'

Karl replied, 'I'm sure I heard a hint of Geordie there.'

'Well, you're nearly correct, but don't tell that to the people of Durham, they certainly didn't see themselves as men from Newcastle.' It turned out that he got his degree at Durham University and was then a postgraduate at the education college in Newton Aycliffe near Darlington. 'I loved it there, I did. Frightened to death in the first weeks and couldn't understand a word the townspeople said. But what a place, what an honour, I still haven't come to terms with the fact that I studied in the shadow of that fantastic cathedral.' He paused and ruminated, 'Perhaps I'll go back one day and share my experience with my wife and kids.'

'Kids?' said Anna.

'Yes, I have five, the youngest is only two,' he said, smiling with pride and radiating fatherly and paternal vibes. He looked at Anna. 'I see that you are pregnant, when is your baby due?'

'August.'

'And are you going back to the UK for the birth?'

Anna, forgetting the fact that only minutes ago she was venting her intentions to be on the next plane back to UK, said that originally her first baby was going to be born at the Evangelical Hospital in Kaduna where they had thought they were being posted. She added that she was still not sure though.

Dr Omega leaned forward and with protective concern said, 'Don't even think about having your baby here in Okene. We have a doctor whose dereliction to duty is as well-known as his love of alcohol. Go here for minor injuries and that's all, but you are better off some 40 miles down the road at Auchi. There is a fine mission hospital there run by nuns. But first we must get you a place to stay, and luckily for you our two American Peace Corps volunteers are leaving one of the cottages in the next day or so.' His statement was uplifting yet caused concern. Moving in a day or so meant another day or possibly even longer having to embrace the dubious pleasures of the Paradise, but conversely the word cottage filled Karl with visions of the quaint and bucolic. Anna obviously had the same thoughts and gave Karl yet another look of concern. Dr Omega read their minds. 'I actually believe they are moving out later today. I am sure that is the case, but wait a while and I'll check. Gabriel,' he shouted. The office door opened and in came Gabriel, respectfully genuflecting as he approached the desk. Dr Omega told him what to do and to report back to him as soon as possible.

Karl felt at ease in the company of Dr Omega. During their brief time with him he had shown courtesy and concern for their welfare and seemed genuinely pleased to see them and to talk to them. He spoke enthusiastically about Karl's role at the college and how he would be working on the micro teaching scheme, more details later he said, and that he would be advising the students about their placements and would then visit them *in situ* to assess their progress and give them advice about their performance in the classroom. 'It will mean some rural travelling, but you will get to see some of the country. And Dr Khan, our VP, will help you out.' He paused, thought again, looked sceptical, then continued speaking. 'He will... he should... I suppose... Probably be able to give you a bit of guidance about your duties... But... I'm always around.'

Dr Omega beamed with enthusiasm. 'Right, accommodation first, then you'll need transport.' He raised his head and looked at the ceiling as though he was trying to grasp a floating idea. He smiled at them and said, 'To speed things up we'll send you to Ilorin, which means you can pick up a government car in a day rather than me writing to them and hoping they will get right back.'

'Ilorin?' inquired Karl.

'It is about 120 miles away to the west at the extreme end of Kwara State. It is as you can imagine big and chaotic but it is nothing compared to the real chaos of Lagos, Ibadan or Abeokuta. But first things first. We'll get you settled in and tomorrow I will introduce you to your colleagues during our short staff meeting and you will get to meet the British contingent we have here. In fact your next-door neighbours on both sides are British. Actually, you mustn't say that to Mr and Mrs Bright, they are ferociously Welsh.' He paused and smiled again. 'You British are just as tribal as we Africans,' and laughed at his own comment. His attitude was one of kindness and concern. It was as if he wanted to put right the administrative maladministration of the Federal Ministry of Education. He looked worldly and you could imagine that if you told him some African horror story he would just nod in normal acknowledgment, but his nod would be one of knowing and appreciating just how frustrating life could be in Nigeria.

Gabriel returned, pretending to puff and pant as though he had been on a mission, pretending to catch his breath. When Dr Omega asked what was happening, he replied that the two Americans were still there.

'Did you find out when they are leaving?' Gabriel did not answer. 'Did you actually speak to them?'

'Sort of.'

'What does sort of mean? You speak perfectly good English. Yes or No?'

'Actually no... I thought that I...'

The good doctor gently sorted him out by saying in a firm, avuncular manner, 'Do not pretend to sprint to the cottages, actually do it, and when you get there find out the time when they are moving out. No guessing, speak to them directly and then sprint back here. Understood?'

'Yes,' Gabriel replied as he dashed out the door.

Karl was impressed by the way Dr Omega had exercised his authority without being aggressive and threatening, something he had seen all too often as he had hung around the ministry.

'The two Americans, a husband and wife team, are returning to Carolina, I think it is. They have done their one year in the Peace Corps and I think the two of them will have some enlightened opinions about their cousins in West Africa.'

'I assume they are black Americans,' said Karl.

'Yes, they are and they will be missed. Like most Americans they were enthusiastic about everything. Josh and Germisha, his wife, were really into walking and trekking and I do believe they must have climbed every small mountain and hill around here.' He waved his arms to demonstrate how they were surrounded by them. 'Now, here is some good news for you. As you probably noticed this looks like a very temporary site and that is exactly what it is. It was formerly a youth camp barracks and we will soon be moving out to our new location at the other side of town to a site on the Lokoja Road. We already have half of our students here and the other half there. Alas, there is a little delay though.'

Karl didn't listen to or fully take in Dr Omega's last remark and it was Anna who spoke. 'How far away is it?

'I get driven there often enough, it is exactly 8 miles, so you will need a car because you will be operating on two campuses. I'll tell you what, after the meeting later in the morning I could take you both there and you will see the site and the fine staff accommodation they are building.' With an extra burst of enthusiasm, he added, 'I'm sure you will be impressed.' He shuffled in his chair and half got up as though to signify their meeting was over, but then adjusted his body and leaned back in a relaxing position. 'I assume you know very little about Okene, especially if you expected to be in Kaduna at this time. But as they say, 'this is Africa' and anything can happen. The government have built four advanced teacher training colleges, and Okene, still unfinished, is the fourth. The other three are in Maiduguri, Pankshin near Jos, and the other is in Yola.

Karl and Anna listened and wondered about the location of Yola and Maiduguri. As they looked at each other their thoughts were interrupted by Dr Omega, who continued talking. 'Now Yola is in the extreme east of the country, on about the same latitude as we are, but it is virtually on the Cameroon border in a heavily forested, mountainous area. There is only a very long strip road winding its way to the town. To put it simply, it is a remote location.' Karl leaned forward to ask a question, but Dr Omega took the words from his mouth. 'Maiduguri is also a remote location, but Pankshin is not, it has a nice climate as it is high up like Jos. But back to Maiduguri, though it is a decent sized town and bigger than Okene, the college is situated in the far north east corner of the country. It's on the border with Chad and virtually on the edge of the Sahara.'

Karl tried to make a little joke. 'Are you trying to tell me that we are lucky to be here?'

'No, that wasn't my intention but compared to the other two colleges Okene does have some real benefits. You see, the reason the government chose these four sites is because each area is so underdeveloped and needs a boost – the other three because of their location and Okene because...' he paused and took in a warm breath, wafting his hands across his face in a futile effort to take in cool air, and continued, 'the Igbira have proved to be seriously reluctant to change. They are an intensely parochial people and other regions of Nigeria make jokes about them just as you do in the UK when the Scots are always referred to as mean or the Irish as being simple. But here, the comments are less of a joke and more scathing. It is because of their reluctance to have outsiders in their community that the college, the new part, has yet to be finished. Things are fine now and the builders are hard at work, but negotiations, maladministration and, dare I say, big dashes had to be sorted out.'

He took a handkerchief out of his pocket and wiped his forehead. The energetic fan was not quite doing its job. His office was warm but free, thank goodness, of the enervating humidity they had put up with for the last two days. A glance through the louvered window revealed an endless blue sky, almost too clear and bright to look at. There was a knock on the office door and this time Gabriel, like his name sake, brought some good news.

'The Americans are leaving today,' he said, and with a nod from Dr Omega he left.

'It seems as though we can get you in there in a day or so,' chirped the principal.

Anna was knocked out of her comfort zone, a wrinkle of panic spread across her face, followed by a furrow of concern. It seemed as though, temporarily she had lost the ability to speak. She uttered, 'The Paradise... the Para... Paradise...' she went on, her mouth and eyes wide open. Dr Omega's response was perfect. He stood up, took one step towards her and with a perfectly timed avuncular hand on her shoulder, said, 'Don't worry, we'll have it cleaned today, after all it is only early and we'll get you in before nightfall.' Magical relief spread through Anna's veins and she gave an involuntary sigh of deliverance as her fears were assuaged by his kindly words.

Dr Omega gestured that it was now time for him to deal with the masses outside and as they stood, Karl, ever the diplomat and not wanting to put anyone to any trouble, told the Doctor about the offer of accommodation at the BICC camp that evening. Dr Omega nodded gently and said to him, 'Don't worry it will be fine.' As he opened the office door, letting in a cavalry charge of heat, he looked them both in the eye and said, 'How can I get the best of the talents of your husband if you are not happy? Get settled and when we formally meet again tomorrow with Dr Khan you'll find out just how you will be helping our students. My driver will take you over there to see the house, it is only 250 yards away. I will see you later.'

They walked outside into the searing sunlight, passing a large group of people huddled in the shade waiting to go in and speak to the principal. The rays of sun felt like daggers piercing Karl's skull, but though it was seriously hot it was so much better than the sodden heat of the coast. The Peugeot, with the driver leaning against it, was parked about 50 yards away up a small rise. They turned and looked back at the office and from their vantage point could see clearly a small lake to their left on the other side of the Okene to Benin road. To the right the college grounds petered out into scrub. Every detail and every texture was clearly in focus in the bright light. It was uncannily silent until they heard a shuffling noise made by some cows that were wandering about in the sparse grass and rocks close by. A woman, balancing a large cardboard box on her head, walked across the track they were about to follow, moving effortlessly and gracefully even though there was a baby swaddled on her back. She paid no attention to them.

Karl looked around and exhaled a breath of satisfaction; he had forgotten how real heat smells and just what clarity ferocious sunlight can bring to the nearby world. In the distance at the foot of the hills, colours and forms disintegrated as they were consumed by the heat haze. It was like an impressionist landscape. He loved the view and the thought that their future home, not yet visible, was on the edge of a natural, barely populated landscape. In the distance he could just see the herdsman who was attending to the cattle. He looked tall and skinny and wore a straw hat that seemed to have a cone shape on the top, and he appeared from this distance to be carrying a spear – or was it just a long pole. This sense of visual satisfaction was also enhanced by the positive conversation they had just had with Dr Omega. Anna must surely have been reassured by his caring words and obvious concern. My goodness, they had only been in his office for a few

101

minutes before he was dispensing advice about Anna's pregnancy and in another breath wanting to organise a car for them as soon as possible.

They walked up to the parked car where the driver informed them they would have to wait a few minutes as he had to go and see his sick uncle. Karl and Anna were seriously unimpressed by this surly individual who was supposed to be helping them. What a contrast to Dr Omega. 'You are going where?' Karl stated firmly and unsympathetically.

'My uncle, he is a sick...'

'And just where does he live, Lagos?' was Karl's sarcastic response. His wife gave him a look that asked was that necessary.

'Just nearby in the town,' he said, with a gesture implying it was somewhere behind him.

'Do you think I'm going to let you drive off with our luggage in the car? You'd be a real target for every thief in Okene, and you're not going to leave us here at the side of this path! Your job is to take us to the house and when that's done you need to go and see your boss and ask him for permission to go and see this uncle of yours.' He muttered, 'If he exists,' under his breath. Gabriel truculently moved surreptitiously towards the car. Karl, reading his mind, deftly opened the car door, took hold of the keys, ushered Anna into the front seat and said to the flabbergasted and seriously pissed off driver, 'Are you going to show us the way, or do I leave you here while I go and find it myself.'

The door slammed and with a face like a spoilt child and wrinkled with resentment, he took the back seat. He grunted and nodded his head in a silent indication that Karl should drive straight ahead. The road was gravelled, narrow and wide enough for one car. As they drove up the gentle hill the wide-open space of the seemingly uninhabited countryside spread out before them, looking exciting and full of potential adventure. Within a minute a large open space about the size of a couple of football pitches spread out before them. The field had a gentle slope and four identical houses with an equal amount of space in between them were visible. There were no gardens, no delineation of where the grounds of one property started and another finished. There was no sign of habitation, no washing lines or cultivated plants, no noise of kids; just two cars parked outside one of the houses.

Anna examined them with a potential purchaser's eye. They had no 'curb' appeal, no well-established or well-stocked gardens or useful vegetable patches, no feature bay windows with the latest craze for panels of stained glass, and no apparent easy access to all amenities, but what they did have in abundance was a very rural and peaceful location. Each house was cube-shaped, with a flat roof that sloped gently to enable the rain to run off. She wondered what they would be like inside. They were nowhere near the standard that they had had in Uganda, but one of them was to be their allocated home.

The conversation with Dr Omega had cheered her up. Here was someone who to all intents and purposes wanted to get things done and for them both to be happy so that he could get the most out of her husband. Her thoughts on catching the next flight home were put on hold for a while. She thought it would be a tough and disrespectful decision to just walk away, or run away more like it, after their warm welcome. But then again, Dr Omega had plenty of words, was he full of hot air, was he like many Africans telling her what she wanted to hear so she wouldn't be upset? Their bags were safely in the car, the area looked beautiful, and one of these little houses was going to be theirs.

Outside the house with two cars were three or four people talking at one another. Two were white and two were black. A tall black man dressed in a shirt and tie stood at the top of the three steps that led into the kitchen of the small house. He had his hands on his hips as though he was frustrated by what he had heard. At his side, though partially obscured, was a woman who gently held his shoulder in support. She had tired, weary eyes and her skin next to his was dull and greying. 'Let me get this clear,' he was saying in an easily detectable American accent.' You want me to hand over the keys of the house to you.'

'Yes!' was the firm response from the white man. 'Because I can guess or know what has happened or is about to happen.'

'Like what?'

'That some of our shiftless, less honourable colleagues will be clamouring for this house, and you know what that means.' He didn't wait for an answer. He added, 'The first thing that will happen is they won't live in the house, they will stay in town and will just sublet the place and claim the house is occupied by them and their close relations. Another bloody Nigerian scam.'

'If you have the keys what are going to do with them, you have a fine apartment of your own in town,' said the American.

'Come on Josh, you know me better than that. Of course they're not for me, I just want to make sure they go to someone who needs or deserves this accommodation in the future.'

The woman standing next to the white man interrupted. 'Look what happened to the house next to St Georges in town, it ended up being full of goats and it took ages for that new teacher and his family to get them removed.'

The white man laughed. 'Can you imagine, they probably had to serve an eviction notice on a lot of noisy goats.'

Even Josh smiled. 'Okay, I'll get my boy to drop them off with Dr Omega.'

'What, are you mad? Your boy is more than likely to scuttle off to one of the teachers who have been clamouring for this place, take his dash, and hand over the keys.'

'You don't seem to have much faith in humanity.'

'No,' was the response from the white man. 'I know Nigeria, I know what happens here and so do you, you're just blind to it because you're euphoric that you're leaving.' With a bit of sarcasm, he added, 'I hope you're not trying to get a nice roll of money for those keys, are you?'

'Come on Jack, that was totally uncalled for,' Josh replied, somewhat affronted.

Jack's wife nudged him to make sure he made amends for his contentious remark.

'Sorry about that Josh, it's just that I was talking to some BICC guys who told me that an English couple had just arrived in the town to work here at the college and they're being put up in the Paradise.'

'What, with mucky Mustapha!'

Jack's wife commented, 'And she is, so we've been told, evidently pregnant.'

The word pregnant made the woman behind Josh take notice and listen, and then she pointed to a car that was slowly driving up to their house. Josh, barely noticing the vehicle said, 'We're leaving anytime now. I want nothing to do with the free-for-all for this house and, I may add, I have been approached by three or four of our shiftless colleagues as you call them, and no, I have not taken a bribe.'

'Nor would he,' his wife stated.

He carried on, 'And neither have I promised them anything despite them being over-pushy and slightly unpleasant. I'm washing my hands of this, here, take the keys, I know you would never try to profit from our premature departure, so here, give them to Dr Omega or the new couple. No one deserves to stay in the Paradise.'

The timing was perfect, although neither the American couple nor Jack and his wife were aware of the coincidence. The car pulled to a halt. A seriously angry skinny youth sat on the back seat, and out stepped Karl, holding the door open with one hand whilst keeping his hand on the steering wheel with the other. He reached back inside the car and put the car keys in his pocket. 'Good morning' he said as Anna emerged from the car. 'I'm Karl and this is my wife, Anna.'

Jack's wife looked straight at them and said, 'You're not the couple from the Paradise are you?'

'Yes,' was Karl's response, 'how did you know?'

'Jungle drums,' smiled Jack. 'There are no secrets in Okene.'

'Dr Omega sent us down here to see a house. He didn't make it absolutely clear which one it was.'

'This is it,' said Josh, waving his hand in an over-dramatised gesture. 'Prime real estate, in unspoilt countryside, only 120 miles from the nearest golf course or swimming pool or air conditioning or a shop with a window. Welcome to FATCO. I'm Josh, this is my wife Germisha, and that's Jack and his wife Mary.'

Karl and Anna were confused. 'What's going on? We are at the right house, aren't we?'

'Yes, you are,' replied Jack. 'The timing is perfect. Josh here is getting ready to leave and there was just a chance that the keys of this place could have gone missing.'

Although their meeting with Josh and his wife lasted only a few minutes, they were told that the couple were leaving the college only because Germisha had been diagnosed as being dangerously susceptible to the effects of malaria and that living in a malarial zone like this was a danger to her health. Jack and Mary were both thin and scrawny, and had such deep-set eyes they looked like a pair of night owls that should still be in bed. Jack wore the ubiquitous colonial-type khaki shorts and well-worn hippy sandals. He sported a little unkempt goatee beard and was quite the opposite of what you would expect a senior education officer to look like. Mary wore a brightly coloured sarong. She carried no weight at all. Her cheek bones were clearly visible and her face gave the impression that the cigarette she was smoking was a substitute for food. Her shoulder-length hair hadn't seen a hairdresser for some time, but at the age of around 40 she could still be considered an attractive woman as long as you didn't like them meaty.

Jack explained to them both how he and Mary had met Jim and Trev from BICC who had told him about them. He also clarified his position as the requisitioner of keys and how far too often he had seen houses being allocated to the greedy, to the bribers, to the undeserved and the exploiters. 'Dr Omega's wishes shall be adhered to,' he said formally. 'Once you get interlopers in it takes months to get them out and a lot of money changes hands as well as a lot of unpleasantness despite the efforts of Dr Omega, who is, by the way, a seriously overworked man. Some of your future colleagues, who you'll get to meet soon enough, will stop at nothing to acquire a house.'

'I can well understand that,' said Karl innocently.

'Hear me out. Basically our fellow workers have no intention of living there, they all have accommodation. What they want is to sublet it to as many people as possible and make a huge profit.'

'Is that allowed?' asked Anna.

'Of course not,' was the reply. 'But once they're in it takes a lifetime to get them out and more often than not little is done about it because there seems to be some tacit agreement that purloining an extra property to make some money is a legitimate perk. Quite frankly it pisses me off and that's why Mary and I are here now.'

Josh and his wife started to load their travel bags and cases into their estate car, a battered Peugeot with FATCO written on the side. They shook hands with Jack and Mary, ceremoniously locked the door to the house and turned and handed the keys to Jack, wishing Karl and Anna well. Jack and Mary had smiles of satisfaction on their faces. For two people living in the centre of hot and arid Nigeria they were remarkably white, appearing somewhat miraculously to be able to avoid the sun. Despite being spare and ascetic looking, they exuded friendship.

'A job well done, I think,' said Jack as he opened the door of the house. 'Twenty-four hours in Okene and you have a place to stay. Unheard of,' he said.

12

Gabriel was instructed to help unload their bags and take them into the house. He had been practising his scowl, trying to make it even more contemptuous. He half dragged, half carried the one case he removed from the car. He huffed and puffed while trying to pretend it was too heavy for him and then had the nerve to stand there with his hand out expecting to be tipped. Jack walked towards him, stopped, and with great deliberation put his hand deep into the pocket of his shorts and rummaged around. Gabriel smelled money. Jack leaned forward, as if offering him a note or two or a hand full of coins, but as the expectant Gabriel presented his open palm, Jack merely shook his hand, saying thank you before he unceremoniously turned away. Gabriel was livid. His face was like a snake that had been trodden on and he turned away with clenched fist, muttering unrepeatable Yoruba curses. 'He's a real cheeky bastard that one,' commented Jack. 'Thinks he's important because he drives Dr Omega around. He won't last long; he'll be fired soon.'

Karl and Anna entered into the small, compact house which was warmer than expected, but it was nevertheless a relief from the blazing sun outside. It consisted of one large room with two doors, a mirror image of each other, leading outside. There was a tiny kitchen of submarine proportions containing a bulbous fridge, a gas hob with three rings and, taking up the majority of counter space, a huge brown porcelain water filter. A few pans hung on the wall. In the living room was some very basic furniture, a sofa and two arm chairs, a coffee table and at the end of the room a table and five chairs. 'Only five chairs,' commented Anna. Mary was quick to respond and said cynically, 'The sixth one was probably stolen or chopped up for fire wood.' Off the living room were two small bedrooms, one of which had a double bed and a set of drawers and the other was empty.

The fan on the ceiling remained redundant, even when Anna went over to the wall to switch it on. Jack read her thoughts and decided to let them know about some of the issues at the college. He told them that the college was not attached to NEPA's grid system and nor for that matter was most of Okene. The college electricity was powered by a huge generator about the size of a double-decker bus which they had unknowingly passed as they came onto the campus. It was diesel powered and was only switched on from 7am to 9am, from 12noon to 1pm and from 6pm to 10pm. Occasionally, if electricity was needed in a classroom for, say, the demonstration of a scientific experiment, the generator would be turned on if the young man who operated the machine was told in advance. Evidently he was always there and lived next to the generator in a very small room with a bed and a small cooking device. Once the generator was running he could go off and do something else, such as going into town and selling a few 'unneeded' gallons to anyone wanting diesel on the cheap. A blind eye was turned to this little perk.

Jack told them about the water supply and explained why the bathroom was as dry as sandpaper. The last time water had come through the lone tap in the kitchen or through the homemade shower head was when the King of the Igbiras, also known as the Ata, celebrated his birthday and ordered the pumps to be switched on. The water came from a natural lake less than a mile away, but unfortunately the Lister pump that had been installed by the British some 25 years ago had run perfectly until some rogues dismantled it and sold it for scrap.

'But what do we do for water?' asked Anna.

She was told that once a week the vintage college water tanker went and filled up at the lake and then delivered the water to each cottage on a weekly basis. Just outside the kitchen door was a large galvanised iron water tank that held 400 gallons of water, their ration for the week. Karl and Anna looked slightly aghast, *only 400 gallons,* they thought. 'Don't worry,' they were told, 'it's amazing how little water you use if you're frugal and it'll make you realise just how profligate we are in the UK when it comes to water usage.' The water was brown and contained all sorts of bacteria, which meant before putting it into the filter it was necessary to boil it in order to kill all the nasty things that perhaps could kill you. Jack laughed as he said, 'One thing is for certain, you won't get constipation drinking African water. Even after filtering and boiling you'll probably still have the shits.'

They checked the rooms. Pillow cases and sheets were needed and a couple of good builder's cups with which to drink tea. They dumped their bags, securely locked the doors and went with Jack and Mary to get some basic supplies. Mary told them there was no need to worry about food that night as she would be cooking for them. 'At least you've got decent neighbours, she said. 'The Bright family lives to your left.'

'Bright by name, not by nature,' interrupted Jack with a wicked grin on his face.

Mary went on. 'On the other side you have Will Christie, he teaches geography and lives there alone, his wife and 3-year-old went back to the UK a couple of months ago and there's no sign of them coming back. And finally, in the end house, is David Jackson.' She paused, cleared her throat and added, 'He too lives alone.'

'Officially,' commented Jack.

Mary ignored him. 'Yes officially, but... Well he does have some company now and again.'

'Basically, David is gay and has the most pretty servant stroke driver stroke gardener.'

'But,' said Mary, 'gay or not, he really is a nice man and very bright, public school, Cambridge degree etcetera, and he's very knowledgeable about the history of Africa. Personally I think a brain like his is wasted in a place like this. He should be back in Britain lecturing at some university.'

'He actually really likes it here. Yes, he has his young man,' Jack winked, 'but he's a professional and he dedicates his life to the welfare and education of the young men and women we have here.'

They found out that Jack and Mary were from Ireland and their surname was O'Driscoll. They had two boys at boarding school near Belfast, who spent their holidays in Nigeria. Jack was a teacher of science and in the last year of a three-year contract. They swapped tales about their arrival and how they too were buggered about – Jack's phrase, before being sent to FATCO Okene. Their circumstances, however, were a little different. They knew in advance where they were going to be posted and there'd been a car to collect them from the airport, but on arrival at the Ministry they were told there would be a short delay in going to the college because of building work yet to be finished. The official they dealt with had apparently been unaware that only half the college was functioning and the building work he referred to was still in progress eight miles away on the Lokoja Road. As a consequence they had been housed in the Federal Palace Hotel for quite some time. Karl immediately told them about their gruesome experience of trying to get a room in a decent place and how the Federal Palace was one of three hotels that had laughed at them and refused to accept the Federal Ministry's voucher, and how they ended up at the Phino-Hotel.

'How long did you have to stay at the Federal Palace?' asked Karl. 'We were in a grotty little place for four nights.'

'Four nights!' exclaimed Jack. 'Do you know we had to suffer the horror of air conditioning, a swimming pool and a 5-star restaurant for four months!'

'And we had our two boys with us at the time, it's a good job they gave us a suite,' added Mary.

'At my insistence,' retorted Jack. 'Ah, those were the days when the government had more money than sense.'

'You stayed four months!' Karl said in a state of disbelief.

'Four months is an awfully long time to be stuck in a confined space,' commented Anna.

'It was fine, the boys went back to school after a couple of weeks so we had double the space to live in.'

'Didn't the hotel object to you taking up that much space?' questioned Karl.

'Don't be daft, they didn't care as long as they were being paid, and knowing the hotel and its management very well, they no doubt screwed the ministry for as much as they could.'

Mary embellished the information. 'The worst thing was that we were very comfortable staying there while the housing got sorted out in Okene, but then the ministry stopped paying and the hotel demanded the rooms.'

'Oh how awful,' sighed Anna ingenuously.

'Too bloody right,' said Jack, as his Belfast tone filled the car. 'But we sorted that out by just refusing to move until the ministry could give us a written guarantee that there would be fitting accommodation for us in Okene. I may add that the dozy bugger who was organising our posting eventually found out that there was a functioning campus in this remote corner of Kwara State. But we stayed a bit longer.'

'What, even longer than four months?' said Karl.

Jack carefully handled the steering wheel and slowed down as he started to negotiate the narrow roads of the town as well as the pedestrians wandering all over the place, He said to Mary, 'Are you going to tell them or shall I do it?

'You tell them,' was her response.

'Well, in total we actually stayed eight months. It was brilliant. The ministry kept paying our salary into the bank, the British kept giving us a hardship allowance, and staying in a nice hotel we had nothing to spend the money on, though we did take a two-week holiday at the Tropicana Hotel on the beach just outside Lomé in Togo.' Mary had to have her say, telling them that eight months in Lagos would have been misery, but due to the endemic maladministration at the ministry they managed to spend all of their time on Victoria Island, which, if they didn't already know, is the only area of Lagos, or even Nigeria, that is bordering on being functional.

Jack found a place to park outside a small corrugated building whose signboard read Kabba's Kabin, 'Purveyors of Imported Foods and Luxury Goods.' The shop was rickety and without windows and taking up the whole of one wall was a set of doors opening out onto the street, giving Mr Kabba a place to present his wares. Mary commented, 'Don't be fooled by his imported goods, no one counts the junk that comes from China. Imported goods must come from Europe or America, which is why he occasionally sells, for example, Weetabix full of weevils or out-of-date Marvel milk powder. Once there was a rush for Oriole Cookies that he got from somewhere but they'd been on a boat so long they'd disintegrated into crumbs.'

'Don't forget that consignment of cheese that had hair on it,' added Jack.

'But what he does get every now and again, and he keeps it a secret because he pretends to be a good Muslim, is a few crates of Scotch or London gin. He gives his regular customers the nod and plenty of them call in on the way back from the mosque. That's why he asks his European customers, every white guy in town, to be discreet. We're not too sure but his goods probably come from the back of a lorry.'

Mr Kabba came to greet them, and leaning on a pile of tins of Blue Band margarine his first words were, 'Mr Jack, you have brought me new customers. Have you told them I have the best store in Okene? Very cheap prices, always good service, and with a smile.' At that point he smiled and showed a huge set of fine white teeth like icebergs. 'You tell me what you need,' he continued, 'and I will try to get it for you. Mrs Mary will tell you that even Valium and Prozac are no problem.'

'Okay, Yolah, enough, they get the message, they've only been here a day so they probably don't need Valium yet.'

Karl smiled at the conversation and the claims of 'Yolah,' and then said, 'A few days ago we could have done with a packet of Valium.' He nudged his wife, looking for a smile or glimmer of agreement.

From Kabba's shop they could just see the Paradise hotel on the corner of the road leading up to the market. From Yolah they bought what they might need for a day or so, including a packet of Omo washing powder which was no longer sold in the UK. *Is it still made here,* Karl thought, *or is it an import that has been in a ship's container for years?* Jack and Mary led them up towards the market area. The place was packed with colourful people who seemed to have a sense of purpose. It was noisy. It was crowded and had a distinctly different feel to the atmosphere of Lagos. As they walked past people there was no feeling of threat or aggression. They were not ignored, but neither were they objects to be exploited, to be shouted at, to be intimidated. Karl remembered the nearest market to Kings College, Budo when they were in Uganda, in the village of Mengo, and it too had had a colourful, exciting and non-threatening feel. In fact, Anna had loved going there to buy their vegetables and even getting to know the roadside traders. Okene seemed to be similar. No one thrust their faces into you and shouted oyibo, their clothes weren't tugged, items for sale were not thrust into their faces, and nor were they pointed at or followed.

This was no tourist market, with masses of mass-produced Africana. There were no heaps of masks, jewellery, 'authentic' drums, elephant hair bracelets or trinkets to take home and put on the walls or sideboards of suburban England. This was a market without frivolity. Everything for sale had a use or a purpose. They passed a man sitting cross legged on the ground, displaying his useful local medicines in front of him on a sheet of cardboard – obviously an amateur chemist. At his side, written in the local language as well as English was a list of ailments he could cure. Great if you couldn't get an erection or you had aches in the joints, or wanted rid of warts or wrinkles, or you couldn't sleep or your neighbour' dogs were noisy. No doubt the last concoction would be clandestinely administered to the annoying beast and it would mysteriously die, hence solving the problem. His rectangle of cardboard was covered with an assortment of feathers, bones, horns, hooves, fungus, hair, bark, fibres that were desiccated and shredded, simian body parts, odd coloured rocks, aromatic powders and fur and of course a homemade mortar and pestle in which to mix them.

The smell of wood smoke filled the air. The locals as they passed smelled of it and the fumes from their cooking fires had impregnated their clothes. There was the odour from dried flaky whole fish with huge dead, silver, sad eyes. There was an all-pervasive smell of roasting meat, the irrepressible odour of rotting vegetation and the stink of decay. Okene too had drainage ditches filled with detritus. Women in exuberantly coloured kente cloth marked with abstract, geometric patterns walked elegantly by, even with children strapped to their backs. There was grace in the way the women sauntered through the crowds whilst effortlessly carrying on their heads a large pot or a basket full of beans. They passed stacks of firewood, a man selling one packet of Bazooka chewing gum, a stall dripping with blood and the remnants of a dismembered cow. Two vultures looked down licking their lips.

Karl and Anna stopped at a pile of coloured plastic objects and bought, on Jack's advice, a plastic bucket 'to help with the water' and a washing up bowl, and Mary presented Anna with a fly swat. *What is she telling us about our home?* Karl thought. He did his first bit of bargaining and bought a pair of flip flops. It was hot, very hot. The sky was ablaze with light and completely cloudless. The sun's rays felt like small sharp probes on your skin, but the heat was dry. There was no dripping with sweat as they had done in Lagos. This wasn't a world of condensation and salty white stains on your clothes and there was no sense of having to wade through air thick with invisible droplets of hot water. The luckier or more wealthy stall holders had the luxury of a folding umbrella or a large garden umbrella to keep the sun off them. Women sat in front of their wares, and for some it may have been a small pyramid of six or seven misshaped tomatoes, waving a piece of cardboard metronomically from side to side to create a cooling draft or deter some lazy flies.

As they walked on smells of food meandered through the mass of humanity. People smiled, chatted and shouted in an atmosphere of conversation and commerce. Looking around there were piles of sorghum, all types of coloured beans, peanuts, sweet potatoes, yams, cassava, maize and palm oil in dirty beer bottles, onions and huge odd-shaped sweet potatoes. But where were the Irish potatoes, as they were called here, or carrots and cabbages?

The market was actually rather exciting. Karl noticed that Anna looked interested. She was smiling at Mary, whilst Jack tugged at his arm and said to him with a wicked look, 'You haven't been using that have you?' as he pointed to a concoction for sale that guaranteed conception. Karl felt a change in his mood, the exciting benign atmosphere of the market in stark contrast to the threatening, chaotic world of the megalopolis of Lagos.

There was no doubt that their experience in the first five days had generated culture shock. Had they really gone to the British High Commission to enquire about repatriation? He was adjusting, he thought, but that didn't mean everything was okay. There was still so much uncertainty to be coped with, and just how did Anna feel? It was less than 12 hours ago that she had been ready to leave and go back to the UK. But a friendly, sensible and positive Dr Omega had helped, as had the jovial friendliness of Trev and Jim. The appearance of Jack and Mary and their unruffled attitude to life was calming and reassuring. They had a house, even though they had only been in it for a few minutes. He had the reassurance of the keys in his pocket, and with a car they would have independence, and when their baggage arrived this 'space' could become a home. All speculation, but certainly his mood was a lot better than it had been some three hours ago when Mustapha offered him eggs and cornflakes on the same plate, and his wife was distraught. So many buts, but he felt the need to give the place a go and try everything he could to get Anna to give it a try as well.

Calling into the Okene post office to collect stamps they watched Jack expertly weave his way to the front of the crowds, and his untamed pushing and shoving were a text book example of how to get served in a crowded institution where the concept of a queue is missing. On the way back to the house, Jack and Mary reminded them of the need to boil and filter the water and gave them some matches they had forgotten to buy. Even though parts of Okene had sporadic electricity, they were reminded again that the college was not on the national electricity grid run by NEPA. *Was this a blessing or a disaster?* Karl thought.

'Right,' said Jack, 'you're sorted for a while. Don't forget about food this evening, Mary and I will sort it out. Perhaps we'll have an 'indescribable kebab' at the Paradise. We'll pick you up around five before it gets dark and then we'll take you to meet everyone of consequence and have a few drinks on top of the hotel.' With a sweep of his arms he went on to say, 'And you'll get to see the architectural splendours and vistas of our internationally renowned town.'

Mary reached into the car pulled out a lump of red plastic and said, as she handed it to Anna, 'Don't forget your bucket.'

13

They were left to unpack and briefly explore their house. There wasn't much to see, but it was reassuring that at last they seemed to have a little control over what was going on in their lives. There was a free-standing fan in each bedroom but alarmingly no door on the bathroom, nor had there ever been one. In the main bedroom there was a rail that would have to act as a wardrobe. But at last there was some privacy and they could surround themselves with their 'stuff,' an act that would help to reassure and settle them.

Karl found the kettle under the sink and just about filled it from the water filter before the water ran out. Thankfully there was enough for a cup of tea each. Anna looked almost cheerful at last. In an attempt to put more water into the kettle she instinctively turned on the water tap. It coughed and groaned and nothing happened. Angst and consternation appeared on her face, but making the best of it she went out of the kitchen through the screen door to the water tank outside. There was a loud expletive. Karl investigated and there stood his wife, furious and shaking with frustration. She squinted in the bright sunlight. 'How the bloody hell am I supposed to get water out of this tank? It hasn't even got a tap. It's just plonked on the bloody floor. I've had enough!' she shouted as she threw the kettle down. Karl now understood why Mary had insisted they had a bucket. The only way to get water out of the tank was to remove the heavy lid, stand on tip toe or a chair and lean over the edge while scooping a pail of water from the murky depths.

Anna looked disconsolate as she went back into the house. Just as she seemed to be accepting to a certain extent of their circumstances, she took another couple of steps backwards. The situation was compounded when the drone of the generator in the distance came to a stop and at precisely 2pm the electricity was switched off. It took a lot of diplomacy, hugs, arms around shoulders and lots of gentle words of encouragement and reassurance. They sat and had some tea and Anna then lay down on the bare mattress in the bedroom to rest, to sleep, and no doubt dream that she wasn't really there.

Karl sat down and wrote to his father.

Dear Dad,

I am really sorry I haven't been able to call you, especially at a time that is so upsetting for you. I can't tell you how many times I wanted to call, but Nigeria, well, we never got near a phone that works, but now that we are here in Okene, not Kaduna as you and I expected, (that is another story) I have been told that the post office can get an international line.

To be honest we have had a tough week, it has been very difficult for both of us, but you have always been in our thoughts and every day I am consumed with guilt that we left the UK so soon after mam's death. I'm sure we've made the wrong decision.

I know how good you are at writing letters and I look forward to your regular weekly letter, like when we were in Kampala, and I promise to phone ASAP and write every week.

FATCO. P.O. box 1046, Okene, Kwara State, Nigeria,
Karl

He then wrote to Tony, their old friend from Uganda.

Tony,

I hope you got the letter we sent you from our time in Lagos, a lady we met at our hotel maintained that half the letters sent are destroyed. You were right, Nigeria is definitely not Uganda. It's been chaos, but we've coped well and are now in Okene, not Kaduna as we thought. Okene, if you have no idea where it is, is about 50 miles south of the confluence of the Niger and Benue rivers at Lokoja. But the good news is that I have to come to Lagos regularly as part of the job. Does that offer of a bed still stand, and do you have a phone that works? By the way after seven years of marriage Anna is pregnant.

Has your wife joined you yet?

116

Karl. FATCO. P.O. box 1046, Okene, Kwara State, Nigeria.

He looked in on Anna. She was asleep and looked completely worn out. He found his sunglasses, carefully opened the screen door to the kitchen so it didn't creak and stepped out into the mid-afternoon sun. The heat took his breath away. The heat haze in the distance caused the hills to lose visual definition but the rocky hills and cliffs nearby were clearly delineated by the bright sunlight and the resulting chiaroscuro. The air felt clear and untainted by carbon monoxide, noxious fumes and the evil of humidity. The rocky outcrops sparkled. He could only just hear the engine of a large truck somewhere in the distance, but all was quiet except for the whine and hum of insects, and even they were relatively quiet. It was too hot even for the flies. The countryside went on for miles. It was referred to as MAMBA in East Africa, that is Miles And Miles of Bloody Africa, and here it was the same. It was empty apart from some invisible college buildings hidden amongst small trees behind a small rise in the ground in front of the house. He just loved the silence, the space and blue sky that went on forever. The view was bucolic, ideal for poetic words and in his case contemplation. The earth was sandy and strewn with tufts of sharp grass. The ground felt soft under his feet and he made no sound as he walked. Every step he took disturbed a myriad of small white butterflies that sprang into life. A buzzard hovered overhead, effortlessly hanging there, supported by rising hot air.

He looked around. Just what was he doing here? A distraught, pregnant wife, a father alone mourning the loss of his wife, a house in the middle of nowhere with no running water and at the moment no electricity. Yet amazingly at this moment he loved it. What a place for reflection, for rumination, for contemplation and adventure. Those hills were crying out to be climbed and explored. Just think, no frost or snow, no bitter freezing winds here and the joy of being alone in rugged country.

The silence was broken. To his left, going past the house belonging to David Jackson, was a small motor bike making a put-putting noise, ridden by a Nigerian in traditional dress who was carrying a pile of large boxes out of which appeared a hoe, rake, scythe and a huge bundle of canes. Would they stay here long enough to find out who he was or where his plot was situated?

He had to try and make a go of it. He didn't really want go back to the UK with his tail between his legs. To his friends, he was an old hand in Africa, full of stories about the time they had spent in Uganda, even when Idi Amin Dada was ruining the country. One week in Nigeria and then

117

giving up, well that would be hard to explain. The five people he'd met so far in Okene were positive and cheerful. Perhaps they were just making the best of it. It was his wife that was his concern. There wasn't much point in staying if she was monstrously unhappy or felt in danger. She needed to be reassured about the state of her pregnancy. He made a resolution. If Anna still wanted to go back to the UK after one week in Okene, then that is what they would do, and, well he'd just have to find a job, any job until his secondment was over.

He briefly called in to see Dr Omega who was surprised that they were already installed in the house, and he nodded knowingly when Karl told him about Jack and Mary's involvement. 'Now there's a couple who really know how Nigeria works. It is typical of them the way they go out of their way to help people.' He handed Karl a huge basket containing new sheets, pillow cases, towels and cutlery. He asked them what help they needed and told him about the staff meeting he should attend at 9am the next morning. As he left, Dr Omega called to him, 'Make sure you look in the bottom of the basket, there's a piece of Nigeria for you.'

The piece of Nigeria turned out to be a bottle of Guinness, which proudly announced on its label 'Brewed in Nigeria.'

They were picked up by Jack and Mary at 5pm for the outing to the Paradise Hotel.

14

The roof top of the Paradise Hotel, only three stories high, was one of the tallest buildings in Okene. As they looked across the town's rooftops, which seemed to consist only of a couple of minarets and two church towers, towards the north side of the town the Ata's palace did seem to be taller. The sun was going down and the odd small clouds in the east glowed pink like candy floss. As he climbed the stairs Jack cursed constantly about the quality of their construction. Mary was fighting a battle to get oxygen into her smoke-filled lungs and Karl was carefully holding Anna's elbow so she didn't slip. At the top of the stairs, their skin covered with a gossamer layer of sweat, they saw around ten Europeans, each of them nursing a bottle of beer. They were greeted with a tray of unidentifiable pieces of meat, bone crushing handshakes, welcoming smiles and two bottles of ice-cold Star beer that almost hurt when you handled them.

Anna, not a beer drinker, tentatively asked if there was wine. This was greeted with laughter and great guffaws. The conclusion was that there was wine, but of a dodgy vintage, from a dodgy vineyard and from a dodgy country. The only credibility it possessed was that it came from Cameroon where the French had been in charge rather than the British.

'A couple of glasses of that will soon get that baby moving.'

'Not for me, it would melt your tonsils.'

'Great if you want to shit through the eye of a needle.' The comment maker was given a jovial slap and told not to be so crude.

Anna declined the wine and opted for a gin and tonic, but deliberately didn't ask where it came from. Of the ten Europeans only Trev and Jim were recognisable. They were told the hotel was a regular after-work meeting place because the drinks were usually cold, the view was fantastic and it was worth coming just to witness the rush hour madness going on in the streets below. They were warned not to lean on the railing, and on close inspection they could see it wasn't properly attached to the roof. A Nigerian woman, built like a retired middle-weight boxer, delivered another tray of drinks. She had a face that would frighten a vampire, well-formed biceps and a chest the size of a wardrobe, and the incongruent name of Pearl. She was also Mustapha's wife. She had an unforgiving, stern look. One of the BICC workers noticed Karl looking at her and said, 'She serves all the drinks, not Mustapha, because one death stare from her and everyone pays up. I reckon it would be a flight over the railing if you forgot to pay.'

The mood was jovial. The air was full of quick quips and the men insulted each other as men everywhere are prone to do. There were the irrevocable Nigeria-bashing comments but they were not spoken in a vindictive or hurtful way. The critical comments served only as a catalyst for wit. It was a place to relax and have some fun and the fun as far as they were concerned consisted of joking with one another or commenting on the mad things they had seen in their time in West Africa.

A huge yellow bus, a reject from the school run in America, pulled up on the road below. It was heavily covered with rust-coloured dust. Out poured the passengers, all men, with their bodies and clothes stained a nicotine colour from the iron ore they had been working with all day at the steelworks in Ajakuti. They tumbled out of the bus. How did you get nearly 100 people on a bus so small? Arguments broke out. Yelling and shouting, wild gesticulations, gurning faces, and those out of the bus first ran across the road with no acknowledgement of the traffic. A man tumbled from his moped to the cheers of the Europeans on the roof. Another worker fell after he was hit by a market woman with a body the size of a wheel barrow. Both men got up, one to pick up his bike and the other to try and join the throng dodging the traffic. The ensuing chaos generated a discordant symphony of car horns. 'He shouldn't have argued with her,' said one of the BICC workers. 'It really is a bad idea; she takes no prisoners.'

'Just what is going on down there?' asked Anna, totally confused at the chaos below and wondering why everyone on the roof was laughing.

'It's pay day,' was the reply, 'though they don't actually get paid cash at the steel works. There's a hire and fire shop as we call it about 50 yards behind the Paradise. It's dog cat dog, if they haven't been eaten by the locals. First come first paid and if you're last you might have to wait about an hour to collect your wages.'

'It isn't so bad on normal days but we very rarely sit up here without witnessing some sort of accident.'

A man who turned out to be their next-door neighbour introduced himself as Colin Bright. He said, 'With luck you may get to see Unglikah.' His wife Cindy, another rather ample woman, chastised her husband, saying, 'The last thing you want to see is Horse. He may not be all there and not know what he's doing but he is quite disgusting.'

Everyone laughed. Anna questioned, 'Horse?' and more of the group laughed.

'Yes, hung like a horse. He wanders around wearing only a yellow waistcoat and a pair of purple platform shoes, exposing his rather large appendage to everyone.'

'What, you mean he has no trousers or shorts?' replied Anna. 'That's disgusting, don't the police do anything about it?'

'No, we all think they're frightened of him and believe he has magic powers because he's so well endowed.'

Karl butted in. 'But what about the market women down there, aren't they upset by him?'

'Naaah!' said Trev. 'If he annoys them they just get together and beat him with sticks. You're bound to see him one day, he's known to everyone in Okene.'

Jim immediately made his contribution. 'Just look out for a tall black man, masses of dreadlocks, naked from the waist down, nearly always carrying a boom box on one shoulder.'

'Playing very loud music!' exclaimed someone called Mattie, also a BICC worker. He had a ruddy yeoman's face and was shirtless and sweaty.

Jim carried on, 'You hear... You can't help but hear the loud music, but what is hilarious is that he waves his big co... Sorry, I mean penis, in time to the beat.'

'He should be on TV here, that's if you can find a signal or a TV. Especially one of those chat shows,' said Mattie.

'But he doesn't speak,' Jim commented.

'Of course, I know that, but he could sit there swinging his chopper while he plays his music,' replied Mattie. He had that bibulous look as he fingered his belly button with one hand and held a bottle of Star in the other.

'Mattie,' sighed Jim, 'you're as mad as a bag of bats. If a Nigerian show wanted some daft comments, then you are the man.'

Everyone laughed as Mattie smiled at what he thought was a compliment.

Mary leaned over and whispered in Anna's ear. 'It's just part of the rich tapestry of the crazy cultural life of Okene. A gang of half-drunk Europeans on a roof laughing at the chaos below.' She paused and added, 'You'll get used to it.'

'Whooooah,' shouted two BICC workers. 'Did you see that car? He's just knocked over a huge basket of mangoes trying to avoid one of the running idiots. There's going to be trouble.'

A rotund woman who had been squatting at the side of the road opposite the hotel stood up, glowering with rage. She leaned into the window of the offending car and screamed at the driver. He appeared to be frightened to death. Her lips were inches from his ear. His body contracted and his head slipped into his shoulders, waiting for the first blow from this seriously irate woman. The mangoes rolled drunkenly across the road and under the car. People passing by deftly picked them up as they ran past. Louder and longer outraged screams came from the woman as she left the driver alone momentarily to try and stop the looting. Other fellow traders stood and yelled in support and the terrified driver made a quick getaway, which was more than she could bear. All that remained was a hot road surface covered in sticky, squashed mangoes, her produce rolling around, the culprit driving off without giving her compensation, and skinny nimble little boys opportunistically grabbing whatever fruit they could. She stood in the middle of the road shrieking and shrieking, her face so contorted she looked as though she had eaten a cockroach. There was more laughter from the drinkers above.

The group of Europeans evidently gathered together two or three times a week to socialise, to laugh and joke and to take the piss out of life in Nigeria. Mary told Anna it was like an antidote to the frustrations of life out in the bush. While the majority of them appeared to be friendly and cheerful, Colin and Cindy Bright were somewhat dour and it took a lot to make them smile. They complained loudly about lots of things, none of which they could ever change. The phrase 'flogging a dead horse' came to mind. They moaned more than they laughed and were the butt of many jokes and comments. When out of earshot she was referred to as Moanalot.

Karl and Anna were told there were six to eight Russians in town but they were rarely seen in public places. And then there were the French. This was the cue for snide remarks, face pulling and open-ended comments such as, 'you know what the French are like.' They worked for a company called Dumez and were replacing the dirt road from Okene to the steel works as well as having the contract for widening and upgrading the 40-mile stretch from Okene to Lokoja on the confluence of the Niger and Benue rivers. Their fleet of trucks, earth-moving machines and graders was predominately yellow and blue. They had a purpose-built camp some five miles out of town which was known locally as Petite Paris. The project manager didn't live in the camp. He had refurbished an old stone house just a mile and a half away on the road to the college which was easily recognised because of its huge veranda, its floodlit badminton court and the fact that it had 24-hour-per-day electricity supplied by his own generator. It gave off so much power even the servants quarters were lit up like the Arc de Triomphe at night.

Karl and Anna declined three offers of supper. They wanted to be alone, to eat what they wanted from their small stock of food, to not have another drink and to go to bed when they wanted. The Brights offered to drive them home and said they would point out the French house as they drove by. They had both enjoyed their hour or so on the roof. It was a long time since they had really laughed out loud. At one point Anna leaned over and clutched her husband's hand, not a worrying squeeze but more a gentle touch of confirmation that she was fine and pleased to be in a place that seemed to be, at this moment in time, more stable. They smiled at each other, at the same time providing each other with that warmth of knowing and a strong appreciation of each other. They had had one drink too many. They had had fun and the drink had erased, albeit temporarily, any latent troubles they had. Karl had a warm feeling. He had been in his element laughing and joking, commenting, picking brains and feeling at home. He had a warm feeling about his wife and their future. He looked at her and felt real pride in her fortitude and how under some dire circumstances she had coped. They had supported one another, given each other a shoulder to lean on, and been receptacles for each other's anxieties. They had been in close proximity for 24 hours a day for a week and the experience had, despite adverse conditions and culture shock, brought them closer together. His responsibility was to help her bring their child into the world, but whether that world was to be Africa, he still didn't know. But he was determined to keep the promise made to her, that if Okene was not for her, they would pack their bags and clear off back to the UK.

Colin and Cindy pointed out the house of the Dumez manager as they passed it on their right. It was dark now and the compound was brightly lit with a profusion of lights. Both Cindy and Colin had strong Welsh accents and they told Karl and Anna that they both came from a small mining village close to Pontypridd. They were around 30 years old. Colin, short in stature and thin, was a little shorter than his wife, who was blessed with the figure of a rugby prop. Karl laughed to himself as he mentally compared them to that well-known imagery of seaside holiday postcards depicting a harassed small, very thin man being dominated by his behemoth of a wife. Colin was a victim of premature baldness, and had a small pointy beard and a mouth that unfortunately turned down at the edges, giving him a permanent miserable look. He was the mathematics teacher at the college. When Anna asked Cindy what she did, it was Colin who answered. 'She should be teaching at the college, or better still, in an expatriate junior or infants school.'

Anna carried on. 'What happened?' she said.

Cindy leaned over the front seat so she could speak to them directly, and said, 'I... we were told that they would sort out a job for me at a nearby expatriate school.' She paused and took a deep breath, '...but there isn't one nearby.'

Colin, with a hint of venom in his words, said, 'Nearby, no bloody chance, the nearest expat school is in Benin and it's dying on its feet. What did they think she was going to do, drive 80 miles there and 80 miles back every day? Half the time there isn't any petrol or if there is you have to queue for hours, and what gets me is that the Ministry told us they'd sort it out.' He stopped as Cindy took over the story.

'I did visit the school in Benin but no one had ever heard of me, there were no vacancies, I would have been the only expat and the place, well... It was just a mess.'

Colin went on, 'It is typical of the mess in this place. Do you know, in the ministry they've no idea about their own country, they actually thought there was an expatriate school in Okene.' He said adamantly, 'The quicker we can get a transfer to somewhere where Cindy can work, the better.'

'Don't go on about that Colin, I'm sure Karl and Anna don't want to hear about our little problems.'

'The quicker they find out that they'll eventually be victims of maladministration or incompetence or bribery, the better!'

Karl tried to interrupt to point out that their brief week in West Africa had also been somewhat traumatic, but he didn't get the chance.

'Do you know, Cindy even offered to teach in one of the local primary schools but they wouldn't recognise her qualifications. And see this car? I'm the only one with a poxy VW beetle and it's second hand, we should have had an estate car like Jack and Mary but we were told we weren't entitled.' Without pausing for breath he added, 'We were told I'd be a senior education officer with 40% more money than we're getting now, and we'd have a decent car.'

Cindy remarked, 'Junior education officer, it's unfair. There are only two or three other juniors on the staff and they are Nigerians who've only taught for a year and they...'

She was interrupted again by Colin who was trying to steer the car while looking at his two passengers in the back seat. 'And most of them are useless. You'll soon find out that there are a lot of useless people working here, and Dr Who, when I tried to get him to employ Cindy, came back with some half-hearted excuse.'

It was Cindy's time to talk and she seemed much more calm about their complaints. 'What we're trying to do is get the Ministry to change our status to senior education officer, pay us all the money we should be due and also transfer us. We applied ages ago but still haven't heard from them.'

'What do you bloody expect?' was Colin's reply.

Colin slowed down as they arrived at the college entrance. Karl managed to get a word in before he started talking again.

'How is it going?' he asked.

'Not so good,' was Cindy's reply. 'You can't do anything by letter because they lose them or they don't get through. You can't telephone, you just have to drive to Lagos and speak to them directly. What's your status? Are you intermediate, junior, or senior education officer?'

'Principal,' was Karl's reply, and then knew he had said the wrong thing.

The two bodies in the front seats gasped and in unison said, 'Principal!'

Colin held the wheel tightly with one hand as he punished the gears with the other as he drove on the rutted road into the college grounds. He moaned loudly, 'You lucky buggers. You arrive without hassle, get a house on your first day and you're a principal.' He placed great emphasis on each syllable. 'Just our bloody luck to have wealthy neighbours.'

As they pulled up outside Karl and Anna's cottage, the lights were on and the hum of the generator could just be heard. Colin temporarily dripped with sweat and resentment which was aimed, it seemed at them, but then he paused, seeming to realise that he was upset at his own circumstances. He calmed down after realising he had inflicted his personal problems on someone he'd just met and remembered that in circumstances like Okene expats needed to help one another.

Cindy said the right thing as Karl and Anna moved toward their door. 'Is there anything you need or anything we can do to help?' Colin too offered lifts into town for shopping or trips to the Paradise, and had that sorry look on his face as he visually apologised for moaning so much.

They said goodnight. Colin drove the 50 yards to his bungalow and Cindy walked. Karl looked after her and reflected that Cindy was not an appropriate name for a rugby prop.

In their house the lights were on, the ceiling fan moved the hot air around the room, and their accommodation, – albeit very Spartan, had a cosy feel to it. Perhaps he would make a sign with 'The Cottage' written on it and place it on the front of the house.

15

Sleepy and ever so slightly under the influence of alcohol, they drank tea and were pleased to see that the water from the filter bore no resemblance to the water stored in the tank outside. They prepared for their second night in Okene and Anna, who had crawled into bed as Karl was brushing his teeth, was fast asleep by the time he came out of the bathroom. He lit a candle in preparation for the lights going out at 10 o'clock. He went to the bedroom and looked at his wife in repose. She looked content, yet fragile and vulnerable. He thought of the worries she must be having and how stoic she had been most of the time as great shovel loads of Africa at its grimmest had been jettisoned on them. The free-standing fan oscillated from side to side, gently ruffling the sheet that covered her. He attempted to get into bed carefully so as not to wake her, but it was obvious that alcohol had temporarily replaced some of her worries and tension and enabled her to fall into a deep sleep. His mind was too busy to sleep, so he put the light out, leaving his reading book in the bedroom. He leaned over the bed and listened to his wife gently breathing, then tenderly kissed her on the cheek. His lips silently thanked her for being so patient with him. He went to the kitchen door, pushed it open and went to stand outside in the darkness. He wallowed in the fresh air, so much cooler and more pleasant now that the sun had gone down. There was a dull clunk in the distance as the tone of the generator softened, the dim glow of light from the college dormitories faded, and then silence as the generator stopped and the cottage lights went out.

He looked up into the sky and in the pollution-free atmosphere the heavens were an explosion of tiny flickering lights. They were quite overwhelming and for an instant they took his breath away. Just to think there was a whole new world above him and so rarely did he take time to marvel at the night sky. There was the whine of the odd mosquito, but if he moved around in the grass he managed to evade them. The predominant noise was from all of the invisible crickets and cicadas rejoicing together. This was the real sound of Africa, not the screaming, hysterical demands for money or blaring horns and vitriol and aggression. Suddenly the noise stopped as quickly as it had started. Perhaps a large snake was sliding through the grass and their silence was his cue to stand still or get into the house. He sighed, tiredness overtaking him. He felt that if a stranger saw him they would think he was sad and forlorn.

It was just as he felt when he saw his father for the last time. Joe looked half the man he was, he looked as Karl felt at this moment. Half of him was missing and he was wracked with sorrow. Not only had he lost Tina, his wife, but his only son was going off to Nigeria. Karl flopped against the wall, overcome with grief and guilt again. Just how could he have left? His sister's eyes had revealed her disapproval but she had said nothing. He had left his father just when he needed him most.

His father had a remarkable long term memory and over a beer would tell stories about his youth, the war and his life in the steel works. He rarely repeated a story, and on one visit Karl took a small tape recorder with him and recorded his father talking for an hour about his own father and grandfather.

He said, 'They were the two biggest men in North Ormesby. My dad Herbert was 6ft 5ins and his dad George was 6ft 8ins. When they walked side by side on their way to work they blocked the sun.' Well, that was his father's phrase. Joe was one of eleven children living in a two up two down house with no bathroom and one toilet in the back yard. 'No fancy toilet paper in those days,' he said. 'You just had to wipe your arse on a page of the Evening Gazette.' His mother used to buy a large candle in winter to place in the toilet on freezing nights. It was amazing that that one small flame could stop the cistern from freezing. In the back yard of the house, hanging on the wall, was a huge tin bath that was brought in every Sunday evening so that all the kids could have a bath in front of the fire. That story or experience was not new or shocking to Karl because he too had lived in a similar two up two down house until he was ten – a house without a bathroom and an outside toilet, one of many identical houses in identical streets that provided housing for the steel workers. Karl too remembered Sunday evenings when his father and mother would bathe him and his sister in front of the fire and then in their pyjamas they would make a mad dash upstairs to avoid being attacked by the cold in the unheated house.

Joe told the story of how by chance he became the most important boy in the street. He had been on a day trip sponsored by Cargo Fleet Steel Works for the kids of their workers. Two buses were provided to take about 80 children on a day trip to the beach at Redcar. 'A day out on a bus and to Redcar, that was really exciting, and it was only nine miles away.' They ate prepared sandwiches of meat paste, but the big treat for them came on the esplanade near the beach when they all had to line up outside the fish shop for a huge bag of chips, with scraps of course, and a good dose of salt and vinegar. Then came games on the beach and the final bit of fun was that all the boys had to line up and race down the beach, the winner receiving a big prize. All the boys were bare footed, braces secured their shorts, sleeves were rolled up for comfort and to show you meant business. Joe reckoned they raced about 100 yards and to his surprise he won easily, beating boys two years older than him. He had the prize of a coveted case ball and from then on until it fell apart some years later, he was important. He was the boy on whom all the street football depended.

Karl had asked him if he ever raced again and was told no, there hadn't been another trip and he was busy trying to make a few pence by pushing a hand cart full of pig food from North Ormesby to South Bank every day after school. He didn't get much time to play in the street.

Karl's parents had married just after the Second World War broke out and for the first year or two they saw little of each other. Joe was trained as an aircraft fitter and was then stationed at Barry Island in Wales and later at an airbase in Cirencester. Meanwhile Tina was an ambulance driver on Teesside, often having to brave danger whilst driving during air raids. A weekend pass for Joe gave him little time to get home with all the disruption to train timetables because of air raids. He told Karl the story of how he was injured during the war.

'It wasn't one of those heroic wounded-in action-injuries, it was just an unfortunate accident, just something daft that happened. There were three of us working on mending the fuselage of an Airspeed Oxford. It was a training plane, and I suppose you don't know this, but they were painted bright yellow because as trainers the enemy wasn't supposed to fire on them. It was February 10th I think, yes definitely the 10th. I was looking forward to a Saturday off. We'd finished the repair job and the pilot asked us if we wanted to go for a spin, his words not mine. You spin on a bike and fly in a plane. It was an easy choice, we could hang around and be given something stupid to do or we could fly.'

Karl had interrupted, 'I assume you chose...'

'...Too bloody right we did, and to cut a long story short the pilot got into thick freezing clouds and got lost for a while. Just as we could see the ground again from the observation panels, all hell let loose. All I remember was the roaring of another engine and all of a sudden holes appearing all over the fuselage. It was over in a second or two. It could have been a German or an RAF plane, we never did find out for sure, all I can recall was that the inside was a bit like a colander and we all looked at each other and couldn't quite believe that none of us had been hit. Did I tell you the plane's body work was only made out of canvas stretched over metal strips?' He had stopped and looked at Karl, who showed a bit of knowledge by replying, 'You mean just like a Wellington bomber?'

'Why no man, these Oxfords were far more flimsy, but it was the same principle. Anyhow, with all those bullet holes it was even colder on the bloody aircraft and the pilot landed as quickly as possible. He wasn't happy because he knew he was in big trouble for getting lost, not to mention having three unauthorised passengers on the plane and all the holes in it. All I remember was stepping out onto the wing. I didn't notice it was covered in ice. One moment I was laughing about our adventure and escape and the next I was flat on my arse and the tarmac. The next thing I felt was the pain right from my arse to my shoulders and that's when I found out I'd broken my back. See, you're looking at a real war hero. Bloody agony I can tell you.'

Karl had always been impressed by Joe's memory and how he could recall so much in such detail. He even knew how much he was paid for every job he had had; he still thought in pre-1971 coinage and could instantly change the decimal system back into the imperial system, nearly always sighing at the same time as he thought of how prices had gone up. Karl remembered when, as a young student, his dad had sat next to him holding his pound note as though it was some sort of effigy, and saying with sadness, 'I never thought I'd see the day when you couldn't buy 10 pints for a pound.' *It's a good job he's not in Nigeria*, Karl thought.

He stayed outside in the ambient warmth, alone with his imagination. He thought it would have been nice to be able to relax with a cigar, not that he was a smoker, but in the past on those fine, alcoholic, convivial occasions he loved nothing more than a mild cigar to finish off the evening. His thoughts meandered from wondering why he was here in the middle of Africa to what the following weeks would bring and just where you could get Shredded Wheat, his daily UK breakfast.

The entomological chorus struck up again playing to the audience of stars. His thoughts moved to his mother and her death at the age of only 61. *It had been so unfair*, he thought, but deep down he had known, even at a young age, that his mother was not a well person. She suffered from formidable headaches that rendered her immobile, the only relief for her being Veganin tablets. They were, so he believed, a very strong version of aspirin. Unfortunately they cost a lot of money and if she had no tablets and it was towards the end of the week, quite simply she couldn't afford them until Joe brought home his wage packet on Friday evening.

Tina was the epitome of kindness. She was created without a mean bone in her body and wanted nothing more than to be a grandmother. Her round rosy cheeks enhanced her big smile and she loved to laugh. When Karl had told her that Anna was pregnant her smile was even bigger and she glowed with delight as though she'd had a decent win on the pools. Next to her bed when she died was a little stack of knitted cardigans, socks, booties and an unfinished white blanket with a satin edge. Under the bed was a cardboard box and in it was a brand-new teddy bear and a beautifully embroidered rag doll.

She always had times when she was obviously unwell and had to take to her bed for a few hours. Along with the ferocious headaches, she was often very tired and it didn't help that she was carrying a little too much weight. She was the ultimate cuddly mum, with a warm welcoming smile, an ample body, large boobs and thin ankles. Her shape reminded him of a robin with its spindly legs. There was nothing she liked better in the evenings than to sit in her armchair by the side of the fire opposite her husband while he read the paper. At her side would be a bottle of Lowcocks Lemonade which she drank straight from the bottle (she didn't drink alcohol), a small box of Cadbury's or Rowntree's chocolates that Joe regularly bought for her, or an orange or two. In the winter she added chestnuts that were roasted in the fire to her diet of chocolates and lemonade, and with a long toasting fork she would toast large slabs of bread and cover them with huge amounts of margarine.

She was small, five feet one in height and a stay-at-home mother. Joe thought it was essential that his wife's place was in the home, being there to welcome the kids home from school, and it was not until Karl and his sister were at secondary school that he relented and allowed her to work. She became a dinner lady at the local Girls Grammar School and it was there that she would pass on messages to Karl's first real girlfriend. A mild stroke in her mid-fifties stopped her from working. Even though he was aware of her health issues – 'It's my high blood pressure again,' she would say, it still came as a shock to him that she had died so young.

This was the women to whom he told his secrets. This was the woman who was not afraid to chastise him severely, even with a big belt, when he lied. She was the one in whom he would confide, telling her more about his life, his troubles, his friends and anxieties than most of his school mates would do. His best friend Malcolm who lived in the house directly across the back alley would say disdainfully, 'Your trouble is, you tell your mam everything.' It was indicative of her nature, she radiated trust, she listened and advised, never saying you must do this or you must do that but making gentle suggestions that showed she cared and that she wanted her son to listen and make up his own mind.

The overwhelming guilt Karl felt about leaving his father was exacerbated by the way he had treated his mother. He and Anna had lived 13 miles away. He would ring his parents a couple of times a week, and invariably after Sunday morning football and a couple of pints with his dad and brother-in-law in the working men's club, they would spend Sunday afternoon with his parents, consuming a huge Sunday lunch. He knew she was unwell, she had told him so on the phone, and the weekend before her death, to his shame, he didn't go to visit her. It wasn't as though he had something important to do, it was more a case of inertia, or dare he say it, a feeling that 'I can't be bothered this weekend.' To compound his negligence, he didn't call all weekend. An extra evening class he had to cover was one sort of excuse, but the fact remained that he had not contacted his parents for ten days before his mam passed away. He felt like weeping.

16

The staff meeting was held in a large free standing room adjacent to Dr Omega's office. It was bordering on the ramshackle and the only time it was in regular use was mid-morning on Tuesdays and Fridays when the twice-weekly mail arrived. This was dumped on a large table and, being a social occasion, those present shuffled through the mass of envelopes to see if any of it belonged to them. Letters not claimed during the day were put in pigeon holes by a clerk, who also performed the bi-weekly job of bringing a huge aluminium kettle of tea into the faculty room on those two days, along with an assortment of cups and mugs. There was of course no sugar, milk or spoons, the milk and sugar in huge quantities already being in the kettle. The clerk also brought a couple of packets of Cabin biscuits, which Karl and Anna had discovered during their time in Lagos came from a biscuit factory owned by one of the Ministry's permanent secretaries, and apparently were the only biscuits allowed to be served to the employees there. There were not enough of the battered wooden chairs to seat everyone, but at the front of the room was the one solitary chair with a cushioned seat which was obviously for Dr Omega's use. Just to add a little formality to the room, on the end wall were displayed a green and white Nigerian flag, a framed photograph of the current president of the country, General Olusegun Obasanjo, and the motto of 'Unity and Faith, Peace and Progress.'

The flurry of activity to grab as many of the granite-like Cabin biscuits was halted by the principal's entrance. He sat down, quietening the throng gathered on chairs or the edge of the table if they were lucky. The majority just stood. Karl glanced around the room as Jack O'Driscoll came to stand next to him. There must have been 35 people present who he assumed were all teachers, lecturers, education officers or whatever else they were referred to at the college. The majority were Nigerian, with a sprinkling of

Europeans and Asians, one of whom was adorned in Mahatma Gandhi robes and had the misfortune to be missing his left arm. Karl later found out that this was Captain Majid, formerly of the Pakistan Army, and that he had lost his arm in a small skirmish with Indian troops on the Kashmir border.

Jack took him to one side and gave him an unflattering and somewhat biased view, he assumed at that time, of a few of those who were present. In his soft Irish accent he said, 'Well, you already know Colin Bright and as I said before, it's Bright by name but not by nature. He moans all the time and has a major chip on his shoulder. Oh and yes, his wife is equally as bitter, but to be fair they probably would have been quite nice had they got their status sorted out before they got here. Anyway, when they are not talking about personal injustices they can be entertaining. The one in the corner to your left is of course David Jackson, you met him on top of our 5-star drinking hotel. Nice man. I think I have told you, but he is our resident intellectual, Oxford or Cambridge, one of them. An expert on African history and a genuine desire to be of some help to the students. He's a hint of sanity around here. You see the Asian guy who keeps giving Dr Who those notes, well that is Dr Khan. Beware, it looks as though you'll have a lot to do with him. Not to be trusted. If he screws up, the conniving git will find a way to put the blame on someone else. I suspect our good Doctor can't stand him but it seems he was an immovable appendage when Dr Omega arrived here. For some reason, probably bribery and corruption, he seems to be untouchable. He does nothing unless it's for personal gain. Buy yourself an armour-plated vest and wear it when dealing with him. A back stabber and bloody snake he is and that's an insult to reptiles.'

'Can I assume he's crossed your path?' said Karl.

'Too right,' he commented. 'Just remember, don't trust him, and he's idle.'

Karl was fascinated and went on listening to Jack's tirade. 'Then there's the Asian, actually all our Asians are Pakistanis, sat next to him. That is Javed. He lives in the flat below me. He hardly ever turns up for work, he can barely speak English and his flat is full of chickens.'

'You mean he keeps a few for eggs.'

'No, he might have about 50 or so clucking about below me and he has a market stall and gets a little boy to sell them for him. When you come to my house you can't fail to notice the smell on the ground floor and the noise, though fortunately we hardly hear anything. We would quite like to move but the flat is huge with a great veranda and it has one or two big advantages. We get running water, sometimes all day, but we always get it between 4 and 8pm, and though electricity is a little unpredictable, we get more than the college and it's free.'

Jack seemed to be impervious to the sun. It was roasting outside and already, even in the shade of the room, Karl felt uncomfortable trickles of sweat running down his back. He felt that any movement, other than shuffling from foot to foot, would cause him to be soaked through in a moment. Jack carried on with his cutting comments.

'Then there's Saddiqui, a supposed scientist. If you see him in a car keep away. He's had his car, a brand-new Morris Marina, only three weeks and has dented it three times. I don't think he knows there's a third gear. As for Qureshi, he's very clever and fun when sober, but spends most of his time being drunk and objectionable. Shares in retsina have gone up since he arrived. Thank goodness for Captain Majid, you can't miss him he's the one with...'

It was Karl's turn to interrupt, '...With one arm and clothes like...'

'...That old bugger Gandhi. Do you know, he walks everywhere, even to the Lokoja Road campus and that must be about five miles from here. A real gentleman, he'll do anything for anyone. He has seven kids at home and has the smallest accommodation of any us right in the grim centre of town. He doesn't have a bed. He sleeps on a table rather than the floor because of the mice, which he says are rather annoying.'

As the meeting progressed Karl was introduced to his colleagues, who were told that he would be working on the 'micro teaching scheme' which was designed to help trainees teach interesting topics in a short time, and that he would also be travelling to watch and evaluate the trainees on location. When it was mentioned that he and his wife were already in residence in the cottage vacated by the American Peace Corps couple, there were a few sighs of astonishment and some serious questioning looks between some teachers. When Dr Omega went on to tell them that Anna was pregnant, however, there was a little murmur of sympathy.

Dr Omega went on to mention that a student called Jonathan Bassey had been selected for the Nigerian Student football team, and two teachers from the Philippines were to join the staff, one to teach physical education and one to be librarian; Karl later found out that the two appointments had been made without the good doctor's knowledge. Further announcements were made about a tennis court that had been built to the wrong measurements and was therefore unplayable, and the surface of the basketball court was dangerous and also unfit to play on. The library had no books. Dr Omega asked three or four members of staff to remain behind to talk about it.

His main piece of information was that the Ministry had insisted there should be a 25% increase in the intake of postgraduate students because of the building that was going on at the Lokoja Road campus. This brought howls of protest because all those present knew that the site was far from finished and was, to all intents, still a building site. The issue was further compounded when Dr Omega dropped a little bomb shell by informing his audience that the two companies constructing the new college, a German company called ATP and JAS their Nigerian partners, had run out of money as well as patience with each other and the Ministry. There was a flurry of muttering which grew into a breeze of concerns that changed into a storm of complaints, some of which were so petty and self-centred. It seemed as though everyone had been promised a new house, a new this, a new that, and since it wasn't going to happen many of them demanded compensation. One teacher had the nerve to say they should all withdraw their labour immediately. Another teacher, who was evidently called Freddie and was a biologist, suggested that for compensation they should all be given money to buy items to make their current homes better. No one wanted to miss out on the spoils that they could be grabbing.

This small verbal revolution caused Dr Omega to bring up the point that some 25 dual-function fridges that could operate with either electricity or paraffin had been ordered for the staff and students but they had gone missing en-route to Okene. This resulted in howls of complaint and sighs of disbelief, but instead of moaning at the foibles of the Ministry, complaints were directed at the principal for not supplying them with what they were due. No one mentioned or considered just how 25 fridges could disappear. The commotion spawned complaints about the lack of subsidised petrol, why some staff got free electricity and others had to pay, would salaries go up if they had 25% more students, why do some people get a house straight away, it's unfair that some teachers got bigger desks than others.

Karl was shocked. It was anarchy. The mood in the room was one of what do I get rather than what can I give in return. Dr Omega was a little ruffed at first but with gentle calming movements of his hands and his finger pointing to his lips he got the moaning mass to be silent. They waited with anticipation for him to provide answers to their demands, but his response was not what they were expecting. 'You are all very good at looking after your own interests,' he said firmly. 'You are too busy complaining who has this and who has that, and it means I find it hard to take you seriously when in fact the majority of you here do not teach the classes that are allocated to you. You need to get that element of professionalism right, in other words turn up for the lessons you are supposed to attend and then I may try and consider your minor, self-serving problems. It might be worth reminding everyone of the national pledge.' He stood up, looked everyone in the eye, and in a fine deep voice said, 'I pledge to Nigeria, my country, to be faithful loyal and honest, to serve Nigeria with all my strength, to defend her unity and uphold her honour and glory. So help me God. I ask you: are you serving Nigeria, are you honest?' With that, he left the room.

Jack and Mary arranged to pick Karl and Anna up early the next morning to take them to the mission hospital in Auchi. When asked if he didn't mind, Jack's answer was that it was an opportunity to buy some potatoes since Auchi, some 40-odd miles away, was the nearest place that sold them.

17

They were collected early in the morning by Mary and Jack for the drive to the mission hospital in Auchi. Anna wanted to introduce herself to the medical staff there and make sure she had regular prenatal care.

The first comment of the morning was from Jack. 'It's a good job you are not going to the hospital in Okene, it's a filthy place and fit only to put a plaster on a cut. It's the sort of place where they would bleed you with leeches, believing the bloodsuckers would cure you.'

'Hmmm!' was the response from his wife. 'A slight exaggeration dear, you make it sound medieval.'

'Well, that's a very appropriate word,' was his reply.

'The trouble is that there really is no one in charge. The last administrator left under a cloud after being accused of fiddling the books.'

'That's normal around here.'

'Shhh! Let me finish. He hasn't been replaced and the doctor... I can't recall his name...'

'... Hyde, or was it Crippen?'

'Do ignore him, he's trying to be funny. The doctor couldn't be expected to run the place and treat all the patients. It doesn't help that he's rather fond of his drink and the general rule among the residents of Okene is to go in the afternoon after he has sobered up and before he has his first drink of the day. Thankfully the government has nothing to do with Auchi mission hospital and it's run by Catholic nuns.'

The road to Auchi was quiet and irrevocably bathed in sunlight. Even this early in the morning it was already hot enough to see the asphalt turn into a mirage in the distance. After driving south for about 10 miles the vegetation changed from scrub and savannah to decidedly tropical. There were still views of the hills above the trees but they were largely hidden by the exotic tropical trees and palms.

'What did you think of the staff meeting?' questioned Jack. Karl wasn't quite sure what to say. Should he adopt the cynical tone of the experienced weary expatriate who was always willing to have a good moan or should he be forgiving and understanding by acknowledging that this was Africa and things were different here. He decided to be noncommittal and answered with a word open to elastic interpretation. 'Interesting,' he said.

'Too right, I suppose you noticed your new colleagues were more interested in their welfare than that of the students. Come to mention it, were the students even mentioned?'

'Actually, I don't think so.'

'You certainly couldn't help but notice Dr Who's final biting comment about attendance.'

'Yes, it was a dramatic ending.'

'Your new colleagues are actually not very good at turning up for work. All of them have extra...' at this point he took his hands off the steering wheel, looked over his shoulder and his fingers made a two inverted commas gesture, '... Let's call them commercial interests. Remember I told you yesterday about that semi illiterate Javed in the flat below us who is virtually running a chicken farm.'

Mary interrupted. 'He and his wife and the chickens live in two rooms.'

'And don't forget all that shit.'

'Most of your colleagues are more concerned with their market stall or taxi business or private tuition or selling alcohol or any commodity that might make a bit of money.'

'But we're well paid, why do they...?' Karl never got to finish his sentence.

'The problem is, is they're not well paid at all. Teachers here have a raw financial deal. Fifty percent of **our** salaries come from the British government. Yes, we're part of the aid package to the third world!' He theatrically boomed out the sentence with jingoistic pride.

Mary now had to have her say. 'The irony of the situation is that Nigeria is awash with money. It's the oil money that is building the new campus and the oil money that is trying to get more teachers into classrooms. But the oil money has made this country a greedy place. Everyone wants their slice of the cake. Obasanjo is trying to get some political and moral stability and use the money to benefit the country, but... There must be 80, perhaps 100 million Nigerians, and until a couple of years ago there were only five universities in the country.'

139

'They don't pay the teachers enough and that's just one reason why they have extra commercial interests, but the teachers here at FATCO also have an attitude of disdain for their jobs. They often feel that if they are not being paid what they think they are worth then why should they work hard or even take an interest in the students. Now a lot of them are rather nice people. They are friendly and good fun, and I ask myself if I were in the same financial position would I be looking for extra income. The answer is of course yes. But, I would like to think I'm professional enough to always make sure I was doing my job to the best of my ability.'

'Oh how idealistic you are,' said Mary with a hint of scorn in her voice. 'You have lapsed a little yourself, don't you think.'

Jack thought a moment. 'Well yes, I do feel as though I've been sucked into the apathy of the place to a certain extent. Yes, I could do more and they could give me more to do, but an awful lot of time here is spent on day to day survival. Like the 12 hours I had to wait in line to get fuel for the car. Like the trip I had to make to get my ankle fixed, or scrounging around for fresh water when the taps go off for a day or two. Or doing something really important like taking your wife to hospital... Don't get me wrong,' he said with a big smile, 'we're only taking you so we can buy some potatoes from the market, Irish potatoes as they're known here, so we can make some chips when we get back. Do you fancy goat and chips for supper?'

There was silence for a little while as the countryside went past in a green blur. They passed women in colourful fabrics with large loads on their heads, old men pushing heavily loaded bicycles and others, many with bare feet, just walking. But to where? Some tentatively waved their hands hoping to cadge a lift and others were just grateful the car was not creating a harmattan of red dust. Karl broke the silence. 'What was Dr Omega talking about when he mentioned the tennis court?

Jack answered, feeling good that he was the source of all information. 'What happened is that FATCO was granted a sum of money to improve its sports facilities despite the fact that it is about to close down and move, hopefully to the new site a few miles away. I'm there tomorrow morning, I can take you there if you wish. Really the money should have been spent at the new campus, but no, someone without foresight decided the money had to be spent on a place that was going to be abandoned in the next few months. Not the staff accommodation of course. So tenders were put out and lots of local companies applied for the job, and since they knew it was government funding these 'contractors' came up with some rather extravagant costs, hoping to cash in on the surfeit of money that was supposedly swimming around.'

'Tell them who got the contract,' interrupted Mary.

'I'm about to.' He paused, took a deep breath of the hot air in the car, and said, 'No, I haven't made this up but a company from Benin, some 120 miles away, called... And you won't believe this, though I promise you it's true ... The outfit was called 'Supercon' as in concrete, but in reality their name told us everything about them. They came, measured the area for the tennis and basketball courts then proceeded to dig a large hole for the tennis court. It was about four feet deep and the boss said that was the volume of concrete they needed to use, the four foot depth being necessary to ensure stability or 'firmness' as he put it. It didn't take them long, I'll give them that, but it was pointed out to them by David Jackson – and he knows bugger all about sport – that the dimensions of the court may have been correct but there was no extra space around the lines for the players to play. There was a slab of concrete thick enough to be the roof of a nuclear bunker and no surrounding area in which to play the game. But it gets worse. What they also did was to put the wire netting tight to the edges of the slab to render play completely impossible. And it continues to get worse, because after they realised they had used 95% of their concrete allocation on the tennis court they then had to prepare the surface of the basketball court which was to be built on a piece of sloping land that they didn't properly flatten. Their incompetence was legion but also horrible because they had the nerve to be taking money for a useless job.'

'And it continues to get worse,' said Mary.

'Although they had little concrete left for the raked-over area of the basketball court they proceeded to simply put the remaining amount of concrete down to create a surface. It was about one inch thick at best and within a week it had begun to crack and now it's a dangerous unplayable mess.'

'When was this done?' asked Karl.

'About two months ago, and guess what? Dr Omega found out that the authorisation for the contract was given by a federal ministry official in Benin who just so happened to be daft enough to have his name as a director on the invoice that was paid. It cost 80,000 naira for three days' work at most, for two facilities in the wrong place that were basically useless.'

'It is normal here. No wonder your new colleagues, as Jack calls them, are not motivated.'

'Dr Omega was livid,' said Jack. 'He really is trying to do his best to create a purposeful college but he's hampered by greed, incompetence and apathy.'

There was an all-round sigh of disbelief in the car. They shook their heads in astonishment and as far as Karl and Anna were concerned it was hard to know whether to be angry and indignant or just to laugh it off as 'it could only happen in Africa.'

Instead of taking the turning directly into Auchi they drove left up a shady, well-maintained one-track road; after a couple of hundred yards the trees parted in an act of welcome, and in a clearing was a rather fine faux Romanesque building that would have been more at home in the south of France or Andalucía. It was painted white and the supporting stones around the round arches had been left as natural stone. There was a bell tower with a functioning clock. Stones were carefully placed to delineate flower beds and at the side of the building was an explosion of red, yellow and purple bougainvillea. Notices pointed to the parking area, the chapel, and the clinic. A man tending a flower bed waved as they stopped in a car park with painted white lines. The whole atmosphere was ecclesiastical and medical. A nun in her blue and white habit with a complexion that by some miracle was untouched by the sun floated past.

Jack and Mary disappeared to the market some three miles away in the centre of Auchi, and Karl and Anna took seats in the waiting room. It was the epitome of order and calm, like being transported to a different country. The heat was the same, the vicious sun still created deadly shadows and the people were still predominately black, but the atmosphere within the hospital was ordered, civilised and gracious. They were interviewed by an old European nurse who wore the nun's habit. The origins of her English accent were indiscernible. Her voice was full of experience and assurance as she reassured Anna that she was in good hands and that they had helped with the births of many expatriate children. Her temperature and bloods were taken, a stethoscope listened for unusual sounds and her arm was squeezed to measure her blood pressure. The nurse pointed to Anna's ankles, having noticed they were a little swollen, and asked her how long they had been like that.

Anna wasn't sure, and with another reassuring comment the nurse proffered the opinion that heat, fatigue and stress could be the cause. 'Nothing to worry about,' she said. 'But if they get worse or the swelling hasn't gone down in the next few days then you must come back.'

The doctor had a typically romantic-sounding French accent. He pondered over the nurse's findings and came to the conclusion that the baby was healthy and that Anna should lower her stress levels by resting as much as possible. He too thought the baby would arrive at the beginning of August. 'Twelve or thirteen weeks,' he said, 'and then you will be proud parents. Have you any idea of names yet?' The response was no. They looked at each other and couldn't quite believe that they hadn't even discussed this since they got on the Nigerian airways fight to Lagos some nine days ago.

The doctor pointed out that there would be no formal charge for the regular check-ups nor for the birth of the baby, but since they were employed a small donation to the charity's coffers would be really appreciated. They arranged another check-up in two weeks' time. Anna felt reassured that she was in good hands and reflected on how in the future she could tell her child how it was partly African for having been born in a small bush town in the middle of Nigeria. For a moment or two the idea of packing their bags and going straight back to the UK dissolved. Although life was a little better she wondered how she would cope in the next few days. Three or four more days she said to herself, and then I'll decide.

Jack and Mary returned and cheerfully entered the waiting room, proudly showing their prize of a basket full of very small potatoes. 'The size of monkey's bollocks,' declared Jack, 'so it's chips and something for supper.' Karl looked at them both. Thin like a pair of whippets. He wondered when they actually ate anything, or was alcohol their source of nutrition. Their friendly disposition, Jack's wit and Mary's serenity, had been so welcome over the last day or so and he couldn't thank them enough for the excursion to the hospital. Jack glowed when being thanked, and Mary did point out that he really disliked Thursday mornings as the only class he had would never make decent teachers in a thousand years and he'd also had a meeting scheduled with the so-called (according to Jack) mendacious Dr Khan. 'Your pregnancy has done him a favour because he can claim he was on a humanitarian mission.'

As they drove back into the grounds of FATCO the row of four little houses appeared and there in front of their 'cottage' was a rather large wooden box. The car pulled up, the dust settled, and the box turned out to be, by some miracle, their baggage which had been sent a week before they flew to Nigeria. Jack and Mary looked at each other in astonishment. Jack stood next to the box, lifted up his leg and planted his foot firmly on the top. Then, with theatrical gestures and much arm waving, he declared,

'Ladies and gentlemen, and the unborn, you are now the witness of a miracle, an event so rare in the annals of Nigerian administration that it could, in fact, be that the presence of this box must be an act of God.'

Mary added, 'I suppose you can't help but notice that we Irish have a lot to say.'

'Did you really only send your stuff a week before you flew?'

They both nodded.

'Well, let me tell you, our baggage took three months to get here.'

Mary made her contribution. 'Our baggage was also sent by air freight.'

'And Colin Bright's stuff took just as long but it had been left out in the rain for days and the contents were ruined.' He paused. 'Another gripe they have... But with some justification.'

The box was manhandled into the house, farewells were said and something and chips was arranged for the evening. Their box had already been opened, hopefully for checking and not pillaging, and with the aid of a stout knife from the kitchen they prised the lid open. Prior experience in Africa had given them some indication as to what was and was not needed when you arrived in a new country and had to settle in. The first item they pulled out was something that every expatriate article about Nigeria suggested was a necessity – a pressure cooker. Karl was unconvinced. When his wife went out and bought one he had assumed it was just for making tough meat edible. There were other useful kitchen items like an iron (as long as there was power), a set of sharp knives and their favourite tea drinking mugs and a teapot. Since there was already one in the kitchen, they laughed as they declared they were a two pot household.

Within an hour they had transformed their spartan 'cottage' into something almost homely. They spread the four cheap durries they had bought from Habitat on the floors, assembled the four self-assembly picture frames, put in their images and hung them on the wall. There were two landscapes by Corot, a Turner painting of Pegwell Bay, and a dramatic image of Middlesbrough's transporter bridge at sunset. The coffee table was moved and the two most expensive items, the music centre with its pile of cassettes and a short-wave radio were placed on it near to one of the two electric sockets in the main room. The Chinese lanterns had nowhere to go so were temporarily left in the spare bedroom. The four colourful cushions brought the dull fabric of the sofa and armchairs to life and the final touch was the two bunches of artificial bright red and yellow flowers that Anna had been crafty enough to pack.

Finally, in the bottom of the box under a bed cover, towels and a huge heap of baby clothes and equipment, was a washing line, some pegs, and a jar of poppy seeds. Karl had seen them in the local delicatessen and had bought them on impulse because he had had the romantic idea of sprinkling them on top of their very own home-baked bread.

They both stood back and admired the front room that had been transformed in such a short time. The power had now gone off for the afternoon and it was time to eat. What to have before the evening's chips and something. They settled for fried eggs on toast. The sweet local bread was cut into slices, toasted and covered with margarine from a tin which, rather disturbingly, was the colour of daffodils. Wow, they had cooked their first meal, and Karl resolved that after tasting the toasted sweet bread it really was essential in the future to bake their own. They talked about what they could bake, what they would use the pressure cooker for, what they needed from the market. Then they looked at each other and Anna, after reading Karl's mind, said, 'Just because it looks almost nice in here doesn't mean we're going to stay. Just look at where we live?' She grimaced, introducing reality into their thoughts. 'We live in the middle of nowhere, one of four isolated houses literally on the edge of the bush. I'm not sure I feel safe here.'

Karl interrupted. 'How can you say you don't feel safe, what danger have you been in since we've been in Okene?'

'It's not that,' she replied. 'Look outside, twenty feet behind us is just... well... emptiness. We can go outside and see three other lonely houses and the roof of the college buildings and all we can hear is a bit of road noise. It's the isolation that worries me. And then there's the town. It doesn't even have a shop with a window, the market has been constructed with kindling and the only place that sells imported food has weevils attached for free.' They both laughed at her remark, which was evidence that they were a little less tense about their circumstances.

'Look, if we get a car in the next few days we can drive down to Benin. It's a huge place with an expatriate club, golf courses... it even has – so I've heard – actual supermarkets with air-conditioning. It's worth driving there just to get cool.' He smiled, hoping for reciprocation.

'I don't like huge!' was her stern response. 'Lagos was huge and that place was created by Dante. I made a decision this morning in the hospital. I'll give it a few more days to see how we fare and if the place is intolerable then we'll go.'

'That's fine with me. Let's just take one day at a time and see how it goes. We have our own place and when we get a car... what a liberation that'll be.'

At that point a vehicle pulled up outside and out stepped a Nigerian dressed in a black suit, *in this weather*, they thought, and sporting the white dog collar of a priest. 'Good afternoon,' he said cheerfully. 'Let me introduce myself, I am Doctor Akinjede and I teach ethics here at FATCO. I am also the college chaplain.' The sun bore down on him. There was a pause and he shifted uncomfortably as the sun changed him from rare to well done. Karl was slow in recognising his discomfort and slow in offering him shade. Anna, being more aware of his discomfort, opened the kitchen screen door and invited him in to the house.

'I will be your next-door neighbour in the next few months.' He looked behind him towards Will Christie's house. 'He will be leaving shortly, so I hear, and I have my eye on it. In fact it has been nearly confirmed by Dr Omega that it will be for my family. I have a wife and two girls. I also have two sons but they are at school and stay with their grandmother in Ilorin.'

'Ilorin,' repeated Karl aimlessly.

'Have you not heard of it? It is the state capital, you will probably get to see it some time.'

He was ushered into the main room where he suddenly went very silent. It was as though he wanted to say something but his vocal chords no longer worked. He made two or three attempts to start a sentence but his tongue temporarily failed him. He looked at the empty box and Anna, thinking she could read his mind, said, 'Oh we'll be getting rid of this later today, that's why the place looks a mess...'

He remained speechless and his head turned slowly from side to side as though he was making a mental inventory. Gazing aimlessly at the ceiling and the silent static fan he thought a little, and then said, 'Do you believe in the devil or will you be coming to church on Sunday to recant?'

His incongruent question left them silent for a second or two, and Karl said, 'Christians... We are not...' He didn't get to finish his sentence. Dr Akinjede turned on his heels, walked out of the house and got into his car. They looked at each other in astonishment. Had they said something to upset him, was their stuttering response about their religious status upsetting? They didn't know.

This wasn't to be the end of their relationship with the Doctor of Ethics.

18

Dr Omega radiated charm and concern as he listened carefully to the outcome of their trip to the hospital, raising his eyebrows when Karl told him they had been advised to keep an eye on the swelling in Anna's feet. He suggested that she should really consider going home to the UK for the birth of the baby. 'Did you tell me when it is due?' he said. 'If you did then I am afraid I'll have to apologise because I have forgotten.'

'The beginning of August,' replied Karl.

'In that case, since term ends the last week of July you should send your wife home. There are relations to help her, I assume?' Karl nodded. 'You could send her home well before term ends and then join her later on.' Karl thanked him for his concern, before idly mentioning that they had received their baggage and were getting settled into the cottage.

'You must have sent it a year ago if it has arrived already. It is excellent that you are so settled so quickly because I need you to be teaching soon,' he said. 'Therefore you will need a ministry car. With luck they will allocate you a Peugeot 504, it might be used, but they run forever and even if it is second hand it will only be a year old, probably handed back in exchange for a new one by some pseudo VIP. I have also got Gabriel to go into town to get a taxi organised to take you to Ilorin tomorrow and you will probably need to stay the night. You know Africa, things don't happen easily, except for the miracle of your bags of course. I'll give you a voucher for a night in the Kwara Hotel.'

Karl instinctively gave an internal groan which registered on his face. Dr Omega couldn't fail to notice and quickly said, 'FATCO has a decent relationship with the Kwara Hotel, I know the manager so you'll be fine. Why don't you take your wife with you? And before I forget, you should use the opportunity to go to the tax office to get a statement, otherwise when we pay you you'll lose a huge amount of your salary.' He paused. 'I have told Gabriel to get the taxi driver to be here outside my office at 7:30 in the morning.'

'Will the taxi driver stay with us?'

'No, no, he'll drop you off at the hotel and come straight back here. To get around when you're there just get one of the taxis outside the hotel. Keep your fingers crossed and you may get a Peugeot 504.'

Karl turned around. Dr Omega's office was like an emergency care unit with people, employees and locals lining the walls waiting to speak to him. *Nothing has changed,* Karl thought, *he's just like a big chief dispensing his justice to all his vassals.*

Sure enough, the next morning at 7:30am the taxi arrived. Punctuality and Africa did not go together in his experience. They had packed an overnight bag and embarrassingly, next to his feet, was a large Calor Gas container the size of a small child. Even though it was empty it was still heavy and awkward to carry. Perhaps he should have tried putting it on his head. Will, his next-door neighbour, had informed him that he must never miss an opportunity to get some gas. He also said that usually when someone went to Ilorin they took it upon themselves to collect the empty gas bottles on campus and swap them for ones that were full.

'You mean to tell me they don't sell gas in Okene!' Karl exclaimed.

Will's response was to be expected. 'Actually, they used to but a couple of thieves broke into the place and fiddled about with the containers whilst having a fag, so one was turned into crispy bacon and the other lost all his hair and the back of his shirt and trousers. He's in prison and the other dimwit was buried. If you go into Okene to the big flat area near the mosque you can see the burnt-out place. Some of the bottles exploded and flew all over the place. Some of my students heard the bangs and explosions and thought the Biafrans were here. It's all part of the rich tapestry of life that is West Africa.' He handed Karl a 20 naira note and said, 'If you find the Kingsway supermarket could you pop in and get some imported toilet paper, I'm sick of having a sore arse... Oh, and a bottle of whiskey.'

To Karl's chagrin, Gabriel was in the taxi. 'Are you coming?' he asked in a slightly contemptuous manner.

'No,' was his abrupt and uncommunicative reply. He ignored Anna and Karl in the back seat and talked to the driver furtively in Yoruba. The taxi, a battered Peugeot 404, stopped in amongst lines of equally battered yellow and purple cars. Suddenly people started getting into the car. Before he knew it there were two huge women clutching baskets and getting into the front passenger seat and another woman clutching a baby and a tethered goat fighting to open Karl's door. Anna, who had left her window open, was fighting with a huge black arm that was trying to open her door from the inside. In the mayhem Karl turned to see that the boot was open and figures just visible between the car body and the boot lid were evidently rummaging around in amongst their bag, a sack of cassava and a big blue Calor Gas canister.

He was having none of this. He had assumed the taxi was for their sole use and now there was a big sweaty arm and a wave of bad breath striving to open a door, and the two women climbing into the seat alongside the driver were big enough to eclipse the sun. They were excited, their flesh vibrated, they were very loud and they wiggled their huge backsides like chickens settling on their eggs to get comfortable on the small front seat. Their bodies spilled all over the front seat and consumed the gear stick which looked as though it would never be seen again. With a surge of strength like Popeye after a jar of spinach, Karl got out of the car, grabbed the driver and shrieked. The driver looked aghast. He obviously had no idea what was wrong until Karl, in very forceful terms, told him that this was their taxi and he didn't want half the population of Okene and a bloody goat sitting on his knee.

Bloody Gabriel, he thought, *time for a bit of revenge.*

It was thirty miles of dangerous strip road from Okene to the next town of Kabba. The driver drove with one arm hanging out of the window and Anna assumed that this was because, in normal circumstances, this car with five seats could accommodate ten passengers and hence there would be no room for another arm. The traffic was light but it was still very un-nerving when he careered towards a slow, dilapidated truck and then overtook it through a barrage of impenetrable red dust and small stones. She almost said another prayer as he performed his overtaking movements time and time again at a fast speed, his car half on the asphalt and half in the ditch.

They finally reached the newly-built main Lokoja to Ilorin road which was blessed with smooth black tarmac. After a quiet mile or so, when they had to slow down to go around a tight bend, they came across a crumpled body stretched across the white line on the road. The driver slowed and veered to the right so as not to hit it, and before he could speed away Karl's natural humanity caused him to grab the driver by the shoulder and shout, 'You have to stop, he may need help.'

'Masta,' he said, 'it is too dangerous to stop, there are too many people nearby.'

'We're in the bloody middle of nowhere, look around, I can't see any people. It's just miles and miles of grass and thorny trees.'

It was then he recalled the consternation and advice of Wellington when they had passed the carnage just outside Okene, which was to ignore the accident and report it to the police if possible.

The new road undulated up and down the small hills and from their summits you could see for miles. The horizon was broken only by huge outcrops of rock as big as council tower blocks, known as inselbergs. They passed very few cars and occasionally saw Nigerians walking in the middle of nowhere, some with enormous loads on their heads and others seeming to be wandering with no sense of purpose. The driver asked if he could stop to pee, giving them time to stretch their legs. They were assaulted by the orchestra of insects and birdsong – buzzing, clicking, whistling, chattering and squawking noises that became an unstructured cacophony. The road was like a long black snake wriggling its way towards Ilorin. To think this was the most populated county in Africa and in the 80 miles of road they had covered since leaving Kabba they had passed through only two small villages, only one of which was big enough to have stalls alongside the road. There was not one petrol station on the 120 miles between Kabba and Ilorin. The heat radiated off the black road surface and from the car, and the engine made ticking sounds as it cooled down. There was a fantastic sense of being the only people in the world and all this was meant for you to explore. 'At one with nature,' was a quote Anna remembered from something she had read.

The city of Ilorin appeared suddenly. There were no very tall buildings revealing its location in the distance and for a city of 250,000 it seemed to be a bigger version of Okene. But it did have a GRA – a government residential area. These were set up by the British years ago to house their officers in planned areas of arboreal splendour and the Kawara Hotel was fortunately apart of the GRA. It had previously been the expatriate club but when the British left, that building and a few cottages alongside it were converted into a small hotel. A seven-storey tower block was then added, and this was the hotel they saw, set serenely in amongst the trees and tended gardens.

To their great relief their voucher for a one-night stay was accepted. The manager, a rather suave, suntanned Italian, offered them a room on the top floor with a view over the gardens or one in the small rondavel in the grounds. They chose the view, collected the key, picked up their overnight bags and pressed the button for the elevator. The doors opened instantly and there, right in front of them, were two rather pale, tired-looking individuals, one of whom seemed to carry in her countenance the worries of the world and the other to be in a state of minor anxiety. The lift was mirrored and the sudden sight of each other, as well as seeing themselves as other people saw them, was quite a visual shock. They said nothing and just looked at each other. The mirror didn't lie. The doors creaked shut, some cogs and wheels and pulleys and cables aching and creaking like an old man. The floor juddered as the lift moved slowly for thirty seconds and then stopped. Weak emergency lights came on, and they were reduced to two shadowy forms.

'Oh my God, we are trapped,' exclaimed Anna. 'Are we still moving?'

'Just our bloody luck.'

'We could be stuck here for hours and I need to pee.'

In normal circumstances Karl would have immediately laughed about it and advised her to cross her legs or stop moaning and get squatting behind a bush, but this was the wrong time to be frivolous. The lights got slightly brighter, flickering between one-matchstick power and painfully dim, and there was some upward glacial movement. The brighter the lights the quicker the lift moved, which meant all they had to do was to be patient and wait until the lift reached the next floor and then push the open button. It took five long minutes to reach it and the lift grated and scraped to a halt. The lights dimmed as he pressed the button. Nothing happened. It was obvious that the doors wouldn't open because of the lack of power. All they could do was to hope the lights brightened when they reached the critical point at the next floor. Karl's fingers tried to prise the doors open but they remained shut and the lift was inert. Cogs above them started to grind, the lights got brighter, he pressed the button and because the lift had gone past the floor, even by a few inches, the doors wouldn't open.

'How much longer, how much longer?' said Anna in a voice tinged with a hint of panic. 'What about the emergency button?' Karl couldn't believe he had overlooked something so fundamentally important. He pressed the button. The result was a squeal of cables and the lift moved, inexorably making its inch-by-inch climb up the shaft. It took twenty minutes to move three floors. Anna was bursting with anger and for the toilet and Karl was livid. He had pressed the emergency button ten minutes ago and there was no sign of help. The lights brightened at the right time and the doors opened. The widening glimmer of light was a delight to behold. As soon as the gap was big enough they were out like a shot, and there in front of them was a uniformed hotel employee.

'My goodness, I have never seen the lift move in the afternoon, how did you get it to work? There is no electricity in the hotel from 1pm to 5pm. I wondered what all the groaning noises were.'

They walked down the four flights of stairs and Anna ran to the ladies' room. The suave Italian said, 'You didn't go on the lift did you? Did you not read the notice?'

'What notice?' said Karl indignantly.

He took Karl by the arm and walked him over to the lift doors. On a grubby piece of paper held up by some yellowing sellotape, a notice said, 'Occasionally the lift can be very slow between 1 and 5 pm. Please use the stairs.'

Karl looked at him and said, 'But I pushed the emergency button.'

'Oh,' he replied.

'What do you mean, oh?'

'I mean the emergency button doesn't work.'

Karl sighed, somewhat aghast. Remember, he said to himself, patience, politeness and persistence. He turned to the suntanned one and said, 'Could we have a rondavel in the garden?'

Before the excitement of collecting their car they decided to call into the tax office since it was close to the Kwara Hotel and on the way to the 'Trusty Garage.' They took the first taxi available and Karl put the ever-present blue gas bottle in the boot.

The tax office had had a former life as the Colonial Administration Office. It was built from imported very suburban British bricks, but was now a little careworn with a few cracked windows in frames that were rusting and had never been meant to cope with the harsh heat and the regular blasts of Harmattan dust. It was chaos. Trying to enter the building up the impressive steps they were assaulted by 'local' tax experts who could guarantee, after a payment of course, that following their advice you would pay little or no tax. They realised that for Nigerians, tax was regarded as optional and something to be avoided on the grounds that they shouldn't pay anything when there was loads of oil revenue. Avoiding tax he found out later was a national pastime for those who had a salary.

They battled their way up the stairs after making an enquiry about where to get the forms. They were taken to an office where a bona fide government tax official would help them fill in their documents, a story they would recount for many years to come.

The tax official congratulated Anna on being pregnant and then asked how long they had been married. The response was seven years. He continued by asking how many other children they had. Karl replied that this was their first one. The reaction was unexpected. He went on to say, 'You have only one child and you have been married seven years. Are you a man?' he said. 'Are you a man without libido?' Karl was struck silent. 'Ah,' he continued. 'I know, they are all at your home in Okene or being looked after in England. You **do** have more children at home?' And with even more emphasis, 'Don't you?'

Anna caught on quickly and recited the names of her sisters and brothers. 'There is Brenda, Kath, Heather, Eric and David and,' patting her stomach, 'another in a few months.' She remembered all of their dates of birth, reciting them efficiently. The tax man winked at Karl and said, 'Ah, I knew a big man like you had plenty of power in his loins.'

'Now, what about your parents at home? I am sure that you look after them and send them money.'

Karl got into the act. He referred to his 'aging 'father but when asked about his mother he couldn't force himself to lie and declare that she was alive. The tax man consoled him and said not to worry, he would make sure he got an extra allowance to help look after his widowed father. It ended up with them having eight dependants who needed their support, and because 'the oil industry should pay all the taxes' attitude, they were told they would be taxed only on 550 naira of their annual salary. Oh, and they would only pay 10% of that 550 because Okene was in a developing region. They had to smile. It was worth having one's sexual performance gently mocked in order to receive such a wonderful exemption. Things could only get better. Now to get their government car, find Kingsway and buy some Calor Gas.

They got back to the taxi remarkably quickly, sat in the back, gave the driver instructions and looked at each other with a mixture of mirth and shock. The driver advised them to get the gas first as the 'Trusty Garage' was a mile or two further on. The taxi stopped at the side of the road near an informal market, where the driver told them that the depot was some 100 yards down a road that he either couldn't go down or didn't want to go down. Karl was sure it was the latter because he had yet to come across a driver who would allow unenforceable rules to stop him from going where he wanted to go and in the direction of his choosing. He got out of the car, struggling to get the canister out of the boot, and told Anna to stay where she was and he would be back in five or ten minutes. She wasn't happy, but Karl soon realised why the taxi driver would go no further. The road was in really bad shape, and the impromptu market had encroached so far onto the tarmac that there was actually no room for any vehicles. He had to admit the market traders would have been very unhappy with a car trying to drive along the narrow strip that remained.

On either side of him was an array of broken shacks, lean-to structures, makeshift tables, rudimentary shelters, and women squatting on the floor protecting their piles of onions, yams, sweet potatoes, trinkets and bric-a-brac under huge colourful golf umbrellas. Behind the makeshift stalls was the communal rubbish dump with children and women pawing through the debris searching for anything that might be of value. It stank. But here and there little tufts of greenery survived. The trees were long gone, having all been consumed for fire wood. One lonely mango tree remained. People fought over its shade and its fruit was on a first come first eaten basis. The romantic view was that this was a colourful and glorious example of third world entrepreneurial skills. To the objective, it was an unhealthy, smelly, asymmetrical mass of humanity: barrow boys, a man dressed in animal skins and trying to sell them, scrap iron merchants, tailors on their treadle machines and men changing discarded tin cans into lamps and cups and bowls. There were sandals made of old tyres, mounds of rubbish, and one enterprising seller of rags had even laid out his wares on a mound of discarded corn kernels in the sunshine. Merchandise of all kinds was strewn on the ground. Clothes donated from charity shops in the UK and Europe ended up here in huge bundles. In amongst the heaps of clothes could be found colourful blouses, perfectly good jeans, even a pair with a 'Super Leeds United 'badge on a back pocket. There were floral dresses, old boiler suits, and shirts that would disintegrate in the first wash. Piles of shoes, like a mine slag heap, varied from huge black wellies to delicate slippers. Finding one thing you liked was all well and good, but the next challenge was to rummage through the pile to find its partner. Traders shouted, and haggled with customers, every little boy had something to sell, and for the second time since they had arrived in Nigeria a puppy was thrust into his face in the hope that he might buy it.

It seemed to be as chaotic as Lagos but didn't have that in-your-face, buy this or get stabbed look. Just as they did in the UK, the traders shouted their inventive jingles, there was an element of fun in the air, and some were dressed up in a mad array of clothes of different colours that couldn't fail to attract attention. There was even a heap of battered old picture frames next to a slaughtered pig, next to dirty bottles of palm oil, next to a pile of dried mice and lizards, next to a man with a compendium of concoctions including recognisable bits of animal that could cure anything. Was this market really less threatening and bellicose than Lagos or was he simply becoming more receptive to the disorder, noise and stink?

He was hot, he was very sweaty and the cylinder was heavy and awkward to carry. He declined help from little boys, holding the cumbersome hunk of metal with one hand and his back pocket and wallet with the other. The hundred-yard-walk left him with a wet shirt and a crotch containing two hot suet dumplings, and a determination to accept some help on the return walk. He cursed as he collected and paid for the full gas cylinder. If he thought the empty one was awkward and heavy, it was nothing compared to the blue piece of metal shaped like some World War Two bomb. He looked around. Where was a boy with a barrow when you needed one? He hoisted it onto his shoulder. A sharp edge made a cruel indentation in his trapezium and a drop of salty sweat dripped into his eye. He cursed again. He managed 25 yards with the handicap on his shoulder until a small school-age boy, seeing a monetary opportunity, offered the service of his barrow. He wanted one naira for a minute's work. One naira was nearly a day's wage, and after Karl had lifted it into the barrow the boy got 20 kobo, a fifth of what he had asked for. He was very happy.

He emerged from the market, damp and red faced. 'Bloody gas bottle!' he said. 'There must be a simpler way of getting it from somewhere closer to Okene. Christ, Ilorin is 120 miles away. It's like lugging a body around.' He was about to go on even longer but his wife smiled and shushed him as she said, 'Look on the bright side, we can go and pick up our car now.'

'Trusty Motors was an unimpressive, single-storey, corrugated iron construction. Under the word 'Trusty' were the words 'Showroom Inside'. The roof was supported by a mixture of wooden poles and pieces of metal, some of which were old railway lines. The poles were conveniently placed so that each pair created a booth for a vehicle. The interior of the garage was quite big but there was only one car in a space that could accommodate about 20. The owner/manager who greeted them was tall and statuesque and elegantly dressed in a brown lace agbada set, the lace being a symbol of his wealth and status. They shook hands and went through various polite and elaborate greetings. After assuring each other that they were in fine health, Karl handed over his set of official documents which were carefully perused by the owner. He made little grunts and groans as he turned the pages and found the official stamp, the final thing he was looking for. He looked Karl straight in the eye. He paused, ruminated, and said, 'I am sorry, you are PEO, and the type of car you want, well, it is just not available.'

'What?' Karl exclaimed, exasperated. He didn't get time to voice a tirade of disappointment. The manager calmly explained the circumstances. 'You are an important man. You are Principal Education Officer, a PEO, and you should have a 504, you know, a Peugeot... A very fine French car. But we don't have one and the next delivery could be two weeks, two months, who knows.'

'What about that car?' said Karl, pointing to the white car behind him.

'Oh no sir, that car is for someone who is only a SEO, a Senior Education Officer. You couldn't possibly want that car; you will be a man of no esteem. You will not look important and if I gave it to you I would be ashamed that it will be a reduction of your big man status.'

'But I'll just have a look at it,' said Karl. He didn't wait for an answer, and he and Anna went purposefully towards the white vehicle. It was a VW Igala. It turned out that igala meant antelope, and to confirm this there was a little chrome prancing deer on the bonnet and tail gate.

'It is too small for you, it is not a car of importance, you can see it is not French, it is made in Brazil, sent here in boxes and put together in Apapa.'

'You mean it is assembled, put together in Nigeria?'

'Yes boss, sometimes they don't do a very good job, forget things you know. But this one is A-Okay, I have driven it.'

Karl got in the car. It smelled like a new car should, pristine, clean and with the smell of vehicular virginity. It was smart inside, had everything a car needs, its engine at the front, not like a VW beetle, and there was a huge amount of space behind the back seats. It was just like a British estate car. 'Look,' he explained to the owner. 'I am entitled to a car. This one is free. Am I right?' The owner nodded in agreement. 'In that case I will take it. I can't afford to be in Okene for a month or even longer without a car. Look at my wife, I need a car to take her to hospital for check-ups and for the birth.'

'So the baby will be born here. Well, that means it will be a Nigerian.'

Anna looked horrified, and Ken cut the topic short by saying, 'Okay, it is not the car I was supposed to get, but this car is perfect. With all that space in the back we can carry the baby in a cot and take her to nursery school when she gets older.'

The deal was done, documents were signed, and a hand-written note stating that Karl was happy with the car was included. The owner nodded to one of his underlings to reverse the car out of the bay. It was at that point when things went rather awry. Two youths scuffled with each other to get in the car and drive it. They shouted wildly at each other, one was firmly pushed away, and the other, – all bluff and bravado, commandeered the driver's seat. The car jerked forward nearly hitting the wall then suddenly came backwards towards them. There was a terrible crunching and grating noise of metal wrestling with metal. As the car went backwards, the side of it glanced against the sturdy vertical railway lines, the outcome of which was the removal of both the back door and driver's door handles. They were left spinning and deformed on the garage floor.

The driver, not quite so cocky, in a swift movement opened the window to lean out to see what had happened. This was a big mistake. Four hands grabbed hold of his hair, ears, neck and shirt and tried to drag him forcibly out of the car window. The width of his shoulders, jammed against the edge of the car window, prevented this from happening. The owner and his formidable foreman were not about to give in. Tightening their hold, they each put a leg against the body work to get extra purchase. It was a little like the birth of a baby. One final push was needed, though the push in this case was a violent pull. His shoulders were released and out he came like a baby whose head had finally cleared the vaginal obstacle. He fell into a helpless lump on the floor, tried to mouth the equivalent of I didn't mean it, and put his hands up like a pleading beggar. The first blow was with a welding rod that bent, the next four or five were blows from a 2 x 1 piece of wood wielded by the owner, followed by his assistant who attacked him this time with a bunch of welding rods. They shouted at the other young man. He dared to answer back and his reward was a monstrous blow on the side of his head from the piece of wood, He collapsed instantly, oozing blood from his head wound. There was lots of shouting. The driver lay on the floor in a foetal position and Karl was handed the wooden weapon and invited to beat him. Needless to say he declined most emphatically.

The owner, after flailing a lump of wood for a minute was sweating and out of breath, and was full of apologies. 'I'll order you a new car immediately and make sure it comes within a month. I will even go to Apapa to collect it myself.' Karl looked at the battered handles on the floor. *Wait for a month or more*, he thought. *The car still drives, I'll order new handles and we'll just have to get used to getting in from the passenger side*. It would be a catastrophe not to have transport. The owner was staggered that they were willing to take the car and Karl had to write yet another note saying he accepted the damaged car and had been a witness to the appropriate punishment.

After listening to a long bout of apologies, he drove the car gently out of the garage. The owner ran alongside and said, 'You need to know how to drive in Nigeria. Remember, you need good brakes, you need a good horn, good luck and the blessing of God.' He stopped and waved them good bye. It wasn't until they got out of the garage and onto the road that Karl noticed the fuel gage was firmly lodged near the empty sign. The garage had no fuel, they didn't sell it, and they were advised to go to the Caltex garage a half mile away, where they were sure fuel would be available. The taxi driver outside was paid off. Karl collected the big blue gas canister, their shopping – including toilet paper and whiskey, and plonked everything in the large space behind the driver's seat. He had his car. It was new. It was damaged and it was running on fumes.

The Caltex garage had one pump and one long rubber hose. There were two lines of cars going in two different directions. A car from one line would fill up and move on, and the same happened in the other line. Karl was about twentieth in line, meaning almost 40 cars would fill up before it was his turn. He just hoped there would be some fuel left. Some cars in both lines were completely empty and had to be pushed. It was the end of the day. The sun would go down in an hour and hopefully the temperature would drop, to be delightfully replaced by nocturnal biting flies.

As they waited they took stock of the day. Get a tank full of petrol and it could be classified as a success. They had their car. Without any duplicity they would pay hardly any tax, the hotel voucher had been accepted and they could look forward to a meal and beer in a decent hotel. They had a huge container of gas, had found a supermarket with half of its shelves full and they had bought soft toilet paper, a bottle of Baileys for Anna, an assortment of British jams, flour, yeast and a huge tin of Nido milk powder. Their final purchase near the counter had been a stick of French deodorant (well that is what it looked like) and a couple of bars of Imperial Leather soap.

The sun was about to create a fabulous sunset. There were three cars in front of them, but an argument had broken out and the garage had temporarily stopped dispensing fuel. It was bad enough that two people were yelling at each other, but an audience soon gathered around. It seemed to be everyone's business. They all had an opinion and each of them wanted to be heard. The driver next to Karl and Anna opened the car door, stood next to his vehicle, and in a deep, sonorous, authoritative voice called for order. He was obviously a man of substance because they looked at him and the yelling stopped. He looked at Karl, let out a deep sigh of resignation, and said, 'Do you know, Nigeria is the fifth largest producer of petrol in the world and it is a disgrace that we have to queue like this. We have all the oil in the world and yet we fight like animals for it. I am ashamed.'

The end of their day in Ilorin was marked with a full tank of petrol, a comfortable rondavel at the hotel, an ice-cold beer and a club sandwich eaten whilst sitting on the bed under the mosquito net. The next morning, following a breakfast where real butter had been served, they navigated their way out of Ilorin in their new, shiny car, albeit one missing two door handles. It was a relief to get out of the city and on to the smooth road to Kabba. They were relaxed as they talked about how, to a certain extent, they had actually enjoyed Ilorin. They talked of the immediate future, although after almost two difficult weeks Anna was still in two minds about whether to pack her bags and go back to the UK. They decided on a wait and see policy. It was obvious they weren't going to replicate the high living standards they had enjoyed in East Africa, but things were getting better. For the first time they really enjoyed the solitude of the countryside, its vastness and excitement, and they enjoyed each other's company. This good feeling lasted until they reached the last half mile of the tarmac before it got to Kabba and changed into a strip road that would eventually arrive in Okene.

There on a bend in the middle of the road was a large object almost hidden by four or five huge black birds. It took them a second to realise what it was. The body they had passed yesterday had been stripped of its clothes and lay naked and hugely bloated from the sun, inflated into an absurd Michelin-man shape. The skin stretched over the balloon-like form and the body was leaking fluids from holes created by the vultures. There were two deep and vacant eye sockets and a toothy grin that seemed to mock the viewers. It was very unpleasant indeed and brought them back to reality with a sickening jolt.

It wouldn't be the only dead body they would see in Nigeria.

19

The work Karl did at the college was quite undemanding. The students were on a one-year Teacher Training course and it was his job to accelerate their teaching abilities with the use of a micro topic scheme. He also had the task, along with a few others, of observing many of the students on placements in nearby rural schools and giving them advice on their communication abilities, organisation and general teaching performance. This meant he was not confined to a classroom and was able to get out and about and see the really rural Kwara State. But a downside of his role was that every six to eight weeks he would be asked to attend a progress meeting at the Federal Ministry of Education. It was not a journey he relished and he pondered on what sort of accommodation he would be given and what impact it would have on Anna should he have to be away from home for three or four days. His first action was to write to Tony to ask if there was any chance of sleeping at his place. A week later the reply was positive.

Tony wrote, *'If you can't give me notice it doesn't matter, just stay anytime you want. And make sure you bring Anna with you. As you will recall, Ikoyi and Victoria Islands are a little less chaotic haven in Lagos. Make sure to remember when you can drive your car into Lagos – even numbers Monday, Wednesday and Friday and odd numbers Tuesday, Thursday and Saturday. Or if you have the wrong number for the day, you can arrive in the city before 6 am or after 7 pm.'*

Micro teaching involved either allocating a topic to the students or asking them to choose a relevant topic that could be taught, explained, and would result in an outcome within ten minutes. The topics they chose would depend, of course, on their intended teaching subject and must also be age-appropriate. There were many universal topics to choose from. One student, who came with a bit of wealth, a big shiny watch and expensive Levi jeans, wanted to teach village kids how to load a film in a SLR camera with a plethora of knobs and dials. It was pointed out that it would be better if they were taught how to cook cassava.

On Karl's first day he worked with a dozen students, all of whom had a great time preparing their 10-minute lessons and delivering them to their peers. The topics ranged from the not-so-useful, like how to make a paper airplane, to what is erosion, what is friction, how to spell ten words ending in 'tion,' or how you get oil out of the ground.

Karl quickly managed to develop a rapport with them, and at the end of a class they wanted to know more about England and how they could get a job there. They were enthusiastic but there was a universal dissatisfied streak running through all of them. They needed little prompting to complain to Karl in the hope that he, as a new and enthusiastic teacher as opposed, – so they said, to the current abject attitude of the faculty, would listen and do something about their concerns.

They told him they were neglected from a teaching/learning point of view. It was here that he had the evidence to endorse their concerns. The demand on his time was very small. He didn't even teach on a Friday and the other four days amounted to about two hours per day and two trips to the semi-built new campus on the Lokoja Road on the other side of town. They explained that many of their teachers didn't turn up for classes, or if they did they were often late, and they would be given some topic to write about which was then graded in a sketchy, subjective way. They resented the fact they had been sent to Okene with its half-finished campus, and they were stuck in makeshift accommodation with no amenities. When asked whether they could be more specific, they went into a bit of a tirade.

No football field, a basketball court with a dangerous surface, one tennis court for 120 students and a tennis court the wrong size that had been so badly built that it was unplayable and cost a staggering 80000 naira, the contract for which had been given to a fly-by-night contractor. But these were minor issues compared to the lack of running water and how they had to shower with reservoir water from a bucket with holes. The food was fine when propane was available, but often it was barely cooked and they had few facilities to enhance their diet because of the poor supply of gas.

'Do you know we had only tomatoes, uncooked onions and peanuts for three days when there was no gas...'

'... And electricity,' someone forcibly added. 'It is hard to study when we are not looked after and are basically unhappy.'

'I know we have our own generator for our power supply but it isn't switched on enough.'

'Surely we are not expected to do assignments by candlelight or to buy our own fluorescent lights with very expensive batteries when the power supply goes off early in the evening.'

'We were promised a fridge for each dormitory. They were paid for months ago, but where are they?'

Karl recalled Dr Omega mentioning the non-appearance of 25 fridges.

They had grounds for complaint and, being new, Karl was a good sounding board, but he could do little about their circumstances other than be sympathetic. At their invitation he went into their living area. It was only 150 yards from his own house and he was quite shocked at the cramped conditions in which they lived and studied. There was little privacy unless you hung up sheets around your bed or, as one student had done, found a battered sheet of ply wood and erected a partition wall. Toilet facilities were overwhelmed and the students, male and female, had designated areas in the surrounding bush in which to perform their daily communal shit.

No wonder they complained, they were all graduates.

There was an inadequate library and it wasn't easy going three miles into town when the FATCO bus had broken down. Their only means of transport was to scrounge a lift from a passing vehicle or wave down a taxi that may just have the room to squeeze in another passenger. 'Just think,' one of them commented. 'If only we had been sent to Yola or Maiduguri. They may be miles away but at least they have a fine, finished, new campus and we wouldn't be treated like kids in a remote rural school where you can't expect running water and power.'

They summoned up enthusiasm for classes and their teaching excursions, but once out of the classroom they seethed with resentment.

Some of them were never going to make it as teachers and that was obvious to Karl in the first few days. This echoed the thoughts of Dr Omega who had commented about the 120 intake. 'Let's observe them and make a judgement about their abilities in the first week, then we will send the 40 hopeless ones home, give some quick advice to the 40 naturals and send them out to teach, and we will keep the remaining 40 and try to make them into teachers.' What the students didn't know was that the Federal Ministry wanted to increase the intake by 25% as quickly as possible.

Even though Karl was shocked by the small teaching demands made upon him, there was a major bonus in that he was able to spend a lot of time giving support to Anna. The car and house helped but she was still basically unhappy about their circumstances – the lack of basic amenities, the remoteness, the lack of sophistication and the fact it was so different from their time in East Africa. Along with most of the expatriates, as well as the black Nigerians (other than the Igbira clan) and the few whites who lived with the Igbira in Okene, she thought that the local people were a miserable lot. They were intensely parochial and largely unwelcoming when it came to anyone who was not local. She tolerated their circumstances but the thought of just packing their bags and leaving was still on her mind.

They had made another trip to the mission hospital in Auchi. Her ankles were still swollen and she had been given some appropriate tablets to take down the swelling. But on the advice of Dr Omega and the hospital medics, they had decided to fly back to the UK for the birth of their baby. Their deciding visit to Auchi was made at the end of May, after only five weeks in Nigeria. A quick look at the calendar meant that in another four or five weeks she could fly home, followed by Karl she hoped, or with luck fly together, so that he could finish the term at FATCO and be home for the birth.

There was still the question of whether she wanted to bring up a tiny baby in the middle of nowhere in fairly arduous conditions and how much longer she felt she could cope with the frustrating day-to-day challenges. It wasn't as though they were on their own. The O'Driscolls were helpful and friendly, as was David Jackson two cottages away. He had spent a lot of time in West Africa and was well acclimatised and at ease with life in Okene. A frustration for him only resulted in a resigned shrug of the shoulders. He would often sit and read under a huge umbrella outside his kitchen door, or he would wander into the bush and spend an afternoon reading under the shade of a tree. He gave sensible advice and had a non-alarmist attitude to conditions at the college. All was not doom and gloom for him. He used his considerable free time to write or to spend time with his live-in driver, who drove his Renault like a mad man. You could always tell when David's driver was at the wheel by the fact that he drove too fast and always had the emergency flashing lights on. David was a fine host, generous with his alcohol and always interesting to listen to. He would lean forward over the table, revealing his thinning hair and peering over his small glasses when he wanted to make a point. However, he rarely associated with the BICC workers who congregated on the roof of the Paradise Hotel three or four times a week. He didn't appreciate their sense of humour and their constant flood of jibes about Nigeria.

Karl and Anna enjoyed an hour or so on the roof of their former residence with Trev and Jim and the ingenuous Mattie, Jack and Mary, Colin and Cindy, as well as Will Christie before he left for good. Mattie was rather odd. He had a vacant look about him. Evidently he was fearless when climbing up the huge electricity pylons BICC were erecting. He seemed to relish the dangerous work and hanging onto a steel cable over 100 feet above the ground was not an issue for him. He worked hard, the heat never bothered him, and as long as he had a few beers at the end of the day and a meal made ready by the camp cook he was happy. Karl really thought Mattie had no idea where he was. Yes, he knew he was in Africa in a country called Nigeria, but he was unsure of where it was exactly in the world and had no idea where Okene was in Nigeria. Nor did he know what was going on in the world. He just arrived on a flight, was collected and taken to some remote place and asked to connect transmission lines some 150 feet above the ground. Before the BICC workers abandoned their camp and moved on to set up another, Karl and Anna got to know him better. He was a man of few words, but in a few cathartic moments he revealed that he had once been married and had an eight-year-old daughter, and one of his pleasures in life was to receive a letter from her that she had secretly written to him.

Anna barely touched alcohol now that she was pregnant, but there were times of frustration that would drive her to drink. 'A bloody blocked up water filter again and I'm the one who has to remove the slime from the damn thing,' she would yell. Sometimes the only thing that could calm her down was a glass of wine (from a bottle bought 120 miles away at the Leventis Supermarket in Benin). She put up with Nigeria, but had Karl not been around so much to give her support she would, by her own admission, have been on a flight home. Now that the decision had been made to fly back for the birth she felt as though she could manage for the remaining few weeks. As long as there was water delivered and the electricity was on when it was supposed to be, she tolerated it.

It had taken Karl nearly three weeks to sort out how to make their water supply easier to access. Outside the house, some four or five feet from the kitchen door, was a 400-gallon galvanised iron water tank. The problem was that it was on the ground and when Karl was not there to help, Anna had to stand on a chair and lean over the tank with a bucket to get water. It was just okay when the tank was full but as the water level went down she would have to lean further and further into the tank, causing her a lot of frustration and discomfort. What they needed was a tank with a tap at the bottom and some supports to raise it off the ground.

When Will Christie's contract ended and he had left to fly home to be with his wife and daughter, Karl immediately decided to requisition his water tank which had the luxury of a tap. He had to be quick. It was no easy matter. The logistics were worrying. He had to do it before the next tenants arrived. The plan was to empty Will's tank sufficiently of water to ensure he had the strength to drag it 50 yards down the small gradient to his house, which would also mean the same thing happening when he dragged his own tank the 50 yards up to the empty cottage. They would also have to wait nearly five days for the water tanker to come around and give them their weekly ration of 400 gallons, so they stored as much water as they could in pans and buckets, supplementing it with a few journeys made to their old tank outside Will's former house. Karl just managed to complete the laborious exchange before Dr Akinjede and his two daughters took up residence there.

Unfortunately, the acquisition of the less battered, partially filled tank with a tap had now exposed another problem. It had to be raised off the ground and put on breeze blocks to a height that enabled a bucket to be placed under the tap so it could be filled without them having to go through the ordeal of leaning over the rim. With the aid of his wife, a lot of tipping and shoving, some elementary physics like a fulcrum and an hour's struggle, the partially filled tank was raised some 18 inches off the ground and all they needed to do was to try and make the small amount of dirty brown reservoir water last the next few days. Even though the clandestine removal and replacement of the tank had made life a little easier, when Anna realised they would have to carefully ration the water she let her frustrations temporarily overwhelm her. With a shaking head, hands on hips and a few stomps, she let Karl and every other living thing near the cottage know how she felt.

'Oh yes, thank you for a tap, a bloody tap that's virtually on the sodding floor.' He tried to interrupt. It was a bad move. 'But it doesn't solve the fact that all we have is about a foot of filthy water. Great for the complexion, great for keeping clean, great for cooking. The toilet will stink even more, we will end up eating uncooked food... Fresh fruit is all well and good but it needs washing because everything here is covered in crap, and it has to be washed with what looks like bloody mud. You think you solved one problem but you've created another. I don't want to live here like some bushman. I didn't come to Africa to live in a place where I can't keep clean, what about hygiene!'

Her torrent of words dried up and she stood and cried. All he could do was put his arms around her, make sure he said nothing and hope the physical contact would give her a little reassurance that he cared and understood what she was going through. It was not the only outburst over the next few weeks. Karl grabbed the two five-gallon plastic containers, went to Jack's house, and while their water was turned on he got ten gallons of water that was actually transparent.

During the first few weeks it had not all been anguish. They appreciated the silence. In the afternoon or early evening they would take little walks away from their house onto some of the dirt tracks and sit on a rock in silence, enjoying a world without noise of people or traffic. They enjoyed those peaceful moments in the midst of countryside that was actually beautiful. There was the gentle swishing of the grass, the susurration of the leaves on the trees, the hum and whine of insects and the chatter of birds. What is more, most of the views were wonderful and Karl could imagine the English romantic poets being inspired by the whole ambience of the place. There were no regimented fields with organised rectangles of green crops, but there was a plethora of exotically-shaped trees adorned with leaves as large as umbrellas and aromatic, some as small and shiny as a stickleback and others full of aggressive yet edible thorns. Here they came across small areas of tilled ground tended by a lone farmer growing a few maize plants. The hills that encircled them cried out for exploration.

One afternoon after a short walk, as they turned to go home they heard the almost oriental sounds of bells ringing. As they got closer to the line of four cottages, they saw above the tall grass the massive horns of cattle which were being tended by the nomadic Fulani tribe. The cows were huge and white and the young men were tall and elegant. Each of them carried a very long stick to guide their cows, as well as a sword in its scabbard or a seven foot spear. They wore something similar to a Roman tunic, they all carried a small leather water pouch around their necks and all of them wore a distinctive woven conical hat. The cows had surrounded their house and that of the Brights. They were close enough to touch. The close proximity was a reminder that here in Africa there was little concept of personal space and there was certainly no curtilage around their house. The cattlemen realised that access was being blocked to the house of the oyibos and gently moved the cows on, leaving behind shorter grass and some piles of dung that were already being eyed by the waiting flies. It was at times like these that they silently appreciated the help they were giving to one another.

Karl enjoyed the regular trips he made to see and assess his students' teaching abilities, although he felt guilty about doing so. He rarely had to travel more than 100 miles, though on a couple of occasions he had visited a huge school in Benin which presented him with the opportunity to buy some proper bread from the Leventis supermarket and make a quick dash along the aisles to see if there were any other gastronomic luxuries he could take home. Apples were one such delight, as was a jar of Bisto gravy and some soft oval rice which looked as though it would make a perfect rice pudding.

His first visit was to St Joseph's, a huge Roman Catholic school which had been built in the early 1900s, to see a student called Ebor. They both stood on the balcony outside the classroom, initially to discuss Ebor's performance and that of his pupils, and in mid-conversation their eyes turned to the break-time football match taking place below them. Even someone with no love of sport would have appreciated what they were watching. The players seemed to be between 10 and 12 years old, and, for identification purposes, the players in one team were wearing a red ribbon around their waists. A slight young man on the halfway line, with his back to the goal, received the ball. Finding himself trapped with nowhere to go, he was challenged by two larger opponents. What occurred next was a mixture of art, ballet, gymnastics, athleticism and magic. He swayed one way and the other without touching the ball and the two defenders, falling for the feint, only managed to kick one another. Another swift turn, and with the ball seemingly stuck to his bare feet he was confronted with another defender who, unfortunately, was standing with his legs slightly apart. It was perfect for a nutmeg and that is exactly what happened. As he moved elegantly towards the goal he left another player on his backside in the dust by pushing the ball past his left side whilst running around him to the right. With the goalmouth in sight he stepped over the ball and performed a move that Karl later discovered was known as a rainbow: with his instep and heel he flicked the ball over his head in a glorious arc and as it reached knee level he volleyed it into the net.

His skill was quite breathtaking. His team jumped all over him as the opponents sat in the dust looking bemused. Ebor looked at Karl as he said, 'That was no fluke, he plays like that all the time. He plays for the under-16 team and he's only 11. All the local teams are watching him. Can you imagine how good he would be if he had shoes, or even boots?'

'Do you know his name?' asked Karl.

'I don't know, but I'm sure I can find out if you wish. Why do you want to know?'

'He is brilliant. That really was the most astonishing 10 seconds. My local town's team in England could do with that sort of talent, in fact a tenth of that talent. I might just write to them and tell them about this "wonder kid" I have just seen.'

Karl's jaw dropped as they continued to watch him for a while longer. The boy's skill level did not drop. He was half the size of some of the opposition but time and time again he left them for dead. Karl was staggered by his skill. He was brave, he could pass the ball accurately, and he had the natural ability to run into the space where he could cause the most damage.

'I'll get his name for you,' said Ebor.

But nothing materialised, and Karl's time at the school was about to end. He never did push Ebor for the boy's name. He meant to do something about it later and didn't. He meant to write to the school and didn't, and many times he wondered what had happened to that little maestro with the ball and the swerve. To think that he could have discovered another George Best.

Another visit involved one of his trainee teachers called Belinda. His morning at the four-room mud and corrugated iron-built school had been excellent. Belinda was one of the 'top third' students, as described by Dr Omega; she possessed such natural talent that after a couple more weeks' training she could easily be placed in a school in the knowledge that she was a 'natural' and would fit in wherever she went. He had watched her most of the morning. There was little cause for him to interrupt to give discreet advice and so he just sat and enjoyed her consummate communication skills. She radiated enthusiasm and the pupils responded by hanging on to her every word and gesture. Her micro topic was for them to describe and then write creatively about what they did when they got up in the morning. She acted out the parts, showing them her morning rituals. She made them laugh, she kept their attention, and after the first ten minutes the kids couldn't wait to describe what they did when they got up in the morning. Later, many of them read out what they had written. Karl found it quite humbling to hear that they might have to walk a mile to get water before breakfast. Sometimes there was no breakfast before school. Some of them had to jog three or four miles to get to school, all the while clutching a treasured pencil and notebook. Assessing Belinda was easy. Apart from accolades he could barely think of a word of advice to give her.

It put him in a good mood for the journey back to Okene. He needed to write a short glowing report, he had finished early, and he would try the short cut home. The chosen road turned out to be an ordeal of his own making. He took a corner too fast, failing to avoid a large protruding rock in the road and, with a mighty sound of stone being dragged over metal, the back end of the exhaust was ripped off and left dangling on the rough road.

He stopped to examine the damage and waited for the expected hordes of people to materialise from the bush. He stood alone under the unwanted company of shafts of hot sunlight which felt like daggers in the lack of shade in this rocky environment. His plan of action, after lying underneath the car to observe the damage, was to remove the exhaust or to try to fix it back on. With a roll of galvanised wire in the boot and some basic tools, including an essential pair of pliers, he was sure he could create enough wire loops to hold the exhaust to the bottom of the car.

The only problem was that he needed three, perhaps four, hands to do what was necessary, and there was still no sign of pedestrian help, and a total absence of passing vehicles. He contemplated just driving on until the part fell off but decided against it, worrying that if the car hit another rock the exhaust could be ripped from the engine block. Dust and sweat were firmly attached to his good trousers and professional shirt. The sun actually hurt and the sweat rolled in salty rivers into his eyes. He opened the car door, on the passenger side of course, and sat half-in and half-out of the car, feeling disconsolate and pondering how he could grow another hand.

Help came around the corner of this unfrequented road in this desolate part of Nigeria. A scruffily-dressed old man appeared, bearing a resemblance to John the Baptist's father. He was as old and as textured as a gnarled tree and positively antediluvian. He walked slowly with the aid of a large pole and when Karl greeted him he replied in a language Karl definitely hadn't heard before. Like a good Samaritan, with gestures, a brown toothy smile and positive sounds, he made it apparent that he was willing to help. Alas, it was obvious that the last time he had washed was many months ago. Not only did his stained, stiff clothes smell awful but he was also surrounded by a blur of black flies, some of which had settled on the back of his possibly formerly white shirt, in long writhing black stains. The smell caused Karl to recoil and had the power to make his eyes water.

Trying to hold his breath, he jacked up the car and mimed what he intended to do using the galvanised wire. The old man bent down, taking an age to get on one knee, and then wriggled painfully slowly underneath the car. His movements were punctuated with grunts and groans, and the thought crossed Karl's mind that the old man might never get out from under the car and he would be left with a corpse on his hands. They were both on their backs, grovelling in amongst the dirt, dust and stones, and it took them 30 minutes of sweaty discomfort before they managed to fix the beaten-up exhaust to the chassis of the Igala.

It was then that Karl realised he was faced with a dilemma. The odorous old man was obviously travelling somewhere and he could hardly leave him at the side of the road now that his stiff, filthy clothes were covered in red dust and a further soaking of perspiration. He was of course very grateful and needed to show it by offering him a lift. He got in the front passenger seat, shuffled across to the driving position and beckoned the old man, who unfortunately brought the cloud of fat, black house flies with him into the car as he sat down. Karl drove tentatively to avoid damaging the exhaust again, but even with the windows wide open the flies remained loyally attached to their pungent friend. The old man sat in the front seat with his large pole sticking out of the window, leaning forward so he could feel the hot wind on his crumpled face. The flies stayed where they were. After 20 extremely smelly miles he was dropped off at the village of Ososos and given a 5-naira note for helping. His smile and gratitude were so genuine that for a moment the smell almost disappeared. Karl arrived home later than expected and was quizzed by his wife about why he was so filthy and smelled so bad. It was a long story that had them laughing.

On another occasion Karl was driving home from a small town in the hills, and just before he got to the Niger valley and the town of Lokoja he came to a small village picturesquely set amongst some dramatic rock formations. A dwelling close to the road in the shade of a rocky outcrop displayed a notice temptingly offering 'Cold Beer Here.' He stopped the car. Should he or shouldn't he? If it was really cold then it would be worth it, but a cold beer in the bush usually meant it had been kept in the shade and was close to the temperature of a cup of tea, though it might have been cooled by immersion of the beer bottle into water in a porous pot, the water staying cool due to evaporation. He went in and to his pleasure he really did find a cold beer, the owner proudly showing him his paraffin fridge. With a wonderful hissing sound, the bottle of Crystal beer was opened and his hands luxuriated on the cold glass that was instantly covered in condensation.

With beer in hand he wandered over to the door and looked out over the sunlit dirt road below. There were mud and wooden buildings sprawling along either side of it and he was reminded of a dusty American cowboy town out West, missing only the tumbleweed.

'Masta, masta!' A cry interrupted his thoughts. He turned to see what the owner wanted.

'Masta, do you like rabbit?'

'Do you mean do I like rabbits or do I like to eat rabbit, which one is it?'

'Rabbit is very good chop, very liked here in Nigeria.'

Before Karl answered he tried to think of when or where he had ever seen or heard of rabbit for sale, either as a pet or as a meal. He had never seen one running across a road despite spending lots of time on quiet, bumpy country roads.

'Are you sure you have a rabbit?'

'Yes, it has rabbit's teeth.' He gave a demonstration with two fingers near his mouth showing that it had the typical buck teeth of a rabbit. 'Yes, it was caught in a net coming out of its hole and is still very alive and is very good eating. You could make a rabbit pie, that is a white man's meal isn't it?'

'Well yes,' said Karl, but before he could say any more, the owner said, 'I will get it for you.'

'Wait, just wait, did you say this rabbit is alive? Because if it is alive and is a rabbit, are you prepared to kill it and skin it for me?'

'Oh yes, it is without a problem.' He turned to look behind him and grabbed a huge knife from the shelf and started waving it about. 'It will die very quickly.' And before Karl could respond he disappeared into the back of the bar. This gave Karl time to think. Did he really want a rabbit? Would his wife actually help him eat it? Did he want to stand here and watch it being butchered? Did he want to drive home with a carcass on the back seat? No, he thought, I'll give the rabbit a miss. His father, had he been here, would have bought it in a shot, peeled a few onions and had it in a pie or a stew. It was one of his favourite dishes.

With lots of huffing and puffing the bartender struggled through the doorway into the bar. He was awkwardly carrying a cage the size of a small armchair and with a final grunting display of strength he lifted it on to the bar. He stood and looked at Karl, spreading his arms as though presenting a superstar, and said, 'Rabbit.' It was the biggest rabbit Karl had ever seen. It was a monster. It had fur. It had the prerequisite buck teeth, it had a tail, but there the resemblance ended. The tail was hairless and 18 inches long, and through the bars of the wooden cage stared the biggest, most monstrous, fearsome 'rabbit' he had ever seen. It looked as though, if it got out, it would tear him apart. Without its tail it was about three feet in length and the bloody thing had claws.

His bottom jaw dropped. He took a step backward. He forgot the beer in his hands as he struggled to say a simple sentence. 'That's not a rabbit, it's a bloody rat!'

'No masta, this is a rabbit, a very fine rabbit.'

'It's a bloody rat, a huge bloody rat.'

'But rabbit is good eating, really good eating, you agree?'

'Yes, I agree, but it isn't a rabbit!'

The 'rabbit' was getting irritated and thrashed about, shaking the cage in an attempt to escape. There, in front of Karl, was not the furry little tail of a bunny rabbit but a tail like a bull whip which was agitating wildly from side. 'It will stop moving when I kill it,' the bar owner said as he picked up the knife. 'How much will you give me for this tasty rabbit?'

'Once and for all, it's not a rabbit, it is a bloody big rat. I don't eat rat, I've never seen a rat this big and I don't want you to kill it, I just want to finish my beer.'

The barman looked disconsolate. He couldn't understand why the white man was not more appreciative and it seemed as though he wasn't going to get any money for the monster in the cage.

The so-called rabbit was actually a cane rat, and this particular one was a normal size. If caught they were classed a real delicacy and were an excuse for a feast.

Karl was still in a state of shock as he left the bar, carrying a vision of two huge gleaming teeth trying to eat their way out of the cage. If he told Anna about his encounter he doubted she would believe him. 'Rabbit!' he mumbled as he left the bar. He laughed to himself and then smiled when the barman shouted after him. 'I'll give you a very good price.'

20

Karl's work at the college required him to make the 15-mile round trip to the Lokoja Road campus at least twice a week. The problem he faced was to do with the over-manning of the police force and the government's inability to pay them enough or even on time. On the short drive into Okene, just before the town started to become built-up, was the police headquarters building on the left hand side of the road. By Okene standards it was a rather elegant, very long bungalow with a wonderful shady verandah wrapping itself right around the structure. However, whenever he drove past on college business or with Anna for a trip to the market in town, the railings and steps were festooned with uniformed police in various stages of repose. There they were, neatly dressed in their sharply creased khaki shorts, long woolly socks and khaki shirts with lots of pockets, but each of them was in a state of serious relaxation. Most of them were asleep, which prompted a comment from the Brights that, 'the Okene police could fall asleep on a clothesline.'

With the government trying to spend its huge quantities of oil wealth on creating jobs, the police force – one of the sections designated for enhancement – had become massively over-staffed. The employees reported for work and then sat or lay around waiting for something to happen. If indeed an emergency did arise there were always plenty of personnel to help, but unfortunately there was no transport for them. One could imagine some disaster a few miles away and an army of heavy-booted, sleepy policemen jogging earnestly to the site of the disaster, arriving worn out and soaked in sweat. So they were inert, mostly horizontal, underemployed, bored, underpaid, and often had to wait for their wages.

However, in order to supplement their incomes the police had decided they should extract money from the local communities and in particular its drivers. During the last few days of the month, when money was short, they would set up 'security' road blocks and once someone was stopped it was irrevocable that at least one law had been broken, such as a car without lights or the all-important horn deemed as inefficient. This resulted in a relatively small amount of money changing hands, but it wasn't the real issue. Disturbingly, the policemen, now flush with cash, would spend it on beer or palm wine and the effects of bravery induced by the alcohol caused them to frequently become very unpleasant and threatening.

The teachers at FATCO were of course wise to this, and Jack and Mary had shown Karl an awful dirt road that skirted the town and came out on the Lokoja Road past the road blocks. Whenever there was a torrential downpour the road became impassable for a few days and there was no alternative but to go on the main road through town. The general advice when dealing with road blocks was to go armed with a few small notes to pay the police before they tried to extricate larger amounts.

At the grocery shop in Okene, Anna was quite shocked that Karl bought three packets of the cheapest cigarettes he could find. To his list he added a packet of boiled sweets and a six-pack of imported beer, although it was a five-pack because one had actually been consumed by someone unknown and it took Karl a few minutes to convince the owner that the pack should consequently be cheaper.

'What is all this in aid of?' asked Anna. Joking with her he said, 'There are times in life when one's progress in the world needs a little oil on the wheels. You don't have to drive the journey to the new campus three times a week.'

'What?' she interrupted. 'You mean to tell me about how arduous it is having to drive 12 or 15 miles.'

'No, just listen. It is all to do with the fact that the poor police get paid monthly and sometimes their money is late, but most of the time, when the last few days of the month arrive they have no money at all and that's when there are road blocks where they gently, so I am told, try to extract a little dash from everyone they stop. I have been informed that it is much easier to comply than to refuse.'

'You mean bribery.'

'Well yes, but on a small scale. I suspect the refusal to hand over a 'gift' could result in fabricated charges of bad driving, a faulty car etcetera, and therefore you end up paying more. And evidently they can get a little scary, so I have been told, if they are drunk or if you don't hand over a little donation.'

'That is so wrong.'

'I agree, but the cost is small and most of the time a cheery smile and a couple of fags works and you are on your way.'

In his second month working in Okene he was used to avoiding the road blocks, but when the bush road wasn't passable he found that a big smile, a bit of banter, a warm beer or a few naira would send him on his way. Today however, there were not only plebeian policemen manning the road block but also an officer who was rather smartly uniformed. He was obviously in charge and seemed to warrant real respect from his minions. He came over to Karl's car. He looked at the damage on the two doors and the lack of door handles and said, 'Was this the result of an accident?'

'Yes,' replied Karl.

'I take it that you reported the accident to the police.'

'Well, no actually, but the accident happened some time ago in Ilorin.'

'But did you report it to the police?'

'No,' he replied in a weak voice.

'Do you know it is an offence not to report every accident, no matter how small?'

Karl was about to try and make a hopefully funny comment like there wasn't enough paper in Nigeria to report every car accident, but thought better of it and kept his mouth shut.

'Could I see your driving licence please?'

Karl fumbled in his back pocket, extracted his wallet and showed the officer a pink piece of folded paper. It was his UK driving licence.

'Where is your Nigerian licence?'

'I was going to get one this week, but...'

The police officer looked at him firmly and said, with a very stern look in his eye, 'You were on the way to the Lokoja driving test centre weren't you?'

A bit of confusion washed over him but trickled away as the officer in charge repeated the words, 'Weren't you?' even more firmly.

'Oh yes, that's where I was going, I was just on my way.'

'Good,' was his reply. 'I have noticed you a few times coming through this police check and I think it is about time you took your driving test in Lokoja. Do you know it is against the law in Nigeria to drive with a foreign licence?'

'No about the licence, and yes, I'm off for my test in Lokoja.'

'And just to make sure that you do as you say, I will inform these policemen that you should be detained if you don't have a proper licence, not a foreign one, on your return journey.'

Karl expelled a lot of relieved air and was about to drive on, when the officer said, 'You will of course be making a donation to the funds of the police football team. Let's say 20 naira.'

Apart from the odd naira or packet of cigarettes or the odd pack of beer, Karl had to pay out his first dash. He was glad he had enough fuel to drive the extra 40 miles to Lokoja. He would miss his two classes but told himself that he had no choice and as for his absence, well everyone missed classes.

He found the driving test centre. It consisted of a rusting shipping container. Situated next to it was an old British caravan, laughably with the word sprinter written on the side. Its colours were faded and stained with mould. Even though it was askew and the tyres were flat, out popped a man in a green uniform who was evidently the driving licence tester. He pointed out the area where the test would take place, a small area of flat land devoid of tarmac. Some lines had been drawn into the dirt with what seemed to be tar and here and there were some bent and faded traffic cones. One especially was smashed and distorted to the point where it was barely recognisable as a cone. *Typical of Nigerian driving,* he thought.

So what does he want me to do, he thought, *drive around a few cones, perhaps show him I know where the reverse gear is and of course I must remember to reveal the importance of the horn.*

The driving licence tester gestured with a sweep of his arm. 'This is where you will take your test...' He paused, looked at Karl and gave a wise and knowing smile, before concluding, '...But you will fail!' Karl was astonished at the remark.

'You do not look like a good driver,' he went on to say. 'I know who will pass or fail, and you look like a failure to me.' Karl was not having this. He got out of the car and was immediately hit by the sunlight. From his back pocket he took out his wallet and brandished his folded pink UK driving licence. The instructor scrutinised it, stuck out his bottom lip, rocked his head from side to side a little as though he was weighing up his thoughts and said, 'But this is a British licence.'

'Yes, and I am just trying to show you... Did you see it on the licence?'

'What?'

'It says I have been driving for many years, in fact over ten, and I have driven in East Africa.'

'Yes, but this is Nigeria, it is tough to drive in Nigeria, driving is different here, you have to be quick and skilful, know how to use the horn, carry heavy loads. Your licence is no good here and I don't think you will pass.'

'But I have been driving for ten years!'

'But this is not England, this is Nigeria where only special people are good drivers.'

At this point Karl had to work hard to keep his mouth shut. He was dying to give his personal opinions about the chaos on the roads, the ignorance of the driving laws, the incompetence, the danger and the fact that within their first hour in Nigeria he and his wife had been in a car accident in which their taxi nearly overturned. He remembered the threat made by the police officer that he was not to be allowed through the road block and would be detained unless he had a Nigerian licence. Was he going to follow it through? Would he even be there? Would he actually give his minions instructions to stop him? If he went through with his threat and Karl arrived back from Lokoja without a licence, what would be the consequences?

'But I really need a licence. I really want to be as good a driver as Nigerian drivers, so I would really like it if you would let me take the test.'

How hard could it be, he thought, *driving around a few cones?*

'I am sorry,' the driving test instructor said. 'I have a very important family party to organise, I am too busy now so come back tomorrow.'

'But I really need Nigerian documentation today.'

The instructor didn't seem to be listening. He continued to moan about all his problems and how hard it would be to solve them, muttering loud enough for Karl to hear. 'It is my youngest son's birthday, all his friends from the Ali Akbar school are coming and how am I going to feed them all, where am I going to get all the drink I need?' He looked Karl in the eye and said sadly, 'My salary is very small and I have seven children and they are very costly and then there is the party at the weekend and...'

Karl interrupted him. 'Is there anything I can do to help?'

He rubbed his chin thoughtfully and said, 'A case of beer would help.'

'How much is a case?'

'Just 20 naira.'

The note was handed over. The instructor put his hand in his back pocket. He took out a green piece of paper, asked Karl to turn around and placed the paper on his back, flattening it out with the palm of his hand. He felt a wriggly motion and a little pressure and was then presented with a green piece of paper that had been stamped and signed.

'Don't forget to write your name in the empty space,' Karl was told, as the instructor walked away looking very pleased with his 20 naira note.

There was no road block when he drove back.

21

Following two further visits to the mission hospital in Auchi, they had been given firm advice by the mid-wives that it would be far safer for Anna to give birth in the UK. Although they were very confident about bringing into the world any baby without complications, they thought that pre-eclampsia could present unnecessary risks. Karl immediately spoke to Dr Omega about this, telling him he would need to return to the UK with his wife for the birth. The Doctor lifted up his rotund face and stared at Karl as though he was mad. 'Look Karl,' he said, 'pre-eclampsia or whatever you call it is not an issue. Personally I think you were mad, as do many of your colleagues, black and white, for even thinking about using the hospitals here. I am saying nothing against Auchi mission hospital, but quite frankly...'

He paused for a moment and thought before he went on. 'You might have been okay if you had been in Kano or Enugu or Kaduna or Ibadan and even Lagos – though that's if you could have got near the hospital through the traffic. At least they are teaching hospitals with lots of top Nigerian doctors and expatriates. But yes, you must go home to UK. I can't think of anything more important in the life of a family other than looking after the family. When do you need to fly?'

Karl was quite relieved to hear Dr Omega's positive response. In all of Karl's dealings with him he had been a beacon of common sense and understanding. 'We hope to leave about two weeks before the end of term, say mid-July,' he said. He looked at the Doctor's friendly face as he raised his chin and ruminated.

'End of term, end of term.' He paused. 'I am sorry, that is the time... You know, final exams, marking, grading etcetera... It's when I need you most.'

Karl wanted to interrupt to try and plead a case for a problem he had never thought of, but Dr Omega held up his arm as if to silence the words he was about to speak. He said, 'It is mid-June now, by the time I write to the ministry to get you a travel voucher, even if they were willing to give one, it could be September before they get around to saying yes or no and releasing the funds. You see, you are not entitled to free flights to the UK until your mid-contract leave which is next April, am I right?'

The normally loquacious Karl was never at a loss for words, but at that response the good doctor's office seemed to become even hotter as he thought of the ramifications. A lazy fly also felt the heat as in slow motion it bashed itself against a window. There was a short silence as Dr Omega tried to point the fan in his direction as though he felt Karl's discomfort. The blast of slightly cooler air (thankfully it was before 10am and the generator was still working) prompted his idea. 'Couldn't we bring forward our mid-contract flights to July and then next year when we are due for leave pay for them ourselves?'

Further ideas were bounced around before they came to the conclusion that even the Federal Ministry of Education would not be sensible enough to pay for and bring forward their mid-contract leave, but as Dr Omega constantly pointed out, such was the way the ministry administration worked, and the travel vouchers may not appear until well after the baby was born.

The solution was that Karl and Anna would pay for the flights, which would mean a drive of 120 miles to Benin City, the nearest place that had something resembling a travel agent, to buy tickets to the UK. Unfortunately Karl couldn't go until the end of term. Cost was not an issue. They were paid quite well and with little to spend their money on, other than petrol and food, they had more than enough money to cover the cost. The plan was hatched. They would have a day visit to Benin to buy the tickets, and to save changing planes at the time of departure they would travel by car to Lagos and Anna would be able to take a direct flight. Karl would follow two weeks later. The big bonus to the pair of them – and it was Dr Omega who mentioned it first – was that at least they wouldn't have to fly with Nigerian Airways because by paying for their own tickets they could pick and choose the carrier.

The deal was done. A day in Benin to buy the tickets, the nearest place that had a shop with a glass window, or a place that resembled a supermarket, or that was connected to the national grid or had a car showroom or traffic lights or a roundabout for that matter or a semi

179

functioning phone system. They would fly British Caledonian Airways there and back and Karl would fly from Benin to catch the BCal flight at a later date.

The trip to Benin was fruitful, although when they found the travel agent they had to double park and pay for a little boy to guard their car. It was his job to yell if someone tried to steal it and if you were naive enough not to offer him a naira then an unfortunate scratch or flat tyre could be the result when you returned. Good old capitalism! It was also sensible, if possible, to leave your windows open when parking a car, otherwise on return the vehicle would masquerade as a small kiln and nearly scorch your eyebrows when the door was opened. It was sensible economics. He paid for the airline tickets in cash, and to his surprise some months later, as Dr Omega had promised, they received a refund from the Federal Ministry of Education.

Their plan was for Anna to stay with her mother when she got back to the UK, and when Karl got home and the baby had arrived they would stay with his dad. They wouldn't be able to phone each other as it would entail a round trip of 240 miles to the post office or the Plaza hotel in Benin City and anything up to an hour to get a connection. Phoning was not cheap. Anna would only know what flight he would arrive on.

Two weeks later they left Okene for Anna's journey to the UK. Their drive to Lagos had been cleverly planned. After 300 miles of travel on dirt roads, strip roads and the new Benin to Ibadan motorway, they arrived on the outskirts of Lagos around 6.00pm. They went to the Ikeja Airport hotel to have a quick drink and to wait until 7pm when the traffic eased and they would be able to drive their car with 'odd' number plates into the city. Anna's flight was on the Sunday when the traffic in Lagos was only marginally congested. It also gave them the opportunity to stay on Victoria Island with their old friend Tony. He hadn't minced his words when they told him the birth of their first child was originally planned to take place in Nigeria. Like Doctor Omega and many others, he had thought they were mad.

Tony was wiry with protruding eyes and a sharp, cleaver-like nose. He looked as though he could peck you to death and reminded Karl of a Marabou stork. He could eat for England. He had an infectious sense of humour based on cutting remarks about life rather than jokes. He laughed a great deal and when it came to alcohol he had hollow legs. Karl and Tony and their respective wives had been good friends in Kampala and though Tony didn't play rugby or football (he thought the former was for gays –

'too much squeezing and hugging and fun in the showers for my liking,' he had said), he did play a mean game of squash and was a half decent golfer. Every sentence he uttered revealed his strong London accent. His wife and two kids were at home in South London because, as he said to Karl, he thought Lagos was far too dangerous to bring his family, though he did go on to point out that his wife hadn't wanted to come with him. On his lucrative two-year contract he flew home for three weeks every three months and as he pointed out, by then he was, 'gagging for it'. He carried on to say, 'After three months I won't know whether to kiss it, poke it, lick it, squeeze it or play a tune on it.'

Two days in a nice apartment with running water, close to the facilities of the Ikoyi Club with its smart restaurant, 24 hours' electricity (they had their own generator) and a swimming pool was the perfect way to relax. Tony was an engineer for Otis, the lift and elevator company, and was part of a team installing high speed lifts into a 20-storey building in downtown Lagos. He reckoned he could jog to work quicker than drive, such was the congestion. The company solved the problem by starting work at 6:00am each day.

He was, as ever, a fine raconteur, full of stories, never short of a comment, and totally aghast at the thought of living somewhere in the bush, or with bushmen as he disparagingly called the locals. Any mention of Nigerian hospitals propagated a profusion of horror stories. 'You see all those people sitting around on the steps outside the hospital?' he said as they drove past a small hospital just over the Carter Bridge. 'They are not there waiting for relatives or treatment you know.' And without waiting for the obvious question, 'what are they there for?' he went on to indignantly say, 'What that bloody lot are doing is selling blood.' There was no chance for a comment from Karl while Tony was in full flow. 'They just hang around waiting for one of the doctors or nurses to come out and say they need a pint of A, BB, or whatever blood type they want. Now here is the sinister bit, the rarer the blood the more expensive it is, and get this, if they can ascertain how needy the patient is, then if some poor bugger is on death's door unless they get the right blood, the price goes up. They don't give a fuck... Pardon my expression Anna... if someone lives or dies, they are just interested in making money. I heard that one such donor – change that word to vulture – who had a rare blood group and sold, so they say, about five pints of it in one day, died of a heart attack on the steps, his pockets full of money... Well, for about one minute until the money was taken off the body. His fellow 'donors' even pinched his shoes, the poor bugger was left with only his undies on and no one collected the body for days. It got a bit ripe in the heat and nearly everyone started to use the side entrance to the hospital. Don't worry though, the vultures sorted out the mess. But enough of these humanitarian acts, let's go and have a bottle of Star at the Ikoyi Club.'

The Club, as with all British clubs abroad, was a temple of organisation and civilisation. It had a democratically-elected committee, squash and tennis courts, golf courses, socialising and food and drink, and the usual old colonials at the bar moaning about the country, wherever they were, that was going to the dogs. As the three of them sat looking out over the 18th green from inside the bar, Karl thought to himself, *Air conditioning, sunshine and a cold beer, civilisation at last.*

A few weeks later Karl found himself embroiled in a little confusion at Benin Airport as he waited for his connecting flight to Lagos for the onward BCal flight to Heathrow. The airport was a building site. Arrivals and Departures were in the same concrete block and iron shed which was in the process of being demolished. He cast a glance outside and saw tractors, diggers, bulldozers and graders that were altering the main buildings and constructing the new runway. Noise, dust and heat filled the air and any announcement of flights was done by a uniformed man holding a megaphone and standing on a chair. All he needed was a bell like a town crier.

It was hot as always, and the terminal building offered some respite from the sharp daggers of sunlight. Initially there was some confusion as to the time of departure. A rumour whipped around the sweaty, frustrated congregation that there was a huge delay, but to his surprise the half-empty plane took off on time for the 90-minute flight. There was only one thing that concerned Karl as he sat at the very front of the plane – for the whole journey he could see inside the cockpit. In itself this was fascinating, but what really concerned him was that as preparations were made to land at Ikeja Airport, he could see the co-pilot lift up panels on the floor of the cockpit and with a huge spanner, similar to that for removing a wheel nut from a car, he started to turn something that was hidden under the floor boards. The co-pilot looked up and recognised Karl's consternation. He smiled and said, 'It's okay, I am just winding down the front wheel, the mechanism has been broken for months.'

Lagos airport was a human traffic jam, a beehive of humanity. He was accosted by scruffy, assertive, dodgy teenagers who declared they could get everything he needed to fly while he waited in peace; for the right price they would take your tickets and passport and – no doubt by dodgy means – get you a boarding pass very swiftly and much more quickly in fact (because of who they bribed) than standing amongst the mess of people who were supposed to be in line. He said a convincing 'no' to all of them. All he could envisage was some teenagers buggering off with his passport and selling it for a case of beer, dirty magazines or the purchase of some high heeled colourful boots and then to never be seen again.

He was patient. Eventually he got checked in, handed over his bag and looked up at the fan losing its battle against heat and humidity. Where was the departure gate? He looked around and noticed that behind the baggage scales and check-in desk, through an open door a few feet behind the desk, the BCal 707 plane was sitting on the tarmac, about 100 yards away. Hopefully it was being re-fuelled and would soon be ready to go. *At least it is here,* he thought, delighted that he had an aisle seat number printed on his boarding pass. He knew that Nigerian Airways rarely allocated seats and at times there could be a bit of a free for all when getting on one of their planes, but thank goodness that wouldn't happen on a BCal flight.

As he tried to work out which direction the departure area was in he couldn't help but notice that a crowd was building up around him where he had checked in his bag, He was close enough that, at a stretch, he could touch the weighing machine. A man of some importance, judging by his buttoned-up blue jacket, shouted at the growing crowd. *Another town crier,* Karl thought. 'Shortly we will open the small gate next to the weighing machine, so make sure you have your boarding pass and as you come through you will be directed to the right where your passport will be examined.' This caused a flurry of conversation, none of which was understood by Karl. The crowd started pressing forward and he was pushed against the metal grill, where only 10 minutes earlier he had handed over his ticket and received his boarding card.

The important man in his sweaty blue jacket called for order. 'Sorry, it is all to do with the building work that is going on.' *More building work!* thought Karl.

'Do have patience and we will be boarding shortly.'

More people appeared. He was like a piece of moraine being slowly pushed by a glacier of people. More and more arrived. There was more and more noise and he was getting a little worried. His small piece of hand baggage was at his feet and he didn't have room to bend over and pick it up. And then it happened. Someone quite close to him saw that through the scrum of people in front of him, behind the wire grille and weighing machine, was an open door and beyond that was the airplane. By stepping on the weighing machine and ducking under the grille you could make a dash for it and be first on the plane. That was where the Nigerian Airways mentality came to the surface. Why hang about waiting to get on a flight that may be too full and perhaps get turned away. A wily passenger took his chance, a push here, a bit of abuse there, a heave and kick there, and he was on the scales, all 92 kilos of him. Then he was on his feet, through the door and sprinting for the aircraft. He was followed by a snake-like charge of fellow passengers who were equally determined not to be left behind. Swollen hand baggage, pots and pans, small children, loaves of bread wrapped in plastic, a bag of dried fish and a push chair all went through the small gap. The pressure of people soon forced open the temporary gate

The man in the blue jacket tried to stem the onslaught with his voice. He was ignored, as was the hand-written notice directing passengers to the right for Immigration, and he was pushed out of the way by the volume of moving bodies. Karl was jammed against the wire grille. At one point as he tried to turn around, his fingers caught on some sharp metal wire. He yelped in pain and saw his blood on the counter. How does a small cut like that bleed so much? With a surge of strength he got his body in the right position and with the onslaught pushing behind him he was forced to duck through the gap between the weighing machine and the grille and was spewed out towards the open door. It was mayhem. A free for all. A mad crazy rush. He had had the air squeezed out of his body, he was soaked in sweat and his hand was bleeding profusely. He staggered onto the tarmac and watched passengers running past him clutching their massive lumps of hand baggage. The sunlight rendered him temporarily blind and the heat wrapped around him like an eiderdown. He had been about fifth in line and must have been the 50th person onto the flight, without going through Customs or having his passport checked. If he thought, as he shunted up the gangplank, that there would be the relief of the air-conditioned plane, he was in for a shock.

There were two sets of stairs onto the plane, one at the front and one at the back. Each was full of people who, once they got on the plane, grabbed the first seat they came to or looked about aimlessly for a seat number, some even made camp at any empty seat and almost put up a flag declaring it taken. Within minutes of Karl fortunately getting into his allocated seat, the hosepipe of humanity from the back entrance scuffled, argued, shouted and threatened the passengers who had entered at the front. As the two belligerent lines met, tempers frayed and fists waved. They verbally fought over where they were going to sit, even though there were still empty seats. In the ensuing heat and chaos the fashionably-dressed and well-made-up air hostesses vanished for their own safety, whilst the pilot – who thought at one point he might have a passenger on his knee – called for help from the police.

Police with bare knees, heavy boots, long woolly socks and carrying batons struck a few blows for civilisation in an attempt to calm things down. Whistles were blown, yelling and counter yelling started to die down, and with the protection of the police the shocked stewardesses tried to put everyone in their allocated seats. It was like solving a Rubik's Cube puzzle, and they gave up when they realised there was no one without a seat, no one left hapless on the tarmac and there were even a few empty seats. The pilot registered in his log something he could hardly believe he had written.

Flight delayed 54 minutes due to fighting on the aircraft.

Immigration officials made a cursory visit to the plane when calm was restored, but they were aware that any issue of contention should be avoided and diplomatically gave a whimsical glance to the majority of passports.

In the seat next to Karl was a Nigerian who introduced himself as Amos. He was on a visit to his father in London and explained that he had left a job at Ibadan University in order to be an entrepreneur. At that point he leaned over and gave a great wink. He apologised profusely for his countrymen and how they had transformed, for a while, the aisle of the plane into a market place squabble. 'Bushmen, nothing but bushmen,' he said, and after some contortions in the crowded seat he managed to recover his hip flask from his back pocket. With great ceremony he proceeded to unscrew the lid and take a huge swig, which resulted in a grandiose satisfied sigh. Next to him in the window seat was a guitar. Karl thought of BB King and how he would always pay for a seat for his precious instrument. He asked Amos if he had bought the seat for the guitar. His answer was a firm no, but he leaned over, exhaled his whiskey breath and said, 'I use this trick all the time on Nigerian Airways. Passengers come along, see it, and usually move to another seat.' He relaxed, and after another gulp or two sat with his huge sausage-like fingers caressing his flask. Before they had reached their maximum altitude he was grunting and making small animal snorting noises.

A stewardess, seeing Karl's bleeding hand, kindly supplied him with a small bandage. It was either an act of kindness or to make sure the seat fabrics were not stained with his blood. He was a little concerned that since his passport had received only a cursory glance it wouldn't have been stamped to prove he was departing the country. It was too late now to worry about that and he smiled when his thoughts turned to the fact that in a few days' time he would be a father. He had felt awful letting his wife go back to the UK on her own, leaving her without his support, but he also had a sneaking hope that the baby would be born before he got home and he wouldn't have to be there at the birth. He was squeamish, but Anna had stated, understandably, that she wanted him there for moral and loving support.

Their three months in Nigeria, in such a backward place as Okene, had brought them closer as a loving couple. Karl's commitments at the college were far from arduous which meant they had managed to be together far more than they would have been in the UK. The hardships of living so far from anything that resembled what they considered to be a normal functioning town meant they had supported each other when the endless frustrations of Africa got the better of them. Yes, they were closer emotionally and each knew that they were spending a huge amount of time worrying about and caring for the concerns of the other. There was an intensity to normal everyday living in the north of Kwara State. Nothing could be taken for granted, nothing was guaranteed, nothing was predictable, only that the unpredictable would happen. They shared their worries about personal safety. They shared their worries about travelling on such dangerous roads. They shared their worries about being lonely, about their health, about clean water. But most of all they shared their worries about their child. Should they actually return after the birth? How would they manage? They were aghast at the decision they had made to go to Nigeria, assuming that life would be easier with a decent wage in a nice colonial house and having an ayah to help with the chores and the care of the baby. If only they had done a little more research. Every day seemed to present them with an irritation or at times a serious worry or anxiety. But they had supported each other unconditionally. They were more patient with each other, more caring and loving. Karl felt warm inside for the love of his wife and how much he had missed her over the last two weeks. Alone, he had felt very lonely. Now he felt an excitement grow in him, knowing that in about six hours he would be at Heathrow and able to get out his pocketful of ten pence pieces and phone his wife and talk personally to his dad. He closed his eyes and pictured his reunion with them both. His reverie was broken when the stewardess, the saint with the bandage, offered him a drink.

'Actually I can't decide. I fancy a cold beer, but could also murder a vodka and orange.'

'Why not have both, sir?'

'Is that okay?'

'Of course,' and she proceeded to rummage through the trolley and presented him with an ice-cold Tennent's Lager, after which she handed him a small carton of orange juice and then screwed the top off a mini bottle of vodka. 'Is there anything else, sir?' she said.

'Tennent's?'

'Well, we are a Scottish Airline. Are you sure there is nothing else?'

'No, I'm fine thank you.'

She took two steps forward, stopped the trolley and turned her head to look over her shoulder at him. She reached towards him with a small bottle in her hand. 'Do have another vodka.' Bemused, he accepted. She then retraced her two steps and offered him a third bottle. 'You may get thirsty,' she said firmly, and then after a short pause said in a very deliberate manner, 'Here, have a fourth, it's the last bottle.'

Puzzled, he stated, 'I don't need four.'

She looked him firmly in the eye. Her face lost its saintly countenance and she said with a hint of exasperation, 'Just take them.' She paused for further explanation and added, 'If you have them then I won't be able to give them to one of them. There are enough drunks on the flight as it is, and you look as though you've got the common sense to keep them for another occasion.'

He was shocked at her racial inference but not quite as shocked as when they arrived at Terminal 3 at Heathrow and all the passengers from BCal 23 were kept to one side before they were even allowed through immigration. They stood in line for some twenty minutes with a couple of policemen keeping a close eye on the weary passengers. An immigration official, and alarmingly another six policemen, all armed, walked down the line of passengers and embarrassingly selected all the white people to go through immigration, directing the remaining 200-plus Africans to stay behind.

Karl was puzzled and embarrassed, and it was only later when he picked up a copy of the London Evening Standard that its secondary front page headline was, 'Police Arrest 13 Nigerian Passengers attempting to bring drugs into the UK on a British Caledonian Flight.'

The train journey up north had no such drama.

22

Their daughter was christened Kate Jane, after Jenny Lauren had been rejected. She turned out to be a stressed little baby and her early temperament was endorsed by a brush of fiery red hair that unfortunately had the shape of a Mohican cut.

Karl had a couple of theories as to why she never smiled at anyone other than her parents. When she was in her baby buggy or on the sofa she would sit with her arms bent as though she was going to lift some weights, with her fists tightly clasped. You could go up to her, gently prise them apart and then watch her form her little fists again. On Christmas Day at lunch at the ATP new college building site, she was in her home-made high chair at the head of the table; there she sat with a fixed scowl and in each of her immovable fists was placed a rather fat cigar. She held on to them for ages. The resulting photograph was hilarious.

Theory one, and by his own admission somewhat spurious, was that at the very time she was born on that Monday evening, Coronation Street was on TV in the waiting room and two of the characters – Suzie Birchall the cynical teenager and the headstrong and flirty Tracey Barlow, were having a really loud, stressful argument. Or it could have been the stress her mother had gone through in Nigeria which had been transferred to her in the womb. Perhaps being delivered by forceps was a stressful first few moments of life. It could also be the fact she was permanently hot and sweaty, or perhaps it was because she spent her first few nights in a wicker washing basket after the new carry cot had broken. Karl, following Anna's wishes, had agreed to witness the birth. He wasn't happy about this. In fact while he was in Nigeria waiting to join his wife in the UK he had secretly hoped that by the time he arrived the baby would be well and truly on the scene and he would escape the painful bloody bits. He was very squeamish and knew from past experience of cuts and blood and breaks that he would be in danger of passing out. He vividly remembered doing so when watching his dog get stitched up; one moment he had been helping to keep the dog calm and the next he swooned, fainted, and banged his head on the wall. He was not attended to until the dog had been sorted out. But, there he was, all dressed up in surgical garb waiting to be called into the delivery room. His mind was a mixture of excitement and anxiety.

A doctor approached him to tell him that he would not be allowed to witness the birth of his first child because of some complications. He was assured that there was no danger but they were going to have to perform a forceps delivery. Karl masterfully feigned disappointment, but now felt relief and worry. Discarding his medical outfit, he sat in the waiting room and idly let noises from Coronation Street pass over him. Other fathers consoled him when they heard that he was unable to witness the 'life changing event' or 'the unforgettable moment in time.' He was patted on the shoulder by a couple of expectant fathers and smiled wanly as he faked his disappointment.

He was eventually called in to see his wife. She looked absolutely exhausted. Lying in the concavity of her arm and body was his daughter. She was not a pretty sight. She had an asymmetrical wodge of bright red hair and her head had two semi-circular red indentations where the forceps had been used. His look of concern was recognised and the doctor reassured him that the marks would disappear in a day or so and that forceps were needed because the rather longer than expected labour had sapped Anna's strength. She needed that final bit of help, he reported. Anna looked so tired but she managed an elated smile and said, kindly and softly, 'If only your mam could have lived a little longer to see her first grandchild.' She dropped into an exhausted and drugged sleep.

He went out to the car and just sat. *How will we cope with a baby in Nigeria?* he thought. He laughed to himself. Every day in Okene he saw plenty of women with very small kids, some of whom had one strapped to their back and a gaggle of toddlers following behind. A baby on your back and labouring with a hoe all day in the fields? Not an issue! The issue for Karl was that he felt helpless and ignorant. He knew nothing about babies and had shamefully done little about it. His mother would have been the natural source of advice and oh how she would have loved to be involved with her first grandchild and would have glowed with delight at being asked for and able to give advice.

She was a patient woman but she worried too much. She was also artistic. She had no formal training but she drew quite well. Once, when at the seaside, she had had a quick portrait sketch done of her. She took it home, pinned it on the wall, and proceeded to alter it. She said she had recognised some flaws in the drawing, the main one being the size of her nose. She rubbed it out and replaced it with something more to her liking.

What she could do really well, however, was decorate cakes with icing. We are not talking about two-mouthful cupcakes, but engagement cakes, birthday cakes, and especially tiered wedding cakes. When the latter was in a state of creation the dining room table was commandeered, and for the time it took her to finish the decorations all meals were eaten off your lap. Her icing technique was superb and she was wonderfully creative. Her cakes were festooned with icing flowers and swirling decorations and the corners of rectangular cakes were embellished with structures made from netting that was iced and ended up looking like flying buttresses. In fact, a three- or four-tiered cake looked like a white marble cathedral. Karl described them as decorated Gothic, which prompted his dad to ask for an explanation. 'What the hell is gothic?' Often she would not only decorate the cakes but would bake them as well. Even his dad loved the brandy soaked aroma of a rich fruitcake mix invading the house. She never had a critical customer, but as a business woman she proved herself to be far too generous to her customers and took scant reward for all the effort she put in. The big treat for Karl and his sister was that she would make hundreds of icing swirls that she would squeeze from the icing bag on to greaseproof paper and, if they deserved it, they were presented with a real sweet calorific treat.

She also painted pottery and every Thursday evening she would go to a neighbour's house where five or six women would sit around the table, chatting and having a glass of wine or two, except for his mam of course, and they would paint decorations on the plain white crockery. The cups, saucers and plates were then fired and in Tina's case they were taken home. She made no attempt to sell them and slowly but surely the cupboards became full of her unused painted creations. Karl could remember all of these things about her and he tried to think of one adjective that would capture what she was like as a person. He came up with the simple but complimentary word 'kind.' My mother was a really kind person was the phrase he used if asked what she was like.

After 10 days Anna was released from the hospital. She had recovered her strength and the unsightly indentations caused by the forceps had disappeared from Kate's head. As much as they had admired the care and

191

concern given to them at the Auchi mission hospital they were truly thankful that the birth had taken place in the UK. The taxi took them out of town and up a steep hill to a small housing estate consisting of small bungalows. They pulled up at number 12 and could just see Joe tending his tomatoes in his greenhouse. In the 12 to 14 weeks since their departure for Nigeria, he had changed. Lines of grief, not previously there, were etched onto his face. He saw them coming down the drive at the side of the house and he smiled. It wasn't the smile of a saucy or wicked remark he had just made or a sarcastic comment about the Tories, or jubilation that he was about to meet his first grandchild. The muscles on his face were restricted by grief. His smile was welcoming but encrusted with sadness.

He had also put on weight. As he stood before them in his collarless wrinkled shirt and trousers held up with braces, his newly formed belly hung over the waist band. He was 63 and looked 75. He was newly retired. He was wifeless after 38 years. For the last four years his job at the steelworks had been in the office where he had responsibility for ordering everything that was necessary for the construction yard. He wore a collar and tie each day and a clean, ironed shirt. *Does he actually know how to iron?* Karl thought.

As if he had read their minds he tucked in a piece of renegade shirt and fingered his collarless neck line. His first words were, 'Bit of a mess, but only in the garden.' There was a short pause before he explained his scruffy state. 'Sandra will be round soon with all my washing and ironing. She has been such a great help since Tina...' He stopped, recovered his composure, and said, 'Right, let's see my first grandchild.'

At a loss for what to do with himself, his salvation was liquid. For the past couple of months he had walked down the steep hill to the working men's club and sat and drank half a gallon of beer before he ate his dinner. He found himself getting to the club earlier and earlier and was horrified that one day he was stood outside waiting for it to open. He had looked at his pocket watch and felt guilty that it was only 11.15 am. His routine of a few beers at lunch time was replicated in the evening when he made the trip to the club for more beer, but most of all for company. With his newly acquired bus pass he would always catch the bus that took him back up the long, steep bank where he arrived home to an empty house. His diet of bacon, sausages, fried eggs, meat pies and sausage rolls and pork pies from Newboulds the butchers added to his weight gain.

His father was lonely and grief stricken, and even on the very first day of them sharing his bungalow, he couldn't conceal his sadness. Karl would see him staring out of the window at his garden, and on hearing them come into the room he would turn to acknowledge them, but not before he had wiped the tears from his eyes. In the following days they would hear him get up in the middle of the night. They would hear the creak of his armchair, the scraping and banging as he tried to stir the embers of the fire with a poker, accompanied by a gentle sobbing.

Three extra people in his house was, to a certain extent, a diversion for him. He had to make conversation, he had to show interest in baby Kate. He was dragged on short trips to the sea side or visits to the local markets. Sometimes he would inadvertently say, 'Tina and I used to...' and then stop, and the tears would well up in private and in public. Her clothes still remained, not just stored in the wardrobe but her coat and pinnies were hanging on the back of the kitchen door, her slippers were still near the fire place, as was her unfinished bottle of pop, and her knitting was on a shelf in the living room. Joe had pinned up more photographs of her and her presence seemed even more tangible after her death.

Karl's sister Sandra had been an angel. She had taken on the role of counsellor, carer and companion in the first few weeks while he was in Africa. He had often wondered if she thought, *it's all right for him gallivanting around in the sunshine while I am here looking after him and trying to teach him how to look after himself.* Sandra admitted that she was very concerned about him because he was still so inconsolable about his loss. But she also pointed out something of which Karl too had been aware. As a couple their parents had never gone out together, there were very few signs of physical affection and they had never heard him speak to her directly in an affectionate manner. But he worked all the hours that were available to him so he could give her the comforts of life. He was financially astute but always put her and the kids first. If she wanted or needed something he could afford he would buy it for her and he regularly brought home small treats, usually a box of Dairy Milk chocolates or Murray mints that she loved so much. Was that love, they both wondered, because now that Tina was gone at the age of 61, only now were his words full of love.

Sandra, her husband Paul, and Karl and Anna all agreed that they needed to get him off the beer, or more to the point, go to see his acquaintances at the club but drink less and go less frequently. They all agreed that he also needed other things in his life. He was introduced to the library, a ten-minute walk away, something he would always be thankful for. He was encouraged to go to the pensioners' lunch at the village hall three times a week and to take an interest in the scraggy poodle dog that had sat on his wife's knee so often. If he bore a grudge with them for going to Nigeria he certainly didn't reveal it, and in fact he did say that he would have been alarmed if his words had caused them to stay in England and become unemployed. He was no longer game for a laugh. He just slowly but surely, like a man lying in the sun, sweated droplets of melancholy.

Karl felt inadequate as a father. His dad had been somewhat similar. When Anna asked him a question about what to do in certain situations he was short of words and could give little or no advice. It seemed apparent to Karl that Tina, out of necessity, took full responsibility for her kids while Joe worked all the extra shifts he could at the steel works. He was well known as a grabber, someone who was first in line when overtime was offered. Baby Kate and their presence, and his sister's constant help, helped him to cope over the next four weeks until their return to West Africa.

They debated long and hard about whether they should actually go back. Karl spoke to Joe for advice and in an attempt to erase their guilt, but his response was to say, 'You know best,' or 'It will be bloody hard here if you don't find a job.'

There was no doubt that they'd been scarred by their initial seven days in Nigeria, even though things had got so much better. They had the liberation of a car, an easy job, a decent amount of money, but there was always that underlying element of danger, of chaos or worry about being so far away from the safety nets of life. Karl thought he had a purpose at the college. Even though he felt as if he was swimming against a tide of inertia, he was still of beneficial help to the students. They seemed to appreciate him and often invited him back to their dormitories. Every time he went there he was shocked at how they had to live. It wasn't as though they slept on the floor of a mud hut as did many Nigerians, it was the fact that these students were already graduates, the top 1% of the nation and if they had been to grand universities like Ibadan, Abeokuta or Lagos, they would have had accommodation fit for the potential leaders of the country.

Their accommodation was dire. Lines of old metal bunk beds with no privacy apart from hanging fabric between each set of beds. Forty people and two toilets, both of which had to be flushed by hand, if there was water. There was no designated work area and many of them had rigged up jury desks. The food was fine, but there were times when a lack of petrol hindered deliveries and thus food was short for a few days. Although they were cheerful in class they rightly complained a great deal.

Would he be missed if he didn't go back?

He made tentative enquiries about returning to his old job and was told his temporary replacement was doing a fine job and had signed a two-year contract until his return. He rang a few schools nearby who had advertised vacancies for September, but they were few and far between, and it seemed that should he remain in the UK he would probably be jobless as well as unable to move back into his own house until the current tenancy ended.

Anna was quite depressed about the thought of going back. She enjoyed the company of her family and was worried sick if on their return Kate became ill.

They received a short letter from Tony who was just going back after his three-week leave.

'How is that daughter of yours? I hope she looks like you, Anna, and not Karl, that really would be a handicap in the future. With bright red hair every local will be fascinated by her. Are you actually coming back? I'm here for the money and the thought of my next leave. Spent most of the last three weeks in bed making up for all the lost opportunities. My kids have been brilliant and it is amazing just how much they change in three months. If you do fly back drop me a line, give me plenty of notice and I'll pick you up from the airport, and remember all three of you are welcome at my flat any time.'

Tony

Anna cried. As the days went by and the return to Nigeria loomed she became more and more worried. She was full of worry and concern. She was sure she would never be happy there, and having the massive additional responsibility of Kate she would gently weep when she was alone. Staying in UK with her mother was considered. Karl would go back and fly straight home at every opportunity and whilst in UK he'd look for a job. But she both wanted and didn't want to share his burden. They were so close and in some ways going to Nigeria had cemented their relationship and given them a more mature empathy. They were so supportive of each other and they had both made the decision to take the job. If she stayed in England she would deprive Karl of seeing his daughter, she would need his support and he would need hers. True, things had improved once they were in their concrete 'cottage' but she couldn't disassociate herself from the isolation and the un-nerving and volatile atmosphere in Nigeria. Her mind meandered when weighing up options, but in the end she decided they would go back together and take the opportunity to fly home every college vacation, and if things became intolerable they would leave and take their chances back in England.

New born baby Kate's first flight was on the 5th September 1977. She was four weeks old. She spent most of the time swinging around in a little hammock that had been slung above them on fixings near the air vents underneath the overhead lockers. She was fed once and quietly slept for the remainder of the time. Swinging above everyone, wrapped up like a cocoon, she was the star attraction as numerous passengers insisted on gently pulling the little hammock towards them to look at her little pink face and the bright red hair, and gasp 'oooooh.'

She would also prove to be a star attraction wherever she went on their return to Nigeria.

23

What a difference it made to have someone waiting for you at the airport. Ikeja Airport, soon to be rebranded as Murtala Mohammed Airport, was unchanged. It was no cooler, no less crowded, no less noisy and it still had an odour of sweat and shit. It was even gloomier in the dark, yet Karl looked around with so much more confidence. Yes, the place was full of hustlers, con men and thieves, but what was important was that he didn't look like a victim. Tony was there to meet them and he made a great fuss of all three of them while telling numerous villains to 'bugger off.'

They had left their car with Tony for the duration of their 4-week stay in the UK and there it was in the parking lot, guarded by a young man who was given a couple of naira for 'not' damaging the vehicle. Karl didn't ask to drive. He was tired and Tony was, as ever, loquacious and full of banter, information and tales of woe about Lagos.

Arriving on the B Cal flight early in the evening meant that after 6pm any car with any number plate could be on the road in Lagos, but it was still a slow, turgid, hot and sweaty drive to Ikoyi some nine miles away. Once over the Carter bridge the traffic became normal, and before turning into Adeleo Adeku Street, Tony took a diversion to the Bar Beach Road, where he pointed out the view out to sea. There were so many stationary ships lined up with all lights blazing that to all intents and purposes it was like looking at a city built on water.

Kate was asleep. Tony stopped the car and asked them to join him outside where it was cooler because of a refreshing wind blowing off the Bight of Benin. He explained that most of the ships were full or pretending to be full of cement. Such was the surfeit of money from the Delta oil fields that there was a profusion of building in the country, and as a result there was a demand for cement. Nigeria had to import ship loads of it. The port, some four miles away down the coast, was small and inefficient and

197

couldn't handle the volume of ships. So with lights ablaze they sat on the surface of the sea waiting their turn to discharge their cargo, and in the meantime they got paid for doing so. In fact so much money was being given away that it was actually more profitable to sit and wait and get paid handsomely for waiting. What made the situation worse was that some ships arrived completely empty. They reported their arrival to the port authorities and were given massive lumps of compensation, all paid in pounds or dollars. What these empty ships did next was as good as printing money. Off they sailed to load their cargo and whilst they were away for a few weeks they continued to get paid. Tony said there were over 150 ships, many owned by Nigerian entrepreneurs who had suddenly become shipping magnates, sitting there coining millions per day. 'Now if we had this much money in the UK I'd like to think we would be a little better at looking after it.'

They slept in late and had a restful day in Tony's apartment as they were unable to drive out of Lagos until the following day. They left very early in the morning so they would arrive in Okene before dark. Lagos, like New York, was a city that didn't sleep. Even at five o'clock in the morning the roads were busy and every part of the highway was filled with pedestrians walking immense distances to work or carrying their wares on their heads to be sold in a market or at the side of the road. Music played from ramshackle bars and even at this hour men sat around drinking beer. The place was as ever noisy. It had to beat New York for insomnia.

As they travelled on the new expressway from Ibadan to Benin the horizon was dominated by huge low grey clouds. As they got closer the clouds rolled and heaved and changed their form aggressively as if warming up for a fight. They flexed their muscles, groaned a little and got darker and darker. The sun shone behind them as they travelled towards the grey mass, creating the spectacular sight of lush vegetation which was lit up as though being attacked by spot lights. All the time the sky ahead changed into a threatening and very black ominous shape. The contrast and beauty was breath-taking. They almost stopped to take a photo, but as they passed beneath the clouds the sunlight disappeared and the clouds regurgitated what was agitating them. The downpour was on a Krakatoa scale. The rain fell like thick welding rods, creating mini craters in the brown earth at the side of the expressway and landing with such force the drops bounced two or three feet. The thunder made the trees cower and the lightning cracked like a whip. In seconds the road surface was a river and visibility was just a wall of grey stripes. The windscreen wipers pleaded for help and the torrent was so severe it felt as though it might actually break the windows. Almost out of fear of this meteorological display of vengeance, and worry that the engine might flood, they stopped and pulled over. Baby Kate slept through it all.

It was always a visual thrill coming over the hill towards Okene after passing the palm line that ended a few miles behind them. It was a relief to see the open vistas of scrubby trees and rocky outcrops and space rather than endless tunnels of trees. It was the end of the rainy season and the grass oozed fertility. Gone was the parched yellow look. As they turned into the college drive they were excited to see some members of the nomadic Fulani tribe who tended their long-horned white cows in the long grass. Each of them carried what looked like a long spear. Alas there was unlikely to be a predator left in Nigeria to threaten a cow or a scrawny sheep, so the spears had become poles to lean on or prods to move their beasts.

The Fulani were thin and athletic like marathon runners. They were elegant. They were handsome, with finely defined angular facial features. Their wives and the young girls made a colourful spectacle in the market place in Okene where they would often break into impromptu dancing to the rhythm of a small drum that was beaten whilst held under an armpit. The girls had elaborately platted hair that was intertwined with coloured beads and ribbons and each wore a wildly coloured tight top that enhanced their breasts, and with skin decorations of henna and white paint they added an exotic feel to Okene and even more energy to the market place.

Anna turned to Karl and said, 'Look at that herdsman, he looks so imperious and independent,' as they slowed to let a small herd cross the drive. This was a vision of an idealised Africa; colourful, armed hunters and herdsmen wandering wherever they wanted, impervious to governments, taxes, petty rules and chaos. Just them and their cows and the freedom to wander wherever they wanted.

They approached the college buildings which were barely recognisable, such was the growth in the short time they had been away. They turned to see the Bright's house and next to it some 40 yards away their cottage which was only partly visible. It was engulfed by an entanglement of high hyparrhenia grass that reached the eaves of the house. The doors and windows were barely visible. To gain entrance would require a prince with a sword big enough to rescue the sleeping beauty.

They were shocked. The grass in places was almost six feet high. They got out of the car and were speechless. Two minutes ago they had been enjoying the picturesque romantic Africa, Africa at its best and now they stood in front of their house which looked like a grass hut. Anna cried. She went from smiling to feeling sorrowful and horrified within a few moments. She held Kate in her arms and looked at her four week old daughter forlornly as if to say sorry I have brought you here to this primitive place. Karl put an affectionate arm around her shoulder and she shrugged it off. She looked him in the eye and said, 'Just look at the place, am I supposed to live there? It's a dump! We should be at home in UK, not having to worry about...' She paused at this point, so emotional she was lost for words. 'What do we do now, cut down the vegetation with nail clippers. What sort of college is it that can't even keep its buildings from being overrun by bloody weeds the size of triffids, what do we have to do, wait until all those cows eat it?' Karl was once more consumed with guilt and felt helpless. It wasn't as though the house had squatters or had fallen down, it was just an image of abject neglect.

From behind them a couple of Karl's students appeared. They were about to give a fine welcome accompanied with a big smile when they caught Anna's mood. Looking at their house they understood her distress. 'We will be the rescue people,' they said, and off they went. Minutes later a small army of students appeared, some of whom he barely knew, all armed with big staves and machetes. They looked like a riotous mob, but their aim was not revolution but restitution as they proceeded to hack down the grass. With a dozen of them working in unison the grass and weeds were soon cleared and the door to the house was freed from its prison of fast growing plants. Karl unlocked the door and went into the house which was just as they had left it weeks ago. He found eight bottles of beer. They were rather warm, but the group of smiling students, hands on hips, admiring their work, eagerly passed the beers around. This too was Africa at its best.

24

Kate's arrival in Okene was a sensation. Whenever she was wheeled about in her Maclaren baby buggy, smothered in suntan cream and sporting an eruption of bright red hair, she really was the centre of attention. A trip to the market proved to be the making of many a Nigerian child's day as they could run home and tell their parents about a fat baby that was wheeled instead of carried and who had this amazing brightly coloured hair. Traders would strain their necks from under their umbrellas to see her. Customers prodded each other as she passed to make sure they didn't miss seeing the 'oyibo' baby. If Anna stopped, smiling people would come up and ask for her name as a prelude to touching her very white skin; the ultimate treat was to be able to touch her hair. One memorable incident took place when Kate, aged around three months, was being pushed by her mother towards the bank. In the middle of the road they were stopped by an exotically-attired Nigerian. He placed his hands on his hips and pointed at Kate. He looked Anna straight in the eye and in a serious tone said, 'I want to marry this girl and you must save her for me.' It was the first of her many proposals.

On another occasion as Karl and Anna headed to their car, escaping the throngs of people in the market, they were approached yet again by a Nigerian who asked for Kate's hand in marriage whilst proceeding to brag how much money he had. 'I am a wealthy man, I have visited Mecca,' he said, as if his trip to Saudi Arabia and the cost it incurred would favourably impress them. Karl, enjoying this, said to him, 'I am sorry, but this girl will not be carrying wood and water on her head for you.'

'Do you think I am a peasant?' was his indignant reply. He then stroked his clothes, inviting them to feel the quality of the fabric as if to prove to them that he was wearing only expensive cloth. 'Do you think a peasant can afford clothes like these?'

'Your clothes are fine, but do you have a car?'

'Of course I have a car!' was his forceful reply. 'I have a Peugeot 504.' He paused and then said with a flourish, 'And it is an estate car.'

'What, only a Peugeot!' commented Karl. 'My daughter needs a man of substance, someone who can keep her in style and comfort. Her future husband needs to have a Mercedes and a house with electricity, and don't forget you have to give her a *dowry*.' He placed emphasis on the word dowry.

The Nigerian was suddenly flummoxed and turned pale as he absorbed the implication of the last remark. He stuttered a little, trying to form his words, 'But a dowry is from the woman...' he croaked.

'Sorry, but a dowry in the UK means **you** have to pay my wife and I for the hand of our daughter. And if you want her, if you want to reserve her, then it will require a big deposit which I'll look after for the next 18 years until she is ready. Now, if you want to continue this deal I need to know if you will be paying in cows, goats or money, or all three?' Karl was really enjoying this. He continued, 'She would make a fine wife, everyone would admire your woman with her white skin and red hair and her own car. Oh, by the way, do you have servants?'

'Of course I do but...'

'No buts, that is the deal, and the next thing we have to do is negotiate the exact price of the deposit.'

The tall Nigerian didn't quite know if he was being wound up or if the white man was serious. But when he saw Karl's smile getting bigger and bigger and Anna failing to hide a cheeky grin he realised that it was a big joke. Far from being insulted by Karl's imaginary demands he roared with laughter and smiled at passers-by, wanting to tell them about his failed attempt to buy a bride.

'You'd better go and trade in that Peugeot and save up for a Benz, and remember, she won't be chopping wood or rubbing two sticks together to make a fire.' The man laughed even more, and the next time Karl saw him in town he introduced himself as Tayo and insisted that they went 'to wet the future marriage', in other words to have a beer. Two bottles of Star lager at midday did Karl no good at all.

Baby Kate opened doors. Mother and baby were often escorted to the front of the African version of a queue. Anna was often served first, the traders ignoring the fact that there were others waiting to be served who had been in front of the oyibo woman and her startling baby who was always unsmiling in her baby buggy, clenching her two fists like a weight lifter.

She was six or seven months old before she stopped sitting in that rigid position.

In Nigeria, Kate had her mother all to herself. There were no distractions for Anna such as having to juggle work and a child. Her days in an environment she didn't like were blessed by Kate who, after she overcame her highly stressed state, was a delight. It made Karl's day when he walked into their house and was greeted with a cheeky grin. She slept through the night after nine weeks, and her glowing contentment was manifested by the fact that she was rather fat, like a little Michelin man. He took some photos of his daughter being bathed, and eventually got the images back after the 120 mile trip to Benin. They were a brilliant source of fun. There was Kate in a purple plastic wash tub that had been purchased in the market. Her form looked like it had been created by a compass and she reminded him of one of the Roly Polys from a Les Dawson show.

In mid-afternoon when there was no electricity and hence no fan, Anna would take her outside to sit on the crazy paving patio Karl had created under a shady roof made from palm leaves – another one of his trying-to-make-life-easier ideas. It was always hot, very hot, but the ramshackle veranda provided some relief from the sun. Kate was always sweaty. They laughed at how in the future they could threaten to show these voluminous images to a future husband or try to imagine just what sort of objects you could hide in her rolls of fat. But she was healthy. A net at night protected her from mosquitoes and, just like all babies, the older she got the more pleasure she brought to their lives. They used to laugh with each other about how she would never be aware that she had lived her early years in the middle of Africa, in the middle of Nigeria, in the middle of nowhere. No disposable nappies here, just the terry towel version secured with a huge safety pin, that had to be washed daily in a place without running water, hot water or a basic washing machine or the servant they would have had, had they lived in Kenya. There were none of the little luxuries they would have taken for granted back home.

25

Timothy was tall, terribly tall actually. In fact he was probably the tallest man in Okene, easily over two metres and thin as a cricket stump. He sat at his desk dressed always in a long-sleeved white shirt and tie, his long fingers whispering through all the documents on his desk. He looked like a cross between a businessman and a professional basketball player. He was an Igbo from the eastern region of Nigeria, but unlike other members of the same tribe who were well built but rarely over six feet tall, he was literally 'head and shoulders' above them. Timothy was known to the locals in Okene as Igi, which is the Yoruba word for tree. He was the assistant manager of the Bank of the North, one of only three banks serving a town of 80,000. He was unfailingly polite. His size made him look magisterial and he walked around looking elegantly aloof yet friendly. He was always present in the bank and this caused new customers to assume he was in charge. It was not really the case.

The manager, Alhadji Fat Wallet, as he was known, was a shareholder, a man who flashed around his money, a man who possessed an extravagant Mercedes and who rarely, in the bank, did anything of consequence apart from sitting behind an ornate desk and peering over his glasses to routinely sign documents with a flamboyant flourish that made observers think that what he signed was of major importance. Most of the documents had been signed on many previous occasions and were brought out from his desk drawer on a regular basis for re-signing. He also made sure he was to be seen fastidiously polishing his gold rings. One of Alhadji Fat Wallet's other enterprises was a bar he owned in the town. He had made friends with a young Scottish VSO and had asked him to make a sign board for it. The sign proudly announced that the bar would be known as the Mubroypu Bar, an exotic east African word meaning 'good taste,' according to the young VSO, and anyone who took the trouble to read the sign backwards would have recognised his sense of humour. He would often leave the bank abruptly, telling Timothy he was now in charge, a fact that was already obvious to the regular customers. He would waddle a short distance to his car, presenting his huge belly to the world as a symbol of how rich he was, and then disappear to his ostentatious house a couple of miles away which was surrounded by a high wall. He had the luxury of a generator noisy enough to let everyone know there would be no dark nights for him.

Karl and Anna felt a real empathy with Timothy. Not only was he thoroughly nice and helpful, he also had a four-month-old daughter about whom he talked endlessly. On one occasion he arranged for his wife to arrive at the bank at a pre-arranged time and the four of them had a baby talk session. It was one of many. His daughter Koti and Kate had one thing in common – a massive head of hair. They were photographed together with their heads pressed against each other, the afro mop next to the red brush. But Kate was not a happy smiling baby, she just wouldn't smile unless she was in the company of her mam and dad, and Karl's wiggly tongue or facial antics always got her giggling. It was as though she had decided that the pleasure she could generate with a huge smile or laughter should be reserved for her mother and father.

The bank was a one-storey building with an almost shiny iron roof. Either side of the double doors were two rectangular windows, each with a set of iron bars, so spaced that a mouse would have had to hold its breath to get through. Like most of the official buildings in the town, the bank suffered from aesthetic amnesia. From a distance it appeared to have a weather vane on its roof but on close inspection one could see that it was in fact a huge vulture waiting for an opportunity; the pork butcher's stall was situated just behind the bank. Above the door was a professional-looking green and white sign saying Bank of the North, and to the side stood a skinny guard in his green uniform and peaked cap, wearing tattered plimsolls and supporting a truncheon which hung from his belt. That was all he had to ward off or fight the armed robbers that were the plague of some of the big towns and cities. The menace was so bad that a person convicted of armed robbery would face the death sentence. He and another guard shared the duties, each doing a 12-hour shift of either standing there during the day suffering the heat or curling up asleep on the doorstep during the night.

The bank was always crowded and disorderly since the people of Okene had not grasped the concept of an orderly queue, and all transactions involved sums of cash as they did not seem to be familiar with a chequebook. This meant there was always a lot of pushing, shoving and shouting. Karl had initially hated going there but had no option as it was where the ministry deposited his salary. One day, however, when he went in with Kate in his arms, the mass of humanity opened up like the Red Sea and he and the baby were ushered to the front. They came face to face with Timothy and it was then that they became friends. There was one thing that was universal in Nigeria and that was the wonderful love of children and, in the case of Kate, total fascination.

Kate became a very useful tool to have in the chaos of the bank or indeed any public place that needed the order of a queue. If the bank was a writhing mass and he and Kate were temporarily unnoticed, then Karl, to his shame, gently pinched the top of one her fat thighs and she cried. This was the signal for everyone to push one another out of the way to make a passage through for the oyibo and his red-headed baby. That trick must have worked 50 times at least, he told his friends. They thought it would have been easier just to hide a tape recorder with sounds of child's distress and press play at the appropriate time.

Timothy, as virtual bank manager, had the power to approve the remittance of money from Nigeria to the UK. Expatriates were always complaining that it was hard to get permission or you had to give a dash (a percentage) to the manager, or the bank staff had no idea what you were talking about. Timothy knew what he was doing, he knew what Karl was entitled to, and without hesitation he made sure that any of his surplus naira were sent back to the UK and changed into sterling. Timothy asked for nothing and, like Dr Omega, stood above everyone in the integrity stakes.

Timothy often bemoaned the fact that because he was so tall it was difficult to get clothes to fit. Karl could only agree, as he had noticed that usually his trousers were that bit too short and revealed a large expanse of sock which made him look rather silly. Timothy had tried to have clothes made to measure by various tailors in Okene, but most of them were men who merely possessed a sewing machine but hadn't got the skill to use it properly, and consequently nothing quite fit him.

'Did you actually get them to measure you?' asked Karl.

'Yes, of course I did,' was his reply, 'but they don't know how to convert what they measure into two dimensional shapes.' Usually he would follow this up with the comment, 'It wouldn't happen in Enugu.' He was quite convinced that his tribe, the Igbo, were so much more worldly and sophisticated than the Igbira of Okene. Although he was a polite, intelligent and dignified man, he had plenty of disparaging comments to make about the locals in Okene. He referred to them as bush men who were ignorant, parochial, lazy and untrustworthy. On one occasion after a typical short tirade, Karl asked him why on earth he had come to Okene.

Timothy explained that it was his first posting and a good one. Rather than starting off as the head counter clerk he had been appointed as assistant manager and had found to his delight that his boss, Alhadji Fat Wallet, mostly just let him get on with the job, though annoyingly there were times when he took much of the credit for what went right and conversely passed the blame on to Timothy if there was criticism to face. Timothy also explained that Okene was classed as a hardship post. Karl remembered that conversation well and had roared with laughter at Timothy's disparaging remarks, causing the bank customers to laugh at his laughter. Kate in his arms remained as uptight as ever.

'Too bloody right it is!' was Karl's reply.

'It will help to enhance my career, I thought. If I can make a success in this difficult place then I will be highly regarded at head office and should, in theory, get a better posting. Who knows, I could be sent to Enugu, Onitsha, Port Harcourt – you know, big towns full of sensible Ibos... Or even to head office in Lagos.'

Karl uttered a groan. 'Lagos,' he said sardonically. 'Okene is like the St Tropez of Nigeria,' using the BICC phrase, 'compared to Lagos. Lagos, well it is horrible, it is like a chaotic dream that's very noisy and smells bad.'

'But Lagos could be a stepping stone to who knows where. Perhaps London or New York,' Timothy added.

'Are you trying to tell me that Bank of the North, this up-market mud building with a tin roof has branches abroad?'

'No, of course not, but Bank of the North could lead to Bank of America or Chase Manhattan.'

'Well at least you'd find a decent tailor,' responded Karl, as he grinned.

A deal was made. Timothy should give up on the tailors of Okene and get his wife to do all the measurements that she considered necessary to have a suit 'tailor made.' On Karl's trip to the UK he would go to Jacksons the Tailors and get one or two made for him and bring them back to Okene. Tall Timothy looked tremendous in his new suit. His wife's measurements were perfect and he now possessed two suits, one in a revolting brown (Timothy insisted) and one charcoal grey. He looked even more like the manager, and it seemed to Karl that he walked around a lot more than usual just to make sure everyone was aware that he was a man of taste.

Timothy commented, 'Taste, taste as you know it, doesn't exist in the Igbira language if you ask me.'

Karl and Anna had thought long and hard about their decision to buy the suits for him. Was it bribery that enabled their remittances to carry on going to the UK, or an act of friendship? It was a bit of both, but what a pleasure it was to see Timothy looking even more elegant and assured. And it worked. He never failed to send their remittances to the UK and he even managed on a couple of occasions to get them some foreign exchange in cash to take home with them.

Timothy remained a friend. Neither of them went to each other's houses; that would have been classed as collaboration. They appreciated each other, and so what if Karl found a bottle of scotch in Lagos, why not buy two and give one as an unsolicited gift to someone he respected. They always had time for each other in the bank, Timothy invariably moaning about the inhabitants of Okene and Karl, after a couple of months there, agreeing that they were hamstrung by parochialism. The locals distrusted anyone who was not an Igbira, they hated the fact that other towns 30 miles away were richer than theirs but they hadn't got the energy to do anything about it, and their attitude seemed to be that everyone who wasn't born into their tribe should leave as soon as possible.

And then, of course, Timothy and Karl also had football in common. Karl was interested in hearing about the Nigerian teams that Timothy followed and in turn he would wax wonderfully about Middlesbrough FC. Unfortunately it fell on deaf ears as Timothy only wanted to hear about Liverpool, now that they had won two European Cups in succession. He was equally forthcoming when Anna went into the bank without Karl but he tended to omit the football talk. If only he had known she was as equally passionate about it as her husband.

26

Ken got home after taking one of his early morning classes. He smiled at his wife but it wasn't reciprocated.

She stood next to the dining room table staring at the battered wash bowl that came with the cottage. There was water on the floor and on the table. Rolled up into tightly packed sausage shapes were some of the clothes she had washed and then squeezed out.

She turned and looked at him as though something was his fault and said very firmly, 'This is like living in the 18th century!'

Just how should I react? he thought. *Make a riposte like 'at least it's not the 17th' and risk a smile or verbal assassination or put on the understanding face and utter apologetic words.*

He opted for a suggestion. 'We need to get a servant, a houseboy or someone to help.'

'Help!' was her frustrated response, 'When I think of all the people who have come to the door asking for work, all of them were, quite frankly clueless. I'll just have to manage,' she said, 'but now we have Kate, as lovely as she is, she still produces bloody shitty nappies and I'm the one who has to deal with it.'

'It's not that I mind washing by hand, we don't actually wash our clothes as much as we should, it is the fact that you can't clean clothes when the water is brown.' With her fists on the table and her head peering into the bowl she said, 'You do know, don't you, that it takes all morning to filter the water so that it is clean enough to wash our clothes and if I don't boil it Christ knows what bugs and creepy things will survive and infest our clothing. The only good thing is at least we've got a tap on the water tank.' She turned on her heel and flopped despondently onto a chair. Karl was impotent on this occasion.

A few days after this exchange, as if to pay for the nefarious nocturnal excursion that had enabled them to exchange tanks a few months ago, which Dr Akinjede and his family were unaware of, a bit of a disaster happened. Karl was teaching some 150 yards away and as he looked up he saw his wife outside the classroom, holding baby Kate and waving frantically.

'The water tank has burst!' she exclaimed. Students were left with the instructions that they were to carry on and he would soon be back.

Sure enough, water was leaking from the bottom corner of the tank. It had just been filled with its precious brown cargo and the pressure of the water had burst the seam which had probably been damaged when he had dragged it the 40 yards in the middle of the night from Will's house.

Nothing they had at hand could solve the problem. The best thing they had was some gaffer tape, and just as Karl was about to give it one more try he had a brain wave. Chewing gum would seal the hole from the inside. Anna was sent into Okene to Kabba's Kabin to buy some and told to get chewing on the way back. What happened on her return some 20 minutes later was that the gaffer tape was useless, and what was about to happen then would entertain many people for a long time. Karl took the malleable, well-chewed gum from his wife, then got a chair from the dining room and placed it next to the tank before stripping off down to his underwear. Thankfully there was no audience, but he knew how to solve the problem. He climbed on the chair and lifted his feet over the edge. Archimedes Law was proven and a wave of water slopped over the edge as he disappeared under the water. It was a bit like watching Houdini trying to escape from a sealed canister of filthy water. After three attempts at diving like a duck into the 5ft x 5ft galvanised tank he was able to stay under long enough to stem the leak by using soft chewing gum and letting the water pressure keep it in place. It worked.

They looked at each other and laughed, and laughed even more as his hair dried out. There was a layer of sediment on his body, and his hair made him look like Dennis the Menace. The tufts were set like concrete and it took a bucket of filtered boiled water to return it to normal. Anna dashed into the house, grabbed the camera and took a photo of the damp pearl diver in his underwear with his solid spiky hair.

He never did make it back to his class that day.

One afternoon whilst Anna and baby Kate were having their afternoon siesta he walked the mile to the lake to enjoy the environment and to see how many types of kingfishers he could spot. He didn't need his binoculars to see that something quite large was floating in the water. It actually looked like a body. *No*, he thought, *it's probably a tree trunk*, and he walked on. On his return the wind had blown the object a little closer to the shore and on closer scrutiny he realised that the two visible humps were buttocks and the two smaller ones were the heels of a body. *A body in my bloody drinking water, what bloody next!* It needed removing. He had no thoughts of sympathy, no ruminations or conjecture about how it had got there, if it was a result of violence or too much alcohol. He just wanted it gone before bits of it appeared in his water tank.

He went into Okene to the police station and without wasting time telling the minions what was going on, he pushed his way past to see the inspector. He managed to get him to put his newspaper down and told him about the body. The inspector looked at Karl and said, alarmingly, 'Why did you put it there?'

'What...what are you talking about, I didn't put the bloody body in the water, I haven't touched it, I'm just reporting it.'

'But if you didn't touch it how did you get it there?'

He decided not to answer the question and replied, 'I just saw it as I walked past. I don't know who it is or even if it's a man or a woman.'

'You don't know the difference?'

'Of course I know the bloody difference, but the body parts were not all visible'

'So am I right in saying you are innocent and didn't put it there?'

'Yes!' he exclaimed.

'But you found it and therefore it is your responsibility to remove it. I think you should bring it into town. You have a car don't you?'

'Yes, but I'm not going to wade about in the water dragging around a body that could fall to bits and then put it in my car. No way.'

'I think you are being very unhelpful.'

'What, I've just driven all the way here so you know about a death and you say I'm unhelpful. I'm just trying to make sure the body doesn't pollute the water that a lot of people rely on.'

'So you won't use your car to get rid of the body.' And then as an afterthought he added, 'I can get someone to help you. I know it will be heavy.'

'No, I have no intention of having a body in the back of my car.'

'Then I might have to requisition it.'

'No, I'm bloody sure you can't do that.'

'Well actually I do have that power.'

'Then requisition someone else's car or truck.'

211

'Oh! Then could we borrow it?'

'Definitely no and no again, I came in here to help and now you want a body – and Christ knows what state it is in to be put in my car!' And at that he got up and walked out of the office. He felt as though he had just been involved in a situation created by the Goons.

A few hours later, as he drove back into Okene with his family, he had to slow down to check what he was actually seeing. There on the driver's side of the road were four police men manhandling a bicycle that had, over the cross bar, a naked body. Its feet and hands at times dragged on the ground and they had to make constant adjustments so that it wouldn't fall off. Karl had told Anna about the conversation at the police station and she was, frankly, a little sceptical, but now there it was, a body being wheeled into town completely devoid of any dignity.

Unfortunately, the clandestine commandeering of the water tank was about to rebound on them again. Yes, they had solved the problem of the leaking tank with chewing gum, but the next incident made their blood boil.

Dr Akinjede could never speak a sentence without a reference to God or the scriptures. It was if he felt he would be punished if he didn't, on every occasion he spoke, invoke some sort of reminder that God was watching and ready to damn the sinners. The staff found him annoying, and even if they had wanted some ecclesiastical salvation he was not the man to go to. He was a fanatic. He was considered to be somewhat bizarre and was clueless about the normal everyday things in life like timekeeping or personal hygiene. He was also hopeless at conserving his water. One morning, as they walked the short distance to the college together he moaned to Karl about the lack of water, but said he would accept God's decision even though he was about to run out and there were another three days to wait before the tanker came. But that afternoon there he was, leaning into the tank, getting the last few buckets of water to wash his car. He either believed that God would come to his rescue or he was just completely ingenuous.

That evening Karl and Anna and baby Kate, together with most of the expatriates in the town, sat in the cooler air on the roof of the Paradise. Mad Mattie was there, as usual without his shirt, and his mounds of radish coloured flesh almost radiated heat. Evidently he climbed about in that state nearly all day. He was genuinely ingenuous. He had no idea what was going on in the world or where he was or the location of the nearest airport in relation to the rest of the country. He seemed to live in his own world yet at the same time he was gregarious. Karl often wondered why, as nice as

Mattie was, he had been employed. When asking that question the reply had been, 'Because he is as agile as a monkey when climbing up those electricity pylons, he is fearless, he tells the gaffers exactly what he thinks, really knows the job and works like a demon... And as you have witnessed, he drinks like a demon.'

Karl and Anna didn't often go to the Paradise, and on this occasion they had cause to regret it.

As they drove home, with the sun going down behind them, they saw two figures hanging over their water tank. The tank had a lid on it, another acquisition, secured by a very small padlock and the tap itself had a locking device worthy of a bank. The lid was bent badly out of shape, and there were two people standing on chairs, leaning over into the tank and enjoying themselves as they washed their hair. And they were doing it properly. Mounds of soap suds and bubbles were everywhere and a pan was being used to swill the soapy water from their heads back into the tank. The two culprits turned out to be Dr Akinjede's daughters. They were having a fine time and as the car drove up they would have seen, had they not been so happy and intent on hair washing, the faces of two Europeans. One had her mouth open as wide as a ventriloquist's dummy and the other had let go of the wheel, his hands formed into two fists and his eyes protruding from their sockets.

They bounded out of the car Baby Kate on the back seat giggled and waved her squeaky toy. Karl's first words, somewhat inappropriate since the two girls looked about 12 and 13, were, 'What the fuck are you doing here, get the fuck out of my water tank!'

Anna, normally sensible and placid and not prone to using foul language, applauded her husband's reaction. As she said in a later conversation with him, 'Do you know I didn't swear until I came to Nigeria.'

The incident didn't end there. It turned out that Dr Akinjede, having used all of his water, had actually told his daughters to wash their hair in Karl's tank. He obviously thought they wouldn't mind their water being polluted with soap and piles of black crinkly hair. It was never established who had used the tool to open the lid. They had a confrontation, with Dr Akinjede protesting about Karl's language, calling it ungodly and that it would bring down God's wrath upon him. Karl's response was to say, 'The only fucking wrath around here will come from me if you steal my water again. Remember this, you religious dimwit, "Thou shalt not steal!"'

The appallingly ingenuous doctor protested to Dr Omega, who, diplomatically and with a dose of tumescent wisdom, told Karl that his reaction was understandable but unacceptable. He heard later that Dr Akinjede had been told that he had brought the out-pouring of expletives on himself, and that his children and he and Karl should meet and shake hands. This they did, Karl mainly out of respect for Dr Omega, but he avoided his next-door neighbour and thought that he was a liability in the college with his extreme version of Christianity.

Water, or the lack of it, and the growing inconsistency of delivery was becoming a nagging issue. All the time they worried about it. They had two large jerry cans and never failed, should they visit the BICC camp, to get them filled with decent water, though it still had to be boiled for drinking and cooking. The water tanker was supposed to come every Wednesday, usually in the morning, but if its trundling gait and rough sounding engine had not been heard by late afternoon then consternation and anxiety built up. *There is nothing we can do about it... or can we?* Karl thought.

His solution was appallingly simple. The house didn't have gutters. So all he had to do was to go into town and buy some. However, no such thing was sold in Okene, and he also noticed that not one single house had a system of guttering that would help to collect rainwater.

He proceeded to improvise. He bought a second hand sheet of corrugated iron, a pair of powerful tin snips, some galvanised wire and a small hand drill and a bit big enough to create a hole through which you could pass the wire.

The roof was made out of, well he didn't know. He hoped it wasn't asbestos, and on closer inspection he discovered it was iron with a coating to prevent rust. So, with the table carted outside and a chair placed on the top of it, he proceeded to drill holes in the roof so that he could attach his home-made gutter.

Cutting the corrugated iron into long U-shaped valleys resulted in cuts, a bit of blood, sore hands and a lot of cussing. It took him all afternoon to make the necessary adjustments, and the result was that the final piece of ersatz guttering would, should it rain, pour its contents into either the 5-gallon jerry can or through the hole he had made in the lid of the water tank. As he and Anna stood back to proudly look at their Heath Robinson contraption, they were approached by some students. They were as friendly as always and asked him what he was doing. When he told them what he had done they were in shock. It appeared to them to be an idea and invention of Leonardo proportions, and they went back to college to bring back more spectators. This glow of admiration was all very well, but as yet he had not tried it with water. With a dozen of his students watching and waiting for success or failure, Karl filled a bucket from his tank, got on top of the table and threw the contents on the roof. It did what it was supposed to do; the water, carrying the sediment from the roof, poured into the water tank. His credibility improved no end that afternoon.

All he had to do now was wait for rain.

27

They had bought the big purple bowl from the market in Okene. There it was, in amongst a kaleidoscope of coloured plastic shapes that blended in with the extravagantly coloured costumes worn by the market ladies. Anna, despite being a self-confessed inept haggler, got 30 percent knocked off the price. There was no baby bath on sale so this huge purple bowl proved to be a perfect size for a clean baby and all the washing that she and the heat of Africa generated. Anna was now much braver in the markets and would almost happily wander about, ignoring the shouted-out bargains and comments on the very pink baby with red hair. She was also learning how to select decent cuts of meat from butchered cows that had actually walked to market before being slaughtered, but as to where it happened, she didn't want to think about that.

The market was like every market in Africa – noisy, rumbustious and colourful, and the heartbeat of the town. It wasn't short of unpleasant sights and smells from ditches full of animal skins, bones, discarded vegetables, offal and the ever present flies, as well as opportunist vultures. Rubbish was thrown everywhere, but the stalls themselves or even just a blanket spread out on the floor, were tastefully tended so as to look attractive. The one exception was the butcher. He had an unkempt beard and his clothes looked like they had been made from the skins of the animals he butchered. He looked like John the Baptist, wielding a rather heavy cleaver.

On his table, which happened to be a rather large used door, was the carcass of a cow. Now had this been Europe the cow would have been steaming; it had after all walked to the market and had probably been dead for only an hour. It had been hacked apart without any anatomical consideration or knowledge of what constituted a fine cut of meat to be fought over by some gourmands. This lack of knowledge about what was tough or tasty meant that every pound of meat (or even gristle) cost exactly the same. The knee joint, the liver, the ears and even the fillet cost the same. It did mean that with a little bit of butchery knowledge you could point to a part of the cow that you knew was tasty and have it hacked off for you. Karl and Anna had soon found out that the local term for rump was 'niache' and by pointing to the meaty hind quarter you could buy huge steaks for the same cheap price as offal.

Just as Anna was about to select a choice cut, she was startled by a huge vulture that flew down from the roof of the bank behind the market and nonchalantly settled itself on the edge of the horizontal counter as it proceeded to tear at the bits of meat. This scraggy necked bird with aggressive eyes must have been nearly four feet in height. The butcher completely ignored it until Anna, quite staggered that a huge dangerous bird was ripping apart tendons and ligaments only a few feet away from her, uttered some incoherent sounds of disapproval. The butcher recognising her concern, reached under the table, took out a long thick stick and with a mighty swipe hit the bird firmly across its breast, knocking it to the floor. In the most ungainly and noisy manner it managed to fly off. The butcher said nothing. He gave Anna a nod of his head as if to say, *sorry about that madam*, and proceeded to wrap the huge piece of meat in some brown paper which had the letters CEM written on the side.

Back at the house the big purple bowl was given a place of prominence inside the dry, concrete shower cubicle. The food was unpacked: SMA baby food, a packet of Italian rusks from Kabba's that they hoped would be weevil-free, huge misshapen tomatoes, onions, some brown rice wrapped in an old newspaper, two huge sweet potatoes, and a second plastic bucket and colander. The meat was unwrapped with some difficulty. It seemed to be somewhat rigid as though it had rigor mortis and the brown wrapping paper was proving hard to remove from the joint. There was an absence of blood, and the meat that only an hour ago was looking succulent and fresh was now covered in a dirty grey skin that was barely flexible and quite hard. Karl got a sharp knife and as he started to scrape the surface the thin layer came off in gritty lumps.

Anna, watching with an appalled look in her eyes, gave it a sniff and a faint touch and indignantly remarked, 'I'm **not** eating that!' She turned away to attend to Kate and heard her husband burst out laughing.

'Look at this, look at this,' he shouted. In his hand was the brown paper in which their precious and very large rump steak had been wrapped. She looked at it.

'Well, what's so funny?'

Look, see what it says, no wonder it is...'

He was interrupted by Anna, who by now had read all of the fully exposed letters – C E M E N T, preceded by the words High Quality.

The mystery was all too easily solved. Instead of just putting the slab of meat into her basket she had asked for it to be wrapped and it duly was, but the only wrapping available was a cement bag and by the time she arrived home the blood and the cement had created a formidable cocoon around the meat. They couldn't help laughing. The meat turned out to be delicious with sweet potatoes.

The big purple bowl was in constant use for washing their laundry, but in the heat of the afternoon when the power went off and the fan slowly jerked to a halt they would fill it up with the cleanest water they had and bathe Kate. As she got older and could sit up, they plonked her on a towel at the side of the shower cubicle, got undressed and stepped into the bowl and proceeded to wash and shower each other using a plastic colander. It was delightful to get cool as another shower of water was poured over their heads. However, that close proximity and privacy on many occasions would result in mid-afternoon intimacy that would, had she been older, have made Kate blush.

The water that remained in the bowl was then carefully carried to the toilet and poured in vigorously in the hope that everything that had been deposited that day would disappear round the U-bend.

28

The cottage was almost on the verge of being cool. It was just after 6am, the sun was about do its job, withering the crops and drying up water holes. The local reservoir grew smaller every day as everyone waited for the rains to come and regenerate the earth. It had been ten days without a cloud in the sky. This morning whilst his wife and baby daughter slept, he got up, padded his way into the living room and peered out of the window to see the sun just poking its head above the horizon. The horizontal shafts of light made the view look quite dramatic.

He adjusted the louvered windows so he could get a better look and decided that he should be part of this golden experience. There was a line of trees about 50 yards in front of the cottage that hid the college buildings from view. They had been transformed into a gilded mass of stationary leaves. There was not a breath of wind in the air. He walked behind the cottage to a small rocky promontory and savoured the calm and serene view. The country opened out here and only ten miles back down the road to Auchi and Benin was the palm line. Here he was surrounded by rocks and scrub and wide open spaces, not unlike the wild countryside of Provence. The small mountains to his left glowed in the sunshine and had a mysterious aura as if they were being viewed through stained glass. Insects caught in the sun's horizontal rays flew about in asymmetrical and unpredictable flight patterns. Small wagtails ferreted around, and the silence shocked him, silence that seemed to separate him from real life. He felt that to make a noise now, even a small cough or a gentle clearing of the throat would be sacrilege and break the spell. No insects buzzed and the early morning bird call had ceased as though they too wanted to enjoy the silence before the sun rose high enough to heat the ground and make the air rise fast enough to flutter the leaves. He felt good. They had settled in remarkably well. He tried to convince himself that Anna was happy but he knew that she would rather be in cold England. Within minutes the sun caught him as the temperature rose. He thought about what an enjoyable evening they had had the night before with the Brights. They had all travelled to Lokoja some 40 miles away to have their supper at the new BICC camp and then watch a film.

The film was called Deliverance, but was not quite fully delivered. Close to the end of the film when they were about to sink a body into the river, the projector coughed and spluttered like an old man with flu and the image started to break up and metamorphose into a flickering abstract pattern on the screen. The room went black and there was a smell of burning accompanied by violent coughing. Mattie, who at times seemed to have the IQ of a carrot, had insisted with his usual bravado that he knew what to do with a film projector. He had put himself into the position of projectionist and had screwed up. The light went on and there he sat, futilely holding some shredded film in one hand and trying to wave away the smoke with the other. One thing for certain was that no one would see the end of the film.

The evening had otherwise been excellent. The cook had made a giant curry with eight or nine side dishes and there was beer and wine a-plenty. The generous men at the BICC camp had also made sure that their visitors' cars were topped up with petrol. All evening, Kate was dutifully behaved as planned, and took her milk and went to sleep.

As Karl made his way back to the cottage he was sure he saw some movement in the trees but the figure was barely discernible and its movements seemed to have no purpose. A few steps in one direction, a hesitant turn on the heel and a few steps back again. He saw clearly a small person, definitely a boy in a green shirt. Karl moved towards the kitchen door and as the door swung open and the screen door creaked on its spring, the image moved back into the trees.

Later he told his wife about the figure in the trees, the green shirt and the sharp exit. 'Probably someone looking for something to pinch,' he said.

'Hang on,' was Anna's response. 'Green shirt you said. Well yesterday afternoon before you got in I saw a boy, a school boy, walk past our delightful residence two or three times.'

'I wonder what he wants or if he is up to no good.'

'Perhaps he is looking for our rubbish tip to see if he can find anything valuable.'

Karl had tried to hide the previous owner's rubbish dump by building a small wall of concrete blocks to hide the view of the refuse from the bathroom and bedroom windows. What shocked him was that every other day a middle-aged woman came and rummaged through the refuse looking for anything at all that she could recycle, such as old tin cans that could be recycled into oil lamps, small bowls, sieves, spoons and ladles. He had gone out to see her and had given her the fright of her life. After an initial few seconds when she was about to run for cover she realised that his calming gestures were movements of friendship and approval. His body language said take what you want, and from that point onward cardboard, wood, tin or plastic were placed in neat little piles so she could take them away. That is what they thought the boy in the green shirt might be after.

Later that afternoon at around 4pm the boy in the green shirt re-appeared. He looked anxiously at the house and in his hands he gingerly held a rolled-up piece of paper. They watched him from behind the window as he took some tentative steps through the scrub towards the house before walking backwards again.

'Well he wants something,' Karl said, 'and the only way to find out is to ask him.'

He opened the fly screen door which did its duty and screeched, and the boy came to a sudden halt. He looked as though he was about to run until, from the back of his Yoruba phrase book, Karl dragged the words 'Beru, ni motile ran o' -- can I help you? The boy tipped his head to one side and raised his eyebrows, seeming not to understand. He gave a weak smile as he walked two or three paces towards Karl and handed him the piece of paper. Anna came out to join them as he unrolled the paper. Written in large, dark, pencilled letters, it said, 'My name is Mohammed, I am Honest, I can work.'

And that is how Mohammed came into their lives for a short while. He was twelve years old and went every morning to the Akbar primary school some three miles away. He also spoke rather good English. He explained how he was the oldest in a family of six including his mother and he had four younger brothers and sisters. When asked about his father he said that he left some six years ago and had never come back. They lived in a two-roomed concrete house and his mother made 'kekere akara' – small cakes – which she sold at the side of the road. They also had a small garden at the back of their house and the use of a deep pit latrine.

Karl and Anna had had plenty of people looking for work, but here in remote Kwara State there was no culture of the 'house boy' as there had been in East Africa, someone who could do laundry, wash, clean, polish, cook and iron. Most of the callers who claimed a multitude of domestic

221

skills were gently rebuffed, but Mohammed had a charm about him and he was bright and a quick learner. It was about time that Anna took a rest from doing all their washing in the big purple bowl and only being able to do the ironing when there was power. One day Mohammed even brought a small sickle and kept the rough grass down around their cottage because he thought it would look nicer.

Mohammed had never been anywhere more than two or three miles outside Okene. He asked to borrow books from them, especially if they had images of life in other countries around the world. He had never seen a traffic light, a shop with a glass window, nor a four-lane highway or a machine that produced music from circular black pieces of plastic. He got to love the Saturday Night Fever Album and especially the songs of the Bee Gees.

He appeared every afternoon after school and did what was asked of him, and afterwards he would make sure that he hung about for a while and asked endless questions about everything. He had a real hunger for knowledge and there was nothing he liked better than to pore over one of the three maps they had – a map of the world, Nigeria, and the United Kingdom. It was this hunger that made Karl decide to take him along when he had to travel the 120 miles to Benin for the day.

He was so excited. He arrived at the house far too early even for the proposed 7am start and had refused to, as he said, 'make trouble for master by refusing a lift from home.'

Benin was a large city of some half a million people, and had at one time been one of the main cultural centres of West Africa. It was renowned for its bronze cast sculptures and carvings and the longevity of its traditional rulers. Like nearly all Nigerian towns it had its huge markets, swarms of people, slums and the impoverished, but the city also had some fine high-rise buildings in its centre, an airport incredibly close to the centre, an expatriate club, Africa's biggest and most chaotic roundabout, and three or four decent hotels, where, after handing over a wodge of cash and waiting for an hour or so, you could get connected by phone to Europe.

Mohammed sat in the front seat of the car, his window down, and stared open-mouthed at buildings three times higher than the Paradise Hotel or the mosque or main church in Okene. The traffic was frenetic, especially on the roundabout where there seemed to be eight lanes of it going around like a mass of drunken ants. There seemed to be no order and it was a miracle there wasn't an accident every few minutes. It was known locally as the Wall of Death.

They stopped at Leventis, a large Lebanese-owned supermarket spread over two floors. Food downstairs and household goods and clothes upstairs. The entrance was flanked by two huge plate glass windows inside which were shelves piled with colourful tins and packets. Mohammed was aghast, and was also startled when he was given a large wire basket to carry. In the aisles of cans, packets, cartons, boxes and bottles his head darted from side to side trying to read what was in them and what they were. Just what were Rice Crispies and Sugar Puffs, Kit Kats, Oxo, Omo, Daz and Aeros. But then he stopped and became alarmed. He tugged Karl's arm and said to him, 'You must stop masta or we are going to be in big trouble, all these things in the basket and we haven't paid for them. I fear the police!' Karl smiled to himself as he explained the concept of self service. Mohammed seemed unconvinced until he got to the check-out, but even after leaving the store he told Karl that self-service was too dangerous and a bad idea. 'There would be many who would sneak out with goods,' he said.

After putting the food they had bought into the car boot so it could not be seen, together with a cold box that held some properly butchered meat, butter, cheeses and – the find of the visit – a dozen bars of Cadbury's chocolate, they then drove to the travel agents near the airport, a half mile from the supermarket. As Karl got down to business he plonked Mohammed down in the seats behind him and handed him some travel brochures. All was well for a while until the clerk dealing with Karl asked if Mohammed could be brought under control. The office was a rarity in hot, sweaty and humid Benin in that it had air-conditioning, and there behind Karl stood Mohammed, opening and closing the door of the shop and enjoying the unique experience of jumping in and out to experience the feeling of the cool air inside and the serious warmth outside.

On leaving the travel agents, as he was telling Karl how he would tell his family about the supermarket and the freezing air and all the exciting and fascinating things he had seen, they heard a deep roar above them which got louder and louder until, alarmingly, a huge dark shadow passed over them a mere 150 feet off the ground. Mohammed's reaction was indescribable. Yes, he knew what an airplane looked like. He had seen pictures of them, had seen vapour trails in the sky and the odd light aircraft that had flown over, but he wasn't quite prepared for the size, the noise and the speed of a modern airliner. Karl laughed. 'Now you've seen an airplane Mohammed, and it was low enough to see the passengers inside.'

Mohammed was visually exhausted and sat in the car in silence for a change. With about 40 miles to go Karl pulled over. He got out and opened the boot, rummaged around a lot and proceeded to rip off a piece of Lebanese bread, and from the cold box he took a small chunk of cheese along with a couple of chocolate bars. Mohammed thought the cheese was horrible but nevertheless ate it all and then was given a bar of chocolate. He carefully unwrapped it and tried it. It was a taste that made his head shudder. Again he was aghast, his eyes sparkled, his mouth was chasm-like and his bright white teeth were smeared with a brown creamy substance that he obviously loved. He stared at the half-eaten bar for a long time. The chocolate began to melt and Karl said to him, 'Aren't you going to finish it?'

'No, masta,' was the reply. As the chocolate ran down his fingers he said, 'I want to keep what is left for my brothers and sisters because like me they have never tried such a wonderful food.' Mohammed eventually did finish the chocolate bar, but when Karl drove him to his house, and as a surprise, he gave Mohamed another six bars which he was sure would bring an awful lot of delight to everyone in that house.

29

After a long, hot and sweaty journey from Lokoja interrupted by annoying road blocks, the rough track to the college from the main road looked so welcoming. They passed the inert water tanker and stopped at the staff room while Karl quickly jogged inside to collect any mail. There was a fat envelope with his father's distinctive writing on the front.

About 100 yards away from the staff room and Dr Omega's office was the generator. It was huge. It was the monster that provided the school with electricity. FATCO was not on the dodgy mains electricity that lit up Okene sporadically. It was a huge, muscular diesel-powered machine about 20 feet long. It was the biggest generator Karl had ever seen, but then again it wasn't an object that he came across often. In terms of generating power all he had seen was a little petrol-powered Honda that was portable and could produce enough power to light up a couple of rooms. They were almost impossible to buy and if by chance you found one for sale, such was the demand that they were always double the recommended price.

The college generator was run by a rather small Nigerian called Simion. He was just over 5 feet in height, and had a shaved head and an oily look about him. His clothes were covered in dark diesel stains. He stayed in a very small room at the end of the generator shed that was just big enough for a small thin mattress. It was there that he kept his clothes, a small primus stove and a couple of pans. His responsibility was to fill, start and run the generator during set times in the day and tend it until it was officially switched off at 10pm.

How on earth he could stand the noise it made was beyond Karl. Like all of the students and staff who lived on the campus they took it for granted that diesel was plentiful. It was supposed to run from 7 to 9am, then from 1 to 2pm and most important of all, at night from 6 until 10pm. Simion, was also required to switch it on at other times should power be needed for some specific classes or occasions.

When the machine was running, the environment in the engine shed was Dante-esque. It was frighteningly loud, it was insanely hot and humid. The unglazed windows were supposed to catch a breeze but only succeeded in creating a super highway for mosquitoes.

There often seemed to be an issue with the supply of electricity. Simion was unreliable. He was often inebriated with palm wine and his timekeeping was often awry.

The indifferent supply of electricity was a problem that had not gone away in the period since their return from England. There had obviously been little power whilst they were away. The meagre contents of the freezer had gone soft and the inside of the fridge was dripping water.

Consequently the students were still in uproar and no sooner had they arrived back at their cottage they could hear, some 100 yards away, lots of shouting coming from the generator house. Anna just sat in despair with Kate on her knee. The sun had gone down. There was a healthy sunburnt glow in the west and the tide of darkness was about to sweep over them. They had become super sensitive to the noise the generator made. It was nothing to do with its distant drone, but after 6pm the anticipated coughing of the starter motor was the sound that assured them that the lights were about to come on and their fridge would shudder into action. The absence of the noise from the starter motor induced a state of anxiety, and when the supply of power was late Karl would often walk up to the generator house to see what was going on. Lately, invariably, a number of equally sensitive students had been joining his vigil. There was nothing worse than experiencing the wait for the engine to burst into life in the distance as the sun was going down and then finding at 7pm that Simion had only just arrived. It not only irritated the families on the site but also the student body, who rightly thought that electricity should be available for both working and socialising.

'Right!' Anna said, with an air of firm determination. 'That's it. You said if the situation was no better, and it isn't, then it was time for us to leave this place and go somewhere where I can, or we can, bring up Kate without her being stared at, without her life being in danger from bloody awful diseases. Where I don't have to change a nappy in candlelight. I need to be in a place that is civilised, where I can wash her clothes, cook our food without worrying about will there or won't there be water or gas. Yes, and by the way the gas cylinder is nearly empty, and David said there was none available on his trip to Ilorin last week. The bloody fuel station in Auchi had no petrol, so if they don't have it you can bet the service station in town won't have it either. We are trapped! Face it, it's a shit hole!'

Karl listened to her bombardment. He had to agree that they had got to a point where her tolerance, and it had been fantastic, had run out. She sat on the sofa rocking Kate from side to side, looking very forlorn. He felt terrible.

'I promise,' he said, looking at her through the gloom, and before he finished his sentence he went close to her and squatted in front of her and the baby so he was at her eye level. He finished his statement. 'Tomorrow I will arrange for you to go home as soon as possible. You have been a saint, I promise!'

'But I want you to come,' she replied. 'I just can't go on here any longer. Look what it is doing to me. I don't want to leave you here but I am fearful for our safety. I worry every time I get in a car, I worry about will we be poisoned by the food, I worry about hygiene, our health, my sanity and if something might happen to our baby.'

'Tomorrow, tomorrow, I promise tomorrow we'll sort out flights. It will mean a trip to Benin though.' He knew his words at this moment in time were never going to be enough.

The noise outside the generator house increased in volume and it was dark inside the cottage. Candles were lit and with a thin slash of fierce orange in the sky the interior of the cottage looked quite atmospheric.

Karl, leaving his letter unopened, left to find out why there was even more student noise than normal and why there was no power.

If Simion was late there were words of retribution, but more and more the issue had become not his tardiness but the lack of diesel. On three or four occasions a deputation had gone and protested to Dr Omega who accepted their frustration and then shared his own concern about a lack of funds.

The supplier was tired of waiting for his money; Ministry vouchers were dealt with at a nonchalant and glacial pace and he had started demanding cash payments. His resolve about cash did weaken for a little while when an out of the blue payment arrived from Lagos. But the situation was getting worse. Dr Omega explained that after a recent visit to the Federal Ministry of Education he was given a cash amount to alleviate the financial pressure. This source of funds was now about to run dry.

The less electricity there was the more disgruntled the students became.

'Federal Advanced Teachers College,' they would say with venomous disdain. What is advanced about it? We get filthy water, the food is not cooked enough because of a shortage of gas and now there is less and less power.' Their protestations were becoming more and more understandably vitriolic.

The new college that was being built on the Lokoja Road was abandoned after the Nigerian and German companies fell out over funding, and when a group of students asked the Germans what was the issue their response was one that could have been predicted: 'We cannot continue to work unless we are paid what we are due.'

The situation was equally dire for all the workers on the site as they suddenly found themselves out of work and owed wages.

The students, who all seemed to have strong opinions about the politicians, were acidly scornful of ministers, permanent secretaries and in fact anyone in power. 'Where is the power for the common man?' they would say. The cynical belief was that everyone in a position of power was using it for personal enrichment. They hated the culture of the 'dash' but Karl often ruminated about the future of these trainee teachers; would they use any position of power they attained in the future to accept bribes? He couldn't answer that question. However the clan that still met occasionally on the roof of the Paradise or at the British BICC camp near Lokoja had no doubts. They claimed that the culture of bribery was so bad that it seemed the only ambition workers had was to be in a position where they could enrich themselves, and the higher the position the more wealth was available.

They were full of 'do you know stories.'

'Do you know I had to pay x amount to get a permit...'

'Do you know I couldn't get a hotel room, petrol, bags of cement, travel permit, having to employ someone useless who knew someone, the list goes on and on.'

But the most perceptive statement was, 'Why worry about it. We just have to accept that the 'dash' and bribery and corruption are now part of the economy and if you want to do business here, be it small hand-outs or millions, then you just have to factor in another 10 or 15 per cent.'

The students had surrounded the generator house. They shouted abuse at Simion for being late and refused to listen to his pleas that there wasn't much point in coming on time because there was no diesel. This caused uproar and there was an outpouring of anger.

A chant rose up. 'Start the engine, start the engine, start the engine!'

228

Simion fiddled about trying to make his job look much more complex than it was and eventually pressed the one button that would fire up the starter motor, and then a few seconds later he could turn on the fuel. He knew, of course, what would happen. Since there were only dregs of diesel the engine would fire up and then with a splutter, die an untimely death. This is exactly what happened, and through the noise of moans and complaints he had that 'I told you so' look on his face.

The students weren't satisfied. They wanted someone to blame and since Simion had arrived late and didn't seem overly concerned then it was, in their eyes, all his fault. He pressed the starter engine button again, there was a cough of life as the last drops of fuel hit the injection pump and then to his shock and that of the students, the starter motor made a noise like a hoe being dragged over corrugated iron. It got louder, a wisp of smoke appeared followed by a cloud, and with a groan worthy of a football crowd it died, and lay bolted to the generator gently smoking. It had burned out. It didn't matter that there was no diesel, because the generator would never start without the starter motor.

Karl spoke to Simion, 'Can it be fixed, do you know anyone who is able to mend it?'

Simion, desperate for some words of kindness, replied with an enthusiastic *yes* and went on to describe where a good mechanic could be found in Okene. In the dark the students were a mixture of anger, frustration and disconsolation.

'Right!' said Karl, 'Here's what we are going to do. You can unbolt the starter, we will take it off, I'll get my car and we'll take it to your magical mechanic.'

'What, now?'

'Yes, right now. I have had enough of miserable dark evenings and nights with no fans, let's get it fixed.'

He told Anna what he was about to do and she thought he was mad, but she recognised that his madness had a real purpose. He had mentally rolled up his sleeves and thought it better to do something other than sit around being inert and miserable.

The starter motor, about the size of a Lambretta, took all the strength of two of them to lift it into the boot of the car. He imagined he was moving a dead body, such was the weight. Simion took him to an area of Okene he had never been to before. The roads between the huts were virtually non-existent and it was dark, really dark. The occasional glow of a candle or paraffin lamp interrupted the gloom and Simion kept saying, 'It's the next corner. No, no, the next one.' He too found the rough part of Okene hard to navigate. They stopped next to a heap of metal. Car parts and abstract pieces of metal were piled up against a wooden hut that wasn't quite vertical. Outside, painted with a brush with three hairs onto a rough piece of wood was the word 'Mekanik'. It reminded Karl of some lost Russian. A dark body came out of the black hole of the doorway. He passed through the headlights. He had a grimace on his face and his thin body was covered by a bib and brace boiler suit. He exchanged words with Simion, helped lift the starter motor, scrutinised it, sniffed it, and said in English, 'Burnt out.'

'I guessed that,' said Karl. 'But can it be fixed?'

'Yes, big job, cash only.'

Karl didn't care how much it would cost or if it was expensive or where the money was coming from, he just wanted the generator fixed, mainly for his wife and himself, but secondly for everyone else's benefit. Tomorrow was the agreed time to collect it.

The generator was not ready on time, giving him an excuse not to go to Benin for air tickets, and his temporary devotion to a starter motor did not go down well with his wife. But this was Africa. This was Nigeria. This was Okene. But his cancelled trip was mollified by the contents of his father's letter. In his envelope was another letter. It was from their letting agent, who told them that the current tenants had vacated their house and it was now empty. What were their further instructions?

He and Simion collected the 'repaired' motor around 10:00pm and in the darkness of the generator shed, with the help of a couple of lanterns, they tried to bolt the huge piece of steel back into its original position. The heat and humidity were dreadful, as were the flies and mosquitoes. It had been hard physical labour taking turns holding such a weighty object whilst the other tried to slowly bolt it back on. They were both saturated with sweat. A coterie of students hearing the noise and seeing the lights came over and watched.

There was diesel as Dr Omega had personally paid for a 50-gallon drum, and all that had to happen now was for the starter motor to burst into life. It was at this point that Karl had grave doubts about the credentials of the nameless mechanic who had asked for and was given 50 naira from his own pocket for the repairs. Where were his tools, his work bench? How did he get spare parts? Did he make them? Did he have any experience? Did he know what he was doing? Had he taken the money and now disappeared? The next few minutes would reveal either his ingenuity or his incompetence.

Simion pressed the button. There was an unhealthy rumbling sound within the cylindrical shape, then it stopped. He tried again and this time, as though it had taken some life-giving medicine, it sounded so much healthier. Again it stopped. Karl and around 50 students sweated and slapped mosquitoes in the darkness. There was no complaining, there was just the silence of hope and anticipation.

On the third try it burst into a splendid rhythm. Simion turned on the fuel pump, there was an anxious wait and the engine shed suddenly exploded with light. The bulbs shone brightly, the fans created a draught, and the students yelled and cheered. They hugged Karl, and for a while Simion, all his foibles forgiven, was a hero.

It was a temporary solution. Only 48 hours later the generator stopped once more. There was no fuel, and nor was there the money to buy any should it miraculously re-appear.

30

Karl had never thought he would be in a position where he would feel the need to engineer a trip to Lagos. At times the mere mention of the word and the recollection of their traumatic arrival and initial stay in the city gave him a touch of anxiety. They were so much more confident now though, and the thought of entering the chaotic maelstrom that was Lagos wasn't quite so scary. It was also reassuring that they didn't have to rely on the ministry or any other people.

They planned their journey so as to arrive on the outskirts of Ikeja near the airport, and as usual they would wait at the Ikeja Hotel until 7:00 pm when they were allowed to drive their car into the city and the traffic had eased somewhat. They enjoyed Tony's company and his hospitality and the college enjoyed the fact it didn't have to pay for their accommodation. They looked forward to a swim at the Ikoyi Club, relaxing in the bar, service in a restaurant and perhaps holding Kate on their laps as they watched the weekly film that was projected on a portable screen near the bar.

They sat in the hotel lounge trying to keep cool under the struggling fan. Anna jiggled Kate on her knee and she smiled with delight. She was a bit of a sweaty baby, 'Like his dad,' Anna used to say, and fan or no fan, she always seemed to be covered with a film of sweat. At 10 months old she was standing and had made her first steps, 'Just like me,' Karl said, who claimed that according to his mother, he had walked at seven months. That tale always induced a few raised eyebrows.

The lounge was run down. It seemed too damp and there was a musty smell. There was a fist-sized hole in the wall spewing electrical cables. The furniture was threadbare and a trifle stained and the pictures on the walls - images of African animals, seemed to imply they still roamed around the country. The reality was that apart from a few elephants in Yankari game reserve and a few fleet-footed deer that had escaped the cooking pot, all of the lions, leopards, hippos and buffaloes had long since been eaten or shot. However, it was a lot better than the public area of the Paradise Hotel.

Anna looked at Karl and said, 'Here we are at the airport hotel and what we should be doing is getting on a BCal flight home together. Just think, we are only a mile away from the airport.'

Karl remained silent, he didn't know how to respond. Was this a bit of 'if only' or was it a serious suggestion. He looked at her eyes to try and gauge her mood as she carried on with a question. 'It can't get any worse, can it?'

What she was referring to was the situation in Okene. They had made their house look nice. Karl had even made a veranda with a terrazzo crazy paving floor and a palm leaf roof and sometimes there was almost fresh water from their guttering. But the constantly repaired water tanker was staggering about like an exhausted marathon runner and the electricity was depressingly sporadic as the college ran out of cash and credit to buy the 50 gallons of diesel that the generator needed each day. Having Mohammed around to do the washing a few times a week helped, but now that it was the dry season water from the roof was virtually nil and the delivery of water was, well, about to stop. Just how much longer could the tanker keep going? It actually looked as though it had been imported by the colonials just after the war.

Karl tried to answer with the trite phrase of 'it can't get much worse,' but he knew it could.

The student's patience was running out. They had grounds for complaint and they did exactly that.

They didn't want to study by candlelight, they didn't want to go days without washing and they were fed up with mangoes and pawpaw to eat when there was no electricity to cook yams, meat, and okra and sweet potatoes. The place was on the verge of rebellion. *Could things get worse? Yes, they could.*

'It might be fine when we get back. Dr Omega is in Lagos at this very moment trying to get more funds and to complain about the fact more students have been sent than the college can accommodate.'

'Where are they coming from?' she asked.

'Evidently, because of trouble on the border with Chad they have closed the college in Maiduguri and sent them to the other three FATCs, especially ours. We have to hope that money is forthcoming.'

She interrupted, 'Money isn't much good when what is wanted is more space for them to be accommodated. Supposing Dr Omega gets the money, it will take an age to put up buildings, not to mention providing furniture and utilities and whatever else is needed.'

Karl's response was somewhat negative and cynical, 'And I do suspect that half the money will be siphoned off to pay people or persuade them to provide what is needed.'

'You don't think Dr Omega would...'

'No, he is by far the most dependable and righteous person I have met here.'

'Oh, I really hope that things have improved by the time we get back.'

'Well if everything is still in short supply we'll just have to move in with the lads at the BICC camp.'

'But that's 50 miles from Okene.'

'Yes, but at least we'd have 24 hours a day water, gas and electricity.' He went on to add, 'And A/C.'

'Why don't we just go home?'

It proved to be, once again, a hard question to answer.

He wanted to remain silent but she looked at him directly and her eyes demanded an answer.

'We'd have nowhere to live, no job...'

'We were brave enough to come here. Can't we be brave and go home. Someone, somewhere will give you a job, we can stay with your dad or my mum or why can't we just rent. Your dad would be glad of the company.'

'I can't just disappear. I can't just walk out of the job and if we did decide to leave there are things...'

'Things,' she interrupted with a tone of frustration. She shrugged her shoulders as she turned away from him and said firmly, 'What things?'

No answer.

'Go on, tell me, what things?'

'I have just mentioned them, and also handing over the house and car and sorting out future work for the students, and I still have to go on six school visits in the next two weeks and...'

'Okay, okay, but if things aren't better when we return you can arrange for Kate and I to go home and you can follow.'

The few days they spent on Victoria Island were restful and more like the life in Africa they had dreamed of when they chose to work in Nigeria. Kate enjoyed the baby pool at the Ikoyi club. She was a chubby healthy little thing with fat little legs that thrashed away in the water. They suspected she was glad the water was cool and it was a nice change from being covered in sweat.

Karl borrowed some of Tony's kit and was thrashed by him when they played squash. They had a fine dinner at the club with Tony and a lady friend and for the first time Kate was left with an ayah that Tony knew, who looked after her whilst they dined. And then there was the 'Star' night as Karl came to call it when he Tony and a few of his friends, who were very interested in and shocked by life in the bush, drank copious amounts of Star lager.

As one of them said, 'One quenches the thirst, two make you tipsy, three get you drunk and four make you hallucinate.' Karl saw many strange things when he came home from the club.

He was just alive enough the next morning to tell Anna that he had been told the two best things in Nigeria were the quality of the beer and the vultures, the latter because they cleaned up the mess that the Nigerians made, especially on the roads.

If he had a headache that morning she didn't care. She was determined to brave the traffic and go over the bridge to the Kingsway supermarket to get some food to take back to Okene.

As they were leaving, Tony yelled at them from the veranda. 'If you see some fuel get it, there is a shortage in Lagos.'

With a full jerry can in the boot and half a tank of fuel they had enough to get to Benin. But if there was a shortage here in Lagos it could be worse the further into the hinterland they drove.

It was their last day in Lagos. Time to get some calorific treats. How nice it would be to have fresh milk instead of powder that came in huge tins. He really fancied some imported jam and mustard would have been nice, or real butter, which they had never seen, rather than the bright sickly yellow margarine that came in a tin. Ambrosia rice pudding would be nice, or some crisp apples, but what was essential was flour, because Anna had become quite a baker and was now making her own delicious bread. He started salivating, hot bread just out of the oven and some jam to spread on it. Magic.

It was a day without sun. Grey clouds, pregnant with rain, were billowing in from the Bight of Benin. It was humid and hot and they were covered in sweat by the time they had walked down the 13 steps to their car below.

They were about to pull up at the road side just over the Carter Bridge where some young men were selling petrol in jerry cans. Karl thought about it. He started to slow down and the youths, ready for a sale, gesticulated wildly. Just as he was about to stop, an expatriate going in the opposite direction shouted at him, 'Don't touch it, they dilute it with water.' They took his advice, and as they drove away there was a tremendous thumping on the car roof as the men reacted angrily after the loss of a sale.

They drove into central Lagos and parked on some rough ground awaiting redevelopment, and only a minute's walk from the Kingsway supermarket. The odd huge spot of rain hit the ground.

They got their flour, risked buying one tetra pak of 'fresh milk' to try back at the flat, a ton of disposable nappies (that could put Mohammed out of work) and at least a dozen jars of varied jam.

'Rhubarb and ginger,' he said. 'Who would have thought you'd get rhubarb and ginger, and greengage and damson in the middle of Africa?' What had shocked them in the supermarket was the huge number of empty shelves. You couldn't even find an egg, but there were two aisles which were, for some unaccountable reason, laden with rare and exotic jams from the UK. *Who on earth had thought of importing them?* he pondered.

The rain was becoming more intense. In the car park shilling-sized craters appeared in the dirt and the heavy drops were audible as they crashed onto the roof of the car. At a distance and sheltering under a yellow umbrella that said 'Blue Band' were two youths. Karl thought no more of it, and with the rain intensifying they drove out of the car park onto the main road. Within 50 yards the engine stuttered, coughed and wheezed, took its last breath at the side of the road, and stopped. A few expletives were uttered.

Karl knew nothing about cars, he wasn't bothered what car he had as long as it gave him no trouble. So they sat, rain bouncing off the bonnet and cars all around them hooting and honking as they manoeuvred past him. The baby cried and it became a wail. He was at a loss what to do. Even if he opened the bonnet he wouldn't know what to look for. He could tell a spark plug from the distributor, he knew which was the battery, the starter motor and fuel pump, but as for taking them apart that was the job of someone who knew what they were doing. Nevertheless he felt compelled to get out of the car and stick his head under the bonnet and hopefully he would recognise something amiss.

As he bent over in the rain, hearing the noise of the traffic and the claps of thunder, the two youths with the yellow umbrella appeared and said kindly that perhaps they could help. 'After all,' one of them said, 'with a small crying child in the car you need to get going.' They muscled their way under the bonnet. One held the umbrella and the other studiously looked at the engine.

'Ah, I think it could be this,' he said, holding a lead in his hand. 'I'll try and reconnect it.' Karl watched him, hoping he knew about engines, but then became alarmed as he saw him trying to hide what he was doing by leaning over at an angle so that for a moment he could keep his hands out of sight. There seemed to be an awful lot of disconnected leads. Karl smelled a scam and without any justification apart from suspicion he forcibly grabbed the youth by the shoulder and pushed him away from the car. He felt that they had both appeared too quickly and their actions looked more like sabotage than diagnosis. He smelled fuel, and their body language was wrong. The youth feigned shock and gave a look as if to say, '*Who me?*' as the other youth with the umbrella tried to take the place of his compatriot. With one hand holding the umbrella, he was defenceless as Karl put two hands on his throat and with a face full of fury told him to fuck off. They were taken aback by his aggression and stood some six feet away as he tried to rearrange the sparking plug wires into the right positions. It was then that one of them touched his shoulder and as he raised his head to stop them they ran off. He was angry. He was soaked. Every passing car hated him because his bloody car blocked the road, and Kate continued to wail. He could smell fuel. He sniffed inside the engine and saw the tell-tale rainbow colours of petrol in the water that was running under the car. He was already so wet it didn't matter if he laid down in the dirty water under the car. This he did as he wormed his way under the bumper and sump to see where the fuel was coming from. And there it was, the tube that carried the petrol from the fuel tank had come loose. Or had it been disconnected earlier and thus caused the engine to stop? It took twenty second to screw it back on, and two seconds to realise that the car had been sabotaged. Had he not been suspicious about the behaviour of the two youths, they could have been left on the pavement watching their car disappear into the distance.

He was filthy, wet and angry, but surprisingly he had a grudging admiration for their ingenuity. Three or four turns of the ignition and the fuel got to the spark plugs and the car started. He felt like some sort of damp, bedraggled, mechanical genius, and then an idiot as he realised that the tap on his shoulder had diverted his attention while his wallet, with a touch of prestidigitation, was deftly stolen.

The driving license he had had to buy was in his wallet as well as a UK credit card which was totally useless in this cash-only economy, and almost 80 naira in cash. 'That will keep those con men in beer and hash for a few days.' he commented.

His wife looked at him and actually smiled. 'What's so funny?' he asked.

'You would need a mirror to appreciate why I'm smiling. Actually, I'm not sure who that person is in the seat next to me, and don't turn around and look at Kate, I don't want our daughter frightened to death.' She paused at that point to give her husband another visual inspection and said, 'I have never seen anyone look so bedraggled, you look as though you have crawled out of a sewer and you are dripping all over the seats.'

A bit of mirth was called for because it had slowly dawned on them how perilously close they had come to having their car stolen. Losing a wallet was nothing compared to being stranded penniless, car-less and with a babe in arms in a tropical storm on a main road in Lagos. The game of the con men was clever. They obviously knew which cars had an accessible fuel pipe and all they had to do was disconnect it and wait for the owner to arrive. Sure enough, the car would die a death in 50 to 100 yards and they would suddenly appear, a pair of saintly helpers, trying to emanate the image of a knight of the road, who would with their tricky fingers render the car useless.

They were lucky, but the further they drove away from the scene the more insecure they felt. You just couldn't be complacent in this place for a second, for everywhere you looked there were predators waiting, to rob, cheat, con and use violence if necessary.

Kate had a bad night. She slept in her carry cot in between the two single beds in Tony's first floor flat. She wailed and cried and very little would console her. They were due to leave in the morning before 6 am so they could get their car out of the city before the number plate regulations came into effect but with Kate being so disturbed they had had very little sleep. At 4 am they were wide awake, she at last was sleeping and they decided since they were awake to get going.

Driving in the middle of the night in Lagos, surely they were asking to be hijacked. They waited and drank tea until the first vestiges of light appeared.

By mid-afternoon they were past Benin City and cruising along the relatively quiet Benin to Auchi road. Karl yawned, as did his wife. She was worried about what would be in store in Okene and Karl worried about staying awake.

At that moment a motor cycle zoomed out of a dirt road at a 45-degree angle and smashed against the side of their car. Anna was evicted from her private thoughts. The car was knocked sideways by the impact and Karl, looking in his mirror, saw the motorbike head lamp shatter like a blizzard and bits of metal cart wheeling down the road. Uninjured, he brought the car to a halt and looked behind him, where, some 30 to 40 yards away, was a mangled motorbike, and like a comet's trail behind it were bits and pieces of the bike. Next to the wreck was a skinny youth, his left knee and elbow covered in blood. He seemed to be free of major injuries. Karl was livid, the side of his car seemed only superficially damaged but looked a real mess. Yes, he was a little tired but even a very alert person could not have avoided being hit by the bike. As he reversed towards the wrecked bike he wanted to show the callow youth the damage he had done to his car.

It didn't go to plan. The youth may have been bleeding but it didn't stop his howls of protests and fist-shaking threats. As Karl got out of the car to remonstrate with him, he yelled, 'It is new, it is super new and you have broken it.' In an even louder voice he then shouted, 'Give me money, give me money!' The motor cycle had no number plates, the youth was wearing ragged shorts and one flip flop, the other no doubt now a part of the trail of wreckage, and in place of a number plate was a piece of card attached to the dying mechanical corpse with the word testing scrawled on it as if the words allowed him to legitimately drive. The youth, who hadn't been wearing a crash helmet, had long hair twisted into rattails, he wore a shirt that said 49ers and remarkably for an African, he had very few front teeth and the cave that was his mouth made a howling sound as he ranted.

Karl stood near the wrecked bike and looked at his car. The damage consisted of dents and scrapes and there was nothing, it seemed, to prevent them from completing their journey.

The youth screamed and ranted, gesticulating wildly as though he was a mad orator in front of an audience. It was then that a typically African phenomenon occurred. There they were, miles from the nearest town, and suddenly from the bush materialised the audience the youth had been wanting. On top of that, cars travelling the road decided to stop and watch what was going on. Within a minute of the accident 20 people surrounded the scene and those who had miraculously appeared from the forest were ranting along with the rider of the bike. It suddenly dawned on Karl that he should have just driven on but it was a little late now.

Anna got out of the passenger side and unfastened Kate from the homemade car seat. She was shaking with anger and fear. Karl reached into the car and got his camera. It had no film, but he hoped that by ostensibly taking photos of the damage to his car and the skid marks made by the motorbike he would have all the evidence that he had done nothing wrong.

His clicking was futile, and the youth kept ranting and more and more people materialised. In an uncontrollable fit the youth picked up a broken piece of his bike and hurled it at Karl's car. It bounced off the back window just missing Anna. In a brief moment of lucidity Karl realised that the raging youth was like some orator, shouting in a language he didn't understand and stirring up the growing crowd.

Anna, with her arms wrapped around Kate like a suit of armour, yelled at the motor cyclist.

'You probably have no license, your bike has no insurance, just a piece of cardboard and you...' He screamed at her and moved towards her. She stood at the back of the car as the limping youth snarled like a dog.

Afraid, but trying hard not to show it, his face only three feet away, she said to him, 'You could have killed my baby.'

His response was to aggressively step forward, his face almost pressed against hers, and he slowly uttered words that were saturated with venom. 'Baby, what baby, I see no baby, give me money!'

Karl was truly alarmed. One minute he was cruising on an empty road and now they were surrounded by 30 or 40 yelling and shouting people. He knew he had to leave. He felt fear ripple through his body. His breathing grew heavier and quicker as though he was sprinting. His jaw was rigid and his eyes were seemingly stuck wide open and he wanted to pee. He shouted to Anna to get back in the car and had enough of his wits about him to tell her to open, ever so slightly, the driver's door. Should he use his loud voice to try to reason? It was the world's briefest thought as inches away from him was this malevolent, snarling, toothless, youth like a living gargoyle gurning into his face, alternately looking at Karl and then shouting at the crowd, who responded with yells and fists in the air. Karl felt a tap on his shoulder and turned to see an elegant Nigerian beautifully dressed in lace who had abandoned his car to see what the furore was. 'This is really dangerous man; you need to get out of here quick. You could die here... And your family. He wants the crowd to help him kill you in revenge for damaging his bike. You need to get in the car and quick.' Then, as if to remind him of the escalating crisis, a man only a few feet away began hitting the roof of the car with a big stick.

'I'll go in front of you and you get in the car,' he said to Karl, showing his concern for the growing mob mentality.

At this moment of danger under a hot, humid, sunlit African sky, in a glade of trees dappled with glorious sunshine, just for a second calm arrived in the form of a translucent ice-blue and purple dragonfly that landed on the windscreen wiper.

Karl fumbled behind him for the car door which was open enough for him to open it with his fingers, and in one swift movement he was in the car.

He tried to accelerate but a throng of people were standing in front of it. Villagers banged the car with their fists, their faces squashed against the windows, making them look like medieval gargoyles. Their sheer mass and their pushing and shoving was holding the car back and the windows were in danger of being smashed. He slowly built up speed and the people parted, and just as he was about to reach jogging speed, alongside his door ran the driver of the motorbike. He was scrabbling his fingers along the side of the car looking for the missing door handle. His frustration and anger were carved on his face, and as the car was about to reach a speed where he was no longer able to keep up, he saw the two-inch gap above the window of the car door and thrust his fingers through in an attempt to get in.

Karl drove faster with an irate figure hanging from the side of the car. At one point it seemed as though his hand and arm were about to get in the car and then Anna, from the back seat, in a fit of fear and fury, smashed his fingers with the only weapon available, a heavy tin of baby milk.

He yelped with pain and as Karl weaved the car from side to side he fell off.

Panting and out of breath they drove on until they were sure that no one was following them.

Both of them for a few seconds were speechless. Both were dripping with sweat. Karl's head rested on the steering wheel and his heavy breathing made his body shudder. He opened the car door, tumbled out of the car on to his knees and puked on the hot tarmac. On all fours as he coughed out the last remnants of fear, an image of his parents appeared. They were benign and represented all that was kind and normal and all he could think of was how he had left his father alone in the UK to be here in this madhouse.

A warm hand touched his shoulder and Anna asked if he was fine. He stood up as they looked at each other and she swore gently, 'What the fuck are we doing here?' Four letter words were rarely part of her vocabulary and she went on to say, her eyes full of desperation, 'They could have killed us, they could have taken Kate, they could have killed her. Just what are we doing here?'

He never did get to meet or to thank the eloquent Nigerian who had been aware of the dangers and had helped them, but he always retained, long after the event, his image in his mind.

31

The fizz of a bottle being opened, the tinkle of a bottle cap as it tumbled along the iron table, a scrape of an iron chair as its legs were moved across the roof and the laughter of a group of men who were convinced they deserved a cold beer. It was Friday evening.

Even though the BICC workers had moved their camp to the outskirts of Lokoja they still ritualistically stopped at the Paradise at least once a week. The roof was a great place to sit and converse on a Friday evening whilst watching the sun go down and the chaos that went on in the road below. Next week it was the Ancestral festival and the roof would be crammed with locals enjoying the spectacle while they drank the Paradise dry.

Jack and Mary were present, as usual their faces adorned by lit cigarettes. David Jackson, who rarely mixed with the rough BICC workers, needed a drink after working on the micro teaching allocation all afternoon and having to deal with the otiose Dr Khan. The Brights were also there, full of euphoria that at last they were moving from Okene to their version of Shangri-La.

'You're going where?' moaned Mattie, who was dressed in ragged shorts, huge steel-tipped boots and a skimpy vest, 'Abeo-bloody-cuta, you must be mad, it's a right dump, like a mini Lagos, and Christ its hot there and it smells of shit.'

'It is supposedly a seat of learning, they actually used to teach Greek at some of the schools there,' added David, who knew of its history.

Trev, in his blue BICC tee shirt and huge safety boots, looked up from his bottle of Star and said slowly. 'Do you know they arrest white people who don't speak English properly and you two had better keep your mouths shut near the Nigerian bobbies or you'll be inside a cell with 40 others.'

243

He looked deadly serious and for a few moments everyone believed him, until after a silent pause he went on to say, 'Well, you are Welsh aren't you.'

Colin took it well, smirked and said, 'Don't think you'll be getting a beer from me this evening.'

'Nowt new,' was the response.

Everyone was appalled to hear about Karl and Anna's horrifying experience of mob psychology and it spawned a half hour of horror experiences, all of which added to Anna's deep apprehension about living here. This generated the righteous conversation about how it wouldn't happen in the UK which went on to make lots of comparisons of 'back home.'

David made a suggestion and said to everyone, 'Okay, let everyone make their own contribution and tell everyone something you miss.' He started the impromptu inquiry by saying, 'A huge decent library.'

Jack waving his cigarette, immediately added, 'Decent TV, in fact a TV that would work here.'

Mattie interrupted with two words, 'Newcastle Brown,' before adding, 'and my daughter.'

Numerous suggestions followed. 'My mam's Sunday dinners.' 'A proper pub that smells of pipe smoke and furniture polish.' 'Autumn.' 'Cool rain.' Watching Bradford City.' 'Watching rugby in Pontypridd.' 'Our local Italian restaurant.' 'Going to the working men's club to meet my mates.' Gardening in a sensible climate.' 'Driving on safe roads.' Karl added, 'Being able to read a decent intelligent newspaper.'

Everyone looked at Anna who had said nothing. David leaned forward and said, 'Well Anna?'

Her initial response was short. 'Civilisation,' she said without hesitation, but before she had the opportunity to elaborate Mattie muscled in, saying indignantly, 'The bloody word civilisation doesn't apply in this bloody country.'

The air was immediately assaulted with moans and groans and comments of a negative nature as though the word civilisation was the trigger for a tirade of Nigeria bashing.

David was exasperated by this outpouring and, leaning forward from his chair with his hands supporting him on the table, felt it necessary to comment. 'The trouble is that you Mattie, and all of us, hear so many horror stories and tales and comments about incompetence, corruption and objectionable situations, and you don't know if they're true or false, but nearly every expatriate ends up adding their own tales of mayhem and so the negative culture just grows and grows.'

Jack commented immediately. 'So, are you telling us that all the chaos and corruption and disregard for life is untrue?'

'No, it's just that we are guests here and we spend an awful lot of time propagating and exaggerating information and, well, running the country down.'

'But half the time we're just joking,' added Cindy.

'Okay, but how would you feel if at home, say, in London or Birmingham and in your case Wales, and there were groups of foreigners denigrating your town, your country?' David paused before continuing. 'Wouldn't you be a bit pissed off?'

Jim took David's comments seriously and replied, 'Not necessarily, come on, I'm happy to moan about our police, our government, that's part of democracy.'

'But guests in the UK bashing our country – don't you think to yourself, they've got a bloody nerve.'

'Well yes, but here it's different, it's only a bit of fun, and we – or certainly I – are never hypercritical in front of Nigerians.'

David changed tack a little and added a statement that was intended to justify his next subject. 'Just remember, we British, when we governed or ruled half the world, it was us who gave them the gift of English which they HAD to learn if they wanted to get on, as well as that wonderful theory of democracy.' His tone of voice and delivery somehow compelled everyone to pay attention and listen carefully.

'Yes, democracy, but it may be okay for European countries who've had centuries in which to perfect it, along with America, New Zealand and Australia for example.

'And it's not perfect,' interjected Colin.

'Precisely, and it's not perfect in Africa. Sometimes I feel it's culturally wrong, because for hundreds of years government here has revolved around a paramount chief who is all-powerful and who calls the shots in his tribe. It's like benign dictatorship. Look at Kenya, it's doing quite nicely and that's a one-party state. It's just a pity that Kenyatta has just died.'

'But there is no opposition, it's not allowed.'

'The trouble is, you are judging the culture in Africa from a European standpoint. Think about this, when all of these African countries – Kenya, Ghana, Nigeria, not to mention the French ones like Ivory Coast and Mali, gained independence they needed all the talent they possessed in order to run their country and quite possibly there wasn't enough talent to form a questioning opposition. Hey, even in a one-party state everyone gets a vote. What's the point, you might ask. Well, the principle is that there is one party with a selection of candidates who, in principle, have slightly differing views.'

Trev, who up to now had been quiet, wanted his say and said angrily, 'The trouble is that the ones with power are the military, the ones with the guns, and I don't see them as being democratic. The proof is all around us. What we as guests should worry about is not who is running the country but something of real concern, and that's corruption and the fact that you're classed as being successful when you're in a position to extort a dash from people.'

David though for a moment. 'Corruption in Nigeria, 10, 20 or 30 percent or whatever it is, isn't it just like value added tax? The dash, the bribe, the extortion, the extra 10 percent that companies always add to their costings, well it's now part of the economy. It's the way society works here. You know how it works, you give a gift to the paramount chief and you get your piece of land.'

He was about to continue with his definition of civilisation, when Mattie loudly interrupted. 'Corrugated Iron. Corrugated Iron.'

'What are you talking about, we are talking about culture and bribery,' said Trev.

'Corrugated iron, it is a part of the culture, where would Africa be without it?'

'Were you actually listening to David?'

'It's changed everyone's life, it has.' And then he went silent.

Everyone followed suit, slightly mystified by Mattie's incongruence.

Anna raised her hand to get everyone's attention, before saying, 'If I dare repeat the word, civilisation – without being rude to Nigeria, is what I miss.'

She then paused, quickly constructed her thoughts and said, 'To live in a place that works, that has some semblance of order, a place without aggression, a place that feels safe, without corruption or threats or danger. A place where you are respected, where there is hygiene, cleanliness, an absence of filth and squalor, where you can walk down a road or path and not be shouted at, where you can drive and not see an accident and carnage, where there are no intimidating road blocks and where you can buy a decent bottle of wine and be able to drink it cold, and of course all the other things that everyone else mentioned.' Everyone held their breath, there was a few

246

seconds silence then a cheer, and David stood up and quietened the group with a gesture as he proposed a very apt toast. 'May we all continue to have safe journeys.'

Mustapha and his wife Pearl appeared with a tray of some unidentifiable meat on skewers.

'Very fresh meat,' he said. 'No more old meat for my good customers.'

'About time,' moaned Colin.

'Now my meat will always be very fresh,' and then with a huge proud smile on his face, he said, 'I have a very new big...' His sentence was interrupted by his wife who gave him a firm elbow in the ribs and stopped his conversation.

'New what, Mustapha?' Mattie asked. 'Is it a fridge you are talking about, then if it is, then get the bloody meat out the fridge and fill it with beer. Just what sort of meat is it today?'

And so began the 'what are we eating' quiz.

Everyone had a skewer, though some like Anna were reluctant. She nevertheless tried it and then had to suppress the urging of Mattie who wanted to offer Kate a chunk of the 'what could it be' meat.

Numerous animals were chosen, but the reality was that no one really knew. Rat, suggested Trev, as he searched through his portion looking for buck teeth or the remnants of a long thin tail. Everyone agreed that it was far too strong a taste to be some kind of bird and the basic conclusion, after the rejection of improbable ideas, was that it could be snake, cat, porcupine, tortoise or monkey, though for some reason not dog. Jack was sure it was snake, having had it on a trip to South Africa some years ago.

'I am going for snake,' he confidently said. His wife rolled her eyes, 'How can you remember that far back?' was her response.

So it was decided, everyone would put five naira in the kitty, then they would get Mustapha to tell everyone exactly what animal the meat he had cooked for them came from.

There was 50 naira in the pot.

'I'll win this,' declared Mattie, 'I'm going to say, it is definitely dog.'

There was universal disagreement because it was well known that Mustapha and his wife had two dogs and they were well cared for by normal Nigerian standards.

They all fell about laughing when Jack told the tale of Fred Nkomba from the college getting a night in jail because he tried to kill a dog with his car, believing it would bring him good luck.

He went on to say that the only good luck he got was having to pay for the repair of the police car, a night in a damp cell with an egg cup to piss in and the company of about 40 other people.

Mustapha arrived with more cool bottles of beer covered in glistening drops of condensation.

He was questioned. He got nervous and was unwilling to answer the jackpot question about the meat's identity and procrastinated, saying it was his secret or that he would tell them later. This was not good enough for Mattie who barged past him as he struggled with the tray of empties. As he disappeared down the stairs he shouted, 'Don't worry I'll find out, be back in a mo...'

Mustapha looked appalled. He made some futile utterances and then after a minute or so Mattie re-appeared.

'Well, Mustapha, you must be making a lot of money to afford a fridge like that.' He looked at everyone and said in a condescending way, 'And it runs off electricity and paraffin. Now give me the money, the bloody fridge is full of dead dogs, but at least they are not puppies.'

'Dogs!' was the cry from the expatriate choir on the roof.

'But you like dogs... They are not yours, are they?' said Anna anxiously.

'Where did you get the dogs from?' was Trev's question.

'Cash and Carry,' was one response.

'Kabba's Kabin,' was another.

'Was it road kill you scraped up?'

It turned out to be a little side line that Mr Nkomba ran. He used the plethora of relations living in his house to catch as many dogs as they could, especially those chained up because that was of course easy money. They would skin them and sell them to Mustapha, the man with the fancy new fridge.

Mattie collected his 50 naira and promptly bought everyone a drink.

As the evening wound down David reminded Karl that they had not submitted the school visit information to Dr Khan. Karl volunteered to take it to his house the next morning before he went on to Benin. David thanked him and gave him rudimentary instructions, finishing with the words, 'Once you have gone up all the back lanes past the Alhadji Low Profile Bar you can't miss the house because it's green and the largest house in that area by far.'

The next day while Anna and Kate slept, he drove into town with the file of work for Dr Khan. He eventually found the house at the end of a grubby, litter-strewn mud road. He knocked on the door but there was no answer. He wandered around the back searching for some form of life and inquisitively peered through one of the windows. All he could see was a sea of white, and on giving it a further more careful look all he saw was a collection of brand new fridges. He was appalled. He moved along the wall like a burglar until he reached the next window. A piece of cardboard with writing on it blocked his view, but what he did see were two sets of letters 'osci' and 'elec'. It took a few seconds to decipher them and he was sure the words were 'oscillate' and 'electric'. A few more contortions of his neck and he was just able to see the letters 'osch'. *Surely it has to be Bosch,* he thought.

He had, it seemed, solved the mystery of the missing consignment of fans and fridges.

32

Dr Omega had called an emergency staff meeting which didn't go down well with Anna as it would prevent Karl from driving to Benin to get the air tickets. There was also an issue with the lack of petrol as even with the 5-gallon jerry can they kept in the bathroom and the half-full tank in the car there was only just enough to make the journey there and back. He told her he would leave as soon as the meeting finished.

Dr Omega was in a serious mood. He sat behind a table shuffling his papers and trying to get organised. He looked around. Half of the teachers who were supposed to attend were not present, either due to indolence or having returned to wherever they came from until the crisis at the college was over. He had an aura of exhaustion and frustration about him. He sighed heavily, then looked up and coughed theatrically to get attention.

Reading from his prepared notes, he told the gathering about some of the decisions that had been made by the Federal Ministry. He confirmed that FATC Maiduguri had been closed temporarily due to riots in the area and that a couple of its teachers may be transferred to Okene. A grunt emanated from the audience and someone uttered 'out of the frying pan and into the fire.' Dr Omega raised his head and gave a disapproving look.

Keeping the stern look on his face he went on to say, 'The Ministry still thinks that our day-to-day problems can be resolved and they still have plans to increase the number of students by 120, and for those non-mathematicians this is a 50% increase. The date is set for three months but of course anything can happen in that time. I have also been informed that any teacher who leaves his post will immediately have his salary stopped.' He looked up, his stern eyes silencing the gasps, and said somewhat acidly, 'And tell your colleagues who don't happen to be here that they will be substantially poorer if they don't turn up for work tomorrow.'

He went on to talk about the state of the generator, thanking Karl for his recent labouring efforts. He informed them that the Ministry had not been able to solve the disappearance of the consignment of paraffin/electric fridges, adding that there were also 20 fans in the same delivery. No new water tanker was imminent although a cash sum was supposedly in the pipeline to repair it. So hopefully in the next few days, if the funds came through, there should be a regular delivery of water for the classrooms, kitchens, houses and dormitories.

There were outraged cries of, 'just how long will it take to mend that tanker, it's older than the mosque,' and 'how are the kitchens going to be kept clean?' Some staff wanted to know if the tanker could be filled from some other source in Okene rather than the lake, and the final cutting comment came from many of them. 'How come there was water in all the taps when General Obasanjo drove through the town last week?'

Dr Omega waved his hands to get order and carried on as the murmuring eased. 'The tennis court will not be extended to the right size because a new one will be built at the Lokoja site. I have asked for a substantial amount of money to be sent to us to make sure there is a steady supply of fuel for the generator here on this site. I am led to believe that top officials at the Ministry are now negotiating with ATP and JAS, the German and Nigerian contractors, to resume their work at the Lokoja Road site and have been told that the resumption of work is about to start. But, I live in hope. I suspect that until the builders are paid what is owed to them and their differences are resolved, no funds for running this college on a day-to-day basis will be forthcoming. Therefore it could be three or four months before we leave this site.'

A forest of hands went up in the air. More questions were about to be asked but he raised his hand and said, 'It seems that the consequences of this stalemate will be that no more money will be spent on this site nor will there be any more subsidised housing in Okene.' That final clause caused uproar, but he went on to add in a very serious tone, 'Subsidised housing is not a supposition on my part, it is a direct instruction from the Ministry.'

This brought about a whirlwind of fury and recriminations. The atmosphere changed from one of frustration to a room full of indignation and outrage. He held up his hand for silence and continued, 'This will encourage everyone to move to the new site where you will be allocated accommodation in the form of a free-standing house. There will be some rent to pay. I will be the first to move. I have looked at the houses, they are

251

nearly ready and the Ministry will eventually equip each house with new battery-powered fluorescent lanterns until mains electricity is provided.'

'Who will pay for the batteries?' was one shout.

'How much rent?'

'What about our gardens?'

Karl immediately recognised the consequences of this move. Most of the Nigerian staff clandestinely sublet their houses and lived somewhere else cheaper, or took in as many lucrative lodgers as they could. He could think of four or five of them who had their own market stalls outside their houses. Dr Omega finished by saying that anyone could speak to him on a one-to-one basis later in the day.

It was hard to get their attention again since there was a lot of analysis of the financial consequences and how much they could lose by moving.

'But how much would the rent be? We need to know.'

'I say we don't pay rent until all the promises are met.'

'More students, does that mean bigger salaries?'

'Just where are we going to put these students if and when they arrive?'

'Half of our current students have left already because nothing is working.'

'They are not fed properly.'

'Will we continue to be paid, because if not...?'

Dr Omega pushed his chair backwards. It scraped across the floor and it looked as though he was about to leave the meeting. He straightened up his rotund form and leaned over the desk, his body supported on his knuckles. He raised his head ever so slowly, looked at the seething staff and said nothing. This stance induced silence from those who were supposed to be listening to him. He said firmly, 'It seems to me that the college would benefit if the complainants in this room concentrated on helping their students instead of thinking about themselves.'

There was a hush in the room. The fans continued to fight a losing battle against the growing heat.

He went on to say, 'I will be telling all of the remaining students that I have brought forward their placements in local schools. This will ease the burden of caring for them, it will give them something to prepare for, and it will also mean that they will not be around for the 'Ekuechi' celebrations when, as you all know, quite a few of our students disgraced themselves with alcohol last year.

Karl leaned over and whispered to David, 'Ekuechi?' assuming his long experience in Nigeria would mean he would be likely to know the answer.

'It's an ancestral celebration. Men get dressed as masqueraders pretending to be spirits of the dead. Lots of dancing and drinking.' He paused as Dr Omega paused for breath. 'But there are no women allowed and basically it usually ends up as a breach of the peace.'

'Dr Khan will co-ordinate the school placements, and would Karl and David please work with him with regard to the micro-teaching subjects they would use.'

Dr Khan, with an expressionless face and an aseptic voice said, while looking at Karl and David, 'I would be grateful if you could make an immediate start on them. Perhaps you could work all afternoon and get them to me tomorrow.'

The first thing Karl thought was that he wouldn't be able to disappear to Benin that afternoon.

It would be the first time he had had to work directly with Dr Khan, and he remembered the many comments made by the Brights and the O'Driscolls. Their opinion, politely put, was that he was not to be trusted and should be called Dr Khan't. David was a little more subtle and sophisticated with his comments about the emotion-free Doctor, referring to him as being solipsistic. Karl had to look up the word when he later returned home.

'There is, however, some good news I want to share with you, and that is that Colin and Cindy Bright have at last had their transfer approved and will shortly be working at a fine government school in Abeokuta. You also need to know that Dr Qureshi has been taken to hospital. The fact is... and I don't feel bad about mentioning it... he collapsed after drinking far too much retsina. He has, I am glad to say, regained consciousness. Finally, Mr Nkomba is not with us today and may still be held tomorrow after side-swiping a police car with his own car as he tried to chase a dog down the main street, apparently in the belief that he thought it would bring him good luck.' He smiled.

'Sorry,' he said, 'one more thing. Mr Saddiqui sent his apologies. His car broke down.' With a wicked smile that reflected the feelings of many of the teachers in front of him, he said, 'Someone really should have shown him how to get that car out of second gear.' The sour meeting amazingly ended with a burst of laughter and a thesaurus of teachers wanting to speak to him personally.

Karl speculated that Dr Omega must have developed his sense of humour when studying near Sunderland. He was good company and with a whiskey in his hand and a full stomach would often reveal some of the funnier parts of his life. Karl remembered how he told the story of one evening while staying in a cheap hotel whilst on college business in Ibadan, his room had been broken into overnight and his suitcase and all the clothes he had been wearing that day had been stolen. He actually woke up as the thief was climbing out of the window. He made a futile grab for him but only succeeded in catching hold of a piece of cloth. He gave a huge yank and a section of it came away in his hand. All he managed to retrieve was one trouser leg, which meant his list of clothing consisted of a pair of very baggy (his words) underpants and a trouser leg. The only thing left behind of any value behind was his car keys. The following day he had to walk to his car in his underwear, using a blanket he kept there to wrap himself in. He said his body resembled two babies fighting under the blanket. With money borrowed from the hotel until he went to the bank, he waddled to the market in the blanket to get re-clothed. His description of his ordeal had been worthy of that of a stand-up comedian and his self-deprecation was hilarious.

Karl and David worked all afternoon allocating micro teaching topics to each of the students to undertake and self-analyse. They also had to make sure that a micro topic of their own choosing was being presented to a class when the teachers from FATCO came to assess them. It took them all afternoon, and another day went by without Karl going to Benin for the tickets.

33

The tickets for Anna and Kate had been bought. She was excited at first and then the reality of what she was doing temporarily overwhelmed her.

All the dreams of a privileged expatriate life for two years in a developing country had never materialised. It seemed to her that life in the remote location of Okene was spent staggering from crisis to crisis. The one accolade she could give to the Nigerian people was for their love of children. The final crisis had been the incident with the motor bike and how rapidly a dangerous situation had developed, an incident when mob psychology could have resulted in their deaths. It haunted her. Two weeks after the event she confided in Karl that when driving and seeing a group of people at the edge of the road in the distance, even though they may be people simply going about their business, it filled her with fear that it could be a road block, some of which could be very volatile and dangerous.

Then there were the hardships. Well, hardships for Europeans. She felt she had coped well under the circumstances but the constant anxiety about health, food, water, electricity and their safety had taken over her life. Only yesterday an outbreak of cholera had broken out in Minna, just north of them. Even though it was 100 miles away it still added to her concerns

They sat on the tartan sofa with its skinny legs and she looked directly at Karl. With a tear in her eyes she said longingly, 'I don't want to go, you know. I don't want to leave you,' and then she paused, took a breath to regain her composure and said, 'I hate the thought of you living here alone, I hate it that you and I can't pick up a phone and call each other.'

Karl was about to say something, anything in fact to soothe her, but she went on.

'It's awful. It's just awful. I could write to you as soon as we got home and it would take two weeks for you to hear from me. By the time you got my letter... Anything could have happened to you and I won't be there to help.'

Kate crawled over the tartan cushions to try and sit on her mother's lap. Again she looked him in the eye then looked down at the head of red hair as Kate squirmed across her legs.

'You do understand, don't you? I'm sure you can see it in my eyes, my actions, that living here is destroying me, I am leading only half a life and if someone said to me what do you do with your spare time, I would tell them that I just try to exist. And that's actually what we do here. At least you have some work to do. I'm left here with the baby, wiping away the bloody Harmattan dust, or hoping there's enough water to flush the toilet, or that the gas doesn't run out or the Fulani cattle are not brushing up against the front door leaving their ticks all over, or there's no water again, and do you know, while you were out yesterday, Kate toddled to the screen door, leant on it and nearly fell down the steps into the grass where there was a flock or whatever word you use to describe lots of snakes, chasing frogs only two feet from her. But it's the relentless grind of trying to stay clean, healthy and civilised that has worn me out.'

Karl looked at her and saw how she may look in 20 years' time. He shuffled along and stroked Kate with one hand while he placed the other around his wife's shoulders. He said, 'I do understand and I will be back as soon as I can.' He put his hand under her chin, lifted it up and smiled at her, and said, with as much sensitivity as he could, 'I promise I'll be careful,' as he kissed her gently.

Though he too found life quite hard, at a certain level he liked beating the problems, enjoyed the challenges and was quite proud of how he coped, but he felt great admiration for his wife and how she could still muster a smile. Though she rightly grumbled and had understandable outbursts of frustration, he felt that she had coped remarkably well. She had made a home for them. It was a sanctuary and refuge. Her presence, her greetings when he came home from college or a visit, meant stability for him and the added joy was their ebullient daughter.

Kate had brought meaning to their lives. She brought the gift of responsibility, of selflessness and a new dimension of love. They had some friends back in the UK, Maggie and Bill. They were the same age and had two kids, aged 10 and 8. One of Bill's wise and straightforward comments when they discussed the merits of having a family was the statement, 'I would die for my kids, and you would die for yours if you have any.' Karl had been unconvinced. But now, here in the heat, in a lonely cottage on the edge of a remote town, on a road consisting of dirt and stones, next to a college that didn't function, 80 miles from a proper shop and with little or no water, he felt exactly the same – that he too would lay down his life for his daughter and his wife.

As though she had read his mind, Kate squiggled on to his knee, blew saliva bubbles, pulled at his hair and laughed with real gusto. Karl and Anna laughed too. For a while she had broken the aura of melancholy.

'I'll miss you both,' he said. 'And I'll be home before you know it.'

'Do you remember when we went home on leave from Uganda,' said Anna, 'and how we had so much to tell everyone. How we were excited and totally enamoured with our life there. I remember we were so happy that we actually thought about having dual Ugandan/British citizenship. In those first two years there we had so many exciting experiences. Even Idi Amin's coup d'état was exciting.'

'Well, at first it was,' was his answer.

'But will we have nice stories to tell when we get home from here. Perhaps we'll blot out all the bad bits and it will just be happy memories.'

'I doubt it, Anna.'

'And so do I. I'm just letting my mind meander, and as I'm about to go, I want to try and have some positive memories. But... For my sanity I have to leave.'

'But Nigeria has had its rewards you know.'

She looked at him, wondering whether the next statement would be a joke or something serious.

'It has brought us together... Just as Kate has brought us together. Being here has been a sort of test, a test of our relationship. Just think, what did we do with our time before she was born? Nothing with real purpose. We earned money, spent it, earned it, spent it, and on what?'

'You still haven't explained what you mean by rewards.'

'Well, as I said, it has brought us together, we have had to rely on and support each other. You being with me has made me more thoughtful, less selfish. Of course I've always cared for you, loved you, but your vulnerability and mine has meant we've needed the support of each other, and though we have been together for eight years, the hardships and frustrations of this place and the way that together we have coped with them has made me love you more.'

She took his hands, and stroked them as Kate sat quietly looking on, as though witnessing a special moment. She took his hands in hers, lifted them up and rubbed them gently against her face.

Her face was full of sorrow. 'Please, please take care while I am away.'

He forced a smile and repeated, 'I'll be back before you know it.'

He looked at her again. He saw her sadness and again felt guilt. She was right; though she had shown immense strength in coping with the hardships, it was quite simply ruining her life. He had to send her home.

Her flight home was due to depart at 7 am and the plan was to take the long drive to Ikeja airport which was situated some nine miles from the centre of Lagos. They planned to stay in the airport hotel so there would be no desperate and anxious drive from Tony's place on Victoria Island.

Though the hotel was classed as 4-star, it was grubby. The constant humidity had taken a toll on the building. The walls of the lobby were decorated with damp stains and the carpet was threadbare. The hotel boasted air conditioning, but they were told that it was only working in the bar downstairs. The hotel was quiet. There wasn't the usual hustle and bustle of arrivals and departures. There was music and laughter coming from the bar and a joyless-looking uniformed youth stood at the check-in desk. Behind him were the pigeon holes for keys, an advert for luxurious flying on Nigerian Airways and the name of the manager, Mr. Edu.

When they asked for a room, the youth theatrically looked through the room plan on the counter and grunted and sighed as he fingered the plans. He looked up, gave them a quick glance and sighed and shook his head.

'I'm sorry,' he declared in a whingeing voice. 'There doesn't seem to be any spare rooms.' He turned his back on them and fiddled with the key rack, and then turned to say, with great deliberation, that all the rooms were very full.

Karl heard his tired wife's sigh.

'The car park is virtually empty,' he said to the receptionist, 'and there is no one in the lobby, are you sure you are full?'

'I can look again if you wish but I can't make rooms empty. Lots of people are coming later; you should have booked in advance.'

Karl also sighed when he listened to that futile comment and thought it would have been quicker to send a messenger with a cleft stick than to find a phone in Okene that worked.

He then did something he had fought hard against all the time he had been in Nigeria.

'I think I can make you happy,' he said.

The youth's eyes lit up.

'If you actually find a room when you check the list again, because you may have overlooked it or just missed an empty room, and should you give it to us, then I am sure I might be able to make you happy.'

The youth smiled a big smile. The charade went on. 'Ah yes,' he said. 'Here's one I missed. It is very nice and the air conditioning may come on. You will like it, I am sure.'

The smarmy, deceitful look on his face made Karl want to grab him by the throat, but, patience politeness and persistence were the order of the negotiation.

He took the key, handed over the correct amount of money and told the youth that his happiness would be taken care of if the room was nice.

The youth was full of perfidious, obsequious assurances about the 'very fine room,' as he put it. They took the keys and climbed the stairs.

The A/C didn't work but the bed was huge and the cot was ideal. Karl set his alarm and the three of them drifted off to sleep, ready for an early morning start. At 11:00pm there was a knock on their door. A whingeing voice said, 'Where is my money?' Since there was no answer, he said it again and again.

Angry at being disturbed, furious that he had the nerve to disturb them with his whining voice, Karl opened the door, and without giving him a chance to speak he said forcefully, 'Do you realise my baby daughter is asleep.' He pressed one finger to his lips. 'Now if you wake her you will get nothing, do you understand, nothing. Just wait until the morning then 'happiness' will be yours.'

'But I go off duty at mid-night.'

'Be patient,' was Karl's reply as he closed the door in his face.

Unfortunately, it didn't end there. Some 20 minutes later there was another knock on the door, then another and another, each one getting louder. Karl wanted to grab him by the throat. He opened the door and he did just that. The youth was taken aback as, with a meaty hand around his neck, he was pressed against the wall with his toes just touching the ground.

Patience, politeness and persistence were replaced by pugnacity, purpose and pleading as Karl tightened his grip and then pushed an envelope next to his face. It was in big bold letters and was addressed to Mr Edu.

'Now you little shit, how dare you wake up my baby and my wife? You see this,' pointing to the note on the envelope. 'This is a letter to the manager telling him about your bribery attempts, your lack of manners, your lack of courtesy, your disrespect for the guests, for your lies and the way you deliberately woke up my child, and when he reads this tomorrow you, you little shit, will be fired.'

They never saw the callow youth again and Karl never handed the letter in. The alarm went off and Anna and Kate were safely boarded on the BCal flight. As he left Ikeja for the long drive to Okene he stopped the car, and through the perimeter fence he watched the plane take off and whispered to himself, 'Safe journey.'

34

He felt great sickening pangs of loneliness as his VW Igala rattled when it turned into the college drive. It was late afternoon and the place was silent. No students wandering about. No noise from the dormitories and no game of basketball being played on the crumbling court. He pulled up outside his house and opened the door. *How many times*, he thought, *have I come home and opened the door to find that my wife and daughter were not there –* perhaps once, when she had gone over to Cindy Bright's house for a chat.

The place was tidy, just as Anna had left it. There were some coloured wooden blocks on the dining room table, a small teddy propped up on a cushion on the sofa and an image in a silver frame of all three of them smiling. He recalled taking it. He had balanced his Praktica SLR on a wall, put on the timer and dashed into position to get the shot. When the film was developed it had taken four shots to get all three of them in.

The bedroom smelled of his wife. There was a bottle of scented shampoo on the dressing table and she had left behind and neatly placed under the bed a pair of sandals. On her side of the bed were some books she had been reading. He picked them up: The Burning Lamp by Frances Murray and The Look of Innocence by Anna Gilbert. A, a voracious reader, she always said that without her big fat 400-page romantic novels transporting her to another place she might have gone slightly mad stuck in the outskirts of Okene. On his side of the bed was the unfinished thriller The Taking of Pelham 123. At least he could get lost in New York for a while.

He lifted up the last book, *Looking for Mr Goodbar.* They had both read it and loved it, and they had loved the introduction which was a short poem by Rainer Maria Rilke. Before he opened the book he closed his eyes and tried to remember the words.

What will you do God, when I die?
When I, your pitcher broken lie
When I, your drink, go stale and dry
I am your garb, the trade you ply.
You lose your meaning losing me.

He knew there were other verses but these, so very thought provoking, were the ones he recalled. The poem finished with something about, 'Your tired feet will wander bare for want of me,' but he couldn't be sure.

He wandered aimlessly around the house looking for items, for discarded objects that would remind him of her presence. It was easy because everywhere was evidence of her organisation and the small aesthetic judgements she had made so the cottage felt like a home. There was an arrangement of wild and exotic grasses in a glass on the table, an image of autumn in the UK that she had cut out of a magazine and put in a frame that she got from the market. The cushions had homemade covers with wildly coloured cloth which she got cheaply from the market after wearing the seller down until she got the best price. Her last words to him at the airport as he gave the wriggly Kate a kiss was, 'Please stay safe, be careful... Promise me.' He was determined to do exactly that.

Kate had been walking when he put them on the flight to the UK. She was 10 months old. She toddled around their cottage, the soles of her little feet permanently grubby from walking so much on the polished concrete floor. One of the joys of his life... In fact, on reconsideration the most joyful thing of his life, was that whenever he entered the cottage she would run towards him and then stop, standing in front of him with her arms in the air wanting to be picked up. He just loved it. Oh how she had changed over the last few months. Gone was the very tense little baby who used to sit in her buggy with permanently clenched fists. She had even done it when someone she was unsure of came into the room. Now she would dance whenever the power came on and they were able to play music. She would laugh when tickled and stand in statue-like, wallowing, immobile ecstasy whenever her mother ran her fingers through her red hair. The red hair made her the star of Okene as she was paraded around in the Maclaren baby buggy. She opened doors and generated smiles.

The college was empty, as were two of the four cottages. His house was empty and he felt the loneliness and the emptiness of having no family to look after. A melancholy wave washed over him. How strange yet also liberating it was to have as his only responsibility his own welfare.

35

The only flurry of activity at the college was when the remaining teaching staff gathered in the staff room at around 10am on Tuesday and Thursday mornings when the post was delivered. The college was bereft of students as it had been easier to allow them to leave rather than have them hanging around and becoming more prone to protest every day. The office staff were still present and as normal a huge galvanised kettle of hot Nigerian tea was delivered to the staff room as well as a couple of packets of 'Cabin' biscuits. His first taste of them, quite some time ago in the ministry had been like attempting to digest coconut matting. He had however adopted the Nigerian way and now dunked them into the very sweet 'tea,' the taste of which could knock your head back like a baby tasting vodka. There was, however, an air of melancholy in the room. *Surely*, Karl thought, *it couldn't be as a result of the demise of Dr Khan.* He soon found out.

He was addressed by Captain Majid who was dressed in his normal Mahatma Gandhi clothes. His rustic sandals scraped the floor as he came closer. 'Have you heard about Parvan?' he said.

'No, who is Parvan?' was Karl's response.

'Dr Qureshi, his first name was Parvan, well, he was killed last night.'

Karl looked alarmed, repeated the word *killed* to himself and said, 'What happened, who did it?'

Majid took him to one side and said, 'Basically he killed himself. He was in his car last night, you know, that huge powerful Renault. He drove too fast round a corner on the way to Kabba's and the car rolled over several times. The police actually got there within half an hour but he was trapped in the wreckage and dead. Crushed.'

'You said killed himself?' said Karl, asking for clarity.

'Drunk, far too much drink. Evidently some witnesses who saw him get into his car outside his house in Okene said he could barely walk. What a waste, do you know he was part of the Pakistani Nuclear program until he was temporarily suspended, probably for drink, but he was, evidently, very outspoken and ended up here. Exiled to this backwater.'

'And his taste for retsina, wine and beer was there for everyone to see. But he wasn't... Was he a Muslim...?' commented Karl.

'A lapsed Muslim. He wanted nothing to do with religion, any religion, and he had a real taste for alcohol and the women of the hotels in Benin. It has been a terrible few days, what with Qureshi and the Paradise incident.'

'What incident?'

'When the Ekuechi Ancestral masquerades were on a few days ago.'

'What happened?'

'A lot of men were gathered on the roof of the Paradise Hotel to watch the celebrations and dancing.' He added a comment, 'These people in Okene are so superstitious.' He went on to say, 'The men were all leaning against the railing on the roof and it collapsed. About a dozen men fell on the crowd below, along with all the unstable bricks and breeze blocks, and eight of them were killed.'

Karl listened, mouth open wide. The expatriates who used the roof of the Paradise for a social gathering were well aware of its temporary nature, having been told about it by Mustapha. He imagined bodies and sharp-edged breeze blocks falling onto the crowd some 30 feet below.

Captain Majid continued. 'Five spectators were also killed and lots were hurt, but the situation really got out of hand when one of the masqueraders was injured. There was more anger and grief about an 'ancestor' being hurt than for the carnage all around. Instead of helping one another I heard that everyone was fighting and trying to ascertain who injured the ancestral spirit. It was horrible!'

Karl opened his one letter from his wife which had taken 10 days to arrive. She had written it within 24 hours of being back home.

She declared that Kate was a born flyer and was wonderfully behaved on the flight, and said what a luxury it had been getting on a high-speed train without having to fight for a ticket. One thing that did concern him was her comment that the flight had made her rather nauseous, but on the plus side she had called Joe from the phone in her mother's house. Her words were, 'He almost cheered on the phone.'

Since Karl had a full tank of petrol he resolved to drive to Benin to try and catch her on the phone at her mother's.

He timed his arrival at the Benin Plaza hotel when it was around 7pm in the evening in the UK. The hotel was hosting a wedding and the party was in full swing. Alternating Nigerian and Western music was being played very loudly accompanied by frenetic dancing, especially to the tune of *The Rivers of Babylon* and Rod Stewart's *Do you think I'm sexy?* as well as tracks from Saturday Night Fever.

Telephoning the UK was not a matter of having a bag of coins and then dialling.

You booked one of the two phone booths, gave the receptionist the number, paid in cash for the amount of time you wanted to talk and were informed that once the money ran out the phone would automatically disconnect. Then it was just a matter of waiting until a connection had been secured. There he sat in his shorts and sweat-stained tee shirt, surrounded by elegant Nigerians dressed in their lacy finery clutching bottles of beer or glasses of champagne. He couldn't help noticing just how splendid some of the women looked, and it was a pleasure to see that there was a section of males in the country who liked their women thin, athletic and gamine rather than female wrestlers or professional eaters. A beer was thrust in front of him. He was the only *oyibo* in the hotel, and it seemed that one kind gentleman had felt that, even though Karl was sitting in a phone booth in the lounge of this 'luxury' hotel that had been decorated 20 years ago and which now looked rather shabby, he too should enjoy the liquid aspects of the party. One bottle of Gulder became two and two became three as 90 minutes passed before a connection was achieved.

He had been invaded by a slight alcoholic mist and felt guilty as he picked up the phone. After the crackling, and spluttering sounds ended, he heard Anna's voice. He was concerned enough to ask if she had recovered from the flight and the nausea she had mentioned.

'It's wonderful to hear your voice, are you okay, you mentioned not being well in your letter?'

'You've got it?'

'Yes, it came yesterday, how are you?'

'Fine, just fine, mum is looking after me, feeding me well, she says I look skinny, but there is one small problem.'

'Problem, what's the problem?'

'I'm pregnant.'

And this is where the three bottles of Gulder beer he had been generously encouraged to drink influenced what he then said, or so he later claimed.

'Oh, what a nuisance,' was his inappropriate reply.

She repeated his statement as he mentally juggled how to get out of this communication 'faux pas'.

'I mean, it must be awkward with Kate to look after and not in your own home and... Difficult and unexpected and unplanned and... What I mean is great, just great, I hope the baby turns out to be as nice as Kate.'

His mumbling answer was accepted, and there and then he told her he would be home in days rather than weeks.

He was offered another beer, thought it unwise and had champagne instead, and then wisely took a room in the hotel. It cost an arm and a leg but he was too drunk to drive back to Okene, and why not celebrate, he was going to be a father for the second time.

36

He arrived back from Benin to find an unfamiliar car outside the Bright's vacated cottage. They had accepted their long-awaited transfer and had left Okene, declaring that Abeokuta was the promised land whilst deliberately ignoring the negative comments from the BICC workers.

The car was a large Peugeot 404 estate displaying number plates from Bornu State. He assumed correctly that this must belong to the transferee from Maiduguri.

Bob Allen was a slim Irishman from Dublin. He was an African veteran, having previously worked for numerous Catholic aid agencies in Tanzania and lately in Ghana. He was genial, worldly, and unassuming and had that wicked look in his eyes when he told a joke or an improbable story. He was older than Karl and his hair, formerly dark brown, was strewn with strands of grey. As soon as he saw his neighbour's battered VW Igala pull up, he walked the 40 yards, fag in hand, to warmly greet him.

Bob's circumstances were very similar to Karl's, in that the situation in Bornu State was such that he thought his wife and 3-year-old daughter would be safer back in Ireland where they also had two older boys in boarding school. He too was a teacher trainer and his base subject was Mathematics. The Federal Advanced Teachers College in Maiduguri had been closed down, not because of a lack of basic facilities like in Okene, but because of rioting in the streets between Christians and Muslims.

The wanton massacre of Christians leaving a church by men wielding machine guns was soon countered by a mosque being set on fire as the congregation was worshipping inside. This civil unrest had made normal life extremely dangerous and though there were troops on the streets trying to keep order, the mayhem continued. It was more than one incident sparking a reprisal; it had become an endless tit for tat state of violence and retribution with a few personal vendettas thrown in. There was an unofficial curfew, people remained indoors and it was decided that FATCM would be closed until order was restored.

Over the last few months Karl had taken it upon himself to explore the locality in the afternoons when there were no classes and Anna and Kate were taking their afternoon siesta. He had lost weight in Nigeria. There was no place where he could buy a Mars bar or a bag of Maltesers. In Okene there was no such thing as a bakery that provided anything other than bread (most of which was sweet) and therefore he had to miss out on calorific custard slices or sticky flapjacks. But there was plenty of meat and vegetables, and in the absence of any organised sport he took up jogging, discovering to his delight that his trousers had room around the waist as his stomach receded.

The local landscape was one of hills with sharp, knife-edged ridges, rocky and craggy. Rocks full of fissures and fractures looked as though they had been thrust into the air into a chaotic mass of rent, and split and grey boulders, some the size of his house and others which seemed to be balanced on top of one another, were full of nooks and crevices, making ideal nesting places for the profusion of buzzards in the area. He loved climbing around 500 feet and then sitting watching the birds glide and hover below him. He was awed by the prelapsarian splendour. Noise, squalor, corruption, chaos and urban development were invisible below. Each walk or climb of two hours was a taste of solitude and introspection. From here all that was visible was nature at its most splendid. There were steep V-shaped valleys and thin soil where crops of sorghum and cassava and yams were grown in little plots next to the small rivers. There were no huge farms, just little fields here and there being tended by one man with a panga and hoe.

As he sat on his high vantage point he felt the soundless breeze and luxuriated in the pleasant sunshine. With nothing to disturb him his mind turned to the 'If onlys'. *If only*, he had thought. *If only I had stayed in the UK and helped my father with his loss. If only we had gone somewhere organised like Kaduna and not backward like Okene. If only I'd been brave enough to turn my back on Nigeria after the first traumatic week. If only we'd gone to Brunei or Zambia.* His eyes swept the serrated horizon and he felt guilty that he actually felt more relaxed, now that the big responsibility of looking after Anna and Kate had been removed from him.

Once the students had finished their weeks in local schools, they, like the staff, had drifted away. His neighbour Dr Akinjede had left with his two daughters for his home town of Warri and David Jackson and his 'friend' had gone to Yankari Game reserve. There was only Bob Allen and himself living on site and they had been informed that once the last of the students had gone, the generator would be shut down. With the water tanker heading for a museum, they were left to their own devices to find water. It was usually a trip into town with a plastic five-gallon container and then a wait at the O'Driscoll's house until their water supply came on early in the evening.

Bob was appalled by the state of the college, but as he said, 'At least there are no fanatics running around the streets trying to kill each other.' He was very critical of the administration, even though Karl defended the integrity of Dr Omega who, he said, 'was fighting a losing battle with the Federal Ministry of Education which appeared to have abandoned the college.'

One of the many things Bob had become aware of in the time before Karl's return from Benin was the supposed demise of the dodgy, deceitful Dr Khan, a man with no anomie. He had heard that he had kept a large shipment of fridges and fans in his house and had then sold them discretely to the local population. For such fraudulence and theft, surely prison or at the least instantaneous deportation was what he deserved, but the rumour was that money had changed hands and he was now on his way to Port Harcourt. Evidently some school was 'lucky enough' to have him as their vice-principal.

Bob was also aghast that the welfare of the students was of such low concern and appalled at the fact that someone in power somewhere had not banged together the heads of the two building companies to get them to see sense and work together to finish the new college. After only a few days in Okene he found the place depressing and missed his wife and daughter, and like Karl he had very little work to do. Except to moan, of course.

In their evening analysis of all that was wrong with Nigeria, Bob easily introduced Karl to the pleasures of a hot whisky. Spirits were something that he didn't drink, but a wee dram, heated up with sugar and honey soothed the frustrations and relaxed them to the point where they were alcoholically sure they could solve all of Nigeria's problems.

One delight that Bob did introduce him to was the generosity of the Catholic church. He was a practising Christian and had decided, uninvited, to visit a Catholic church some 40 miles away on the road to Ajaokuta, and he invited Karl to go along with him.

'If you think I'm going to start praying with you, you must be mad. By all means have a good pray, but don't expect me to join in,' was Karl's reaction.

Bob responded by smiling and saying, 'You could always say a few words about helping Nigeria and...' Bob was winding him up, and the response was firm: 'Pray for Nigeria, God wouldn't listen to the words of an atheist like me, any improvement for Nigeria would need the entire nation on their knees praying for hours.'

He went with Bob, really for a change of scenery and to avoid the thought of sitting alone in the cottage.

Father Murphy was a fine host. Nothing seemed to worry him. He was kind, gentle and forgiving and when he too got involved in conversation about the state of the nation he was accommodating and hospitable, even to the non-Catholic in his presence, and just like David Jackson, he was an optimist who felt that one day the country would emerge from this swamp of corruption with leaders who would go out of their way to improve the lot of the people rather than continuing to inflate their Swiss bank accounts. Karl found Father Murphy's attitude refreshing and when listening to him he did feel a little guilty that by criticising everything all of the time he was turning into a typical cynical expatriate. Karl would read the Irish Times during the late morning service and then he and Bob were treated to a fine meal and huge quantities of alcohol. He wondered where Father Murphy had found such a competent cook and house boy who served copious quantities of whisky. It was obvious that to drive home with blurred vision and a lack of coordination between brain, hands and feet meant they could become another accident statistic, but not to worry; as was the case with all Catholic churches in Kwara State, they were given pleasant, clean and functional rooms to stay in, and a bowl of hot water and a hot cup of tea brought to them in the morning.

Father Murphy got very interested when Karl talked about jogging and how, in the absence of an organised game of football or rugby, it helped him maintain his weight loss.

'Now, is it actually running?' enquired the good Father. 'Do you just shuffle along or actually lift your feet off the ground?'

Karl tried to explain that it was a sort of running but he would never go so fast whereby he was gasping for air.'

With a whisky laden voice, Father Murphy asked for a demonstration. He became most enthusiastic and jovially dragged Karl to his feet. The room moved a little, but all three of them went outside, and Karl and the

Father went for a jog on the path around the church. The fact that his religious garb almost touched the floor was somewhat of a hindrance to him. This induced the farcical sight of a man of God in his cumbersome religious clothes attempting to jog. He was a vision to behold as he held up his clothes like a housewife about to perform 'Knees up Mother Brown,' and with an alcoholic haze inhibiting his sense of balance he jogged, and staggered, along the path. He declared afterwards that he would fly around the countryside once he had bought himself a pair of shorts.

Back in Okene, the college was to be officially temporarily closed in the near future and typically no specific date was given. The instruction from the ministry was that all employees should remain at their posts until the official closure otherwise they wouldn't be paid. Bob and Karl laughed at this. There were only five or six remaining members of staff out of a faculty of 40.

Their ruminations extended to thoughts of how long would it take for the closure decision to be made and would the situation arise in which it would take a committee or a sub-committee to be organised before a decision was made. Could they actually monitor who was here and who wasn't, and if those who were absent should ever be named, just how long would it take for their wages to be cancelled. Then there was the issue of the government cars they were driving, where were they all?

They visited the new college site on the Lokoja road. It impressed Bob with its possibilities. The staff houses and classrooms and dorms looked nice and new, but all were uninhabitable with building debris strewn all over the place and only partially fitted interiors. All but one remained unfinished.

The only finished and occupied house was Dr Omega's. As an expression of his status he occupied a nice three bedroomed bungalow with his wife and family, although it had no running water or mains power. The only privilege he had given himself was a subsidised Honda Mini generator.

They visited the workers at the BICC camp near Lokoja. After sweeping out the debris of bird droppings, feathers and rotted leaves from the abandoned colonial squash court, they had to take into account when they played their game that the entry door had long since disappeared. They visited the overgrown and melancholy colonial grave yard and from its high vantage point watched the cable ferry cross the huge confluence of the Niger and Benue rivers far below them. Africa went on and on in the distance. Bob insisted that they visit yet another local Catholic church, where they received yet another generous and alcoholic welcome.

Getting petrol was becoming a real issue. No sooner had it arrived at the one garage in Okene, after a flurry of queues, impatience and anger, most of those in the first 50 yards of the line had got a full tank. Bob and Karl were both running low and they had used up their extra jerry can supplies. The men at BICC had offered to fill Bob's tank the last time they were there, but out of pride or something equally stupid, Bob, with Karl's full approval, declined the offer.

The problem with getting fuel in Okene, was that they only found out if a tanker was there well after all the petrol had been sold. It wasn't as though there was a daily delivery, the last one had been a week ago. Things were so desperate that drivers had started to queue outside the petrol station and sleep in their cars. The police, at the behest of the owner, got all the cars removed, some of which were so empty of fuel they actually had to be pushed.

Karl really wanted to make the 240 mile round trip to Benin so that he could ring Anna, and Bob too wanted to contact his family in Dublin, but how to ensure they would get a full tank? Mohammed came up with the answer. Since he lived some 200 yards away from the fuel pump, he would keep watch and as soon as he saw the tanker arrive he would cycle the few miles to the college to tell Karl.

'Bicycle, bicycle, I didn't know you had a bike,' said Karl quizzically.

'I don't masta, but I can borrow one but I would have to pay.'

Karl raised an eyebrow.

'Only 50 kobo master.'

Karl replied in an exaggeratedly serious voice, pretending to be astonished at the price, 'What! 50 kobo!' There was a pause, a big smile from Karl and an even bigger one from Mohammed, and the deal was done. Well, after all, 50 kobo was only around 10 English pence.

Around 6 pm the next day a puffing, skinny Mohammed arrived on a barely functioning bike shouting 'Masta, fuel, it done come.'

There was chaos near the petrol station and Karl must have been about 20th in line. Bob was just ahead of him and like everyone else he had made sure that the gaps between their cars was an inch or less. Should a hand-sized gap appear you could be assured that a car would try to push into the gap ignoring the scratches and scrapes each vehicle would receive. Their cars moved tortoise-like towards the pumps.

There were two pumps. One was powered electrically. It had a price gauge and a volume of fuel gauge, and displayed the familiar bright yellow

273

shell image on top of the pump. But as they said in Okene; 'De power it done quench.' In other words, no electricity, no fuel.

That left the hand pump which was a worthy museum exhibit. It stood like some science fictional sentinel. There was a glass reservoir that held one gallon of fuel. It was about six or seven feet above the ground and stood on top of a sturdy metal tube that served as a support and the means of sucking the fuel from the tank below ground. The attendant would vigorously use a hand pump to fill the glass reservoir then place the nozzle into the car, open a valve, and let the fuel be delivered by gravity. This was painstakingly slow, and the attendant kept count of the gallons he dispensed to each vehicle by moving pebbles, one for each gallon, from his left pocket to his right so he knew what to charge. Even though the attendant was working quickly and efficiently it was not quick enough for the drivers. The owner stood back as his job, of course, was to take and hold the money.

Someone appeared at the front of the queue holding a jerry can and was seen to give the owner money. Since money speaks, the interloper was allowed to fill up. Others with empty clanging cans or fragile plastic containers immediately seized the opportunity and bundles of naira were thrust into the owner's hands. There was outrage. There was a hooting of horns, yelling, screaming, shouting and protestations, and then someone had the audacity and idiocy to try to grab the fuel pipe, unaware of the dangerous situation he was causing. He was sensibly pushed back into his car by some drivers with common sense, although not enough to switch off their engines and put out their cigarettes. After an hour went by, and in twilight, Bob and Karl got their full tanks. They were about to move out of the station when another altercation erupted. Again there was a fight at the pump. Blows were struck, the attendant was thrust to the ground and they proceeded to wrestle with the open delivery fuel pipe. Karl was in a position where he couldn't move, and Bob's car was across the street. Fuel flew in the air, great splashes of petrol landing on Karl's car. Some came through the open window and doused his arm. More people carrying containers were converging on the pump trying to get hold of the nozzle while someone pumped furiously.

Then to Karl's horror, a man with a cigarette in his mouth scrambled over the waiting cars to join in the fray. As the nozzle swung about like a dancing cobra more fuel splashed onto his car. He was for once thankful there was no electrical power or the big yellow pump would have sprayed petrol even further. The air stank of petrol, it attacked the back of his nose and throat, fuel ran down the windscreen and the dangerous situation

274

frightened the life out him. He felt sick with fear. With the driver's door not functioning as a means of escape and a passenger door that was rendered inoperative by the renegade car only six inches away, he was trapped. Cigarettes near fuel! Instant combustion! He was in danger of being trapped in a burning vehicle. It was far more than disquiet; he was seriously afraid that he was part of this horror show. He was on the verge of panic. He was overwhelmed by a situation he couldn't control. Scenarios ran through his head, burnt alive trapped in a crappy car. How he would never get to see his wife and daughter again. How he could be another victim of the madness of Africa like the poor missionaries whose graves he saw in Lokoja. Dying miles from home. He tried to wind up the door window to prevent more fuel coming in as the nozzle swung in another arc towards him, fortunately now only spewing drips. He was going to vomit, piss and shit himself at the same time. He had a moment of clarity and leaned across the passenger seat to wind down the passenger window. He banged on the car next to him and shout 'Fire, fire!'

The man had enough common sense to realise that he too would be incinerated should there be a conflagration and he moved his car far enough away for Karl to drive away from the garage, leaving behind the petrol-soaked fighting individuals who were in serious danger of being caught up in Dante's inferno.

He was now twenty yards away from the mayhem at the garage. In the fracas, somehow the glass fuel dispenser on the gravity pump had broken and fuel had formed a small lake under a couple of cars. No one had the sense to stop pumping. One electrical spark, fuel on a hot exhaust, a careless cigarette end, would result in the barbecuing of about 20 people.

He lay with his hands and sweating forehead on the steering wheel. He stank of fuel and felt sick, and just as he had some three weeks ago following the mob and motorbike incident, he stepped out of the car, knelt on the ground and vomited.

Bob wandered over, looking at Karl on his knees exhausted by fear. He said, 'This is a very easy place to die.'

That day, no one did.

37

Bob and Karl had decided to leave for the UK and Ireland within 48 hours. They were told that they would continue to be paid and should the college get back to normal again they would be contacted so they could return and resume their duties.

Karl went to say a temporary goodbye to Timothy at the Bank of the North. He felt a little guilty for having an ulterior motive, which was to ascertain whether Timothy would continue to convert 75% of his salary into pounds sterling and continue on a monthly basis to send the remittance to the UK every month.

There was no need to worry. It was Timothy who brought up the topic by saying, 'I think you'll be needing me to send your allowance to your bank in the UK, after all it's not your fault the college has closed down.' Karl had always enjoyed his weekly chats with Timothy, or Igi as the locals called him. He was highly critical of General Obasanjo's government and the parochial nature of the Igbira and Karl would listen rather than comment. They did however collectively moan about the general lack of organisation in the country and how difficult it was to get anything done. The empathy between them, with both having a small child and a love of football, had been constant. It was Timothy who told Karl that Ipswich Town had won the FA Cup final 1-0 against Arsenal, as well as the sad fact that one of the FATCO students called Bassey, who was a current Nigerian under 21 international had died, though not as everyone was told, from some mysterious undisclosed illness, but something as curable as lock jaw from an untreated scrape on his leg.

Karl also took out a large amount of accumulated cash to pay for his air ticket at the airport. He was cash rich in Nigeria, because here, in the middle of Nigeria, in the middle of Kwara State, in the middle of Okene, there was precious little on which to spend your money.

Utilities, for what they were worth, were free, except for Calor Gas for cooking. The car belonged to the government and therefore there was no outlay for it. There was supposedly a reasonable rental charge for their cottage but maladministration had dealt them a kind blow in that the powers that be had forgotten to take the rent from his salary and he wasn't about to tell them of their error.

Their money was spent only on food, drink and fuel. and since there was hardly any expensive imported food for sale, most of what they had needed came from the market in Okene. It had often seemed to them that they hadn't eaten chips for months, nor had they seen a fine chocolate biscuit or a bag of crisps. Okene was just too hot for potatoes to grow. It had meant that their diet was one of fresh meat and vegetables and if they went to Lokoja there was fresh fish. The consequence was that both of them had lost weight; no big scoops of ice cream, no treacle pudding from a tin, no trifles with rich layers of cream and custard, no bars of chocolate, just a treat of rice pudding now and then that they cooked in a pressure cooker.

Karl gave the two cheap carpets they had brought from the UK to Captain Majid along with a fluffy pillow. Karl liked him. He was honest, with high moral standards and an air of dignity and righteousness about him. He was one of those ascetic individuals who saw the good in everyone and was grateful for what he had. His small flat in a rather run down area of Okene had a well-used and dirty bed. 'Too awful to sleep on,' he had mentioned. He didn't replace it, but simply slept on the dining room table. He was wise and courteous and his whole attitude as a Muslim was so different from that of the avaricious, discredited Dr Khan. *Dr Khan made him feel ashamed*, he commented. He couldn't drive as he felt that having only one arm was too much of a handicap and until recently he had walked everywhere, or in extreme circumstances he would pay for a taxi. However, he now had a bike but had yet to master the skill of defying gravity and steering with one arm and he was a shaky presence on the roads of the town. As he told Karl, he missed his family but he was in Nigeria to earn enough to pay for his kids to go to college.

With his cash Karl went to the local primary school near the south end of town and paid the next two years' school fees for Mohammed who had been a star at helping them out. He made sure to get a receipt and waited for an official document to be created to say the fees had been paid. Yes, it was generous, but only in Nigerian terms. The cost to Karl was the equivalent of £60. Mohammed's family also profited from a barely used set of pots and pans, cutlery and china, and when Karl dropped it all off at their modest house Mohammed's mother cried.

He woke up early. There was no point in calling at Bob's cottage at this time because Bob could sleep for Ireland. The sun was just rising and already it was hot. It was the dry season and the grasses and leaves had that faded, thirsty look about them. Massive variations of green were still prevalent, though slowly being transformed into yellow ochre. The low sun caught the tops of the trees and made them glow like precious gems. There was a delightful lack of humidity, it hadn't rained in the last couple of weeks and Karl's now famous guttering was redundant. Bob had told him, and he had thought it was just another Irish yarn, that the air was so dry in Maiduguri the lack of humidity could actually shrink a pair of leather shoes.

He took a walk on the dusty, farinaceous path behind the cottage that went towards a small rugged hill about a half mile away. The hill was his first goal when he had started jogging up the slope from his house to the base of the hill. If he could make it without stopping, and he had struggled at first, he would then have the pleasure of running downhill on the way back and with the aid of the slope, feel somewhat athletic. His trainers made foreign prints on the path as he followed the tracks of a small motor bike and someone with bare feet. He climbed the hill, which was a scramble, with a mixture of stretching, reaching, gripping and securing his legs and arms from one foot and hand hold to the next. The top of the hill was only about 250 feet above the path below but the view at this time of the morning, with the sun sending horizontal rays like a huge yellow spotlight, was visually majestic. The jewel of this visual experience was silence. There wasn't a cloud in the sky. He loved being alone. He could faintly smell wood smoke and the gentle aroma of the sparse stringy grass.

On his first climb up the hill, and on the other side in a rare flat area he had found a pile of football-sized stones about six feet in length. It had obviously been made by the hand of humans, and it was only after further inspection following the removal of a few stones, that he found the skeleton of a human foot. He had replaced the rocks over the very white bones and felt a little uneasy at his very small act of inquisitive desecration.

There was a light hot wind. He was being gently cooked and he closed his eyes and enjoyed the warmth on his face before it became unbearable. He saw some vultures circling some way into the distance, and then in a flash the pure colour of the ice blue sky was interrupted by a moving, amorphous, ever-changing black shape. He had seen this phenomenon before in the United Kingdom when a flock of starlings flew near his house in ever changing forms in front of his kitchen window. What he had witnessed was a murmuration of birds flying in choreographed unison, some thousands of them together, in an ever-moving and changing formation in an attempt to avoid a predator. Were they starlings? Perhaps they were skylarks? They never got close enough for him to tell. But now the noise of the thousands of twirling and flapping wings kept him engrossed. At this moment in time, in this quiet place, with this awesome view, with the warm sun, with this visual phenomenon, he wouldn't have been anywhere else. He was also proud of how he had coped. He was proud of his wife. He also got a thrill when he mastered one of the many frustrations thrown at him. Just working at the college and doing some good, so he hoped, was, as far as he was concerned, an achievement.

The college was ghostly silent, only he and Bob were on the site, and since he had run out of Calor Gas he decided they would have breakfast at Bob's. Karl bought some pork at the market. He wasn't quite sure which part of the animal it came from but he had it cut into strips, and with some eggs and a loaf of bread that tasted of condensed milk, that would be their breakfast.

Karl was surprised to find Bob awake, and what's more he was sitting outside on an upturned cool box tending a fire.

'What are you doing? Impersonating a boy scout?'

'No bloody gas!' was the response. 'Can you believe it... Sit on the crate... I got it out for you... No water, my plastic container has enough water left to brush my teeth after saving some for tea. The power has been off for days and days and now my bloody gas tank is empty. So you see it's a good job I smoke and have a lighter and a good job I was scrabbling around to get some kindling while you, no doubt, were communicating with nature.'

Karl dragged the crate upwind of the smoke, while Bob held a frying pan over a small open fire which Karl fed with sticks. They looked a pitiful sight. They resembled a pair of tramps sitting in the scrubby grass outside the little square house tending the pathetic little fire.

'Here we are, two educated, intelligent adults in a centre of post graduate learning, and to get breakfast we have to light a fire outside and sit around like bloody tribesmen or vagrants.' Bob went on with his mini rant.

'Just look at us, how low have we fallen? We should take a photo and send it to the Nigerian Embassy in London and Dublin to use in their 'come and teach in Nigeria' campaign.'

279

'We must look rather pathetic,' said Karl.

'You're right,' agreed Bob, 'pitiful and sad, and sad that one of our final acts before we leave Okene is to be sitting outside like a pair of bushmen cooking bits of pig and some eggs on an open fire 'cos nothing works. This place, this country, it's as though it is covered by a cobweb and every attempt at progress is held up by this huge web.

'Institutional chaos is what I call it.'

'Well, we've brushed against it often enough,' commented Bob.

'Do you know, I suspect, if and when we tell this story to people at home we won't be believed,' commented Karl.

'Can you imagine if we wrote a book about this, what would we call it? Go on, what's your suggestion?'

Karl replied, 'How about, *Welcome to the 17th century*, or *Awful in Okene*.

'Better still, *Orrible in Okene*, and how about *Nothing Works*, or a *Month without petrol*.'

'Now, I have a personal one, one that my wife would agree with.'

'Okay, let's hear it,' said Bob.

'*Another bad decision*,' was Karl's enthusiastic answer.

'Yes, I suppose that could apply to me as well.' Bob went silent for a moment as he thought about it, before finally saying, '*Total Chaos*, or *Creative Chaos*, or wait for it,' he paused again and said, '*A Brush with Chaos*, yes, I like that.'

'And so do I,' agreed Karl. 'Now, if ever I write a book I might just use it.'

Bob went on to say that he would probably do nothing because he agreed that most people would assume he was telling porkies.

'But it's a good day,' He exclaimed as he stood up. 'The food smells good, there'll be no washing up because there is no water, and best of all, this morning we are off to Benin, then on to Lagos, and tonight to Amsterdam and our wives and kids.'

'It's going to be a good day, a memorable day, and my last act as principal education officer in such an intellectual and exciting place is to sit outside cooking dodgy meat from the market on an open fire.'

Bob interrupted 'It almost sounds romantic.'

Karl went on, 'And then get in a rattling taxi, smelling of sweat and wood smoke. Do you think we'd be allowed back in the UK, smelling as we do? He paused and went on to say, 'Now let's hope we don't get food poisoning.'

'Stop worrying, it will be a feast. Now grab a few more twigs.'

38

The new runway at Benin airport had been completed, enabling jet airplanes to land and take off. The terminal building was unfortunately still in a state of refurbishment with areas cordoned off for construction, alteration and destruction, which meant the area for check in was chaotic and more crowded than usual. As usual there appeared to be no order. It was a case of wandering around this sign-free area as though a maze until you came to an area manned by a Nigerian Airways official. One thing that was communicated well to the gathering throng via loudspeakers was the fact that all passengers flying on the new jet service would be transferred to their flight by coach.

What they didn't say, however, was that the passengers would be taken one mile to the end of the runway for embarkation.

It was searingly hot. Only five hours ago Karl had sat at the top of the small hill behind his house, enjoying the view and the flying display, thinking how the day was going to be a hot one.

Benin, some 120 miles south of Okene, had a distinctly different climate, in that it was always humid. It gave that heat-inducing, rivulets of water down the back feeling, with hot air that toasted your throat and today it seemed extreme. The terminal building with its low iron roof, its lack of ventilation and the swarms of noisy passengers made the whole place distinctly uncomfortable and claustrophobic. Ladies in voluminous satin and silk dresses scrabbled in their bags for anything that would wipe the sweat away. Kids cried or looked lost and any object of a decent width and light weight was used as a fan. Even Bob, who had been comfortable in the 100 degree Fahrenheit-plus dry heat of Maiduguri, complained.

They were packed into two brand new buses with A/C which only became effective when the bus stopped at the end of the runway for the mass defenestration. The terminal buildings were not in sight and the two or three hundred passengers sat at the end of the runway had no shade except for two lonely and rather small palms. The noise of a tractor grew louder and louder as a two-engined airplane gleaming with new green and white Nigerian Airways livery was towed by the chugging vehicle to the end of the runway.

The two gang planks were lowered and the uncomfortable, enervated and sweaty passengers shuffled towards the plane. Karl looked around him. He looked at the plane and the volume of people, looked at the plane again and whispered to Bob, 'I think that all these passengers are not going to get on this flight. I think we should get further up the queue. The last thing we want is to be left in this heat in the middle of nowhere with only two skinny trees for shade.'

They eventually managed to get seats together on the plane. The inside smelled new and clean and fresh, and his estimation of the capacity of the plane and the number of passengers proved to be correct.

The aisles were full of people without seats, and the attendants worked in vain to try and solve the problem. There were irritated noises coming from those standing. These grew into complaints, then to shouting, and on to aggression. The end product was that the brave and confident pilot had to squeeze down the aisle to solve the problem by making all the standing passengers sit in the aisle facing the cockpit door. There were still rumblings of discontent and all Karl could think of was *no seat belts for them and what about the extra weight the plane was about to carry*. He didn't really care, he had a connecting flight to catch and a wife and daughter to see. The pilot's actions still didn't accommodate everyone though and some passengers were still outside having to suffer the sun's rays on the gangplank of the aircraft. They were told forcibly that there was no room at the inn and they would have to be transported back to the terminal to wait for the next flight. There were many angry words, especially about their bags being on the flight, but eventually the doors were closed. As the plane taxied, spewing out even more hot air onto the tarmac, Karl looked out of the window and saw five forlorn and forgotten passengers huddled under the inadequate shade of the two emaciated palms. The bus had left them behind, sweltering a mile away from the terminal. The heat rose from the runway and distorted its shape, and the abandoned passengers looked angry and worried. Karl thought there was a good chance that by the time the next airport bus came to get them, they might just find five sets of bleached bones under the trees.

Ikeja Airport just outside Lagos had been renamed as Murtala Mohammed Airport, after the former president who had been assassinated in 1976. Bob and Karl were booked on a KLM flight to Amsterdam, with Bob going on to Dublin and Karl to Tees-side Airport. Some refurbishments had been carried out and departure seemed less chaotic than it used to be. But as Bob pointed out, it was the disorientated and tired passengers who had just arrived who were more vulnerable to the conmen, pickpockets, hustlers and hasslers. Departing was definitely a lot easier. Karl remembered again with some agony their first few hours in Lagos. It had been an overwhelming experience as they were doused in all of the uncertainties of culture, the aggression, the lack of privacy and the deprivations.

Now, he was proud that he felt he could handle Nigeria. He had actually enjoyed some of the challenges and was pleased that he had met many of them. His moments of euphoria, such as this morning, had become more frequent, and he wondered, if there had only been more organisation and more support for the college, the staff and its students, whether they would have had a far better experience.

39

As they waited at the check in desk, they were, as usual, accosted by scruffy teenaged boys who, for a small fee – or more often than not the disappearance of your luggage, could make sure you would be at the front of the check in line, because they knew someone who knew someone that would make sure that you would be at the head of the queue…

Their offers seemed very plausible, so Bob and Karl just played games with them and egged them on with false promises until they had the brains to realise that these two white men were not going to hand over their documents and the 'small' fee.

Bob said, 'I am sure that one or two of them can be helpful, but the worst thing I heard was from one of my former colleagues in Maiduguri who was, I thought, somewhat gullible in handing over his documents only for the young 'helpful' man to disappear. There he was, waiting to get on a flight to Europe from Kano and he suddenly finds himself without a passport.'

'Bloody hell!' commented Karl. 'What a nightmare scenario, it doesn't bear thinking about. What happened?'

'Now, by some miracle another kind young man, an accomplice of course, said he was in a position to find the lost passport that had obviously been taken by an 'evil thief', his words, but he knew he could get it back because all the hustlers were fearful of him and he wanted to help the man.

My mate, totally furious, said a vehement **no** in no uncertain terms. Thankfully he was nudged firmly by his fellow traveller who said, 'You can't win here.' And just as he had finished talking, the 'helpful' young man came up to the victim, looked him squarely in the eye and said, 'Have a good flight.'

It was then he came to his senses. Reluctantly hiding his frustration, they negotiated the price which was payable on return of the said passport.

'I have always tried to avoid giving anyone a dash,' said Karl, 'and over the time I've been here it has been a pack of cigarettes, or the odd cigarette or a couple of naira here and there. But that's extortion!'

They were booked on a KLM flight which meant the seat numbers on their boarding passes would be the seats they would actually get to sit in. Their bags were waiting for them when they got to Customs. Every case or package had a light blue label for KLM and a green and white one for the Nigerian Airways flight whose departure to London was scheduled for a few minutes after the KLM flight.

'Is this your bag sir?' asked the customs official as he chalked some big ticks on arbitrary suitcases that went slowly past on the conveyor belt. 'Have you got anything to declare?'

'I am sure I haven't, but like what?' said Karl politely.

'Ivory tusks, animal skins, especially those of a leopard, precious metals, Nigerian antiquities.'

Karl laughed internally and thought to himself. *Leopard skins, there probably hasn't been a leopard in Nigeria since Mungo Park was here in the 19th century and even if one misguided animal entered the country it would have been eaten.*

Remaining very polite, he replied, 'No sir, I have none of those items in my case.'

'What would I find if I was to check your case?'

'I can think of nothing that is illegal, in fact it is mostly clothes belonging to me.'

'Are you sure?'

'Yes I am positive because I packed it, and should you search my case you will find nothing untoward.'

The customs officer raised an eyebrow at the word 'untoward'. Karl got the visual message and immediately said, 'Nothing illegal.'

'Okay, but I will have to search your case.'

'That's fine with me.'

'What time is your flight due to leave?'

Why is he asking that? Karl thought. He found out soon enough after giving the answer.

'About one hour, in fact 55 minutes.'

'Oh dear, then you may miss your flight... Because if I search it thoroughly, and I intend to do so, it will take me more than an hour and you will have to leave on the next KLM flight.'

'But that's in three days.'

'Yes, I know, but I have my job to do.'

Bob had already gone through customs but Karl stood helpless, with a vice applied by the customs officer gripping his bollocks.

'Is there any way in which you could speed up your search to help me get on my flight?'

'Well I have issues, so many issues.'

'Issues?'

'Yes, my car, it is an issue, you know these mad Lagos drivers scratched it, and there is a dent, and it is so expensive to fix, so I have many issues, what am I to do?'

Karl knew there was no escape this time, the customs officer was determined to get his daily dash.

'Would 20 naira help out?'

'No, but fifty would get rid of my issues,' was his firm response.

It may not have been much, but it was against his principles, principles that had now been obliterated by the smiling uniformed man in front of him. He was in no position to refuse and the money was discreetly handed over.

His bag was immediately given the 'I'm okay' chalk mark and dragged off the conveyor belt ready to be taken by hand to the airplane.

A surly young baggage handler with a huge Rasta hairstyle, stained bell bottom jeans and a reptilian grin, slid up to him and said in an abrupt tone, 'What flight are you on?'

'KLM to Amsterdam.'

He pointed to Karl's case and said, 'This it?'

'Yes, the one with the blue label.'

'What is blue?' was his incongruous reply.

'The label is blue, just like that big airplane behind you, you know, blue like the sky.'

'But if I don't know blue, how do I know which airplane to put it on?'

'I am telling you, the one nearest to you and not the other green one. The nearest plane is blue, like the label on my bag, that is where my bag needs to go, to the nearest plane that is blue.'

'But I do not know the word green. I may put your bag on the wrong plane.'

Karl felt stupid as soon as he mentioned the word green because all it propagated was that reptile face was trying to bugger him about. He suppressed his anger. Again he swallowed his pride and said, 'Would this ten naira note help you to recognise blue?'

'Yes, but there are two blues, the airplane and the bag, so 20 would be better.'

Karl would normally have made a scene and shouted out about bribery, corruption, chaos and the dash. But he calmed down quickly, thought it through and decided that 20 would have to be given to this slithering, thoroughly unpleasant youth.

He saw Bob ahead of him disappear past the immigration post and gave him a wave as if to say I'll see you soon.

The immigration officer sat behind a large imposing podium. From this high position of power he was then able to look down on everyone who presented their passport. Karl watched him at work. He was gruff. He was full of his own importance. He gave a very firm look to each passenger as if to say *I am important and I need to be treated with respect.*

He arrogantly flicked through the pages of each passport, giving it a seemingly thorough look before dramatically stamping in the exit stamp and then handing it back in silence.

Karl was rather hot and sweat marks were appearing like big dirty pools under his armpits. After annoyingly submitting to the demands of the customs officer and the baggage youth he was just keen to get to the departure lounge where he could sit under a fan. The airport may have been refurbished since he had first arrived in Nigeria but the general departure area air-conditioning was beaten by the west African damp humid air. He handed over his passport.

The immigration officer gave him a searching stare and then really took his time examining it. He tipped it from side to side, held it up to the light, grunted in disapproval, looked at it again very intently, and then placed it behind him and shouted *next*. Karl was pushed out of the way by a burly African who was quickly dealt with, and before Karl could step forward for an explanation he was once again pushed out of the way. This happened another three times and with the heat, humidity and anxiety he was soaked to the skin and had to pull his shirt out of his trousers and lift it as he bent over to clear the sweat from his eyes. He managed at last to confront the immigration official who stared at him with disdain, and said nervously, 'Have you got... Have you finished with... My passport?'

The officer turned his head slowly and dramatically before leaning forward so he was close enough for Karl to smell his cabbage-scented breath, and said, 'What passport... Who are you?'

This was the point where Karl became sick with worry. He felt as though his central nervous system was being attacked and fought hard to think clearly. He could feel his heart beating faster and his pattern of breathing changing. The heat settled over him and every sweat gland was in full production. He was wet, very anxious and he was nervously fidgeting. Yet another passenger was seen and sent quickly on his way and once again when Karl, trying desperately not to look distressed, tried to confront him in the most diplomatic way the immigration official again refused to admit that he had touched or even seen his passport. *Go away and look in your bags* was his casual and cynical suggestion.

A last call for flight KL88 to Amsterdam was announced as Karl stood looking up at this charlatan who had decided that he was to be one of today's victims.

His hands were shaking; he was finding it hard to put words together. Sweat was stinging his eyes. He was getting to pleading point as he thought of the mess he was in. But he knew that he had to overcome his fears even for a second or two so he could address the officer in a dignified way. When would he get to see his wife and kids? How long would it be before he could get a new passport from the British High Commission? What could he do to make this mental assailant deal with him properly? But in a moment of lucidity he knew the official was playing with him and that he had to play the game. He wiped his brow again as he tried to look calm before saying, 'Would a donation help you to look for my passport?'

The officer didn't answer at first. He just looked at him again in disdain and said very seriously and firmly, 'Do you know, my wife is very sick, my youngest needs new shoes and I am poorly paid and this weekend I have to get lots of beer for my brother's birthday.'

He then looked away and then moved as though he was leaving his post. He could walk away with the passport and Karl would end up stranded. More sweat, more anxiety and another final boarding announcement for his flight.

Karl actually shouted, 'I think I can help!'

He turned again slowly and looking over his shoulder in a slow dramatic way said clearly, 'Perhaps you are a kind man, but how can you help me?'

'Let me make a donation so I can help you solve your problems.'

That statement solved the problem.

He was asked for his wallet, ostensibly to verify his identity, then watched as the officer removed all the money, some 150 naira and some sterling that made him rub his hands with joy. He then handed the wallet and passport back to him.

Damp and shocked Karl reached the departure lounge. 'What have you been doing, running around the airport carrying weights? You look exhausted.' Bob was shocked at his damp dishevelled state and listened open-mouthed to the details of his ordeal.

Once Karl had recovered his composure their conclusion was that although everything in Nigeria seemed to be corrupt and chaotic, it was however organised enough – in pockets – for three airport employees to plan together, pre-select their victim and take him for all he had without actually asking for money. Why wasn't the government that enterprising and organised?

He sighed to himself. *Just when I thought I could cope easily with all Nigeria could throw at me I can't believe I had to pay out all that money.* But it was only as he walked up the steps of the 'blue' airplane did he feel, that at last he was on his way home and it wasn't until flight KLM 88 was in the air that at last he was able to relax.

The hum of the aircraft engines and a strong gin and tonic sent him into a state of semi-consciousness. He ruminated about the future. Soon he'd get to see Anna, he'd be greeted by his daughter and would become a father of two. Following his Nigerian experiences he felt he was in a better state to deal with the demands and frustrations of life. As he recalled all of the challenges and trials, including the last one, he actually felt weary and exhausted.

Was he a better person? *Yes,* he thought. Was he a better husband? *Absolutely,* was his answer. Was he a good father? His self-judgment said yes. Would he make up for all the time he should have spent helping his father? Yes, he would really try. And as for Anna, he could only admire her tenacity, patience and stoicism in coping with the brush of chaos that had been a part of their life in Nigeria.

He shuffled his body and reached awkwardly into his back pocket to retrieve a crumpled piece of paper. It was Tony's first letter to him, containing those ominous words, 'Remember, Nigeria is nothing like Uganda.' *Best tear it up,* he thought.